THE
CITY

THE
CITY

CITY OF VICTORY, BOOK 2

ADRIAN GOLDSWORTHY

An Aries Book

First published in the UK in 2022 by Head of Zeus Ltd,
part of Bloomsbury Publishing Plc

9 7 5 3 1 2 4 6 8

A catalogue record for this book is available from
the British Library.

ISBN (HB): 9781789545784
ISBN (XTPB): 9781789545791
ISBN (E): 9781789545777

Typeset by Divaddict Publishing Solutions

Printed and bound in Great Britain by
CPI Group (UK) Ltd, Croydon CR0 4YY

Head of Zeus Ltd
First Floor East
5–8 Hardwick Street
London EC1R 4RG

WWW.HEADOFZEUS.COM

For Robert

The city of Nicopolis in this story is fictional. Several cities with this name existed in the Hellenistic world, named in commemoration of battles won by a king or Roman emperor.

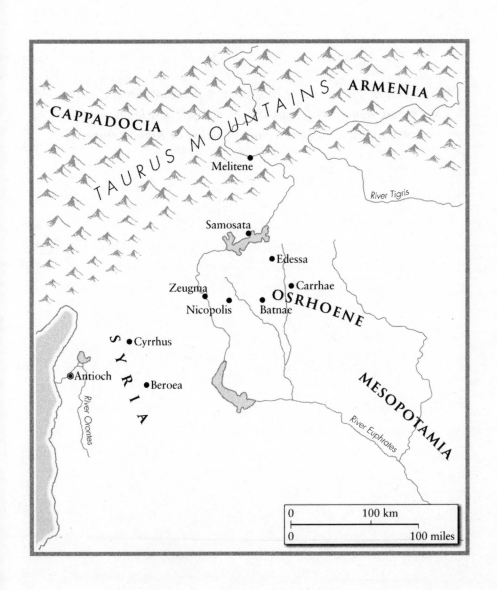

CAPPADOCIA

TAURUS MOUNTAINS ARMENIA

Melitene

River Tigris

Samosata

Edessa

Zeugma
Nicopolis   Batnae
Carrhae
OSRHOENE

SYRIA

Cyrrhus

Antioch   Beroea

River Orontes

MESOPOTAMIA

River Euphrates

0	100 km
0	100 miles

PROLOGUE

WHEN ALEXANDER THE Greek came, the shepherds said it was like a great ram, always enraged, charging at anything in its path. His main army did not come this way, and the shepherds and the farmers heard of battles and slaughter and were glad that such things were far off. One Great King was dead, they heard, and Alexander was Great King. There were Greeks in the cities, satraps who sent their soldiers to collect the taxes as soldiers, satraps and kings had always done. Greek or Persian, what did it matter, for life was hard enough without worrying about anything beyond their control. There was always work enough to keep a man busy.

Trade caravans came and went as before, and the dusty travellers said that Alexander the Greek was waging war in Bactria, climbing mountains that reached up to the Heavens and crossing into India. Traders told good tales, and whether they were truth or lies did not really matter for it was all so far away. After a few years they said that Alexander the Greek was become a god and that he was dead. The shepherds admitted that the boldest rams often fell sick and died before they grew old, but the farmers had heard before that Alexander the Greek had fallen and it had not proved true. So they tilled the hard earth and cherished each drop of rain and waited to hear what the traders would say next year. Instead the soldiers came and laid out their city, choosing a hill to make it strong, for that is how soldiers think.

The men of the caravans had never said much about the Greek soldiers, for what was there to tell? They were savages from the distant west who knew only how to kill. The merchants had not spoken of the warriors grown weary of Alexander the Greek, of the ones who whispered that they should halt and turn back for home, and that the young Great King was too drunk with wine and his own might. They did not speak, if they ever knew, of how Alexander grew angry with these men, and ordered that they be taken from their regiments and formed into a special band. Into it went all the men who criticised him, all those who broke his rules, all those who tried to desert and were caught, and any who disgraced themselves in battle. Few outside the army ever heard of these men, the 'Disorderlies', as they were called, or knew that in the tongue of the Greeks they were called the Ataktoi, and that Alexander gave them all the posts that brought great danger for little honour. Many died, but some did not, and there were always more sentenced to join them.

These were the soldiers who came, sent by Alexander the Greek to make a new city and hold the lands around it in his name. They told the farmers and the shepherds that they were to be subject to this city, that their fields, flocks and herds were no longer their own, but property of the citizens of this new place for whom they must work. The farmers and the shepherds could not hope to match the weapons and murderous skill of the newcomers, so did as they were told, and the colonists had the sense to leave them enough to feed their families. Such is the way of the world.

Yet these Greeks were strange folk, who called their new city

Thebes and said that it was because there once had been a great city in the land of the Greeks of that name until Alexander the Greek had destroyed it. They did not seem happy or sad when a few months later the news came that Alexander the Greek was most certainly dead, and they did not leave but continued to build their city, quarrying stone from the hills rather than baking clay into bricks like sensible men. Many of them had brought women from half the world – Carians, Phoenicians, Egyptians, Persians, Bactrians and Indians as well as Greeks – and the rest took girls from the villages to be their wives and that was as it should be.

The settlers said that the brother of Alexander the Greek was now Great King and that the unborn son of Alexander the Greek would also be king, but that they no longer cared and wished only to live, and that seemed wise to the shepherds and the farmers. Yet kings arose throughout the lands and made war against each other and in time two armies came. The settlers argued for many days, for such is the way of the Greeks, until they decided to arm themselves and join one of the kings, for thus they said their homes would be safer. They arrived late for the battle, when already corpses lay in heaps and the carrion fowl were feasting, and one king, bloodied and weary, was rallying his bloodied and weary soldiers for a last stand. Yet the settlers came from behind the enemy army, and their attack was so sudden and so bold that the enemy panicked. The other king led a charge against the settlers and died on their spears, and his soldiers grew afraid and fled. It was a victory, as if that mattered, and the almost defeated king praised the settlers and renamed their city Nicopolis, which meant 'City of Victory' in the Greek tongue. There were lots of cities with much the same name and some were famous and most were not. The shepherds and the farmers did not mind, and watched their animals and tilled the hard earth and were glad when the armies went away.

The years passed and the first settlers grew old and died. Some villagers were forced and some chose to join them, while craftsmen, labourers, merchants and slaves all came to the city, and lived within its strong stone walls. They mingled together and some worked hard and some did not, and some had skill and some did not. For a while more caravans came, while the armies stayed away, for Nicopolis was neither as wealthy nor as desirable as an outpost to make them scorn the strength of its walls. Though the Disorderlies were gone, their descendants and the other inhabitants kept both their suspicion of Great Kings and their desire to be left alone.

Kings and kingdoms rose and fell and life went on. Caravan routes to the south became safer and some said faster, and the few who still came this way were the stubborn or those who valued the beautiful inscribed gemstones crafted by the Nicopolitans or the fine silk they took and reworked into flimsy gauze. The city was not wealthy and built fewer temples or monuments and did not add to its walls. Yet it was not poor, and like the shepherds and the farmers, the craftsmen endured and had enough and sometimes more than enough.

When the sons of Greece dwindled and the lines of their kings failed, others appeared. The proud Arsacids rode their fine horses out from the east and later the barbarian Romans and their Caesars came from the west. Kings appeared in Edessa and claimed the lands all around as far as Nicopolis and the great Euphrates beyond, calling their kingdom Osrhoene. There will always be kings and their satraps and their soldiers and there will always be tribute. The Nicopolitans paid the tribute, but would not take any of the kings' soldiers into their city and said that they would defend their own walls, and the first king was wise enough to see that the old stone walls were still strong and agreed. Not all his heirs were so wise, but willingly or not they kept the promise to let Nicopolis govern itself and defend itself as long as the city paid tribute. When they spoke of this sometimes the traders laughed, because the same agreement was made by these kings with the great Arsacid king of kings in Parthia.

For four hundred years and more Nicopolis stood on its hill, its stone walls weathered and cracked like an old warrior who still kept some of the vigour of his youth. The citizens were of many races and spoke many tongues, though all were governed by a council and magistrates who wrote laws in the language of the Greeks. Outside the walls, the shepherds and the farmers spoke as their fathers and their fathers' fathers had done back to the very beginning. Just as it had always been, they tended their flocks and tilled the hard earth, cherishing every drop of rain.

I

In the hill country
Fifth hour of the night on the Ides of February
In the consulship of Quintus Ninnius Hasta and Publius
Manilius Vopiscus Vicinillianus (AD 114)

RUFUS' FACE WAS numb, battered by wind and the driving rain. He was soaked through, his clothes heavy with water, cold and clumsy. No doubt the mail cuirass, polished to such a fine sheen by his slaves, was already rusting. It was hard to care, and this barely a month after he had arrived with such pride to take up his commission in the legion. For all the cold, his back was slick with sweat from the sheer effort of climbing, and he was barely half way to the top of the hill, its sandy soil turned into slick mud by the storm. That meant going carefully to keep his balance. Then a stone hit him squarely on the head. Rufus yelped like a child and fell flat on his face.

For what seemed a long while Rufus lay in the slime, no longer caring what anyone thought and lacking the will to rise. There was a sound, perhaps a faint cry, from higher up, and he raised his head, spitting out mud. The rain was slackening, the night becoming just a little lighter, and he thought that he could make out the dark shape of the tribune, with his face a pale blob looking back. The clumsy oaf must have realised

9

that he had dislodged a stone and sent it lobbing back down the slope.

'I'm fine!' Rufus shouted, although he doubted that the tribune could hear, and gave a thumbs up, which the man might or might not be able to see. Either way, the tribune seemed satisfied, for the white blob vanished and the dark shape resumed its climb. He seemed hunched, so must be near the top of the hill, where the slope was much steeper. According to the legatus, the two officers ought to get a good view from the top, and find some landmark which would tell them where they all were before anyone found out that the commander of Legio VIIII Hispana was stranded in the middle of nowhere with a handful of officers and a tiny escort. Rufus was doubtful, although the easing of the storm might just give them a chance, but one of these scrubby ridges looked much like another to him, most of all at night, while they should not be near any city or even village of note. Since they had not yet fallen into the river – an experience that surely could not make him any wetter than he already was – he could not think of any feature likely to tell him anything of use. Still, orders were orders, the legatus an odd man even at the best of times, and since even Rufus' minimal experience of the army made him suspect that as the most junior officer present he was an obvious person to blame, there was nothing else for it. Rufus felt the top of his head and suspected that there was a bruise, perhaps even a cut. With his hair soaked he could not tell if there was any blood.

'Bugger,' Rufus said softly and pushed himself up, nearly slipping again, and started to follow the tribune. The numbness was spreading to his limbs, and he panted as he forced himself onwards when all he wanted was to sit down and rest. No, that was not true. What he really wanted was be two thousand or more miles away at home in Tarraco, with his father – his dear, indulgent father – once again telling him not to be such a damned fool as to take a commission in the legions and having the sense to listen this time.

Soon the centurion was leaning forward and using both hands because the slope was getting steeper. The ground felt different, harder and much stonier, and sometimes he had to go around stretches where it was almost vertical. He could see more, and once or twice glimpsed a few stars between the tears in the clouds. It must be well past midnight, and less than half an hour, even if it felt like days, since the legatus had sent the centurion and tribune on this climb in the hope of working out where they were. With a final effort, Rufus scrambled up to the crest. The tribune was waiting, reaching down with his hand.

'Ah Rufus, my dear fellow,' he said and hauled the centurion up. 'Beastly climb, isn't it? And beastly night too, for that matter. Who'd join the army, eh?'

Rufus managed to straighten up. 'Only the hopeful and the hopeless,' he just managed to say, repeating something he had seen written on more than a few walls. 'And I'm no longer sure that I am either.' He decided not to add any of the riper sentiments that usually followed the slogan.

The tribune grinned, his teeth very white. Lucius Flavius Arrian was a short, stocky Greek from Bithynia. Rufus was twenty-six and guessed that the tribune was a similar age, or perhaps even a little younger, which made his air of cheerful competence as impressive as it was exasperating. Still, Arrian was an *eques* and had spent several years commanding an auxiliary cohort somewhere on the Danube before becoming one of the five equestrian tribunes with the legion, so he must have been through his share of hardships in the past.

'Hard to be sure of anything in that storm. At least we've seen the end of that. Look, there's the Moon herself!' Arrian was pointing up at a thin crescent. The clouds were scattering, the great fields of the Heavens appearing and washing the hilltop in a pale silvery light.

'It really is quite beautiful here,' Arrian declared brightly, sweeping his arm across the horizon. 'And the foulness of that storm makes us appreciate that loveliness all the more... Rarely known worse weather,' he added, now shaking his head, 'or a worse place to be in such a storm. Enough to make a man wish that he was home – or anywhere other than here.' He sniffed and then rubbed his face with his hand. Rufus' skin was still numb from cold and the hours of hammering rain. 'And yet...' The light was good enough to see the tribune's brow crease as if he was in deep thought. 'And yet we must consider whether such wishes are truly justified or even rational. After all, wherever you are, are you not wet when it rains?'

'Sir?' Rufus was puzzled, but sensed the senior officer wanted some response. 'Rain is wet,' he allowed after a while, since he must humour a senior officer especially when they were alone. 'A lot of rain is very wet.'

'Quite so – and it may fall on us wherever we are.' Arrian appeared delighted with the conclusion. 'Wisdom, my dear fellow, wisdom, and in this case learned from the very wise. Wishing to be somewhere else is fruitless and no more than deceiving ourselves. Bad things could easily be happening to us if we were actually where we wished to be. Thus, you are wet when it rains, wherever you are. Far better to accept our lot in life with equanimity.'

Or be under a roof and somewhere warm, Rufus thought, although he had sense enough not to say anything. A small voice inside his head whispered that his despair was obvious and that the tribune was trying to encourage him, but he was too bone weary to be offended.

'Come, we must continue our quest!' Arrian sounded genuinely excited and sped off across the hilltop, only to stop abruptly. 'Wait!'

Rufus froze, staring around him for signs of danger. There was always a risk of bandits in any desolate place on a wild night like this, but he could see no sign of anyone or even any animal, let alone one likely to pose a danger. Bandits, for all their moral failings, could show sense sometimes and who but a soldier under orders would be out on a night like this.

Arrian had bobbed down, crouching on his haunches and scrabbling at the ground. 'Look!' he said. 'They're everywhere. I knew it!' He almost bounced to his feet and held out a large chunk of pottery. 'Look!'

Rufus could see nothing remarkable, but he took the piece and obediently inspected it. There was a heavy rim and the curve suggested that it had been part of a large bowl, which did not explain the tribune's excitement.

'I knew it,' Arrian said again. 'The shape of the hill was so clear – certainly not natural. This was once a city. Centuries ago, perhaps a thousand years ago, men dwelt here and called this home, tilled their fields and fought their wars.' He was almost shouting, and not simply to be heard over the howling wind. 'Thus this hill we have cursed as we climbed amid thunder and lightning was once hearth and home to men not so very different to us. Will one day strangers pick over the fragments of our lives, do you think?'

The tribune strode away before Rufus could respond, leaving him holding the shard and wondering whether he was supposed to keep it.

'Come on, man, don't dawdle!' Arrian called back, so Rufus dropped the pottery and scurried after the tribune. His boots crunched as they broke more fragments, so there was no shortage if Arrian wanted any more of the stuff. 'Hurry!' Arrian sounded impatient, almost angry, and as the wind had dropped away his voice was very loud. 'Come on, we have a job to do!'

Rufus followed, watching as the tribune threaded his way through a series of mounds. Up close, he realised that they were heaps of stones, the remains of ancient houses and walls. Some were still waist high, and he clambered through what might once have been a gate in an outer wall to join Arrian as the tribune stared out. Below them, the slope was almost sheer as it dropped away.

'Well,' Arrian said after a while, 'at least we are still in Syria. That is a comfort.'

'Though we should be well advised to be content with our lot wherever we are,' Rufus replied, trying his best to match the tribune's flat tone. In truth he could make out very little. A deep valley opened below them, with another ridge on the far side and at least one more crest beyond it. The view was much the same in other directions. Rufus knew his eyesight to be less good than that of most men, especially in the darkness.

'There is the Euphrates!' Arrian was pointing. 'See, where the land seems so much lighter. That is moonlight on water and the only water of that size must be the great river. So there is proof that we are in Syria and the kingdom of Osrhoene is there on the far bank. Can you make out the cluster of lights some way beyond? I guess that must be one of their cities. If it were earlier in the night, there would be more to see, but now all good men should be tucked up in bed with all good women.'

'Or bad women?'

'It is a matter of taste,' Arrian conceded, 'and I suppose opportunity... Well, no matter, let us turn to the problem in hand. We have a better idea of where we are, which begs the question of where is VIIII Hispana? Some three thousand of our own men are out there somewhere, with another thousand auxiliaries, not counting all the *lixae* and other odds and sods.'

Rufus shook his head. 'I see no sign. None at all.'

'Yes, it is somewhat disconcerting. Legionaries are noisy creatures as a rule, who tend to make their presence known. It is mean spirited of them to choose this moment to change the habits of a lifetime.' Arrian had the flat accent of his province, his Greek very correct, even old fashioned, but spoken at a steady pace so that Rufus always understood every word. Syrians tended to gabble and since his arrival Rufus had often struggled to understand them. 'Yet there is no sign,' Arrian went on, 'none at all. I fear the inevitable conclusion is that they are all lost. Most careless.'

'Strictly speaking, sir, are we not lost?'

'Not anymore. We know where the river is, and up there in the sky is the Dog's Tail, so we ought to be able to find our way back as long as the weather does not change again. But that is all beside the point. Our task in this merry exercise was to be the quarry. We stole away before dawn. They had been told to keep a close eye on us and hunt us down by midnight at the latest, and that hour has long passed.'

'Does that mean we've won?'

'Don't be flippant, centurion. We have mislaid one of the Lord Trajan's legions, and I do not suppose that they will simply let us indent for another to replace it. So it might be best if we find them before their absence is noticed. Or perhaps steal some soldiers from another legion? After all, there has to be a simple answer.'

Rufus' spirits began to sink again. For a moment he had trusted in Arrian's confidence and hoped that they would head straight back to camp. Instead, he feared being sent off on his own to search for errant soldiers. He doubted that he could find his way in this landscape in daylight, let alone in the remaining hours of darkness.

'Hold!' Arrian's hand shot up as if signalling a column to halt. 'What do you make of that?' He was staring down into the valley below them. Rufus followed his gaze and saw only darkness.

'I am not sure,' the centurion ventured.

'There, man! There!' Arrian was pointing. 'Movement, I am sure of it, and coming towards us. Can you not see?'

Rufus shook his head and said nothing.

'There is a darker shadow in the gloom, one that is moving and moving quite fast.'

'A caravan?' Rufus suggested. 'I hear tell some sneak through at night hoping to avoid paying the tolls on either side of the river.'

Arrian was unconvinced. 'Too fast for camels, and certainly for men on foot. Perhaps some of our own horsemen or men from the cohorts have found us?'

'That is not the way we came.'

'Hmm.' Arrian considered this. 'Yes, chance then, and perhaps an opportunity for us – or better yet for the noble Crispinus – to surprise them and impress one and all with his skill at navigation even in the foulest of weathers. Quite a coup. The Divine Spirit appears to be smiling on us.'

If that was so, Rufus could not help wondering why the gods had been pissing on them for so many hours. 'Are you sure, sir?'

Arrian did not appear to be listening. 'Too far to shout though. One of us had better go down before they ride past and get themselves even more lost.'

'But we don't know they are our men.' Rufus was again thinking of bandits, or *latrones* or *lestai* or whatever they were called locally. As a child he had suffered many nightmares about robbers in the night and out here the old horrors seemed all too real.

'Who else would they be? Still, I'll show the courage of my convictions by going down to meet them. You go back the way we came and inform the legatus. There looked to be a clear route leading from that valley into this one, so I will bring them to you all or you can meet us halfway. Understand?'

'Sir, I am not sure.'

'Not sure of what?' Arrian's tone was sharp. 'The orders or my decision? You will obey, centurion, and do your job while I do mine. I am going down.'

'Go and you'll die.'

Arrian jumped with surprise, and Rufus might have found some comfort in this display of weakness if he had not once again yelped like an infant. The voice had spoken in Latin and had come from their left. Yet he could see nothing there, apart from the dark mound of the old wall.

'Herakles' balls,' Arrian said softly. 'Who are you? Speak!' His voice only wavered a little and Rufus was once again impressed by the tribune. His own heart was pounding. After a moment, thinking that something more practical was in order, he started to fumble beneath his sodden cloak, searching for the hilt of his sword. He could still see no sign of anyone in the darkness, nor had the voice spoken again.

'Do you hear me?' Arrian sounded steadier now. The tribune managed to flick aside his cloak more smoothly than Rufus, but did not make a move to draw his gladius. 'Show yourself! Who are you? What do you want?' The tribune had switched to Latin, which had only a hint of the sing-song accent common to Bithynia.

Rufus fumbled until he had his fingers around the bone grip of his sword. The cloak had fallen back over his hand, so he tried to inch the blade out of its scabbard. It would not move, probably rusted by the rain.

'If you go down there, they will kill you,' the voice said flatly. 'Doesn't matter all that much to me, unless you make them wonder who else is up here.'

'They're our men.' Arrian was so exasperated that he had gone back into Greek, probably without noticing.

'They're slavers.' Rufus thought that he caught a hint of Gaul or even further north in the man's speech. 'They'll kill you just to take your boots – and that fine sword and armour. Be a good night's work as far as they are concerned.'

Arrian drew his gladius. Rufus decided to ask him whether he had greased it with anything special, for it came free with only the slightest hesitation. 'We are in a Roman province,' the tribune declared, 'and there are thousands of soldiers not far away from us.' Rufus had to wonder whether or not that was true, although he guessed it was still possible. 'Why would slavers be here?' the tribune asked.

'Coming home from Cyrrhus. They've sold the people they kidnapped in Assyria and Media. Snatched a few strays on the way to sell once they were over the river and in Osrhoene or beyond. Lot of opportunities for bold men willing to cross between empires and kingdoms.'

'Indeed. And you know this?'

'I do. Killed one of them a few hours ago. Wounded his mate, who was willing to talk.'

'Before you executed him?' Arrian asked.

'No. The deal was for him to live if he talked. He is injured, unarmed and on foot. He might make it, or he might stumble into some villagers or shepherds. They're not keen on slavers.'

'Who are you? Show yourself!' Arrian raised his sword, its blade glinting in the moonlight.

The dark shadows by the old walls moved and suddenly the tall figure of a man loomed up just a few paces away. His hood fell back and he grinned at them. 'What are you planning on doing with that, my lord tribune? If you really want to go down and fight a dozen of them, then that's up to you. But best hurry before they are gone. And if you want to fight me, I wouldn't bother. You'd no longer be breathing if that is what I wanted.'

'Oh.' For once Arrian appeared lost for words. He stared at his gladius, as if seeing it for the first time, then lowered it rather sheepishly. 'That would not seem wise, I suppose.'

'You are a Roman?' Rufus said.

'So they tell me,' the man said. 'Some call me other things. My name is Flavius Ferox. *Pilus prior* in Legio II Augusta, but more than a little detached these many years.'

As far as Rufus knew the legion was stationed in Britannia, and he wondered if that explained the man's accent. Perhaps his family were Britons given citizenship.

'Why are you here?' Arrian asked, marshalling himself at last.

Ferox gave a grim laugh. 'Why indeed, but that is a story for another time. Did I hear you speak of Crispinus as your legate?' It took Rufus a moment to realise that the strange centurion was speaking in Greek. 'Would that be Atilius Crispinus? Short man, white hair, talks all the time?'

'Yes,' Rufus said before Arrian had a chance to speak. 'He commands the Hispana. This is narrow stripe tribune Flavius Arrian, and I am Cornelius Rufus, *hastatus posterior* of cohors V. Do you know the legatus?'

The response was another bitter laugh.

Arrian coughed. 'The noble Crispinus is with his escort in the valley on the far side of this hill. I think it would be best if we all reported to him.'

Ferox sighed. 'Aye. The night can't get any worse, so we may as well. I will meet you there.'

'Better you stay with us,' Arrian said, and while he did not threaten, his stance changed so that he was holding his sword with purpose. 'Just to be on the safe side.'

'I'll be safe enough,' Ferox told him. 'I need my horse, and I am under orders – and not yours, my lord Arrian. So I will join you soon.'

Arrian thought for a long moment, and then let the gladius hang down limply again.

'We have a simple camp near some boulders and a withered tree,' Rufus said, doing his best to be helpful.

'I know. Knew you were Romans, but was not sure beyond that, until I heard you two talking.'

'Is that why you spoke to us?' Arrian sounded suspicious. 'Because you know the legatus or because we are officers.'

'Perhaps.' Ferox turned and walked off into the darkness. Rufus was not sure whether he felt safer with the man gone or when he was beside them.

'At least he seems to know the way,' Arrian muttered. The tribune sheathed his sword, having to force the blade into the scabbard. 'Come on then. Let's hope we don't fall on our arses on the way down that hill.'

Nearer the Euphrates
The same night

D OMITIUS HAD GOT *lost before the storm came in, his fever*
now so bad that he could not concentrate and did not
notice for a long time that he had strayed. A bolt of
lightning struck a tree close by, splitting the trunk, and this and
the deep roll of thunder panicked his horse which bolted, wild
eyed and ears twitching. The young mare ran on and on, mile
after mile, starting each time there was another flash even though
the worst was moving away from them. Somehow Domitius
stayed in the saddle, and that was a minor miracle for he was
no horseman, even by army standards. One hand gripped the
reins and his other wound itself around the beast's mane. Soon
the horse was gasping, but still she pelted along in terror, and
when she came to a gully filled with rainwater, she did not stop.
Domitius was never sure whether he jumped or simply lost his
seat at last and fell sideways out of the saddle, hitting the ground
hard. The mare leaped and screamed as she splashed into the
torrent and was swept away. Domitius never saw her again and
had never even known what the horse was called.

His shoulder hurt and his left arm did not work, so Domitius
had to roll onto the other side before he could get up. The rain
stopped very suddenly, unless that was simply because his
clouded mind took a while to realise. He had little sense of
where he was or of where he should go. The remaining food
had been in the packs tied to the rear horns of the saddle so

had vanished with the horse. A soldier for ten years, and before that the son and grandson of soldiers living surrounded by old soldiers in the colonia at Berytus, there had always been a pattern and an order to his life, with regulations or traditions to follow. That was all gone, and it was not simply the fever that made the change so hard to understand. It had all happened so quickly, and now he was a deserter and fugitive and nowhere would he be truly safe within the empire. Even if the truth came out, his crime was public and could not be forgotten.

Were they still after him? Domitius could not imagine anyone being able to follow his track through that storm. Still, he had heard stories about Ferox that made a man wonder. The centurion could be out there, getting ever closer. Better to be caught by him than the others, for Ferox might listen and understand. The others would simply kill him to make sure that the truth was hidden. Domitius had no armour, but had managed to grab a belt as he escaped, so had a pugio dagger on his left hip and an issue gladius on his right. At least he could make it difficult for them.

There was no way of crossing the flooded gully and it would be hours before the water level started to drop. The Euphrates was the only path to freedom... at least if he could find a way to cross it. That was a problem to be faced if he could reach the bank. Domitius' head was throbbing and each thought came only with effort. He had lost all sense of direction, but the water in the gully was flowing to his right and surely it must lead to a stream which in turn would lead to the river. Nursing his arm, Domitius set off along the bank.

Although Domitius would never know, Ferox had been much closer than he expected, already ahead and hoping to cut the fugitive off, until the centurion had run into the two slavers no more than a couple of miles from the place where the mare leaped into the torrent. The man Ferox wounded and spared was less injured than he had pretended, or perhaps just more determined, and before long was making his own way through the night. After that, his luck took a turn for the better when he saw the little cart and the pair of stragglers from the caravan.

Domitius walked and walked and beside him the gully fed into a stream which led through a shallow valley. The stream became broader and began to meander between little rocky hills. He was somewhere between waking and sleeping, as much staggering as walking, and once or twice he fell and felt his arm and side hurt when he pushed up. He lurched over one of the stony humps and ahead were some tiny, twinkling fires, with a silvery plain beyond them. Domitius stared, blinking at the view as his mind struggled to accept that this was the moonlight on water and that he was so close. Then he heard the screams.

A woman's voice was first, yelling in fear. A man shouted, then another gave more of a hiss than a cry, and the other one grunted in pain. The woman screamed again, and the second man shouted, angry this time. Figures ran towards him, one out in front and another larger shape in pursuit.

Domitius acted without real thought. He drew his stolen gladius and stumbled forward as fast as he could. The woman screamed again, until the cry was cut short and the bigger shape pounced on the smaller one, both of them falling. The man snarled, and when the woman squealed he hit her hard enough for Domitius to hear. He was hunched over his victim, pressing against her legs with his knee and trying to hold down her arms. The woman was sobbing and still struggling, and the man hit her again. He was talking softly now, like someone calming a horse.

The slaver only noticed Domitius when he was close, but

saw the glint of the naked blade. He tried to get up and the woman sensed this and rolled, kicking with her legs. The slaver swayed, lost balance and fell. Domitius closed on him silently, his mind too clouded to think of any challenge or threat or even why he was doing this.

Both the man and woman were on the ground, and the woman's hands were behind her back as if tied. The slaver lay flat on his back for a moment, then groaned as he sat up and his hand flicked forward, flinging a small rock he must have found. Domitius dodged, but was not fast enough and it smacked into his left shoulder, starting a wave of pain. The Roman swayed, then went on again and a decade of training meant that, even without realising, he had his gladius back and ready in an underarm guard as taught by the manual.

The slaver pushed himself up, one hand clutching his side, while he searched for another stone or anything else he could use as a weapon. Domitius took two paces forward, then another, and as the slaver raised his fists like a boxer, the Roman jabbed straight and hard just as he had practised so many times. Whoever had owned the gladius had tended the blade well, even though he had left it lying around for a deserter to snatch. The stubby point was sharp and, in spite of the resistance of thick and waterlogged wool, slid through the slaver's tunic and deep into his belly. Screaming, the wounded man pulled away and somehow Domitius kept a firm enough hold not to lose the blade as it ripped a gash in the slaver's stomach. The man fouled himself, adding to the stench as some of his entrails fell out. He doubled over, clutching at his belly and sobbing louder than the woman had done.

Domitius stabbed him in the throat and the noise stopped. It was the first time he had killed a man, but whether it was the fever or something else, he felt nothing at all. Turning he looked for the woman. She had rolled on her back and was trying to wriggle and push herself up. Her clothes were torn and her dress over her knees from her struggles. Her face was pale in the moonlight and she had lost whatever head covering she had worn, so that her long dark hair was wild. Domitius thought of a beautiful fury from a painting and it was the first real thought he had had for many hours. The woman was staring up at him, wild eyed and defiant.

'It is all right,' Domitius said. His voice was little more than a croak, and for all the drenching in the storm, he had not drunk anything for many hours. 'I won't hurt you.'

The woman was sitting up, and instead of trying to stand she wriggled away from him, pushing with her legs.

'Friend,' Domitius told her. 'I am a friend. Amicus,' he added, even though the chances of someone out here speaking Latin were remote. What was the Aramaic? 'Racham,' he tried.

The woman stopped trying to escape and looked at him properly for the first time. Then her eyes flicked to the side and she screamed. Something hit him hard on the back of the head and the night swallowed him in darkness. As he fell the last thing he heard was the woman screaming words he did not understand.

II

The temporary camp of Legio VIIII Hispana,
Fifty-five miles east of Cyrrhus
Fifteen days before the Kalends of March

'I SHOULD ORDER your immediate arrest and execution! Hercules' balls, I would be within my rights and no one would question it.' Marcus Atilius Crispinus, legatus legionis of VIIII Hispana, was angry, and not making a very good job of controlling himself. 'You have already been convicted and imprisoned, making you an escaped fugitive. Orders are orders, and no one could prove that the second letter had arrived in time to save you.' He slammed his heavy cane against the top of the folding table.

The legatus' rage had bubbled up steadily during the earlier meeting, as he listened to his officers' explanations. The idea had been simple. Crispinus had ordered the whole camp to keep a close eye on him, because he and his staff were going to slip away. When the legatus sneaked off, it was up to the rest to set out after him and track him down. The divine Julius had been fond of the game, and he was one of the best trainers of soldiers in history. People said that he was fond of turning everyone out like this at night, or when they were happily celebrating a festival. They also said that the soldiers liked the challenge.

Crispinus had just taken over a legion that was not in the best of shape. That meant he needed to get them all into good order as quickly as possible, a task made all the more urgent because the Lord Trajan was on his way from Antioch to inspect them at the end of the month. Trajan was very keen on discipline and training, and rewarded imaginative approaches as long as they worked, and that was the problem. No one had found the legatus. Most had lost the trail by the time darkness fell, all as night brought the heaviest rage of the storm. They had also lost each other, with barely any detachment managing to keep all its men together until the dawn.

There were plenty of excuses, and as Crispinus had listened to them he had kept turning the cane in his hands. The weather had been against them and that was bad luck. You got winter storms, of course, but the day had looked clear and given no warning that such a savage one was on the way. No one in the legion had done much training at night, which was fair enough, without excusing the fact that it had taken them three hours to notice that the legatus was gone and that half of them then managed to get lost before sunset. On top of that, one legionary had been struck by a lightning bolt and left a scorched wreck, his cuirass melted and sword twisted out of shape. A dozen men and twice as many horses had managed to break legs or ankles. One of the *lixae* had fallen into a stream and drowned, while eight men were still missing, whether dead, deserted, or just plain lost.

Crispinus had managed to keep his voice under control as he reprimanded the officers, and had the sense to encourage and assure them that they would do better next time, while making sure that he added a dose of fear. There was no sense in terrifying or bullying, since he needed them to make the most of what little time was left before the emperor arrived. They were still subdued when they were dismissed, for all the world like a class of naughty schoolboys. Ferox had watched them go, having sat at the back and in silence for the rest of the meeting. Now it was his turn.

'I've made up my mind!' Crispinus shouted. 'Tomorrow morning, and good riddance to you!'

Ferox said nothing, simply standing at attention and staring at a fixed point on the wall, just an inch or two above the legatus' head. Crispinus was not a tall man, while the centurion was over six foot and broad with it, so the senior officer did not attempt to step close and stare into his eyes. Born a prince of the Silures, the wolf people of the south west of Britannia, when they at long last submitted to Rome, Ferox had been sent to Gaul and then Rome itself to be educated before being made a citizen and commissioned as a centurion. His tribe cherished silence and held a man worthless who spoke when there was nothing worth saying, while army life had long accustomed him to letting harangues from senior officers flow past without really listening. This was a pretty good one, though, punctuated now and then as the legatus slammed the table with his cane. They were alone, but Ferox had no doubt the noise was carrying well beyond the hut. The guards ought to catch most of what their commanding officer was saying, as would passers-by in the crowded camp built by the legion for the duration of these training exercises.

'Yes, I've made up my mind.' Crispinus was almost shouting each word. 'The guards will take you away and you will be beheaded at dawn tomorrow. Jupiter knows it's long overdue. You have plagued this army and this empire for thirty years, Flavius Ferox, and it's time to put an end to it, do you hear me?'

'Sir.' Ferox's face remained impassive, his tone flat.

Crispinus slammed the cane down again. It was a similar shape to the ones carried by centurions, but shorter and thicker, and made from a dark hardwood rather than vine. The sides were richly carved and it had become the fashion in recent years for carpenters in each legion to present one to a new commander. Enough had done this to make it seem an insult if one was not crafted, so that a new tradition had been created.

The table shook when the legatus struck again. 'Minerva's tits, man! Having Hannibal at the gates must have been less terrifying than having you in the service of Rome. How many times have you been there when the army suffered a disaster? Three?'

'Give or take, sir.'

'Three armies routed, thousands of men massacred, and you come out smelling of roses.'

'Is that what that smell is, sir?' Ferox said before he could stop himself. He imagined how his old friend Vindex would have smirked, and suspected that he had spent far too long in the company of the northerner.

Crispinus slammed the cane down and this time the table broke. The legatus hit it a second time just to make sure, and there was a sharp crack as the wood split again. His cheek twitched again and again and it took a while for him to control it. His knuckles were white where he gripped the cane with both hands.

'More destruction,' he said sadly, and his voice was softer. 'And here you are again. If my dear father had known the future he would have left you and your men to die.'

'Sir.' That had been many years ago, when the legatus' father had command of a legion of his own on the Danube. He had marched to rescue Ferox after the Sarmatians slaughtered Legio XXI Rapax. The price was for Ferox to swear an oath to serve the father and his family, an obligation second only to his duty to the *princeps*.

'So now you have murdered a tribune?'

'Only a narrow stripe, sir.'

Crispinus flushed red and raised the cane high before he stopped himself. His cheek twitched just once. Ferox was still surprised by how much the man had changed in the last dozen or so years. When they first met, Crispinus had been a young aristocrat doing his initial spell with the army. Barely twenty, his hair had already gone grey and these days it was pure white, and the creases around his eyes and mouth made him appear much older than his thirty-seven years.

Crispinus shook his head. 'Only a narrow stripe – although from what I hear this was a large and plump example, so that ought to count for something, don't you think?' Here was a flash of the younger Crispinus, always so eager to appear poised and unshockable, no matter what the subject. 'I take it you had good reason and it was not mere high spirits?'

'Yes, sir.'

'Under orders?'

Ferox said nothing.

'Hmm. You have not changed. Just as infuriating as ever and just as closed. I really would be doing the army a favour by killing you, I really would. … Well, fortunately for you the second letter arrived, from a man with whom we are both acquainted and whose suggestion carries the weight of an instruction. So – for the moment – I shall defer your well-merited execution. For a while at least, and then we shall see. Might I presume that you are being useful to the noble gentleman in question?'

'Sir.' If the nature of his service was not in the letter, then Ferox was not about to volunteer any information, especially as he had been set more than one task.

The legatus' face flushed red once more and the twitch returned to his cheek. Crispinus had always been a clever man, who learned quickly and saw to the heart of matters. He was also ambitious, even by the standards of the old aristocracy, seeing politics as a game and playing it to win and win well. Yet excessive intelligence and ambition were dangerous, and even while he was just a tribune there had been plenty of doubts about his loyalty. Ferox remembered the then governor of Britannia, and Crispinus' uncle, more than entertaining the thought that his nephew might be part of a plot to overthrow the Lord Trajan, but suspecting that he would straddle a fine line between treachery and loyalty. As the governor had said, Crispinus was the kind of man who planned to do very well whichever regime was in charge.

Ferox felt tiny drops of spittle on his face before Crispinus regained control. The young senatorial tribune Ferox had known all those years ago would never have betrayed his emotions in this way, but his service in Britannia had not ended well. Crispinus had played both sides during a rebellion headed by a prince of the Brigantes, the greatest tribe of the north. Ferox still was not sure whether the tribune had been spying on the rebels or had joined them or perhaps he had done both and was making sure that he prospered whatever the outcome. The rebellious leaders claimed that Trajan was dead and that the governor wanted to make himself emperor, so that they were the defenders of the true emperor yet to be chosen by the Senate. The leaders knew that none of this was true, but plenty of men had believed the stories, and the defeat of the first column sent against them added to their numbers. By then the Brigantian prince was parading Crispinus as a captive and proof of the empire's weakness. He put an iron slave collar around the tribune's neck and made him walk on all fours like a dog. That may have been the least of the abuse he had suffered, and rumours spread of beatings, torture, and even rape. After the defeat of the rebels, Crispinus could barely walk, refused to talk, and cowered at the slightest hint of threat or loud noise. His term with the legion due to expire, he had been sent back to Italy and the care of his family as discreetly as possible.

'How is your wife?' The change of tack and the studied innocence of the question was far more like the young tribune he had known all those years ago. 'Do you manage to hear from her, these days? I suppose it is some time since you last saw her.'

Five years, three months and – Ferox did a quick calculation because so much had happened lately – thirteen days. He wondered whether the last number was unlucky before deciding that things could not be much worse.

'The queen is well so far as I know, my lord,' Ferox said, remaining at attention and barking out the words as if they were a formal report.

'Ah yes, I believe the Senate is close to formal recognition of her as monarch of the Brigantes and friend of the Roman People.'

Ferox had thought the approval long since given, but simply stared at the wall rather than take the bait.

'There was that business in Moesia. What must it be? Ten years ago? Something like that or close to it. You were all in a fort and besieged by a host of Dacians – and the noble Claudia Enica, your good lady, inspiring everyone by her cheerfulness and high spirits. They say she carried drinking water to the walls even during the attacks.'

Ferox managed not to smile and kept his face rigid. His wife was an eques, as fine and fashionable a Roman lady as any when she chose. She was also a warrior trained in the old ways of the tribes, and during the siege she had fought with deadly proficiency and led the Brigantes from the front. Still, a ferocious woman was not a Roman ideal, and the mere thought was enough to make people uncomfortable, even when the lady in question was on their side. So the official version told of a demure wife bringing food, tending to the wounded, and concealing her fears in a dignified way. In truth there was another lady at the fort who did all of those things and did them well, but Claudia Enica had taken a different path. As reward for her conveniently forgotten courage, and also for her and Ferox's discretion over some less edifying episodes during the siege, there had been the understanding that this would speed her recognition as queen of her tribe. Yet by the sound of it, the Romans still dragged their feet, no doubt nervous of a woman as ruler, even one who had proved her loyalty again and again, not least in fighting against her rebellious brother.

Crispinus slammed the cane against the broken table, and the sudden crash made Ferox look. Silently he cursed himself for such weakness.

'A fly,' Crispinus said affably. 'Wretched things get everywhere. Now where were we? Ah yes, the adorable Claudia Enica. Such beauty, such poise – such an ability to chatter unceasingly.' Ferox did not react to that – after all it was true. 'Such an actress. So keen an intellect is unexpected in someone so fair of face and form, and the unexpected tends to make us all nervous and suspicious. The beautiful really ought to be dull witted, so that everyone else can feel superior to them in that respect and deal better with their jealousy. Well, I should know...'

'Ha, ha, sir!' Ferox said flatly.

'Don't be insolent, centurion – or that second letter goes into the fire and never existed. Still, we will need to find a sharp blade to deal with that stiff neck of yours... Where was I? Ah yes, the lovely, flirtatious Claudia. I have never really cared for red hair, but with her... Such beauty, and married to you.'

Crispinus shook his head to emphasise his dismay. 'Really it is a waste, a shocking waste. And yet here you are thousands of miles away from a prize that other men would envy. It is most puzzling. Most men would surely have retired from service and lived blissfully, even ecstatically, for as long as their strength coped.'

'Duty, sir,' Ferox lied. In truth he had no choice if he was to protect his family.

'Or has she chosen this separation? Leaves her free, of course, and she is so much younger than you…' The legatus let the question trail off.

'How is your health, my lord?' Ferox asked in a voice of deep concern, feeling that two could fight dirty as easily as one. 'You suffered so terribly among the Brigantes. It was said that you suffered from poor health and low spirits for a long time.' Actually, the gossip said that the former tribune was insane, all but sowing his fields with salt like Odysseus, although a few hinted that the madness was invented to prevent public disgrace. Either way, a promising career in public life was felt to be over.

Was there a twitch? Perhaps, but the legatus rallied quickly. 'I believe many said that I was mad, you know. Just think of that!' There was a tick now, but a deliberate one. 'As if that had ever disqualified anyone from the Senate! Indeed, in the army I understand it is a positive advantage.'

'Only for senior officers, my lord,' Ferox said before he could stop himself. He silently cursed Vindex and his sense of humour – and like all northerners, his constant talk.

Crispinus twitched and then roared with laughter. 'Quite true, quite true, although best not said aloud… Well then, since you do not seem to wish to speak of your own family and affairs – and yes, I know you have children…'

'The twins are close to being women now, my lord.'

'Then all the more reason for their father to be close by and keep his eyes peeled and sword sharp to see off those whose designs are less than honourable. And yet you are here on the edge of Syria, so far away – and war is coming.' Crispinus sighed in disappointment at the lack of reaction. 'I suppose war is always coming wherever you are, Flavius Ferox? You seem to have a knack. What was it that old villain Vindex used to say? 'The centurion has a way of making friends.' Yes, that was it. Where you go, trouble follows. And now you are here, and so am I, waiting for chaos and war as usual. Just like old times.'

'You had a choice, my lord.'

'I have a duty, just like you.' By any normal standard, Crispinus ought to have been given command of a legion six or seven years ago. Aristocrats always liked to take each step along their career as soon as they were eligible, but for a long time his progress had ceased and at thirty-seven he was old to command a legion. 'The Lord Trajan has charged me with command of a picked legion when we are on the cusp of a great war, a war that may in time make even his conquest of Dacia appear little more than a border skirmish. Thus we have our parts to play and must do our utmost to prevail for the sake of the *res publica* and for our own reputation. That is our only way home.'

There was a surprising grimness in the legatus' voice, as well as something harder to pin down. 'Yes, sir,' Ferox said. Trajan, or someone close to him, must have decided that Crispinus was sane enough and trustworthy enough to be given a legion. It might be a test, for the emperor was fond of giving aristocrats one more chance to prove themselves. Half the trouble during the siege in Moesia had come from someone given just such an opportunity. Ferox wondered whether Crispinus was facing the same prospect of vindicating himself by distinguished and loyal service or utter disgrace if there was any hint of unreliability. There was also the third option of dying heroically and adding posthumous laurels to the family name. In many ways that was the most convenient from the point of view of the emperor and his advisors.

'I am proud of the Hispana,' Crispinus declared, the orator's love of the dramatic taking over once more. 'Soon we shall add to its reputation. I say we, because you are to be placed under my command – you and your ragamuffin band of cut-throats from Britannia. They are on their way because I suspect that I will need them and you.'

That was news, for the last he had heard of his men they had been in Thrace. Just before the siege he had been placed in temporary command of an irregular unit of Brigantes. There had been almost six hundred of them in those days, and by now barely eighty were left, even though the temporary appointment had stretched on and on. Sometimes they were with him to do yet another dirty job, and sometimes he was on his own. It would be good to see them, but that suggested something nasty was waiting for them, even if it was hard to think where they were going.

'Why, my lord, if I am permitted to ask? I understood that the war was to be waged in Armenia.'

'You understand too much.' Crispinus was smiling. 'But then you always have. And in this case you are only half right. The war will probably start in Armenia, but where it will spread after that is a page yet to be written.' Trajan was known to be concentrating a large force ready to move against Armenia if its king chose not to behave himself, and Ferox suspected that the Romans would make sure that he could not because he sensed that they wanted war. Yet that was all further to the north, and Legio VIIII Hispana was not part of it. Founded by the divine Augustus, it had once had a fine reputation, and had served in Britannia from the time of the invasion under Claudius. Still, the empire never had enough soldiers and a few years ago someone had had the bright idea of stripping Britannia of a legion for use elsewhere. In Ferox's opinion the decision was sheer folly, but it had been made and the Hispana chosen. After that things had not turned out well. They went to the Rhineland just when plague broke out, costing them a lot of men. Afterwards a thousand of the fittest legionaries were taken from them and posted as permanent reinforcement to legions ground down by the wars in Dacia. Then Hispana went to the mouths of the Danube, and hundreds more men fell ill with swamp fever. The survivors were moved again, this time to Syria, to take over duties from other legions earmarked for the war in Armenia. Another cull saw more men and officers posted to bring those legions up to strength and Hispana was flooded with new recruits to replace them. Outside Antioch a new disease met them and many more died, shivering and fouling themselves. In the last few years, Legio VIIII Hispana had become known as a sickly, unlucky unit. Crispinus' new command was scarcely a prize.

'We spoke of one queen,' Crispinus said, 'but I suspect that we both have an interest in one much closer to hand.'

'Sir?' Ferox could guess, but was not about to volunteer anything.

'Or perhaps princess is better than queen. I speak of Azátē, daughter of King Abgarus of Osrhoene. How much do you know of her? And of Nicopolis and the other western cities?'

'Sir? I do not know this country or its kings. Most of my time has been spent near the coast.'

Crispinus stretched his arms up to yawn, almost touching

the tent strung up as a roof over the dry stone walls of the room. It was a style Ferox had never seen anywhere else in the empire, but offered a good compromise between pitching tents and the effort to build more permanent huts. The legatus had rugs on his floor and camp furniture, so that four folding chairs were around the broken table. In a very studied way, he pulled one over to him and then sat down. For a while he examined his cane as if seeing it for the first time.

Ferox remained at attention. Trumpets sounded for the change of watch and he could hear someone bellowing orders outside as the guards outside the legatus' tent were relieved. Crispinus said nothing as the little ceremony was completed.

'Where would the army be without shouting and stamping?' the legatus said at long last. 'They do so love it.' He let out a long sigh. 'And you, Flavius Ferox, dearly love your mulish obstinacy. When I was young I would have coaxed and cajoled you into talking, prising each gem of knowledge from that thick skull of yours... and still you would keep your secrets and play your little games. Are we not both too old for that?'

'Sir.'

The legatus flushed again. 'Well, since I am not going to kill you, I shall choose the easier path for once. Go to the table. My apologies, what was once a table, and next to it you will see a papyrus letter on the floor. Pick it up and examine the remnants of the seal and then go to the final two columns. After that we can talk properly as I do not believe that you will disobey the instructions there.'

Ferox did as he was told. Even though he had known what was coming, his heart sank when he saw the little figure of Hercules on the broken seal, for that sign had haunted his life for the last decade.

'You see, I think,' Crispinus said as the centurion read the last part of the letter. 'Perhaps I should have begun with this, instead of hoping that a reunion of old friends would loosen your tongue. Some hope of that. So I wield the mark of Aelius Hadrian as a weapon to beat down your resistance. Yes, I speak his name, and need not warn you to do so only with great caution. He had more than a little to do with my appointment, and it appears that he has work for us both.'

Ferox did not think that he even mouthed the words, let alone whispered them, so perhaps Crispinus knew him better than he thought.

'*Omnes ad stercus*,' the legatus said. 'Quite.'

III

On the training grounds outside Zeugma
Fifth day before the Nones of March

HADRIAN WATCHED AS the horseman pat his steed's neck and then turned as the trooper came forward to offer him his shield. The rider grinned at the man and said something that Hadrian could not catch, although it was easy enough to guess. After a moment's hesitation, the cavalry trooper leaned his oval shield against his legs and used both hands to unfasten his helmet. It was bronze, with broad cheek pieces which extended back to cover the ears, and a shallow neck guard like all cavalry helmets, because wide ones like the infantry used were dangerous if a man took a tumble. The trooper made sure to lift off the hat he wore underneath with the helmet and then passed it to his emperor. Trajan grinned again, running his fingers over the tinned detail moulded to look like locks of hair, then put it on his own head and tied it fast, before reaching down to take the proffered shield. Hadrian heard the soldier laugh at something the emperor said to him. Trust Trajan to joke with his soldiers whenever there was an opportunity, and trust Trajan to wear a combat helmet – albeit one polished to a high sheen for the inspection – rather than one of the highly decorated ceremonial ones with their face masks.

'They love him, don't they,' Lusius Quietus said admiringly. 'And so they should. That's a man all right, and no mistake.' Hadrian had to agree. Trajan had a knack for talking directly to the soldiers and had done so time and again during a long day of exercises and manoeuvres. Today it was the turn of the cavalry, so that there was more colour and movement than the day before, when a legion had gone through its drills. Tomorrow it would be the turn of the auxiliary infantry, always the last in the pecking order, although Hadrian sometimes wondered if they were more useful. There was attention, sometimes even fuss, when a legion was moved from one province to another, but no one bothered too much when auxiliary cohorts went to a new station – or for that matter when new units were raised or old ones disbanded. By the spring, nine legions would be ready to take the field at the emperor's command, with substantial vexillations from as many more, so that almost half the legionaries in the entire empire were concentrated on the Asian frontier. Trajan spoke of sorting out Armenia, where a king had been appointed without his approval, and worse still by the Parthians. Other than that, the emperor remained tight lipped with all but a handful of friends and confidants, and so far these had not included Hadrian. Day after day they saw preparations for a war not yet declared or explained.

Another soldier was on the other side of the princeps and held out a spear. Trajan took it and leaned back to slip it into the long quiver suspended from the rear horn on the right side of his saddle. He held out his hand for another weapon.

'Oh shit,' someone said under their breath. Hadrian guessed that it was Bruttius Praesens, the new legatus of Legio VI Ferrata, no doubt regretting the impulse to speak up when the emperor had invited his staff to join him in a spot of practice.

'Wonder if he'll try for three?' Quietus drawled, without

looking at Praesens, but it seemed that the princeps was content with two throwing spears. 'Good to see he had the sense to pick a light little mare,' he added once this became clear, and gave a sideways glance at Hadrian and Praesens, both of whom were on taller horses from the senior *turma* of the *ala* on parade.

'Don't pay attention to the nasty man,' Hadrian cooed into the ear of his mare. He was quite fond of big horses, but had chosen this one from those on offer simply because there was something he liked about her, and that was as good a reason as any. 'You're far more lovely than his little gelding.' Hadrian stroked the horse's mane.

'Do you need some privacy?' Quietus asked. 'Praesens and I can wander off if you like.'

Praesens' eyes flicked nervously between the two men, until they both chuckled. Trajan had exiled his uncle, Laberius Maximus, just a few years ago and it was only now that the nephew had received any sign of favour.

Trumpets sounded and a hush spread over the exercise field, apart from the sighing of the wind and the little noises of shuffling and pawing the ground inevitable when more than two thousand horsemen were paraded.

Trajan raised his right arm, the spear pointing straight up into the air. The princeps was handsome enough by Roman standards, his limbs muscular and his chest broad, even though he was of no more than average height. Hadrian suspected that Trajan's fondness for smaller horses, like the one he had chosen today, was deliberate, for when mounted it made him appear taller. His seat was good, as per regulation, with back straight and heels a little back. His borrowed shield was oval, the field red and decorated with double wreaths probably to show the ala's record as *bistorquata* – twice awarded a unit battle honour.

The helmet fitted well, even if it looked odd combined with the solid iron cuirass worn only by senior officers.

Trajan walked his horse in a tight circle, making sure it was warmed up as was usual before any drill, even though a trooper had already made sure that the animal was ready. The hush continued, for he had made it known that there was to be no fuss unless he had earned it. Hadrian and the other two came forward and took position behind him, allowing more space than was usual. Ahead of the emperor was an open, carefully smoothed track some thirty paces wide. On either side stood the serried ranks of cavalrymen, parading by turma each with its own standard. Weapons, armour, and every metal fitting on the harnesses were polished to a high sheen, so that the afternoon sun glistened and sparkled off the three ranks of mounted soldiers. Hadrian hoped that none of their horses would shy or panic at the sight when each made the ride, but there was nothing to be done. It was too late to ask for one of the chamfrons worn with the full ceremonial equipment, fitted with dome-like coverings for the horse's eyes, the metal like a grill so that the animal could see enough straight ahead, but little to the sides; too late, and perhaps it would only have made things worse. You never quite knew with horses. People were so much more predictable.

'May I join you?'

Hadrian turned to see another horseman approaching. He was a slim youth, eighteen at the most, with the delicate features of the East, and his large brown eyes outlined with kohl, even if his hair and thin beard were after the Greek style. Lips a little too full, and inclined to pout by the look of it, while the little pearl earrings were truly barbaric. His trousers and long-sleeved tunic were silk, as was the trapper on his sprightly horse. Hadrian could see a gaggle of riders in eastern dress, no doubt the lad's attendants, and since they were talking amicably with the commander of the *singulares Augusti*, the emperor's own mounted bodyguard, he was clearly of some importance.

'Certainly, if you give us your name? I am Aelius Hadrian.' Lusius Quietus glanced back and did not appear welcoming, but nor was he inclined to intervene.

'Your servant, my lord,' the boy said, bowing his head, although Hadrian suspected that the name was entirely new to him. 'I am honoured – and they call me Arbandes, son of Abgarus.' That made his father the king of Osrhoene, so all the more interesting.

'Welcome, lord prince. Shall I send for shield and javelin for you?'

'I do not need them,' the young man said, and gave the bowcase and quiver behind his saddle a complacent tap.

Trajan had started his run and was already at a steady canter. That was approved by the drill books, for good cavalry attacked in order and not in some wild charge. It was also sensible for a man of his years, his once pitch-black hair now a mottled grey and his forehead a good deal higher than it used to be. Come September the princeps would be fifty-nine, and he was beginning to look it. Today's little show was all part of it, and something Trajan would not have done a decade ago in Dacia. A good commander was supposed to be as adept with sword, shield and spear as he was skilled at combining all the elements of his army and directing them to one purpose, but he did not need to keep proving it. Then a few nights ago, as they talked over dinner of the great generals of the past, someone had told of Pompey, a man by then as old as the emperor was now, training with his soldiers in Greece and outdoing them on the exercise field.

The emperor threw his first javelin some thirty paces from the six foot high post set up as target. That was a fairly long range, but his aim was true and the point struck, although it did not stick in deeply and dropped to the ground. Timing was the key, for the horse was pounding on across the dry earth, the distance closing every moment, and the idea was to keep up the pace while reaching back for the second javelin, hefting it and then throwing before coming level with the target. Trajan did it, loosing the missile when five paces from the post. This time the head of the *lancea* drove deep into the wood and stayed there, as the watching soldiers cheered.

Pompey had ridden, fenced and thrown javelins like a stripling, and his soldiers had cheered him to the skies as well. Still, after a promising start, he had also lost the war in a single day when his much larger army was routed by Caesar at Pharsalus. Hadrian wondered whether that was a bad omen.

'Ah, you are the emperor's cousin,' Arbandes said, breaking in on his thoughts, 'so of the royal blood.'

Lusius Quietus turned his head to watch, paying close attention to how Hadrian responded.

'Not quite, lord prince. My late father was a cousin of the Lord Trajan. I am his kin, but distant. And in Rome we do not have a royal family.'

'Nor a king,' Quietus cut in. 'The Lord Trajan is princeps, the first among us and the chief servant of the res publica, chosen to lead us in peace and war.' Quietus smiled, showing his neat teeth, which were very white against his deep brown skin. 'You will have to pardon Romans our pride, but it explains so much about us.'

Hadrian often thought that Quietus was the finest looking man that he had ever seen, although like the emperor he was not particularly tall. Unlike Trajan, his was a light frame, perfectly balanced, so that he was almost a human version of the ponies so loved by the Numidians. He was prince of that wild African people – king perhaps by right – and Hadrian suspected that you could see the marks where his ears had been pierced as an infant, but from the age of six he was raised as a Roman aristocrat by a father who had proved his loyalty to the res publica and been rewarded with citizenship. Domitian had made the son an eques and an army officer, decorated him several times and then cashiered him. Trajan recalled him to the army, promoted him, decorated him and eventually enrolled him in the Senate. Now this 'Roman' senator was telling an eastern prince about Roman pride. Perhaps one day Arbandes would follow a similar path and tell others what it meant to be Roman, for that was how the empire worked.

'My apologies, I meant no offence,' the young prince assured them.

'None taken, my dear boy,' Quietus' grin was infectious, 'none at all. Romans are not given to apologies, either, so we don't expect 'em from others.' Hadrian suspected that Quietus' face would not quite meet the standards set down by the famous sculptors so revered in Athens, but had an animation that few artists could ever have captured. He must be well into his forties, but did not look it, for his skin was smooth as a child's. That animation gave him charm and whenever he wanted Quietus could be very likeable. 'The point is,' he continued, 'that the Lord Trajan steers the ship of state because he is the best of us. One day – though with the gods' blessing not for many years – he will pass into the Heavens and he, helped by the Senate, will choose the next best man to succeed him.'

Hadrian wondered whether Quietus dreamed of such elevation. The empire could certainly do worse, for the one-time Numidian prince was clever, a brilliant soldier and leader, a decent enough man in his way, and charm could be a great asset to any leader.

'Oh, nearly time for me to go,' Quietus said, as if realising for the first moment that Praesens had started his run. The new legatus managed only a single throw, which chipped the side of the post, and he tapped the target with the shaft of his second spear as he passed it. There was polite cheering and some smiles at the gesture. At least he had not made a fool of himself.

'See you in a little while.' Quietus was half turned, smiling at them, when his horse went from stationary into a fast canter. Hadrian did not see any sign of movement of heels or legs, and only now realised that the reins were loosely looped over the horn of his saddle. It was as if the animal simply knew what its rider wanted and acted without being told – and this was a horse he had mounted for the first time just a little while ago. The beast shot off, faster than Trajan had gone, let alone Praesens, and yet somehow Quietus gave the impression of sauntering along. His first lancea struck low and fast on the target, the second right at the top when he was still fifteen paces short. He simply seemed to have more time than was natural. A little beyond the target was a line of hexagonal shields, each propped up by a spear rammed into the ground. Without the slightest check Quietus went for them and his horse jumped easily over. Trajan led the soldiers in their cheering.

Quietus certainly had style. He would have been an easy man for Hadrian to like, if he had not been an enemy. There was talking behind Hadrian as he waited for the shouting to die down, but he was sweating under the weight of his high-crested helmet and trying to focus solely on the task in hand.

'I am so sorry.' Arbandes had walked his horse alongside. Another older man was a little behind him. 'They say that I should not. I am sorry.' The lad appeared quite distressed, but the cheering had died away and there was no more time.

'Do not worry, and do not apologise,' Hadrian told the boy, echoing Quietus, and tried to give a smile just as encouraging. He clicked at his horse and gave slight pressure with his legs and the beast lurched into a trot which then became a canter. It was not the finest start, but not a disgrace, and he kept pressure on the reins to stop the animal going any faster. The post seemed very close, but he made himself wait, lancea ready to throw. The key, just like riding itself, was to make it all feel natural. He threw, angling the light spear high to allow for its drop, and reached back for the second. There was approving noise from the watching soldiers, so the first must have hit, and now the other was ready. He was close, very close, as he drew back the spear and flung it forward, and then he passed the target and a cheer told him that he had struck true. The row of shields was a little to the left and he stared at it, gave a gentle tug on the bit, and shifted his body to let the mare know where they were heading. She responded, and he felt her strength gather because they were at the jump already and he knew that she would obey so did not urge her on in case he made her nervous. Then the mare stopped.

Hadrian felt himself leave the saddle, flying forward, and he tossed the big shield away, as he went over the row of shields, falling now, and the earth came up and smacked into him. There was a gasp from the rows of soldiers. Hadrian struggled to breathe, his eyes blinked and the blackness started to close around him.

'Who gave you permission to dismount!' a voice called out from the ranks as someone aped one of the army's riding instructors, and laughter spread along the serried ranks.

Hadrian felt his mind clear and decided to make the best of

it. His face was still pressed against the ground, so he took a bite of earth and started to push himself up.

'Need a hand, my dear fellow?' The drawl could only be Quietus. 'Perhaps this is a new technique for us to consider, my lord?' he added. 'If spears don't work jump on the buggers!'

Hadrian was half up, and saw the emperor next to the Numidian. Trajan seemed amused rather than annoyed, which made it easier to play along. 'Well, I do like to try out new ideas,' he explained. 'This way my wrestling skills would come into play.'

Trajan gave a little snort of laughter. 'Not sure that it will catch on,' he said.

'True, my lord, but up until the last moment it was perfect – and by throwing his shield he might knock another foe off his feet.' Quietus was enjoying himself.

'All part of the plan,' Hadrian assured them. 'Although I wonder whether next time I ought to throw the horse at them and stay on the other side of the jump myself!'

Trajan snorted again. 'Might be wiser, my boy. Now dust yourself off. The Games are over and we must return to formalities while the light lasts.' He tapped with his heels and rode off towards the big tribunal.

'Oh look, they have found your proud steed.' Quietus nodded at a soldier leading the animal by the reins. 'Come along then.' He set off after the emperor, without any visible signal to his horse and without bothering to wait. Praesens had appeared, his face making clear that he was happy someone else had drawn attention away from his own modest performance. He gave a faint smile, then noticed that the emperor and Quietus were now some way off.

'Sir?' A trooper was offering to take Praesens' shield from him. The legatus frowned until he understood and let the man have it. He glanced back at Hadrian, who was nuzzling the head of his horse, and decided not to wait any longer so followed the others.

Hadrian felt a little sorry for the man, but only a little. He had known Praesens' uncle when Laberius Maximus had been one of Trajan's favourites. The old boy was a bluff, old-fashioned Roman, with a fine military record and a taste for army life much like the princeps himself. More than once he had acted as intermediary to Hadrian when Trajan was displeased. Then quite suddenly, Trajan came to distrust Laberius. The old man pleaded innocence – quite reasonably because it was true – but he had made a few unwise decisions, become associated with some questionable people and deeply incriminating evidence was discovered involving them and implicating him. Hadrian knew that this was all false, since he had arranged for the material to be made and found, and Laberius had done the wrong thing and lost his temper, saying things to the emperor which could never he unsaid. With great regret, Trajan sent his old friend into exile. Hadrian gained mild satisfaction in avenging himself on someone who had done him several bad turns. Far more important was the simple truth that everyone who fell from the top made room for those below.

Quietus had insisted to the young prince that the Romans would not tolerate a king. Hadrian wondered whether anyone really believed that lie after more than a hundred years of Caesars. Perhaps some did, in the face of all the evidence. Lying in public was essential to civilisation, but only a fool lied to himself in private, and Quietus did not seem a fool, nor did any of the other men Trajan trusted. They knew that Trajan was a monarch, king in everything but name, and decent enough in his way if scarcely the best of them. After all, who was to judge which senator was more capable or more moral than the rest, let alone choose a successor on that basis? Trajan was a king and kings had courts, and when the king was childless, the succession was a matter to be arranged. So far, the princeps had shown not the slightest interest in the matter, which meant that someone else must decide. Quietus and a few others were riding high at the moment, so might well influence Trajan or perhaps dream of rising just as high. The very nature of a royal court was that influence waxed and waned and a man's fall might be very sudden. Laberius Maximus was proof of that.

Hadrian barely listened as the afternoon's events played themselves out. Trajan sat on the podium, with Quietus, Hadrian and half a dozen others beside him. Each ala marched past at the walk, trot and then gallop, and each in turn then halted directly in front while the princeps spoke to them about their performance. There were the usual platitudes about each commander and the care he had taken to keep the men and horses in the finest condition.

'Your prefect Julius has done his duty undauntedly.'

Trajan talked about drill, leavening the praise with occasional instructions for change or improvement.

'I do not care for too much speed where order is sacrificed. If a rider cannot see where he is going, or cannot rein back his mount at will, then he may come a cropper from ditches or traps he has not seen. Nothing must ever be done recklessly.'

The style and the delivery were very familiar by now. In the last month they had reviewed the troops waiting outside Antioch for the coming campaign, before each contingent began its march to the concentration area in Cappadocia. Most units had a lot of recent recruits, and many had not served in a major conflict for decades, apart from the detachments sent to Dacia. The army boasted of its high standards of training, but there were always so many other tasks for soldiers to perform, especially here in the eastern provinces, with their multitude of unruly cities. Eight days ago the emperor and his staff had watched Legio VIIII Hispana march, build a camp, and stage a mock battle. It was the weakest performance so far, and the advice had been fuller and more detailed, without preventing praise of 'Crispinus, my legatus, and his diligent work in training you all', which given that the man had only arrived at the very end of last year was generous. The Hispana was to stay in Syria as the only complete legion left in the province, for even Zeugma and Samosata were to be held by skeleton garrisons. Crispinus and his men were staying behind because Trajan wanted only the best for the real effort.

He was also leaving Hadrian behind, and after the inspections at Zeugma, his orders were to return to Antioch. Last year the governor of Syria had eaten some bad fish and died. At the time Hadrian was at Athens, after a relaxing year as archon of the city, making and listening to speeches of immense grace and no importance whatsoever. He was fairly near, otherwise unemployed, so Trajan sent him as temporary legatus until a proper replacement could be found. That was typical of the man, for he recognised Hadrian's talents, but just could not bring himself to like him. A new legatus was on the way, although delayed because he was assisting with the troop concentration and preparations for war in the north. Hadrian had three or four months left as acting governor of Syria and after that he was not sure. Trajan had not said whether he wanted Hadrian to join him on campaign at this stage or go off to Athens again or to Hades or wherever he liked. Quietus and the others in high favour at present certainly showed no enthusiasm for his company.

With a final ride past, the parade was dismissed and the imperial entourage rode to the pavilion built for them in a temporary camp constructed by one of the legions. Trajan preferred this to staying in proper houses in the garrison at Zeugma, and the dinner that night was like all the others so far, exclusively male, military in tone, with good if fairly plain food, at least by Rome's standards, and very good and very plentiful wine. The emperor enjoyed talking, and enjoyed listening to manly stories and jests. Hadrian wondered whether he got drunk quicker than even a few years ago, but could not be sure. He was doing his best to glean every useful bit of information from the talk and the unspoken signs of precedence in the way men behaved. With just a few months left in command, he wanted to know all that he could so that he could make best use of the opportunity. A plan was already in his mind, so he took care to cultivate the prince from Osrhoene, even though the boy was not invited to the main dinner. Before that began, Hadrian had taken him back to the training area and watched as the youngster galloped and shot arrows at the target. He was lavish in his praise, and had the boy not been bearded might have gone further, even though that was not his purpose. Arbandes was both likeable and rather gullible, clearly flattered by the attention. Trajan had been too angered by the letter from the boy's father to take a good look at the son, who was just the sort of eager young puppy the emperor liked to have around. That too might prove useful, but not for the moment.

Hadrian drank with the others, dutifully laughed as several times someone barked out, 'Who gave you permission to dismount!' He watched Quietus and the others and listened, knowing so much that they did not. A month ago at Baalbek he had seen the future. It was just a question of whether he was skilled enough and fast enough to make sure that it turned out as he wanted.

In the house of Simon the merchant, Nicopolis
The next day

TIME PASSED, AS *it must do. Day and night were as one,
sleep and waking so barely distinct that it was hard to
notice. There were voices, sometimes people, and they
tried to help him drink and even eat a little. The faces were
indistinct, until he dreamed, when all was vivid. He dreamed
of a ladder, climbing high into the Heavens, but as he climbed
a dragon was beneath him, its eyes as coals and its breath like
fire. It snapped at him and grabbed him, biting his heels and
pulling at his cloak. An angel wiped his brow, the touch cool
and damp. She was a tall angel, with long black hair that was
soft whenever it brushed against him. The dragon pulled and he
was falling, falling into the deep water.*

*He dreamed of far-off days and days that may never have
been, but always he came back to the one place and the one
moment and stood in that high chamber off the grand hall of
the principia.*

*Domitius felt their eyes upon him. Most were men he had
known for years, men he trusted, respected, and in many cases
liked. They had toiled together, stood side by side on parade,
taken those magic drinks of men parched after a long march
when anything tasted more wonderful than at any other time.
Many were friends and all were* commilitones, *bonded as
comrades by the shared suffering, joys and plain stupidity of
army life. There was Sextus, squat, broad chested, slow, but*

always got there in the end. He was frowning, as if puzzled. Annius, always on the fringes, always the cynic, had his usual expression of amusement as if everything was one huge joke. Longus was beside him, eyes excited. He had always been a vicious little bastard who enjoyed seeing anyone suffer, but as the others all said, he was their vicious little bastard, and when it came to it, they knew that they could rely on him. That was the army all over – them and us, and you stuck with us. Others he did not know, for there were men from other cohorts.

Then there was old Caecilius, almost a second father to him, and his face was as rigid as only an old sweat could manage, while his eyes pleaded with Domitius. 'Just do it, lad, do it.' He seemed to say, just as he had done the previous night. 'It's nothing. Doesn't mean anything. Just a gesture. No one really cares. Do it, then forget it and think and do what you like the rest of the time. They won't care. No one will be looking, but they're looking now and all you have to do is step forward, pour out the cup and say the words. They're just words, boy – like 'No, sir' when someone higher up asks if you've got any complaints. Doesn't mean anything – not a thing. You're not lying to anyone who matters, are you? This is bullshit, just army bullshit, so treat it like a parade, don't think, obey all the orders and then forget it.

'Step forward, Caius Domitius Clemens!' the praefectus castrorum *commanded.*

'Go on, boy. Do it.' Caecilius did not need to say the words aloud.

Domitius could not move.

'Step forward!'

'Come on, it's nothing. Do it and forget it.'

'I cannot,' Domitius found himself saying.

'This is an order, Clemens!' the praefectus barked. 'Step forward and make the offering.'

Caecilius' face was white. Domitius had never seen him show fear before and this was somehow worse than when he was pleading. Yet how could he deny the truth.

'I cannot,' Domitius croaked. He licked his lips. 'I cannot,' he managed, louder this time and clear to the whole room. 'I am a Christian.'

Caecilius shut his eyes. The praefectus castrorum, a solid, sensible man, stood up and came over to Domitius.

'None of us heard that, lad,' he whispered. 'And none of us will remember, so don't be daft and think of your own skin and the honour of the legion. It's just words, nothing more. So pretend and no one will mind.' He glanced back at the seated officers. The tribune who had pressed for the investigation was not there. Of the centurions, only Festus was hostile and he would not resist pressure from the praefectus. Yet where was Ferox? Even if there was no way out of this, he wanted to pass on all that he had learned.

The praefectus took a step back and gestured at the altar. Beside it was a cup filled and ready to be poured out in libation. 'Do this and renew your oath to the princeps and Rome, and you walk free, honour and rank restored.'

'What of the curse?' Festus asked. 'Should he not revile the name of this Christ?'

The praefectus stared at him. 'That is not necessary. This is no civilian court with all its wiles and hypocrisy. We are a tribunal of soldiers and will act as such.' He turned back to Domitius. 'Let's be done with this, lad.'

'I cannot,' Domitius stammered. He thought he caught a flash of hope from Caecilius. The desperation in his friend's face made him choke and he could not speak, so shook his head.

'For the last time of asking,' the praefectus began, a mixture of sorrow and frustration in his voice, 'make the offering and take the oath. That's it, all you have to do, and no more will ever be said, not ever, so do as you are told and make the sodding offering! Now, boy!' His voice was suddenly loud. 'That's a direct order, soldier, and you will do it!'

Domitius' legs responded to discipline and he took a pace forward before hesitating.

'Go on, boy, go on.' Caecilius actually mouthed the words.

'Obey me!' the praefectus snapped. 'Two paces forward!'

Domitius wanted to do as he was told. They were all watching, urging him on, even Festus seemed caught up with the general mood. He stared around him, seeing all their faces. His throat was parched, his heart pounding.

'Do your duty, man, obey the order!'

'No,' Domitius yelled, 'I cannot. I am a Christian.' He sat up in bed, eyes wide and the sound of his shout echoing from the low ceiling, before slumping back. There did not seem to be strength in any of his limbs. 'I cannot,' he mumbled.

'I know, so you keep saying,' a voice said. It was a nice voice, warm and feminine and as far from the memories of the tribunal as could be. 'Are you staying this time, or did you simply fancy a good shout?'

The angel appeared over him, her hair plaited and coiled behind her head. Her eyes were the palest blue, and her nose was as strong as her gaze, although her full lips and slightly receding chin softened her face without taking anything from its remarkable beauty. Angels should look like that, he thought, but surely Heaven did not have a ceiling.

'I suppose you have a real name,' she said. 'If you are going to stay around this time, then I should like to thank you by name.'

'He's not dead, so he's staying,' said a deep, gravelly voice, 'so we must honour our debt even to a Gentile.' They were speaking in Greek, even though Domitius was sure he had shouted in Latin.

'This is grandfather,' the angel said. 'He is the one who hit you with a spade.'

'You are welcome,' the deep voice said. 'I have not hit a Roman for a very long time. Once I was better at it.'

'What is your name, stranger?' the angel asked. She leaned forward, mopping his brow with a wet cloth. Her dress was a pale grey-blue, over a long-sleeved tunic, and she gave off a faint smell of jasmine. 'We know what you are, but that is not the same.'

'Domitius.' Even smiling felt like an immense effort. 'Caius Domitius from Berytus.'

The angel smiled. 'Good. That is better. Well, I am Sara, and the old fool who enjoys hitting others is my grandfather, who is called John.'

'John of Jotapata, once,' the deep voice boomed, 'until you Romans burned it to the ground.'

'That was long ago, and they would have saved me a good deal of trouble if they had set you alight with it. Not that there was ever much of you to burn.' The warmth in the chiding was obvious. 'Instead you are here, and as a good woman I must have patience and suffer your folly.' She stepped back and made a gesture like a bow, but more fluid for her knees must have bobbed down. Domitius wondered whether this was the custom of the country, whatever this country was. 'Welcome, Domitius from Berytus to the house of my father.'

'In my father's house there are many mansions.' The words ran through Domitius' head and he tried to smile back as he spoke them.

'He is babbling,' the deep voice said. 'I'll get my spade so that I can hit him again.'

'You will not.' Sara shook her head. 'Family can be a burden, can they not? Do you have family, Domitius from Berytus? Perhaps you let them call you Caius? Do they hit each other a good deal? That must get so tiring, but then if they are men or fools – and do not those words mean the same thing – it must be necessary for their own good. Now, sit up, Caius Domitius, for you are not as weak as all that.'

Domitius was not convinced, but forced himself up on his elbows, and Sara pushed cushions behind him to keep him upright. She was the most beautiful woman he had ever seen – his age, or perhaps a little older – and even in his weakened state it was a thrill simply to be near her. In contrast the room was bare neither large nor well maintained. There was a small window, high up on what must have been an outside wall. There was a band of deep red where the walls met the ceiling and the rest was thinly whitewashed plaster. Apart from the bed, there were boxes piled up in one corner and a single chair occupied by a wiry old man whose white beard reached almost to his lap.

'There,' Sara said, fiddling with the cushions, which were soft and out of keeping with the otherwise plain room. 'Now sit up properly.' The tone was irresistible and Domitius did as he was told. 'You are going to eat, and in a moment I shall see to that and also fetch Father so that he can decide what to do with you.'

'I've told you, give me another spade, child, and it will all be over.'

Sara ignored her grandfather. 'First there is something I must do.' She stood up, patted at her dress even though it did not appear at all out of place, and bowed again. 'I wish to thank *you, Caius Domitius of Berytus, for saving my virtue and for saving me from slavery or death.' The words were nervous and her forehead creased in concentration as she tried to remember what she must have rehearsed in her head. 'Whatever led your path to us that night, I can see only the hand of God, and I pray to Him, and show my gratitude to you.'*

Domitius had wondered whether the screaming woman and the fight with the slaver had only been a dream. Yet his left shoulder still felt sore, and seeing the earnestness in the woman's face he knew that it had been real. He felt his chin, and was surprised to find that someone had shaved him.

'It is I who must thank you all,' Domitius said. 'I do not know how long I have been here, but know that I have been ill and surely would have died without your care.'

'No,' Sara snapped. 'That was our duty. You had none to us. You are a stranger and a Gentile. So please accept my thanks.'

'Of course.'

'Good, now I must see to everything – as usual. Keep an eye on him, old man, and take good care.'

'I'll only hit him if it's for his own good.'

'Huh!' Sara's expression took on the air of a determined child. She scowled at her grandfather, then came over to the bed, leaned forward and kissed Domitius on the forehead. With another fierce and wholly insincere glance at the old man, she strode out of the room.

'My grandchild,' the old man rumbled. His pride was as obvious as his affection. 'She could rule the world if she chose, God help us! But she is mine, so that I too am in your debt. If you had not come, then I dread to think what would have happened. I am too old now to protect her, and it was vanity to make the journey, and her kindness to hang back from the caravan because I was so weary. If it was God who brought

you, then I praise him, and I never thought that I'd say that to one of you monsters.'

'We are not in the province?' Domitius asked warily.

'Do you think I could live under Roman oppression? Of course not, when I can be oppressed by other Gentiles. No, my boy, we go to the lands of the Romans when we must, but do not live there. We went there to do business, and because an old fool wanted to see Antioch once more before his bones are laid to rest, and could not keep up when that brigand found us alone, knocked me down and wanted to take the child. Pity the master who bought her as a slave! I got up and chased, saw a man standing over her and hit you on the head. Prudent folk would have left it at that, burying you out of respect, but the child insisted that we bring you with us. We crossed the river the next morning and left your people's lands.'

'And where am I now?'

'Nicopolis, which some say is in Osrhoene and some do not,' the old man told him, and then his voice grew louder and more deliberate. 'In the house of my son-in-law, a foolish, conceited man, who indulges his children.'

'And an old man, who tries my patience every day!' A tall, very thin man had entered. His tunic was a fine one, if a little stained, and he was wiping his hands on a cloth after washing them. 'They told me that you were well, and I am glad to see it.'

The old man snorted. Domitius noticed that Simon, as this must be, stooped and blinked as he stared at him. He came closer until he was at the side of the bed.

'That is better.' Simon pointed to his eyes, which were pale, just like his daughter's but without her strong gaze. 'Too many years of work make it hard for me to see anything that is not close.' He had a short, well-trimmed beard and a thick mop of hair. Both had streaks of grey in them. 'Well, let me thank you

for what you have done – and do not thank me for our care. Sara will not allow it!'

'You should beat a wilful child,' the grandfather muttered.

'You are a soldier?' Simon asked.

'Optio ad spem, Legio VI Ferrata.'

'That means they had promised him the rank of centurion,' the old man rumbled. 'Smart folk the Romans, you have to give them that. They promise a man rank in the future, but don't give him the pay or confirm it until they feel like it. Makes him eager and hopeful so they get more from him.'

'But you have left before they gave you what they promised? And since you have kept on shouting it out, I presume this is because you are misguided enough to be a Galilean, follower of their self-proclaimed Messiah, and the Romans consider that a crime rather than bad judgement. Yet I guess that you have been in the army for some time, so either your religion is new or they have not cared too much until now.'

'Another man wanted the promotion,' Domitius said, for that was true and safe to reveal. 'He denounced me in public as a Christian. They had to respond.'

'And you could not lie? I hear they let you off if you pretend. The Romans care more about appearances than what is underneath.'

'Good thing for you, my lad, because you can sell them rubbish at a high price,' the old man suggested.

'I could not lie when it came to it,' Domitius said.

'So you are a deserter and criminal in their eyes, but perhaps you are also an honest man as well as a brave one. We shall see. For Domitius of Rome you have a choice before you. In a few days you should be up and about, for the fever has broken and idleness will no longer do you any good. That shoulder will be fine now as well.' Domitius had a sudden memory of *sheer agony as the arm was put back into the joint. 'I take it that you know that you are in Nicopolis? Yes, and it is a good city in many ways. There are those here who call themselves Christians and chant their dirges and maul the words of the Torah. When you are well I can take you to one who is a good man for all his strange ideas and he and his wife may help you, although there are others among them I would not trust as far as I can spit. So you may go to them if you so wish.*

'If not, then you can remain as our guest, at least for a while. If that is your choice then you must understand us. We are Jews, and follow the ways of our ancestors as far as we can in this dark world – even this old fool, at least mostly, for his wits have wandered after so many years of idleness. We honour the Sabbath and will allow nothing unclean within our doors. If you stay then you will abide by our rules and respect our customs.

'What did you do in the legion?'

The change of tack caught Domitius by surprise. 'I tried to be a good soldier, and do my duty.'

'Pah! What is that to me? I mean what work did you do, if soldiers do work. You are too young to have chased this old fool through the hills! A good father teaches his son a trade, and from what I hear your army likes to give men a craft.'

'I was mostly with the ballistae *– the catapults we have – and sometimes in the* fabricae.*'*

'Then you have some knowledge of mechanisms and tools, at least. Well, you may be useful and may be able to learn more. So if you wish to stay long you will earn your keep. Think on it. You must decide by the end of the week. You know what a week is?' Domitius nodded. 'Well, there it is. If you do stay we shall say nothing of where you have come from – at least for the moment. Not everyone is fond of the Romans or their soldiers.'

The grandfather snorted in amusement.

Simon placed a hand over his heart and leaned in, eyes no longer blinking. 'Thank you for saving my daughter. I am glad to see you well. Now, I must get back to my work. Think upon my words.'

'You fought against us?' Domitius asked the old man once Simon had left.

'I did – and look where I ended up!' He shook his head. 'God in Heaven help me, but I enjoyed it too. I have no love for Rome or the Romans and pray for the day your City burns as ours did, and even more for the bright golden day when the Temple stands again. But that is not today, and like the others, I thank you, optio ad spem.'

Sara appeared, carrying a tray, and gave him a smile that was almost nervous. Domitius already knew what he was going to decide. There was warmth about this family, something he had not felt since he was a child. For the first time in his life he was beyond the frontier, in a world he did not know. Better to face that with friends and with an angel by your side.

IV

The temporary camp of Legio VIIII Hispana
Fourteenth day before the Kalends of April, the first day of
the Quinquatria Festival

'WE COULD ISSUE half rations, just for a few days. That would—'

Rufus was cut short by the newly arrived *primus pilus*. 'Think before you speak, lad! These are men, not machines, and they can only march so far, carry so much and work so hard in a day. Not if you want them able to do the same on the next day and the next. Press them and they might do it once, or twice or even a third time – the gods know they've surprised me more times than I care to remember – but if you keep on they'll crack in the end and that's the road to disaster! I've seen it!' The chief centurion's face was round, lined with age and very red. He was one of the handful of gifted and lucky soldiers who started in the ranks and made their way to the top of the centurionate. If he was frank, Rufus had to admit that he was scared of the man, and it did not help that he seemed to have a very quick temper.

There was a long silence around the table until Crispinus broke it. 'Thank you, my dear Caecilius. That is wisdom indeed. And it is because of your wealth of experience and your expertise that we are so fortunate to have you. The noble Hadrian chose you himself, did you know that?'

Caius Caecilius grunted. 'Good of him.' His tone hinted that the average senator barely had the wit to put on his own shoes, let alone spot merit in an officer.

'Quite so. We will all benefit from your knowledge. Still, for the moment this is more about considering possibilities, so that we can prepare for what may come, and may come very soon.'

'Can you tell us any more, sir?' Arrian asked. 'You say that we may need to form a column and take the field at very short notice, and that speed could be essential, hence Rufus' suggestion of reducing the rations.' The tribune paid no heed to Caecilius' obvious scorn. 'Forgive me, but I am still a newcomer to Syria, and cannot guess at our purpose.'

'Reasonable question, and I shall do my best.' Crispinus was the only man standing, using his hands to gesture across the unrolled map. It was one fitted onto a scroll, easy to roll up, and representing the empire as a long, thin rectangle. 'Now, where are we? Ah yes. Here is Antioch, Cyrrhus, Zeugma.' He traced a rough line using a stylus. 'The Lord Trajan, has gone from Zeugma to Samosata, and from there to Metilene and finally Satala, where the great army will concentrate. None of this is a secret, so feel free to write it on the latrine wall!' There was dutiful laughter, except from Caecilius, who merely nodded.

'Here is Armenia, where the pretender is at long last realising his peril.'

'Nine legions on your doorstep will do that,' Arrian whispered theatrically to the tribune sitting beside him.

Crispinus chuckled. 'As you say. For generations the king of Armenia may only rule after his coronation has been approved by Rome. This fellow thought that this approval was unnecessary. He's a Parthian, of course, most of them are after the true royal family devoted generations of concerted effort to exterminating itself. In itself, that does not matter, so long as he submits, and he may have left that too late. Come the spring, our legions will march into Armenia and he will surrender and face judgement or fight and be destroyed.'

'Will that mean war with the Parthians?' Rufus dared to ask.

'Serve 'em right if it does,' another centurion chipped in.

'Don't be a fool,' Caecilius snapped. 'Don't speak lightly of the biggest war you're ever likely to see. If there is a great war, then this is the way the Parthians will come, through here, on their way to Antioch and its riches. They've done it before, back in Antony's day.'

Rufus tried not to giggle when the centurion beside him whispered, 'And I bet the old bugger was there.'

'Parthia is a great empire,' Crispinus said, like a schoolmaster bringing an unruly class to order. 'Indeed, it is the only kingdom beyond our borders worthy of the name of empire. You should all know enough history to realise that fighting the Parthians is no light matter, for when well organised and well led they are formidable indeed.

'Yet they are not well led, not at the moment. Their royal family breeds more prolifically than the Armenians, so there are always plenty of princes, and too many heirs naturally produces conflict in a people whose laws and customs are so loose. At the moment there are three kings in Parthia – or at least there were at the last count and who knows, by this time another may have popped up for all we know. Thus their main efforts are devoted to warring with each other, which is good from our point of view. On the other hand, the desperate times of civil war make them unpredictable. They may do something rash, and even if they do it with less force than would be the case if they were united, still it could be dangerous because it would be unforeseen. So Caecilius is perfectly correct to point out that we are in the path of any likely invasion, should it come from the south. There is no sign of trouble from that direction at present, but we must never forget that it just might happen.

'We are the only legion at full strength left in the region. The good news is that we are getting some more auxiliaries attached to us, so that soon we shall have a very handsome little army, very handsome indeed. It will be up to us should they come.

'But…' Crispinus dragged out the word to get their attention. 'But I do not think that such a contingency will arise, not this year, at least. Still, the very uncertainty of power within Parthia causes problems in itself, for it is bound to spread. We guard our empire by strength. Those living outside must fear that strength, just as they trust our faith not to abuse them if they behave properly. Here we deal with kingdoms.' Crispinus tapped with the stylus once more. 'Closest is Osrhoene, then Adiabene and others beyond.' The map quickly grew vague and was tightly compressed to squeeze the names and principal routes and cities into the little space left outside the provinces. Crispinus grimaced. 'Let us change to something better. Arrian, dear fellow, if you could be so good as to unroll the next map. Thank you. That's better, much better.' He helped the tribune weigh down the scroll which kept wanting to fold up.

'Osrhoene is just beyond the river. Its kings rule from Edessa, and on the whole they are usually friends of ours, more or less, but do not require our seal of approval on their power, and it has to be said they have always been closer to the Parthians. That is the root of the problem now. Old Abgarus is trying to pick the winning side when it is not obvious to anyone who that will be. So he is keeping his distance from us. He sent his son with an escort to see Trajan, but had only empty words and no promise of loyalty, let alone agreement to let us have some troops for the coming campaign. What do you know of their warriors, Caecilius?'

The primus pilus sniffed before giving his verdict. 'Good horsemen. Well, most are in this part of the world. Mainly archers backed up by some cataphracts. Not up there with the best of the Parthians, but still decent enough. And they're used to the summer here, so cope better than most of our lads, especially the ones brought over from Europe.'

'Thank you.'

'One thing we all need to remember,' the primus pilus went on, warming to his subject. The first centurion in a legion, let alone one with Caecilius' forty years of service, enjoyed a special status, as the most senior military man. It granted a licence, even if interrupting the legatus was stretching this to the limit. 'You all hear talk of soft and effeminate Asians.' Arrian gestured at himself with an air of exaggerated innocence. 'Won't go toe to toe, fight by running away and shooting arrows as they flee, and when they're not at war spend all their time hunting, humping and eating.'

'But not necessarily in that order,' Crispinus said.

Caecilius laughed with the others this time. 'Well, I can tell you that all of that is true, and it still doesn't matter any more than a sack of shit. You let them fight in the way they like on ground that they choose, and all you'll do is pile up the bodies. Remember what happened to Crassus – and Antony. And when I was a tiro there were still boys who had been with that damned fool Paetus. You cannot give them a chance, not the slightest chance, or you'll die. So let's have none of this effeminate Orientals. Just because they don't fight like us, doesn't mean they're not good at what they do, because, lads, they are... very good.'

'That is sage advice and no mistake,' Crispinus said, judging that the little lecture was over. 'But to return to Abgarus, he has decided to back one of the claimants to the Parthian throne, and is willing to marry his favourite daughter to the likely lad. She won't be his first wife, of course, but still an important one, and who knows, the mother of a future king? In the meantime, his son tries to placate us, and is ready to take soldiers to help out the Parthian in question – or another, should fortune change for his first choice. Neither outcome offers particular advantage to us. If Abgarus succeeds he moves closer to Parthia. In the meantime, it might strike one of the other Parthian leaders that a change of power in Osrhoene would be a good thing. There are bound to be a few noblemen with royal blood and ample ambition knocking around for them to use. Again, not a good thing for us. Is everyone following all this? I know it is complicated, but that is the way with kings?'

'Do I take it, sir, that there is more encouraging news?' Arrian asked. 'For us, I mean.'

Crispinus beamed. 'Indeed there is – for us, for Rome, for the glory of the Hispana!' He made a sweeping gesture in the air. 'Azátē is the name of the lucky princess set to marry a Parthian thirty years her senior, who might end up as the true king, or get himself killed. By the sound of it the head of the Suren clan is the real power behind the man, so our girl might face some stout resistance if she hopes to influence the old boy. This gives her pause, and doting daughter though she is, sufficient pause to approach the acting governor of Syria, and through him, the Lord Trajan.'

'Hadrian,' Caecilius said.

'The very same and known as an excellent judge of character. Well, the beautiful princess has sent word secretly and asked for

Rome's protection. That will permit her to avoid an unwelcome marriage, and in order to do this, she has much to offer us.'

The centurion beside him nudged Rufus in the ribs. Caecilius glared at him. 'What will she give?'

'Loyalty to Rome, is the first thing, and that is nice, if scarcely persuasive in itself. More tangible is this, the city of Nicopolis.' Crispinus jabbed down with the stylus. 'You can see it is some thirty miles from the Euphrates. As Caecilius reminded us, the river in these parts, for all its great width, is not much of a barrier to an invading army. A Roman garrison on the other side could be a thorn in the side of any would-be attacker. And, since we never know how matters will develop, once the emperor has restored good order in Armenia, he may well decide that it is necessary to intervene in the nearby kingdoms to ensure that this order is preserved in the years to come. At the very least, he will be pleased to have a more secure defence in this region or perhaps approve this as a base for a greater advance. Either way, the noble Hadrian is eager to take advantage of the opportunity, assuming the opportunity comes.'

'How exactly does this girl plan to give us a city?' Caecilius' question was blunt.

Crispinus' cheek twitched once before he replied. 'That is still to be decided. At the moment she suggests that we come across the river at an agreed date. The people in Nicopolis love her, so she says, and certainly they are not too keen on her father's rule. Azátē claims that the people will welcome her, and at the very least that her household guards will be able to seize control, so that the gates are opened to us when we arrive. If the timing is right, that should be well before her father or brother can send men to stop us. After that, well, they won't want a fight with Rome, and even if they do, we will be behind the city walls and can hold them off with ease.

Arrian whistled through his teeth, realised that he had done so, and grew embarrassed. 'So that is why we need to think of marching fast.'

'What if it goes wrong?' Caecilius' face was belligerent. 'What if we're late – it can happen – or what if the good citizens aren't quite so keen on the lass, or her brother and her father aren't quite so dumb as she thinks? Treachery is in the blood in a family like that, so they won't trust her no more than she trusts them. What if we end up stuck outside in the plains, and this young prince gallops up with a few thousand horsemen? What then, sir? Do we fight?'

Crispinus let the question hang in the air for a while. He had broken the tip of the stylus when he struck the table and he ran his finger over it. 'Perhaps,' he said eventually. 'None of this may happen. The princess was supposed to send a messenger to us, but no one came to the meeting place. Ferox thinks that the man was hunted down and killed before he could get there.' Crispinus silently cursed himself. He had not meant to mention Ferox's involvement in the business, at least not before it was unavoidable. Rufus and Arrian both sat up at the mention of the name, but he also thought that there was shock in Caecilius' eyes and that made him wonder. Still, he had to make the best of things, even if it worried him to have these lapses of concentration. 'The meeting was supposed to happen on the unfortunate night of our exercise, so those of us who took part can remember the appalling weather, which made everything harder.'

'Was it a deliberate ambush?' That was Arrian, as always to the point.

'Perhaps – perhaps not. There were slavers out there as we know, and they might easily turn their hand to robbery and murder.'

'But the prince or the king or someone else may know that something is going on.' Hadrian had assured Crispinus that the tribune was a clever fellow and likely to prove a capable one. They had met at Athens, and both revered Epictetus, but the judgement seemed a fair one. 'Was the letter concealed or in code?'

'Both. We have no idea what happened to it, none at all, but clearly we must consider every possibility.'

'Which brings us back to the point,' Caecilius cut in again. 'Let's say we rush across the Euphrates to this town, but the gates are barred and they're up on the walls ready to shoot. What then? Slink back with our tails between our legs, saying, will you beg our pardon?'

Arrian chewed his lip as he thought. 'A lot depends on whether we can trust this Azátē,' he suggested.

'She's a woman and a princess,' Caecilius said, his scepticism obvious.

'We cannot fail.' Crispinus' voice was deeper than most expected a small man's voice to be, and he was a trained orator, so the words echoed around the hut. All of them looked at him, so he smiled. 'That is the nub of the matter. If we commit to this, then we cannot fail. One way or another, we must have Nicopolis, so that our position on both banks of the river is made stronger rather than weaker.' That needed to be made clear to them, even if they did not need to know why.

Arrian started to scratch his chin, then realised what he was doing. 'Sorry.'

'Do you understand what you are saying, sir?' Caecilius' voice had all the scepticism of an old hand dealing with a young tribune on his first day with the army.

'Yes, and I need everyone else to understand as well. If we are sent to do this task then we must succeed.' The legatus beamed at his senior centurion. 'That is another reason why you were chosen by Hadrian to join Hispana. He understands that you have served in more sieges than anyone else in the army.'

The others all looked at Caecilius. A primus pilus was always treated with respect, but none had realised that the man had such a distinguished record. He was old for his post, and that was another reason why Hadrian had sent him to Hispana. The ambitious and well-connected rose fast, whereas Caecilius had crawled inch by inch because he had no connections and not the right sort of luck to find them. He had languished for ten years in his last post, and all but given up hope of an appointment as primus pilus. Others saw him as well past his prime, and that was why he had been left behind when the vexillations were formed for the emperor's coming campaign. In a sense that was another reason for choosing him: there was not anyone else available at short notice. Still Hadrian – and Crispinus – hoped that the joy of receiving the promotion would invigorate the man, making him grateful and all the more eager to show his talents.

Caecilius sniffed. 'We haven't succeeded in all of them.' He shook his head. 'Sieges are a mix of science, planning and the luck of the dice. You have to stack the odds as much as you can in your favour, take the pounding you're bound to receive, and hope and pray that it all works out. Sometimes it does, sometimes... *thetatus*.' He drew his finger across his throat. On army records the name of a soldier who died was annotated with a *theta*, and the Greek letter had spawned an army slang word.

Rufus had been sitting up, eagerness redoubled at the mention of sieges, for Crispinus knew the man was obsessed with engineering. Now he frowned until the man beside him whispered an explanation.

'If we are prepared for a siege, then we won't be able to move quickly,' Arrian said, as if thinking aloud. 'We'll need engines, tools, and more supplies than for a short campaign. How much do you think we will need *primus*?' Crispinus was surprised to hear him use the informal name for the senior centurion. The Bithynian was fitting into the army very well.

If Caecilius was offended at the presumption then he did not show it. 'Can't say. Can't say much at all until I know much more about this place and its defences.'

'Information is being gathered as we speak,' Crispinus assured them.

'Ferox?' Caecilius' suspicion and distaste were obvious.

'And others. At the moment, I can only tell you a little. Nicopolis is not tiny, but not large. Perhaps three or four thousand inhabitants. It sits on a hill, and has walls of stone – old ones, it's true, but once we are in it will be easy to maintain with a fairly small garrison.'

'Bet that's what Abgarus is thinking,' Caecilius said. 'My lord,' he added after a pause.

'Do we gamble on being let in?' Arrian asked. 'Send a small force ahead, marching with just the essentials? If they are let in, then all is well. If not they pull back to the main force coming on at its own pace,'

'Perhaps,' Crispinus said. 'Or we send a few hundred riding ahead in the hope Azátē's people let us in, and a thousand force-marching to try a quick assault if that fails. That way we have tried everything, and will still be able to do things the hard way once the main column arrives.'

They pondered that for a while. Crispinus was scanning their faces, and noticed Caecilius doing the same.

'But—' Rufus began.

'Lad,' Caecilius interrupted, 'there are so many buts that I don't know where to start.' He turned to Crispinus and nodded. 'But it is early days, and we don't know enough yet.'

'Precisely. That is why I have held this *consilium*. I want you all thinking. We have to prepare for what may happen, and that means planning, training the men and getting everything ready. Arrian, I want you to think about transport.' The tribune rolled his eyes. 'Yes, I know that's a tough one.' Crispinus allocated tasks to several of the others. '*Primus*,' he said, hoping the informality would reinforce the man's apparent goodwill, 'you get the technical side – engines, equipment, crews and all the other things you'll know about. If you need to spend or requisition, then do – and take your pick of the men. Rufus, here, will be your right hand. He can add up, which is more than can be said for half of us, and knows a thing or two about machinery.' Caecilius grunted, which could mean anything. 'Well, there is plenty for us all to do, so let us get to work!'

As they left, Rufus struggled to keep pace with the primus pilus' bustling walk. He had the sense not to say anything and waited for the old man to speak if he wanted. They were almost at the fabricae when Caecilius broke his silence. 'Well, lad, what do you think?' He did not look at the young centurion and kept striding ahead.

Rufus hesitated, wondering whether to feign confidence before deciding to be honest. 'Tell you the truth, sir, I'm worried.'

Caecilius stopped so abruptly that the other man stepped past him. He was a big man, with a sense of power that belied his advanced years, and as he put a hand on each of Rufus' shoulders it felt as if only a little pressure would drive him into the ground.

'Are you, lad? Well, that's a good start.'

V

FEROX DID NOT much care for cities, even though he had spent a lot of time in them over the years. He had seen Rome when he was young, and after that none ever quite matched the noise, the crowds, the grand buildings and the stench and squalor. A lot of them tried very hard with the stench and the squalor though.

'Stinks of shit,' Vindex said beside him, 'and camels.'

'Then they shouldn't notice your distinctive scent, should they?' Bran added. 'Well, the camels might, but only because they'll think you're a relation.'

It was the same every time they came to a city or even a village, and there had been a lot of both in the last decade. Camels were a recent fascination for them both, but that was the only real change. Vindex was one of the Carvetii, close kin of the Brigantes, and their biggest settlements were rarely home to more than a score of families. Bran was an orphan of the Novantae who lived to the north and they liked their space even more. Together they had wandered over half the empire, unimpressed by what they saw and very ready to show it.

'The Romans are a strange, dirty people,' Vindex went on, following the ritual.

'They live like rats in a sewer,' Bran concluded. Before he had come to join Ferox, the boy had not even known what a sewer was.

'Silence!' Philo hissed back at them. 'Do your duty and hold your tongues!' The Alexandrian was not a confident rider, so sat like a sack of old clothes astride a well-behaved mule at the head of their procession. Everything else about him was impeccable, from manners to movements, and most of all his pristine clothing.

Bran made a face to Vindex who leered back at him. Vindex had a long face, the skin taut over the bones and his mouth naturally open to show his horse-like teeth, so it was hard for him not to leer.

'He used to be so nice,' he told Bran. 'Before the power went to his head.'

'Sad,' Bran agreed.

Ferox was even more saddened to hear the lad talking so much – too much time spent with Vindex, no doubt. He did his best to shut them out, while searching for any signs of danger and gathering all the information he could. This was market day and they were part of a stream of people, animals and carts heading for the western gate of Nicopolis. Most were local, farmers bringing stock from their winter stores, a few driving animals ready for sale and slaughter, and others with bales of wool carried on their backs or on animals. The sun was high, the day warming up even though it was still early in the morning, and the crowds jostled against their horses as they pushed their way onwards. They were a little leery of the mounted barbarians with their armour, spears and swords, but as they got nearer the gate the road went across a bridge and that packed everyone together. Vindex, Bran and the others were free with the butts of their spears, but there simply was not the room to keep people too far back. Other merchants had their own escorts, who lashed out with shaft and clubs, so sometimes people were driven one way then the next.

The bridge spanned a ditch some twenty feet wide and almost as deep. It was dry, man-made, but dotted with bushes and scrub because no one bothered to clean it out. Ferox could see a couple of patches were the bank had worn away and frequent use had made a path, but even so it was still a major obstacle. From here it was hard to see whether it stretched all the way around the city. Beyond it the ground rose a little towards the walls, some twenty feet back. He could not see any sign of obstacles fixed or dug into the earth, but someone had cared enough to keep this ground clear of bushes and even the piles of rubbish and filth you often saw dumped from the tops of city walls and then forgotten. Several men, and an old woman, were squatting on the edge of the ditch, clothes hitched up over their waists, so it seemed that using the ditch as a latrine was perfectly normal.

There was a squeal from beside him. A youngish, rather plump woman was rubbing her behind through her dress, while Vindex winked at her. Ferox guessed that the warrior had tapped the woman with the blunt end of his spear. She spat at him and yelled a word he did not understand, but could easily guess.

'Behave yourself!' Philo shouted back. 'No, off there, off!' Some urchins were around his mule, and fiddling with the harness. Vindex kicked his horse forward and yelled at them, which was enough to make them slip off into the crowd. They were over the bridge now, but the press only eased a little because everyone had to go through the arch of the gate. This was high, of a pale yellow stone, and on either side of the open gateway were tall towers that thrust forward. They were round, or at least round on this outer side, for Ferox could not see the back as yet. There were towers all along the wall on either side, although these were square, but like the ones at the gateway projected out from the curtain wall. He reckoned the walls were close to thirty feet high and the towers double that, and the slope would make them seem taller unless you were right underneath. The stone was well crafted and neat, each block large, but with few concessions to decoration. About halfway up the walls was a row of wooden shutters, which made Ferox wonder.

City guards were stopping everyone, which added to the jerky progress of the crowd. They had two Brigantians riding behind the waggon, which was driven by another tall warrior in armour and helmet. Five guards put them among the stronger parties queueing to enter the city. Most of the other armed men were Arabs, with a few from further afield mixed in, and most likely a couple of army deserters.

'Who are you?' A city guard demanded of Philo.

'Demetrios of Alexandria, with my wife and escort.' They had come up with the story before crossing the Euphrates. Hadrian and Crispinus had suggested that they pose as Arabs, with Ferox as their leader and purchase a few slaves to sell and take money to buy more. It was just the sort of fool idea aristocrats would dream up, presumably on the basis that one barbarian would look much like another barbarian if given the right clothes. 'The head-scarves will cover anyone whose hair is light,' Crispinus had assured him. Ferox had said yes, sir, thank you, sir, taken the money, bought no slaves and instead invested a third of it in good Italian wine, something rare in this part of the world. The rest was to buy inscribed gemstones from one of the workshops in Nicopolis.

'Wife?' The guard licked his lips. Sitting beside the Brigantian on the waggon was Indike, Philo's true wife. Both of them were former slaves, but while he was a Jewish boy from Alexandria, she had been a dancer and entertainer and had been born in distant India, though sold as a child and eventually ending up in Londinium of all places. She was small, moved with a rare grace, and pretty, something obvious even through the gauzy veil that covered most of her face.

'Bet he's going to ask which one is the wife?' Vindex muttered in Greek, playing his part. He knew little of the language so this had taken some coaching.

'Hold your tongue!' Philo snarled. 'Any more insolence and you can forget your pay and I'll leave you here on your own!' He turned back to the guard and shrugged. 'Galatians!' he added, switching to Aramaic and was relieved when the sentry seemed to understand, as you never knew with all the local dialects. 'They are a vulgar folk, but have their uses.' Ferox had decided that they might just pass as Galatians, descendants of the Gallic warbands that raided and then settled in Asia centuries ago. A lot of them joined the army, and he had met a few lads who looked like they had been born and bred in Lugdunum or even southern Britannia for all the generations that had passed. It was at least a little more convincing than the idea of posing as Arabs.

'Aye,' the guard acknowledged. 'Good slaves so I hear, at least as labourers.' At least that was what Philo thought he said in his outlandish dialect. It was a relief when the man switched back to Greek. 'Your business in Nicopolis?'

'Selling wine and looking to buy gems,' Philo said.

'You'll find the best here, sir. I'd try Simon the Jew or Nicocles, if I were you, sir. Thank you, sir.' Philo already had a coin in his hand and was impressed how quickly the guard's fingers closed around it while still supporting his spear. The man raised his voice. 'Follow the rest through the right-hand gate.' He nodded in that direction. 'Up the Cardo, past the three temples, and the market is on your left in front of the theatre. You'll find the clerk of the Agoranomos there and they'll register you.'

'Thank you.' The press was already moving, most going to the right and the main way out. The guards were only stopping those carrying goods, and the rest, local mostly, wove in and out to get past. With effort, and more use of spear shafts, the group managed to keep together. Ferox paid little attention as he tried to commit as much as he could to memory, and only hit out once or twice at the most persistent.

Most cities, like army camps, had grand entrances to impress all who came through with the might and majesty of the place or the empire they represented. Whoever had designed the West Gate at Nicopolis had allowed for this, but had not ensured that the visitor, awed by the height of the towers, was then struck by the dead straight line of the cardo, colonnades on either side, as it led into the heart of the city. Instead, whoever it was had thought long and hard about how to slaughter anyone attempting to break into the city, for if they got through the main gate they found themselves in a semi-circular courtyard, formed by a wall as high as those on the outside. A single wide-topped tower stood on this wall, directly behind the gate towers so that it was invisible from outside. The only ways out of the trap were a small doorway on the left, and a single arched gate on the right. If both were barred, then any assault party would need ladders or a ram to have any chance of getting further. If the defenders still controlled the main gate and were able to block or close it behind them, then the result would be a massacre.

'Good gate,' Vindex called out to him. 'Some of these Romans are getting smarter.' Even the Brigantes made sure there was no direct path into one of their forts, and the tribes of the south had gone to even greater lengths to confuse any attackers.

'Think before you speak, man,' Ferox said as quietly as was possible while still being heard about all the hubbub. They were using the language of the tribes, and had been all day, and it was unlikely in the extreme that anyone in these parts would understand them, but there was no sense in taking the risk. Still, he had known Vindex for more than twenty years and not yet found a reliable way of keeping the man quiet.

'Only saying.'

'Then don't,' Ferox told him. 'And these folk aren't Roman. We're outside the empire, remember.'

'They're not Carvetii, I know that, so what's the difference?'

'The difference is they might see us as enemies,' Bran suggested, then blinked as they came through the smaller gate, leaving behind the shadowed courtyard and coming into the bright sunshine. 'You know, might want to kill us.'

'That's true wherever himself goes,' Vindex pointed out, gesturing at Ferox. 'Remember Scythia?'

'When I get bad dreams.'

'Or Moesia, Pannonia, Thrace, Germania? Taranis, we even went back home to his country and within days they all wanted to kill him.'

'There is a pattern, I'll allow,' Bran said. 'Might be just bad luck though. After all, we're still here.'

'Wherever here is.' They were on the cardo now, and the press eased a little, until the hawkers and idlers from the city itself started to swell the numbers again. 'Anyway,' Vindex concluded, 'we're still here because we're better at killing than most folk.'

'True.' Bran did not boast, and merely stated a fact as he saw it. 'And you have to admit that taking a strong dislike to the centurion tends not to end well for most who try it.'

Ferox glanced back at the walls. They looked wide, far wider than he had expected, so that the walkway at the top offered plenty of room. There did not seem to be any stairs, so they must all be in the towers. A row of well-spaced and open windows ran along the curtain walls, perhaps a little higher than the ones in front, which suggested that there were rooms inside.

'Don't think you can afford me, lass!' Vindex called to one of the prostitutes standing where a side road fed into the cardo and there was a break in the canopied stalls set up all along the colonnade. There were shabbier ones on the side roads, along with other services.

Nicopolis was a tough nut to crack, and even though some of this was the market, Ferox reckoned that the Romans were underestimating the number of people who lived here. There might not be any proper soldiers, but even an old man or woman could tip a rock off the top of a parapet onto someone's head. From that height it would crush any helmet, not to mention the skull inside. No doubt this had happened to one of the Greeks at Troy – everything seemed to have happened to one of the Greeks at Troy as far as educated Romans, let alone the Greeks themselves, were concerned.

The cardo rose ever so gently upwards as it ran through the city and, with the tall houses on either side, was like a tunnel. Ahead, Ferox saw the steps and high roof of a temple.

'Hey, reckon it's one of those cities?' Vindex asked, for once with wonder in his voice. Soldiers talked, as soldiers always will, and years ago the Carvetian had first heard someone talking about the fabled cults of the east, of temples where maidens from the finest families went to lose their virginity in honour of the gods. Men could just wander into the precinct and take their pick, or so the wide-eyed soldiers claimed. Ferox had heard the stories many times, but never seen a place where such a temple existed and wondered whether it was no more than an army myth, like nymphs living in the forests or tribunes who knew what they were doing. Vindex had fixed on the idea, so that it became a favourite dream.

Still, he did not know Asia at all, and was still learning about Syria, let alone the lands beyond. He guessed Hadrian and Crispinus had sent him – and thus the other unfortunates – to spy out the city because they saw him as a clever and capable officer, and because he could not refuse them. He knew Britannia, especially the north, and had spent enough years in Moesia and beyond the Danube to understand how the peoples there thought and reacted. Out here he tried to listen well and see straight, but much remained strange to him.

Nowhere had he seen fortifications quite like these, and whoever had planned and built them had done a good job. They had come through the western side, the easiest to approach, and it did not strike him as easy to attack. The ground sloped enough ahead of them to suggest that it would be even more formidable on the far side, assuming the walls were of similar size. At the end of the cardo the land rose sharply, and he could just glimpse a wall whose battlements faced towards him, suggesting an inner citadel.

The Greeks, or whoever had laid these walls and towers down, had done a fine job, and they looked to be in decent repair. Yet the same people, and all who came after them, had not felt the urge to cover the sewer which ran down the middle of the cardo, and presumably found a way through the walls, even if he had not seen any sort of culvert. The slope made the water flow and carry the waste with it, although in high summer there might not have been enough to move it at all.

Then and now it reeked, and woe betide anyone who fell into it. The gully was a couple of feet wide, and every few yards they had thought to put a stepping stone in place so that people could cross, but it still seemed so rudimentary, even squalid, compared to the walls and the grander buildings in the city. While most of the houses were mud brick, usually whitewashed and sometimes painted decoratively, a few were of stone and this was true of all the temples and public buildings.

'That's Artemis Eileithyia,' Ferox explained, reading the inscription at the base of a statue of a goddess holding an infant in her arms, outside one of the larger temples, and seeing Vindex's interest. 'And no, it's not,' he added. Vindex and Bran's faces both fell in disappointment. Ferox knew that Artemis was not always the virgin huntress of the old poems, but had no idea of the stories associated with this cult, other than the obvious connection with birth and children. Philo might have known, but it would not do for his rough Galatian bodyguards to be heard discussing religion with their employer.

By now they were near the marketplace, a great square of open space – or at least what would have been open space were it not for the little shops set up in rows, each with a canopy against the sun, and each with its goods spilling over an ever wider area. That was not supposed to happen, but always did, and the stall owners carried the risk; anything broken by a passer-by was their loss, counted as an accident and with no chance of recompense through the courts. The buildings around the square were bigger, grander than those nearer the gate, let alone the ones on the side streets. Better yet, there was no sewer, or at least none visible, only a few drains to help carry off the rainwater. Ferox suspected that it would flood whenever a storm came, which meant that these did not come so often to persuade the citizens to do more to deal with them.

They found the clerk, even saw the Agoranomos himself, a sleek young aristocrat who gave every impression of being bored by his duties. Still, Philo, accompanied by Ferox while the others waited, was given a spot to set up his stall. That was a tribute to his apparent status, and his generous gifts to the clerk and the magistrate. Most visitors would be pointed in a rough direction and left to their own devices. Inevitably, others had started to occupy the spot allotted to Philo, but by the combination of Agoranomos' name and the burly presence of the Brigantes, these moved on, albeit after a good deal of shouting on both sides. Once they had unloaded the waggon, the driver drove off, accompanied by another of the Brigantes leading all their horses. Slaves appeared, sweeping up the manure left by these and the other animals, letting other odours take over. When they were ready to trade, another clerk appeared to test their scales and weights. Philo had none, given his business, so instead the man tasted a sample of their wine to ensure that it was safe, and after briefly and half-heartedly assuring them that no further generosity was necessary, departed with his attendant carrying a small amphora. All in all, it was much like any market anywhere within the empire.

Ferox did his best to lounge and loaf with Vindex, Bran and the other warrior, snarling at anyone who became too curious, unless they were a woman and young in which case they flirted and winked at them. Philo gave every sign of enjoying himself, as did Indike, and they both haggled with great enthusiasm. By chance, or perhaps the hints to the clerks, no doubt rewarded by gifts from the recipients, the two merchants named by the sentry at the gate came to call. Nicocles came first, tasted some expensive Falernian, talked volubly about engraving and the properties of different gems, took some more of the wine, spoke of silks and spices as if these were wonders new to his audience, drank another cup, and finally left, having invited Philo to the stall, apologising that he would not be present, but assuring him that his every need could be catered for.

Simon came a little later, followed a few steps behind by a slim woman and a young man. By chance Ferox was at the back of the stall, leaning on their barrels and under the shade of the canopy. He tried not to react, and let his head hang as if half asleep, for, without a doubt, the young man was Domitius the deserter.

Nicopolis
The same day

T HE FAMILY OF *Simon could not have been kinder or more welcoming to a stranger. Domitius thought of the Good Samaritan and of Christians he had met who proclaimed that the Jews were a wicked, greedy and cursed people, going further than the empire which taxed the Jews and no other race just for following their religion, was suspicious of their loyalty and dismissed them as perverse for rejecting the gods. He also remembered Pausanias, the man whose words had first made him realise his need for Christ, and how the old man reminded him time and again that the Jewish race was chosen of God, that the Lord Jesus had lived as a Jew in his time on earth, that his family were Jews, and that for all those reasons the race and the faith were to be honoured.*

Domitius had spoken to Pausanias whenever he had got an opportunity. Men and women like him lived their lives in a way he admired, which only made him puzzled when some Christians were so different, in their pettiness, jealousy and pride. Sin was everywhere, gnawing at every soul, including his. He had met Christians who would not have been anywhere near as generous as his hosts, and worried that he would have been no better in the same circumstances. In truth, he had never owned a house, and could scarcely invite anyone to stay in the couple of rooms allocated to an optio in barracks or billets, so the question was a theoretical one. Still, he worried that he was judging others, when he would probably have done no better or worse in similar circumstances. 'Forget what might happen,' Pausanias had told him. 'That's for the rich and leisured, who'll probably do the opposite when it comes to it, if it ever does. Live your real life, and try to do it day by day and hour by hour in a way your heart tells you is right, and you feel would be pleasing to the Lord. That's a hard enough thing to do, my lad, without dreaming up trials and tribulations in your mind.' Pausanias had been a sailor, then a captain of a trading vessel and spent thirty years at sea before he saw the Light and became a servant of God. That had left its mark on him, and not simply in his strong arms. Pausanias spoke of faith in a way that was real, and had a directness about him that was lacking in others.

It was odd, but in many ways John reminded him of the preacher. The old man spent a lot of time with him. 'Always wise to keep a watchful eye on any Roman,' he said. 'I've seen what they can do.'

Domitius' strength returned quickly, so quickly that he grew restless. Resting just made him think and worry about his faith and his future. He had broken his sacred oath to the emperor and the res publica and gone over the rampart. That would sadden his father when he heard the news, for his attempts to explain his new beliefs had not been welcomed. The elder Domitius was a legion man, through and through, and nothing mattered more than discipline and keeping faith with comrades and the legion. There would be no welcome for him at Berytus, although since his father's health was failing, soon there might be no family left there at all. If ever he went back to the empire – anywhere in the empire – he would risk arrest and severe punishment as a deserter, and once they checked the records and read of his public declaration of faith, he would be once again given a choice between denying the truth and execution.

Rather than sitting or lying in silence and thinking too much, it was better to talk, and John was lonely and starved of company.

'I'm old,' he would say, 'very old, and those younger never really feel comfortable around the ancient. So either they nod and smile and do not listen, or avoid us, because otherwise they will see the path that lies ahead of them and grow afraid. A pity really, since if they paid more attention they would realise that being old is not so very bad. It's not so very good either, but it is what it is, and has the satisfaction of being so much wiser when it is too late to do any good. So what are you doing?'

Domitius was hoping to leave the house for a while and walk. He always felt better and thought more clearly when he walked, and now that he had been up and about inside the house for several days, he was feeling restless.

'Always impatient, the young.' John shook his head sorrowfully. 'Well, you cannot go wandering off on your own at the moment, not until we know you better and know your intentions. No, don't protest, that is the way it is and nothing will change it. It's for your own good. You are a man without family, friends and money in a strange city. And you're a Roman, and this is not Rome, so there are some who will wonder whether you are truly a deserter or really a spy sent to discover our secrets. Yes, yes, I know that you are not, because the Romans never plan very far ahead, and even they aren't so stupid as to choose a man who looks like a legionary and acts and sounds like one.

'So we can go out, but I will come with you and keep an eye on you while you keep an eye on me. That way I don't have to take my spade and should be safe from all the evils my granddaughter assures me are waiting to pounce! Think of that. The two of us have just gone to Antioch and beyond with just

a single servant, and she worries when I walk out in our own city!'

'I'm sure Sara wishes only to protect you,' Domitius ventured.

'Pah! And who needed a stray Roman to protect her?' John sighed. 'I am too old, and I know it, but still it would be kind of a child to be more understanding. Still, there is nothing as ferocious as a young woman sure that she is right.' He laughed his deep, rumbling laugh. 'That was where we went wrong when we fought Nero! If only we'd kept the young men at home and sent the angry young women off to fight we would have won!'

'If you had been real men you would have won!' They were in the central courtyard of the house on their way to the side door, when Sara appeared in an upstairs window. 'So now you have recruited a legion of your own to escort you when you wander for no reason! Make sure he pays for what he buys, Domitius, and does not expect you to open your own purse!'

Much of the conversation within the family took the form of insults, and Domitius still found it strange. 'I am sorry, but I have no money...' he stammered, but neither of the others seemed to be paying him attention.

'Legion, is it? One man and she calls it a legion.'

'He'll have to do. Now, Domitius, you must be in charge and act as if you lead an infant by the hand. Turn your back and he will steal fruit from a stall or go and fall down a well. You are responsible and will answer to me if you fail.'

Domitius wanted to say that he would do anything for her, but Sara had already vanished and closed the shutter behind her.

The old man shook his head. 'May God help the man she marries,' he said with great fondness. 'They tell me that the daughter of the king in Edessa has committed to the one true God and now lives as a Jew. May God help us all if she becomes our queen. But for the moment let us free ourselves of the tyranny of efficient young women and wander the streets.'

John liked to talk, and every day after that, barring the Sabbath, they walked through the city streets, although when Domitius suggested that they go outside or climb the walls to see the view, the old man told him not to be a fool. 'Not yet. This is my home, and although I believe that you are a good man at heart, a lot of terrible things in this world have been done by good men.' The old man often spoke of the great rebellion. 'I killed men much like you, and men much like you killed my friends, my two brothers, and they probably defiled my sisters before they sold them as slaves.'

'Do you hate me?'

'What good would that do? You are too young to have been there or to have done any of these things. Tell me, have you ever been to war?' Domitius shook his head. 'I thought not. There is a hope in you that battles will kill even if you come through with a whole skin. I had that hope, that faith, and that belief that because we were young anything was possible. My father knew better and told me so, but I did not listen. "Wait," he said, "not all governors are bad and you cannot fight Rome and win." "God is on our side," I told him, "so we must win." "Will you give orders to God?" he asked me, but I was young. The Sicarii killed him because they said he was a traitor, but really for his purse and because my older brother was famous among the Zealots. Looking back I often wonder if more Jews were killed by other Jews than by the Romans. Probably not, for you Romans excel at slaughter and destruction, but I have to say that our leaders tried very hard to surpass you.

'I am too old for hate. I don't like Rome or its emperors, but some are worse than others and living here, at least I do not have to follow their rules.'

'*What about your journey to Antioch?*'

'*Ah, the soldier senses a weak spot! Hah! Well, that was no great burden. It is good to travel. I cannot follow young Simon on his travels.*' This was Sara's brother, who had gone away far to the east three years ago and might return with the spring or perhaps next spring. '*For that at least, my body is too weak, but a journey now and again, gives life and pleasure for all its discomforts. I wanted to see the sea again.*'

'*Were you ever a sailor?*' Domitius asked, suddenly wondering whether here was another similarity with Pausanias.

'*Hah! I hate boats, but as children we lived sometimes in Jaffa and I love to look at the sea in all its moods. That seems longer than a lifetime away, in the days when the Temple stood in all its glory. I saw it burn as well, years later, but since I had seen men fight and bleed out their lives on its walls and in its precincts, by then it did not seem the same. Yet my grandchildren have never seen a sacrifice performed, or the smoke from the altars.*' They were passing a temple to Dionysius, and by chance a bull was being killed in front of it. John shrugged as Domitius watched them. '*All right, all right, I mean a proper sacrifice to the true God whose words you misunderstand. Well, you are a Gentile, so what do you know? And no, I am not in the mood to debate the true meaning of the Torah and the prophets with you yet again. Instead I want to talk of war, and tell the stories that are still satisfying or still funny after all this time. You may not have seen battle, but as a soldier you will understand more than anyone at home. So, you will listen and learn...*'

'*Yes, sir!*' Domitius stood to attention.

The days passed with walks, a lot of talk, and visits to the workshop, where he marvelled at Simon's ability to carve intricate details on tiny gems, not least because he had to do everything in reverse, so that they would mark a seal clearly.

His attempts to copy were more destructive than useful, so instead he helped clean and sharpen the tools, and let Simon and the workmen he employed concentrate on their craft.

He saw little of Sara. Once he was well, they had moved him from the room high up in the main house to another above the small stables on the far side of the courtyard. There was a pervading scent of donkey sweat, hay and manure, but that was true of plenty of army bases so oddly familiar. Meals were brought to him by one of the servants, and while sometimes John would come to sit and talk, the others did not. Once or twice he had helped carry bales to and from the family's other workshop, where Sara and a dozen women re-wove and dyed silk, but his offers to help more there had been met by a contemptuous snort.

'She likes you,' John assured him. 'And not just because you saved her. I should run, if I were you, before she makes plans and marries you off to one of her Gentile friends.'

After two weeks, Sara once again called out to them from the window as they were setting out. 'Grandfather, do not tire our Roman out!'

'Hah! He is young and kind enough to pity a poor old man and keep him company. Of course, the poor old man has family, so should not be neglected in the first place...'

'Then he should not weary his family with endless stories about himself! Nor should he feign infirmity and weakness to avoid honest work! But I need our Roman, so you must have him back here in an hour. Do not be late!' The shutter slammed loudly as it was closed.

'She'll have the hinges off one day, you mark my words. But better do as she says, or she will tear down the whole house.'

'Like Samson!'

'You're not wholly ignorant, it seems, even if misguided.'

*They returned in plenty of time, and then Domitius waited
for another hour before he was needed. Simon's eyesight was so
poor that someone had to accompany him whenever he went
out, and Sara went with him if there was business to be done,
with a servant to accompany them. 'Today, everyone is busy, so
you will have to do,' she told Domitius. She had the loveliest
eyes he had ever seen, and the pale green veil she had donned
with her headscarf, because they were going out, only drew
attention to them. 'Try to look intelligent!' she ordered. 'Harder
than that. Well, if that is your best, then it will have to do. They
will think that you advise my father, so will pay heed to you and
less to me, which will let me do what needs to be done.'*

*'No man will notice me when you are around,' Domitius
said, his voice cracking halfway through.*

*'Huh! It is well known that the Romans are a lecherous
people.' Did she smile? It was so hard to tell through the veil,
but at least the tone was the same as the one she used with
her family. 'Do we give you your sword? No, a stout staff will
suffice. You look enough the soldier to make them think twice
before trying to threaten. Good, Father is here, and almost
tidy for once. Remember not to agree to anything before we
have spoken.' Simon could see Domitius over her daughter's
shoulder and gave a little shrug.*

*That was the first time he went with the father and daughter as
they visited stalls around the streets and markets, calling on the
Agoranomos and a dozen or so other city officials or prominent
men. Simon was always very business-like, while Sara always
stood a little back and kept her eyes down, as a respectable
woman – and especially a respectable Jewish woman – should.
Yet once or twice she whispered something to her father, and
his stance in the conversation shifted subtly but inexorably.
Neither of them spoke to him at all, unless giving an order.*

All in all it was much like accompanying a senior officer on an inspection, albeit with a good deal more talking. No money changed hands at any stage, but alongside all the pleasantries – 'Have you heard from your son? Do you know when he will return?' were the commonest ones addressed to Simon – there seemed to be agreements made or modified. Presumably this was how commerce functioned.

No one paid him much attention the first time he accompanied them. A few days later, when he went with them again, the Agoranomos asked whether he was a slave or in Simon's employ.

'He's a Syrian, name of Domitius,' Simon replied. 'Hired on with my father-in-law during the last trip to Antioch. Don't know much about him beyond that, but he has served well, so far.'

'Indeed. Well, that is good to hear.' There was no more, and no question addressed directly to him. Some cities registered anyone staying longer than a month, but so far no one had said anything about that so he did not know whether Nicopolis followed such a practice.

That day they made several purchases, so that he walked home with his stick under his arm and carrying a bundle of fabrics for Sara. As soon as she stepped into the courtyard of the house, she took off her veil and treated him to a lavish smile while indicating that he give the things to one of the maids. Domitius could feel himself beaming for the rest of the day.

'Don't get any ideas,' John said to him later on. 'Her father may be a fool sometimes, but he isn't enough of a fool to let his daughter marry a man not of our faith.'

The third time he accompanied Simon and Sara was to the monthly market, the first of the year to see people coming from further afield than just the chora around the city. Streets were crowded, so that sometimes he went ahead of them to force their way through and one of the servants brought up the rear. Domitius worried about thieves, for sometimes the press was solid, and felt that a lady should not really be walking through all this. He had enough sense not to say this to Sara, whose eyes were bright with excitement over her veil. The pace was much faster, with more meetings and negotiations which sometimes ended with invitations to come to their workshops. Domitius wondered why they did not set up a stall, until he noticed that several of the merchants they had visited in the past were similarly going from place to place.

It was much harder to hear what was said because of the constant talk and shouts of vendors as they tried to draw customers to them. The Agoranomos' clerk whispered something to Simon, money changed hands, and then they were off, into the heaving crowd. The men at the stall they went to had more than a hint of the army about them, though lacking the polish of the legions. It was enough to make him wary, for all that there was nothing the army could do to him here, not formally anyway, although there were men who might go to great lengths to hunt him down. The merchant was a slim, almost elegant, little man with a warm smile that grew even warmer as he and Simon spoke. One of the merchant's guards had a face from a nightmare, and looked him up and down without much interest. Another, younger, smaller, and with a pleasant face even if a hard eye, stared at his feet. Domitius suddenly felt very conscious of his army issue caligae, although they were so comfortable that he did not want to give them up until they fell to pieces. Only after that did the fellow lounging by the barrels strike him as familiar.

'Oh shit.' Since he had found his faith, Domitius had managed to hold back from swearing out loud. He had never

been a great one for cursing, at least by army standards, but he had tried hard and only once or twice failed to keep this pledge to himself. He did not seem able to stop himself from thinking these things, which worried him as so many things worried him.

Ferox showed no sign of recognising him, but that meant nothing at all. Wild thoughts flashed through his head, that the centurion had tracked him down and meant to take him back for punishment or kill him. He realised that he was gripping the staff he carried as if he could break it with his hands, and that his teeth were clenched.

No one showed any sign of noticing anything he was doing. Simon was talking to this Demetrios of Alexandria, and from the snatches he heard they were agreeing a visit to inspect some gems. In turn Simon asked about the wines. The merchant went to an opened barrel and reached for a cup, until he stopped himself and smiled in apology. He spoke softly to the pretty woman who was his wife, and she produced an amphora.

'I am the only one who has touched this,' Demetrios said. By chance the noise around them had grown less, so that Domitius could hear. The merchant held a cup, and let his wife pour the wine into it. Simon took it, and Domitius realised that the merchant must also be Jewish. For all their kindness, the family had made sure that he never touched food or vessel before they used it. Simon drank.

'It's good. May I ask the price of a small barrel?'

'Please accept this as a gift in anticipation of dealing with each other,' the merchant said. His tunic was so white that it almost gleamed, and his teeth even brighter, but there was sincerity in his smile. Still, that was true of so many merchants and plenty of scoundrels. An honest face was easier to trust than a dishonest one, which did not mean that it was wise to do

so. 'And be assured that the barrel will come to you unopened and untasted.'

'That is good of you.' Domitius knew that even dipping a cup used by someone else into the wine would pollute it. They were about to leave, and he glanced at Ferox and knew that he must do something. Simon had bowed to the merchant, and he and Sara were turning when inspiration came to him. Domitius took his staff in one hand, spun it round and rested the tip on the ground. Then he followed.

Ferox did not come with the merchant when he visited the workshop, and Domitius was not sure whether this was a good sign or not. Simon had gone ahead and asked him to escort Sara to join them again after she had visited her weavers and instructed them to prepare several garments as well as rolled silk for sale. On the way, Domitius wondered whether he should mention that the trader was escorted by a Roman centurion disguised as a hired bruiser, and decided that this was not the time. Instead of Ferox, the frightening, leering fellow and the youth came with the trader. That would have to do, and thankfully he had plenty of time, because this Demetrios spent a long while inspecting gems, some of them set in rings and most loose, while his escort lounged about. When Sara was busy with Simon – they had started discussing prices, and she was always involved in such matters – he wandered over to the tall, long-faced barbarian.

'This your first visit to Nikopolis?' he asked, speaking in Greek. The man did not seem to understand, but with his back to all the others, Domitius cupped his hands and crossed his thumbs in a gesture Ferox had shown him months ago.

'Don't speak the lingo,' the barbarian said in strongly accented Latin and gave no indication of recognising the sign, but still took the small shard of pottery Domitius pressed into *his hand. It quickly vanished, and as far as he could tell no one had noticed the exchange.*

Later Domitius wondered whether or not he had done the right thing. He hated the thought of keeping anything from his hosts, even though he could not see how it involved them in any way. Sleep did not come that night, for he worried about Ferox and his intentions, and about Simon and his family, and John's warning.

Perhaps none of it really mattered. Later the day after next he heard that Demetrios of Alexandria had been attacked. No one was quite sure what had happened, but three bodies of his barbarian bodyguards were found, all hacked to pieces. The waggon was there as well, its contents stolen or burned.

VI

On the road to the crossing at Zeugma
Tenth day before the Kalends of April

PHILO WAS NERVOUS and Ferox could not blame him. The lad – who was now thirty, but it was hard to think of him as anything other than a boy – did not lack courage. He was not a fighter, and more than that, he had his wife with him. Romans often claimed that slaves became docile by nature, frightened of everything and lacking courage and that this taint persisted when they were freed. Ferox did not believe a word of it, for he had seen cowardice and courage mixed in folk of all ranks and all races. Philo and Indike were devoted to each other and had come through a lot together. They had wanted to come and the plan of posing as a merchant and escorts was a better one than anything else anyone dreamed up. Yet the risk was always there and now it was catching up with them.

'I think I saw one,' Philo said quietly.

Actually there were at least four and they had been following them for over an hour. Four against their five gave decent enough odds, except that this was the east and the one he had seen closest had carried a bow in a case behind his saddle. More than likely they all had them, and the archers from these lands tended to be good. So the enemy would not need to come close to kill them all. Ferox did not doubt that they were enemy even if he did not know who they were. They could be simple bandits, even slavers, on the prowl for any opportunity. After all, the merchant Demetrios had goods and money and a pretty wife, so there was plenty worth taking for those inclined. One rider had followed them from the city, hanging back in the loose procession leaving Nicopolis on the morning after the market. Ferox had seen him a couple of times, a tall, hawk-faced man in dull green trousers and tunic and a tall felt hat, who did not seem to be attached to any other party as guard. He might have been a horse trader who had sold his animals and was heading home on his own or he might have been a bandit seeking a good target. The two were not exclusive whether here or in much of the empire. An hour out from the city, Ferox had spotted a horseman, briefly outlined on top of a hill to the right of the track. The other two were on the opposite side, and again made brief appearances. Ferox guessed that this was to show the man with the column that they were there, unless they were sloppy or simply uncaring. Four men would not attack so many people, but he could see that the guards with other parties had noticed the threat and were more wary.

Before long, folk from the villages left the main track and the column thinned. There were still over a hundred people, with about a dozen merchants and their escorts and the rest individuals and families. A quarter of them went their own way by noon, while the rest kept going, most heading for Syria and the main ferry-crossings at Zeugma. It was not an organised caravan, for there should not be need for such protection in this area. Even so, when they stopped for the night they camped in a circle, lit plenty of fires and agreed to organise a watch for the hours of darkness. Before they settled down Vindex had glanced questioningly at Ferox who shook his head. This was not the time. The Carvetian did not need to say that the rider in green was no longer with them.

Nothing happened during the night, and during the next day only a handful of people went their separate ways as the procession trudged on. There were two riders either side of them, taking a little more care to hide, but in country like this Ferox still had a fair idea where each of them was, at least most of the time. One merchant left the road late morning. He had a bodyguard, and a slave leading three donkeys, their panniers light which suggested that his purse was full. The four horsemen did not follow him and were still in place by the middle of the afternoon.

Ferox had a plan. So far they had done well and done the two things they were sent to do. Ferox had taken a good look at Nicopolis' fortifications, making some notes, but storing more in his head so that he could explain to someone skilled in making a plan of it all. He had not liked what he had seen, but that was not the point. Although he had begun to doubt, late in the day they had a visit at the stall from a merchant from Edessa, who gave 'Demetrios' a small jar of unguent and said the right words to make clear that this was the message from the princess.

Seeing Domitius had been a surprise, and Ferox was still not quite sure what to make of it. The note written on the broken piece of pottery was short and simple, advising Ferox not to trust Lucius Valerius Messalinus. Given that this was the tribune Ferox had killed earlier in the year, this was of little use, although it might suggest that the former optio was as honest as he had seemed. Ferox had not wanted to kill the tribune, for all that the man deserved it. It would have been better to pressure the officer into talking, for he was not the real chief in all this. The man must have been warned, for he had two soldiers with him and was determined to fight with a courage surprising in a man so fat and apparently slothful. They died and Ferox did not, so there was a good outcome in that sense, even if it left him with few leads.

There was always graft in the army, from officers taking bribes or claiming pay for non-existent soldiers, to men requisitioning anything they fancied or selling off food, equipment, and raw materials from the stores. It was always there, sometimes less frequent and sometimes more, but only now and then did it become a real problem, sapping the efficiency of the army or worse stirring rebellion among communities being plundered. When Hadrian was sent to watch over Syria, he had come across signs of something far bigger, of organised corruption making some officers and soldiers fabulously wealthy, but sapping morale within their units and undermining all discipline and efficiency. That was serious enough at any time, and far more worrying with Trajan on his way to campaign in the region. Apart from making sure the army was in good shape for this, Hadrian suspected that he might come in for blame as acting governor if the truth started to come out. Two of his staff were sent to investigate. One was found, drowned in a canal, and the other had not been seen since. So Hadrian had summoned Ferox, and after some time he had found the tribune and killed him.

Domitius might know more, much more, for the eager young centurion in waiting had accidentally become aware of the widespread sale of 'condemned' army mules, whose health amazingly recovered when bought by new owners. He had been very useful, keeping his eyes open and putting Ferox onto the scent of other abuses, until he was publicly accused of belonging to a proscribed cult and imprisoned. His escape was puzzling, for it had seemed too easy, but Ferox had been too late for the inquest or to speak to the man before he deserted. At Nicopolis he had not been sure that the man could be trusted. There was surely a big temptation to prove himself to the authorities by informing them that the merchant and his party were likely Roman agents. Apart from that, there was no obvious way to speak to him without arousing suspicion about them both, which meant he had the message and no more.

Still, if Domitius had informed on them to the magistrates, it seemed unlikely that they would have sent just four men in pursuit, instead of inventing some pretext to investigate 'Demetrios' and arrest them. Even less likely was that the deserter had the influence or funds to hire the men, unless he had been helped and paid off by someone deep in all the abuses going on in Syria. Which meant that most likely they were cut-throats acting on their own, or had something to do with the princess' message.

'It's time,' Ferox told them.

Philo nodded. 'See you at the crossing!' he called to the merchant ahead of them. 'My load is too big to face that climb, so I'm going round the hills!' The driver had pointed the team off the track to the left. This was pasture land, so there should not be ploughed fields or drainage ditches to get in their way.

The man was surprised, but waved them farewell. They were the only group with a vehicle, and in truth the track did climb up and down some slopes, although they probably could have taken the waggon across with care, and they certainly did not have a heavy load. There was about an hour until sunset, and Ferox wanted to give the horsemen a chance to catch them on their own. Timing was everything. It would be a while before the men from the far side of the road could cross and join their comrades. As he had guessed, they waited until the folk on the track were out of sight and then trotted across. No one was hiding anymore, for the other pair were watching from the brow of a ridge.

'Now!' Ferox ordered the driver, and the warrior whipped the team into a lumbering canter. Indike squealed when they hit a bump and she was bounced out of her seat, and then looked embarrassed. Philo was excited, clinging for dear life onto his mule so tightly that he did not risk glancing behind. Bran was riding ahead, searching for any hazard in the ground, but these were gently rolling plains and they sped across them.

The four riders followed, spread out in a line.

'Go on!' Ferox yelled to the driver, who cracked the whip again. The mules were labouring, and kicked out, but their anger turned to speed and they kept going.

Vindex rode close beside the waggon and was making faces at Indike, who laughed back at him. Their pursuers were three-quarters of a mile away, horses racing.

'Keep going!' The driver whipped the mules again, just as the waggon lurched and this time when Indike bounced up and slammed back onto the seat she giggled.

Hoofs drummed on the hard earth. The mules were sweating, their sides white with foam.

'On!' Ferox yelled. The horsemen were half a mile away, riding with the easy grace of Arabs. 'Keep going!' There was no one else in sight, not that shepherds were likely to intervene on behalf of strangers.

'Keep going!' The sun was ahead of them, a great red ball sinking in the Heavens.

'It'll kill 'em if we keep on!' The driver shouted. The mules' tongues were lolling out of their mouths, their eyes wide, and he had to flog them mercilessly to keep them running.

'On! On!' Ferox yelled. 'Don't stop!' The mules would die and that did not matter if it bought them just a little more time.

'Nearly on us!' Vindex yelled. The riders were barely a quarter of a mile back, and would soon be within bowshot, at least if they halted. Still, they were looking right into the setting sun and that helped no one's aim.

'Go on!' It was getting dark, and for once Ferox was glad of the abrupt sunsets of these southern lands. At home his plan would have had no chance, but here he was counting on darkness to make archery difficult and take away the enemy's biggest advantage. The rhythm of the mules' footfall was irregular now, the waggon lurching from side to side, and when the wheels' rims hit a stone they threw up bright sparks.

Ferox wondered whether the pursuers would try an arrow or two. None came, which suggested that the men wanted to be certain and had patience. It was almost night, stars appearing in the sky above them and the sun no more than a semi-circle of dazzling light.

A wheel sank down into soft earth, lodged against a stone and the axle snapped, bringing the waggon to a skidding halt. Indike screamed as she was flung forward and then gasped as Vindex caught her in his arms. Ferox searched the darkness, a throbbing light lingering from staring at the setting sun, and could just make out the riders dropping back. They were good, by the look of things, willing to wait for their moment.

One of the mules sank onto its haunches with a sigh. The other was struggling to breathe.

'I think I might keep her,' Vindex said. Indike was little more than a child in his arms. She stuck her tongue out at him.

'I wouldn't,' Philo told him, 'for she is very rude.' He slid awkwardly off his mule, rubbing his rear. Vindex lowered the woman very gently to Bran who helped her down.

'We'll camp here,' Ferox said, as the second mule slumped down and died.

'Will we?' Vindex asked. 'Going to be one of those nights, is it?'

They lit a fire and no arrows came, nor any sign of their pursuers. Ferox had read that the Parthians and their neighbours never fought at night unless they could help it, but so much the Romans and Greeks wrote about others was misunderstood or plain nonsense.

'One guard,' Ferox ordered. 'We'll take it in turns.'

'And stay out of the light?' Vindex asked.

'It'll be cold, so make the most of it.' He could make out Vindex's expression. 'We want them to think that we're stupid.'

'That shouldn't be hard,' Vindex muttered. 'Why don't you give us a song?'

'Do you want them to start shooting?' Bran asked.

They started breaking up the waggon to get firewood. Without a team and with a broken axle, it would not be going anywhere. Philo cooked for them and Indike helped, and they sat talking for hours, wondering and waiting.

'Where is Bran?' Philo asked, suddenly noticing that the young warrior was not around the fire.

'You should ask where is your patron, husband,' Indike said. Philo blinked in surprise when he realised that Ferox had also gone.

Vindex smiled. Even he had not seen Ferox slip away, although he reckoned that he had noticed his absence pretty soon after the centurion had gone. Bran had followed a little later, and Vindex was not sure whether or not the centurion had given his approval.

'Well,' he said. 'We had better play our part. My turn to go on watch so the rest of you try to get some sleep. Keep your heads down if anything happens.' He picked up a spear and wandered a few paces away from the fire where he would still be visible, but only just. The two Brigantes rolled themselves in their cloaks and one was snoring away within a few moments. Philo and Indike whispered to each other, but if they could not find sleep at least they had each other to cuddle under the blanket, and Vindex reckoned that they ought to count themselves happy.

Waiting was the key. The Silures trained boys to lie still and quiet, watching and waiting, letting the time flow past them. Ferox often wondered why other peoples did not do the same, but in all his travels he had not met a tribe who did. Yet the skills could be learned even if it took a long time. Bran was coming on, and the lad had been so keen that he had not had the heart to refuse his offer to help. By the time he slipped away, Ferox was already lying flat behind a flat stone, and he only spotted movement once or twice before the youngster found a spot of his own on the far side of the camp.

If it was going to happen, it would happen soon. The night was half spent and he could afford only one more hour before they would need to leave, with Indike and Bran riding double in an effort to get back to the track and some company soon after dawn. If the enemy was really smart then they might wait for daylight, especially if they realised that the waggon was broken.

Ferox had his chin resting on his folded arms. He wore no armour, and had his pugio, the short army-issue dagger, under his arms and his gladius lying beside him, the blade covered in a fold of his hooded cloak because the stars were bright. He was some hundred and fifty paces out from the camp, which was the distance he judged someone might risk a shot. Vindex was a dark shape against the dying fire, hunched as if half asleep and propping himself up with his spear. It was a risky job, but his old friend did it well and had done it so many times that he was used to the risk. Try as he might, Vindex made too much noise blundering around in the darkness to help in any other way.

Another hour passed before Ferox heard a movement. It was soft, and could easily have been an animal wandering about its business, until he heard a breath and knew that the sound came from a horse. This was not a country of wild horses, and their own animals were too far away and not stirring. Then he heard the gentlest of scraping sounds, again and again, coming on steadily. A man was crawling, close by and behind him.

Ferox waited, not moving, but not letting himself become tense. One horse, probably with a rider from the way the sound was swiftly muffled, was close by and another man was crawling on his belly. That one was even closer now, and Ferox caught his breathing; crawling was harder work than anyone realised until they tried it. When younger he might have felt the urge to look around, although he hoped that even then he would have resisted. Only an infant would make such a mistake. Instead he lay still, and simply hoped that the man would not crawl right onto him. Otherwise, unless he was really good, he probably would not notice Ferox at all.

The horse's feet were quiet as it walked a little way forward. Perhaps these men wrapped the feet in rags to muffle the sounds, as the Sarmatians did. The animal was to his right, and he judged that the man was a little to his left, but very close for the noise was getting louder.

Still Ferox waited, staring forward and unable to see much on either side because of the hood. He thought that there was movement beyond the camp and wondered about Bran, but the crawling man was so close that he heard him whisper something under his breath. Ferox's fingers closed around the handle of the pugio as it lay under his arms. The crawling man was beside him, inches away and surely must realise that someone was lying covered in a cloak. Yet he kept going, muttering what sounded like curses. Perhaps he thought that Ferox was one of his comrades?

Vindex jumped back as an arrow whisked through the night towards him. Ferox turned his head, saw a bearded man just a foot or two away, who opened his mouth and said something. The centurion flicked out his left hand with the knife in it, and punched, driving the point through the man's eye, who hissed once before he died. Ferox left the blade embedded, not bothering to wrench it free, for a horse was galloping towards him. He pushed himself up, gladius in his hand, and wrenched off his cloak, snapping the brooch in his haste. The rider was close by, bow up, an arrow already nocked, so Ferox ran at him, yelling as loud as he could and waving the cloak like a banner. There were shouts from the camp, and a piercing scream from further out.

The rider saw the new threat, and since Ferox was coming from his left it was easy to flick his bow round, but his horse reared from the sudden noise and movement, and the arrow flew high. His mount was turning, and he kicked his heels to drive it at Ferox even as he reached back for another arrow.

Ferox pelted towards him, and they closed so quickly that he mistimed his throw and his cloak flashed past the horse's head rather than covering it. An arrow scraped the side of his head, drawing blood, then he thrust with the gladius. It was an old-fashioned blade, longer than the standard ones and ending in a long triangular point, which drove through the scale armour the horseman wore and went deep into his belly. The man screamed and fell out of the saddle onto him, knocking Ferox to the ground. His face was pressed into him, eyes wide, and mouth gasping and his fingers clutched for the centurion's throat. Ferox's hand was sticky with the man's blood, but he still had hold of his sword so twisted the blade and drove it deeper. The man shuddered and went still.

Close by, a horse galloped off into the night. Ferox pushed the corpse off him and saw that the rider's mount had stopped only a short way away. On the edge of sight the shape of a horseman pounded off across the plain.

Ferox sighed, and put his boot on the man's chest so that he could drag his sword free. One of them had got away.

Vindex appeared. 'You all right?'

'I'm getting old.'

'Aren't we all?' the Carvetian replied. 'I count three.'

'Three.'

'Bugger,' Vindex said.

VII

Zeugma
Seventh day before the Kalends of April

'SO SOMEONE WAS watching?' Hadrian said. 'And one got away, so whoever it is will know that Azátē's message reached us?' They were in the principia of the fortress on the edge of Zeugma, the morning after they had come across the Euphrates. Hadrian had been busy at a feast the night before, but Ferox had handed the jar with its message to Sosius, because he knew that the acting governor trusted the man. Personally, Ferox thought that Sosius was as reliable as a snake, and realised that he must tell Bran who had sworn vengeance on the man. He did not want the young warrior to do anything hasty or foolish, like leaving witnesses.

Sosius was his usual surly self, so Ferox left him as soon as he had handed over the message and given a brief summary. Orders had come to report to the principia at dawn and spend time describing what he had seen to a draughtsman. At the second hour, he was summoned to see the acting governor, who studied the plans and drawings, and asked a long series of questions, first about Nicopolis, then briefly about Domitius and finally the message from the princess and the men who had pursued them.

'Pity you did not find anything out about them.'

Ferox had explained how they had cut off the dead men's heads and then dressed them in the Brigantes' clothes before draping them on and around the waggon and setting fire to it.

'Won't fool the man who got away, will it?' Hadrian had snarled.

Ferox remained impassive. He had no choice but to obey Hadrian if he was to protect his family and others about whom he cared a good deal. However, he was not about to let Philo and especially Indike put themselves in danger again and did not trust the senator not to order them to go back to Nicopolis and spy for him. The story would spread that their escort was dead, the cart burned and husband and wife vanished. Even Hadrian should not want to send them back when they would have to explain away surviving such an attack.

'Well,' Hadrian picked up one of the plans and studied it. 'These really are good, very good. You never cease to amaze me, Ferox, you truly do not.' Ferox had lost count of the tasks given to him by Hadrian over the last years. None were easy, most highly dangerous, and if he had survived them, plenty of the men he had led were dead or maimed for whatever life was left to them. Somehow it was never enough, and Hadrian's hold over him remained. Sometimes he wondered whether it might be simpler to kill the man and flee the empire. He doubted that Hadrian would be able to strike at his family from the grave, but could not quite be sure. It did not matter, for he had sworn an oath to serve and could not break it unless it clashed with his higher oath to the empire. Neither had been taken willingly, but that did not matter. His grandfather, the Lord of the Hills, had raised him to despise oath-breakers. So he must keep going, like a hero of legend bound by a curse, or like Hercules or Herakles or whatever you wanted to call him, although the demigod seemed to enjoy himself with a lot of women on his journeys, since so many dynasties claimed him as ancestor. Being a demigod obviously came with privileges.

'What did the princess have to say?' Ferox asked, to break his own chain of thought. Hadrian had made no mention of the contents of the message, and Ferox was tired of playing games.

Hadrian raised his thick eyebrows. Ferox had noticed that several of the acting governor's senior staff also sported beards and wondered whether this was sycophancy or the start of a new fashion.

'Ah yes, I have a bundle of letters for you from your wife. The messenger – who was not the first one to carry them, but had spoken to him – assured me that the queen and your children are in the best of health.'

'The queen?' Ferox asked. 'Has that been approved?'

Hadrian tilted his head to one side as Romans did when they wanted to seem apologetic. 'Ratification of the title is close, very close, although with the Lord Trajan here in the east and involved in sensitive diplomacy'—Ferox wondered how sensitive diplomacy could be when backed by 100,000 heavily armed soldiers, but did not interrupt—'other matters may delay his approval. I am doing everything I can to remind him and ensure a successful outcome.'

Lying bastard, Ferox thought. Like Bran, he was spending too much time with Vindex. Still, it was good to have the old rogue beside him once more. Not long ago the temptation to dive back into a wine cup had grown very strong. Ferox suspected that if he did that again, then he might never come out. That would solve one problem, since Hadrian would not keep an unreliable agent and would not risk him talking, so *thetatus*. It would not help his family though and that was all that really mattered.

Hadrian rang a bell and a slave appeared almost instantly. 'Felix, go to my quarters and fetch the package from the table by the window.'

The slave bowed. 'My lord.'

'Do not think that I did not notice that you said princess rather than queen,' Hadrian said, turning back to Ferox. 'There was a rolled pack of calfskin in the jar, and when treated properly it revealed letters. The code was the one we have agreed, and while I cannot tell you everything that was in it, Azátē states that she will soon be ready and is confident of success.'

'How many men will she have?' Ferox asked. 'Did not strike me that the Nicopolitans were itching to admit a foreign army into their city. So she will need a good few reliable and well-led soldiers to take control of the citadel and one or both of the main gates.'

'And how many hours were you in the city to form such a judgement?' Ferox sensed that Hadrian very much wanted to believe. 'Azátē claims to know her people and is adamant that she will do anything to avoid the proposed marriage. Her bodyguard of fifty men is utterly loyal to her and there are others from the noble families willing to support.'

'So she says.' Silures were well known for their ability to convey scorn and some of this transferred into Latin.

Hadrian's face reddened. The fingers of one hand drummed on the tabletop for a while and he stared into Ferox's eyes, even though experience told him that this achieved little. 'Blunt and to the point as always,' he said at last. 'Well, that is why I pay you.'

'Thought that came from the emperor, sir.'

'Don't be insolent – or obtuse. You know what I mean and for all your usefulness you cause plenty of problems. I can hold off investigation into the killing of Messalinus for a while longer.

If necessary there is – or should I say there will be – a signed confession of his crimes which will justify your acts. However, it would be a good deal more useful if it went into detail about his confederates. Are you any closer to finding them?'

Ferox shook his head. 'Too many possibilities – and they've gone quiet now that the emperor is on the spot and too many others are paying attention to details in every unit.'

'Is it worth your while going back to see Domitius?' There it was, as Ferox had expected.

'Don't know which way he will go. And someone might recognise me. And no sense in making the authorities nervous about Roman spies.'

'No, indeed no. Occupying Nicopolis is the main thing and we must do nothing to imperil that end. Still, once we are in, it would be good if you could find Domitius and persuade him to talk.'

'Sir.'

'Do you think that those men got rid of him?'

'Probably.'

'Hmm. One cannot condone perverted religion, but the truth is that no one is bothered unless it becomes public. The timing seems too coincidental to be mere chance.'

'Probably, my lord.'

The slave returned, carrying a small package. 'Ah, here are your letters. Depart, Flavius Ferox – even take your things and go!' Hadrian grinned at his own joke. Ferox simply thought that it would be very nice to be divorced and free from service to this man. 'Read your letters and then go with your fellows back to Crispinus and plague him with your insolence. I will write soon, but tell him to make haste with his preparations.'

'And to expect a siege, my lord?'

Hadrian sighed. 'If you must. It is wisest to plan for the worst as long as such pessimism does not become too embedded in your soul.'

Hadrian always felt weary after a meeting with Ferox in a way his other agents and servants, let alone his officers, never made him feel. The man's face was so rigid. Noble Romans prized self-control, maintaining the *dignitas* and *gravitas* appropriate to high office and good family. Yet a man was a not a statue, and it was unnatural to show no sign of emotion at all. Smiles and frowns, even tears and laughter, were appropriate in their place.

Ferox just stood or sat there, utterly impassive, back rigidly straight, and narrow eyes taking in everything. It was more than the impassive expression of a soldier on parade, for although you never actually caught him looking at anything in particular, you could sense the scrutiny. Years had passed since they had first met, yet Hadrian found it hard to shake off the feeling that Ferox was pondering just where he would stab you. By the sound of it, this was what it had been like fighting the Silures, before they were beaten down. That was the point. You were stronger, much stronger than they were, and your power meant that they had to do what you wanted in the end. Still somehow they remained cold, impassive, and the only thing you could be sure they were feeling was an immense sense of superiority. Hadrian had briefly considered proposing the recruitment of a cohort or ala from the Silures, before deciding that that was one nightmare too many to release on the army and the empire.

Ferox would do his job, and do it well, if not quite in the way you expected. He had proved himself time and again and was a useful man to have with Crispinus in the months to come. There was not much time left, although thankfully he had received word of yet another delay before the new legatus arrived to take charge of Syria. There was still a chance left to achieve something and Nicopolis was the only real prospect. Hadrian desperately needed a big success, for Trajan was dying. The stars pointed in that direction, although nothing was quite certain and it could prove to be anytime in the next five years. Far more than that, Hadrian had spent a lot of time with Trajan in the winter months at Antioch and had been shocked by how much the man had aged.

Trajan had been friendly by his standards, even to Hadrian who was invited to accompany him when he visited a number of shrines. Together they had climbed the mountain path near the mouth of the River Orontes to the temple of Zeus Casius, Trajan rushing ahead even though the steps were steep. Hadrian had composed a dedication on his behalf, 'from the ruler of the earth to the ruler above' to accompany the offerings of spoils from Dacia. Two slaves carried these, one with a huge golden bowl and the other with several ornate helmets. No one else was with them, and the slaves did not count, so only Hadrian saw the emperor's eyes begin to flicker, and his speech slur as he prayed. Trajan was not the sort of man to make a show of religious passion, even of the mildest sort, let alone the ecstasies associated with the more exotic and vulgar cults. He slumped down, sitting hard on his bottom, and if Hadrian had not caught him by the shoulders he would have fallen flat. There was a stench as the ruler of the earth fouled himself, and Hadrian wondered whether the emperor was dying.

The slaves did not seem surprised.

'Hold him, my lord,' one said softly. 'The fit will pass.'

Hadrian did as he was told and before long the emperor's eyes became steady if unfocused. Then he started to sing. It was an old song, a marching song of the legions about the misadventures of a randy centurion. The ruler of the world was soon bawling out the verses, keeping to the time that helped men stay awake even while fatigue and the rhythmic crunch of boots lulled them to sleep.

'Lift his arms, my lord.' One of the slaves had produced a clean tunic and underwear from a satchel. 'We must be quick.' The haste was not in case they were discovered, but because the emperor was still unaware of what was happening and easier to handle. Hadrian did little, save to take Trajan's weight, and the two imperial slaves swiftly stripped and re-dressed him. By this time the emperor was sitting up strongly and did not need supporting.

'Sit beside him, my lord,' a slave whispered, and Hadrian felt it best to obey.

'Ah, cousin,' Trajan said, as if bumping into Hadrian on the street.

'I slipped and fell,' Hadrian told him.

'Clumsy, but no harm done. Let me help you up.' Trajan got to his feet and reached down. As far as Hadrian could see this was not an act, and he had no memory of what had just happened. That was the only time he witnessed an attack, but the smooth coping of the two slaves made clear that this had happened before. Afterwards, he noticed that one of the pair was always at Trajan's side, along with a second slave who appeared equally competent. No one said anything, not that there was any need, for Hadrian kept the secret. Certainly, the emperor's behaviour did not change, and he took Hadrian with him to visit a number of other shrines. There were no more attacks, not even when one oracle gave an answer that, for all its opaque poetry, clearly meant that Trajan was not destined to return to Rome.

Hadrian was not sure how much the emperor understood. His eagerness for army camps and war was nothing new, but there seemed an urgency about it all. Trajan wanted a war, there was no doubt about that, for all the talk of negotiation. At the very least, if no one would fight him, then he would lead his armies to accept their submission in their own lands. There was more talk of Alexander at court than Hadrian remembered in the past.

Trajan was a man who revelled in weapons, drills, marches and campaigns. He was not someone to relish rest, let alone the gentler life of old age. Armenia was important, as it had been since the days of the divine Augustus, and there was justification for the emperor coming here to assert Rome's dominance. Hadrian was sure that it was more than that. Whether aware of his sickness of not, Trajan resented oncoming age, and wanted to become young or feel young again by going off to war. For all the talk of setting an example, there was something undignified about a princeps joining in military exercises by riding and throwing javelins before a great crowd. Trajan's health was failing and he might just overdo it one day while playing a game like that or sharing too many of the hardships on campaign.

Hadrian studied people, especially those who mattered, and felt that he was a good judge of character. Trajan was refusing to accept old age, and part of this was his utter unwillingness to mark out a successor. No other emperor had lived so long and ruled so long without showing clear favour to someone. He was friendly with plenty of senators, and praised and promoted men like Quietus. He had been nicer than he had for some time to Hadrian, but it went no further than that. Being called cousin was no real endorsement. The appointment as acting governor was a compliment and mark of faith, while also making clear that he did not want Hadrian by his side to share in the trials and glories of his campaigns. Nor did he want him in Syria for a longer spell. Hadrian wondered whether he had overdone his 'but of course duty first, my lord' act last year and his reluctance to leave his comfortable life in Athens.

It was probably too late to expect Trajan to mark him down as closest relative and heir. The emperor was not going to face his responsibility as princeps and admit that his life would end. Apart from that, Hadrian had always known that deep down Trajan simply did not like him. So his path must be a different one. The empress liked him a lot, and he must take every chance to cultivate her while she was in the east. Yet he needed more, for he needed to make himself a plausible – indeed the most plausible – candidate for that moment when the emperor dropped dead and senators wanted the stability of a new princeps as soon as possible. Time was running out. He had spoken to physicians, albeit very discreetly, describing the symptoms as if they were his own. The men blustered as physicians always did, but the clear consensus was that the attacks would get worse and eventually lead to permanent paralysis and death unless he rested and made the right offerings.

Time was short, and he needed a victory, and there was Nicopolis with its appropriate name, and some omens were too clear to ignore. Like Trajan, Hadrian craved a campaign and a success, whether bloodless or gruelling. All that mattered was to win. He feared Ferox was right and that it would not be easy. Either way it must be soon. Sosius said that he had found a man able to reach the princess. The freedman had his doubts about the fellow, so the message would need the most careful wording as well as the usual code. Sosius would go to Nicopolis – the man had a knack of surviving and the risk was worth it. Hadrian would tell Azátē that it must be soon or never.

VIII

The camp of VIIII Hispana
One day before the Nones of April

R EADY OR NOT, there was no more time left, so the trumpets sounded two hours before dawn, and, to make sure, the *tesserarii* went through each barrack room, banging something loud and brass and bawling at the legionaries to wake. Men muttered and growled, and a few hurled insults from the shadows, as they hauled themselves out of warm bedding. The legionaries dressed and got their equipment ready, and each *contubernium* prepared a meal.

When the trumpets sounded for the next hour, Crispinus knew that they were running late. By this time, they were supposed to have taken down the tents, starting with his own and the other tent acting as a principia. Having spent the best part of two months camped here, and given the season, the men had made little huts with dry-stone walls and used their leather tents as roofing. He knew plenty had gone further, packing earth tightly to make a table in the centre and firm bases for their bedding. A few optimists had even begun to cultivate little gardens in the space outside and watched as the shoots started to grow. That made it all the more of a wrench to leave, especially as even the rumour mill had soon dismissed the story that they were to take over the permanent fortress at Zeugma now that its legion had marched to join the emperor. They were going to Zeugma, it was true, but after that no one was quite sure. Perhaps that made them even more hesitant to set out.

Crispinus had hoped to parade the legion and march out before dawn, but everything was taking too long. For all the training they had done, they had not practised getting ready for a long campaign and there was more confusion than he would have liked. Some was his fault because he had not given detailed orders for issuing hard tack and other rations to be carried by each soldier, and his subordinates had not thought to do so. Like him they had assumed that the normal regulations would suffice, but still ultimately it was his fault for not thinking to check. He had not served with the army for more than a decade and he realised that he had forgotten so much. Ferox always seemed to know what to do and remembered to do it, a habit as useful as it was infuriating, and Crispinus regretted not having talked to the man at more length before sending him with the advance party. It was too late now, and better that he was not here to wait in silence, his face so impassive that it was almost worse than seeing him look smug.

Caecilius was even more experienced and here with them; Crispinus was not sure whether the man had not realised the scale of the task facing them or chosen not to speak, wanting to be asked his opinion. The primus pilus was an odd fish, and for all the flattery of recent days, there may have been a good reason why he had been passed over for promotion until now. Caecilius had warned them at the start that they could not be ready for a proper siege and move quickly, and the last days, let alone this morning, had proved him right. He was not a man to crow, and instead the primus pilus shouted himself hoarse as he scurried about, trying to bring some method and haste to it all, yet now and then Crispinus thought he spotted an air of satisfaction about the fellow. Rufus was with the primus pilus, and the two were so far working better together than Crispinus had hoped. His broad-stripe tribune had still not arrived, while the praefectus castrorum had gone down with fever and would be staying behind. Crispinus suspected that the illness was feigned, and neither man was much of a loss in themselves, but it did mean fewer pairs of hands for the biggest tasks. Arrian was shaping up nicely, and by far the pick of the narrow-stripe tribunes, which was why Crispinus had sent him with the advance party. They should be at the river by now, further south to give them a much quicker route to Nicopolis. They were to cross by raft and boat tomorrow night, or sooner if the signal was given.

Taking their cue from the primus pilus, the remaining centurions charged around shouting and often enough shoving or using their canes. Crispinus did not stop them, but made a note to himself to have a quiet word. He had seen enough during his time as tribune in Britannia to realise that officers too ready to strike ended up with sullen, spiritless soldiers. For the moment the centurions could shout, and so could the optiones and anyone else with authority. Most of the time it worked, and men swore under their breath as they moved faster. Shouting and bawling were part of army life, and everyone understood. Now and then the shouting became too frantic, or a soldier too nervous, and that meant buckles not fastened properly, equipment dropped, packs accidentally spilled. A tent was pulled too sharply from the roof of a hut and ended up on top of Rufus, who had the sense to laugh with the men once they had pulled him out. A *signifer* was kicked in the head by a mule, and that was funny too, until he would not wake up. One legionary had his foot crushed by a wheel when a loaded cart was being dragged too quickly towards the waiting team, while another slipped while running to form up and stabbed a comrade in the thigh with his *pilum* – one of those bizarre accidents that Crispinus suspected would be hard to reproduce even if they tried. Thus the first casualties of the campaign were suffered, and the chaos went on.

The animals were even more of a problem than the men, for the army always believed that it was cheaper to keep the bare minimum and find the rest locally on the rare occasions a big campaign was planned. It was a minor miracle to have assembled sufficient to equip the baggage train. Since last year Syria and the neighbouring provinces had been combed for anything with four legs able to carry packs or pull a waggon, as well as for mounts. The well was running close to dry when it came time for the Hispana to begin its search. Hadrian had made it possible, releasing ample funds and allowing them to search far afield. Somehow they had found the numbers, even if this meant a motley selection of gaunt horses, half-wild mules and asses, and more camels than the army preferred. The lixae struggled to manage so many unruly and inexperienced animals, and the soldiers assigned to assist them were worse, so that Crispinus had hired as many locals as he could to help and the volunteers were an even motlier looking bunch than their animals. He guessed that he would have to flog and even crucify a fair few of the fellows before the campaign was done.

At least Hadrian was not here to witness all of this chaos and delay. The acting governor was at Zeugma and had arranged for pontoons to be floated and the bridge put together for a couple of days. Most of the year it was no more than a stub on either bank, so that river traffic could pass freely, and was only put in place a few times a year, when the big trade caravans wanted to cross. Crispinus and the main force would march to Zeugma, arriving late tomorrow, by which time he hoped that everything would look more ordered. They would cross the Euphrates the following day and march to Nicopolis. Hadrian's hope was that the city would already be held by the advance party and they would be welcomed, but Crispinus sensed that this was a thin hope. The main force would carry all the artillery and other engines and supplies, which was another reason why it was so good to have the bridge instead of having to get each waggon on and off a barge.

Apart from the senior officers, no one in the legion was supposed to know where they were going or why. As far as he could tell, everyone, even the clerks who had attended the meetings, had obeyed orders and kept silent about this. Sentries and other men who happened to be in earshot for a moment may have overheard and made the most of letting slip privileged knowledge, so there were tiny nuggets of truth amid the wilder rumours. The favourite still seemed to be that they were to mount an attack on Armenia from the south, marching over some rough terrain through the mountains to surprise this jumped-up king. Crispinus had dropped a few hints that this was the truth. As far as he could tell, the men were reasonably keen, even though VIIII Hispana and the auxiliaries attached to it were a small force for such a task. In truth they were barely enough for their real job, at least if it came to heavy fighting. Crispinus had managed to muster eight cohorts of the Hispana, with a ninth sent on with the advance guard. All counted at least half their theoretical strength, which was not bad, and several, like the first cohort, were much stronger than that. In addition Hadrian had found a decent number of auxiliaries, most of whom were to join them on the march to Zeugma, apart from the ones with the advance guard. There were two alae of cavalry, one of them milliary, a milliary cohort of infantry and four cohortes equitata, adding very useful cavalry as well as their infantry. Hadrian had promised to search for more units or detachments, and try to see whether he could get some allied soldiers from the kingdoms without drawing too much attention, but was not sanguine. Crispinus would have to get by with what was available. It could have been worse, but then it usually could, and it could always be better. Crispinus half smiled at the thought. That was pessimism worthy of Ferox.

As the sun rose the trumpets sounded for the third time. They still were not ready to march, but they were getting closer, with the majority of the men in formation, although allowed to lean on shields or even sit while they waited. Caecilius and all the other centurions were shouting less, and not simply because their voices were gone. Gradually the animals were chivvied into as much order as was possible, and the last men ran to take their place in the ranks. It was almost time, and Crispinus motioned to the groom to bring his horse. He patted her head fondly, before stepping into the cupped hands of his orderly and climbing into the saddle.

In the intervallum, the open tract between the ramparts and the old tent lines, and in the roadways the legion – his legion – was at long last formed up. The trumpets sounded again, a mix of the curved *cornu* horns and the straight trumpets of the *tubicines* in a repeated fanfare, as the escort from cohors I brought the aquila, the symbol of the legion's pride, out from the old principia and marched straight down the road to the main gate, following a path left for them. Without a signal, apart from the fanfares, the soldiers had sprung to attention. Behind the little golden eagle with its wings raised and the lightning bolt of Jupiter clutched in its claws, all atop an unadorned staff, came the other standards. There were the *imagines* of the Lord Trajan and his family, several vexilla with their square flags showing the legion's name and symbols on a dark red field, and finally the serried rows of *signa*, the standards belonging to each century. The fanfare continued as the standards made their way to what would become the head of the column. Crispinus had never thought of himself as of a romantic disposition, but still felt a thrill and a majesty about the moment. He nodded to the herald.

'Are you ready for war?'

'Yes!' bellowed the men of Legio VIIII Hispana as each one stamped his right foot. That was a peculiar affectation of the legion, for Roman soldiers dearly loved to be different and set themselves apart from other units. The question was a tradition for the whole army, performed whenever a substantial force marched out in the spring as well as before a real campaign.

There were plenty of other rumours doing the rounds apart from the one about Armenia. Some said that they were going to Osrhoene, and that was a little worrying, especially when there was talk of overthrowing King Abgarus or indeed of protecting him from a usurper. Other stories – heard it from a despatch rider, from the beneficiarius on the main road to Antioch, from a cousin who had a friend – insisted that they were going to Adiabene to intervene in a similar struggle within the royal family. A few were more ambitious. One of the rivals for the Parthian throne wanted to take Osrhoene or Adiabene or Syria and they were going to stop him.

'Are you ready for war?' The herald had a good, clear voice, if a little high pitched. Crispinus had considered shouting out the question himself, until deciding that at his age there was no need to prove the power of his oratory. There were more important things to prove.

'Yes!' The shout and the stamp were louder this time.

From what the centurions were saying some even wilder rumours had popped up in the last few days. One claimed they were the spearhead of a march down the Euphrates all the way to Seleucia and Ctesiphon. Trajan's talk of Armenia was all a decoy, and the emperor would bring the main army down the Tigris, where he would depose all the rival Parthian kings and appoint his own choice instead. Hispana had the special job of getting there first and capturing the royal harem. 'Think, boys, hundreds of the bints, one for every night of the year and all of them gorgeous, the pick of a vast kingdom. All of them know what they're doing too.'

Crispinus guessed that only the wildest optimists believed the tale, and few even of them truly believed that the emperor would let loose a horde of sweaty legionaries among such a political prize. Still, plenty of others surely wanted to believe. In his younger days, Crispinus would have found it all rather amusing. Instead, the legatus in him worried because if the Nicopolitans admitted them willingly, he did not want the citizens turned against him because the legionaries had run amok. The man felt more sad than anything else. He had been ill for a long time, and much of it he could not remember, which was better than some of the episodes when he had lost all control and part of him was aware of it all, but could do nothing to stop. He could also remember the darkness and despair.

Only in the last five years had he returned to his true self, and that was hard because everyone else remained wary of the madman or worried about the suspected traitor. Crispinus did not think that he was either, not really, and it was hard for an ambitious man to sit idle and watch fools climb the ladder while he stood off to the side. His father had been kind, or at least as kind as the bluff old man could be, as his own health failed him. These days he had to be carried to the table and even the latrine. Three years ago, when his father was still able to walk and talk coherently, he had arranged a marriage. Crispinus' young bride was of impeccable family, reasonable good looks, negligible intellect and a sweetness of disposition that was childlike. She was swiftly with child – in that respect at least he was as vigorous as ever – and promptly died along with the infant, who was a girl to add to the disappointment. During their marriage Crispinus had indulged but thought little of his wife, which made it all the more puzzling that her death left him so devastated. He felt that he should have done more to be pleasant during her brief life, and he dreamed again and again of her cold, still face lying in death.

'Are you ready for war?'

'Yes!' The cry and the crash of hobnailed caligae slamming onto the ground came together and the sound echoed back off the ramparts.

Crispinus was ready, even if he knew deep down that he feared failure and almost expected it. Nothing had turned out well for him for so very long. A year ago he had fallen in love as hopelessly as a schoolboy, with a *hetaira* of all things – one of those elegant mistresses from Athens who expected to be wooed and pampered. He had never been in love before and would have despised himself had he not been so happy. She had come with him to the province, then fallen ill after a feast in Antioch. Two days later she was dead. Strange that while he often dreamed of her voice and heard its sweetness in his head, he struggled to picture her face.

The senior optio marched up and stamped to attention beside him. 'Legio VIIII Hispana requests permission to set out, sir!'

'Password for today is Hercules Victrix,' Crispinus said. 'Noble Caecilius, if you would be so good.'

This was all tradition, and the primus pilus was clearly a man who revelled in tradition.

'The Ninth Legion will advance!' Caecilius must have found something to drink because his voice boomed out. There was a clash of metal and wood as the men hefted their shields and brought their pila onto their shoulders. 'For Rome, for the Senate and People, and for our Lord Trajan. First Cohort, march!'

The eagle and the other standards were at the head of the first cohort, which would lead the column out of the camp. Its remaining centurions repeated the order; the horns and trumpets sounded once more and they all stepped out as one in a rhythmic thumping of equipment. For the moment things were formal, the men marching in silence at attention. Crispinus and the other senior officers sat their horses beside the main gateway and as each file passed, all the heads jerked to face them, the motion like a wave washing back across the formation.

Crispinus raised his arm in salute as the legion, his legion and the basis for his army, marched past. This was not the first time that he had led a column to war. Back in the first year of Lord Trajan's principate he had commanded a column setting off from Vindolanda. The scene with its pomp and ceremony – and this being the army more stamping and shouting than anyone would believe humanly possible – had moved him then and it moved him now, more deeply perhaps because this was a far bigger force and he was in overall command. He had been young then, full less of hope than the absolute certainty that he was destined for great things.

Crispinus was grateful to Hadrian for giving him this last chance for some distinction, both for himself and to maintain the family name. Yet the plan was risky, and although he had to wear the mask with everyone else, he could see its many flaws. Crispinus would play his part, out of duty and without much hope. He wondered whether this was how Ferox felt all the time.

Crispinus gave a grim laugh.

'Sir?' Rufus asked.

'Nothing, dear fellow.' The last cohort was passing them and the baggage train approaching. 'Let us go.' Crispinus nudged the mare and led them through the gateway. On their left, just beyond the ditch, a cohort was waiting to fall in behind the baggage train. Tomorrow Crispinus would insist on more precautions for the march, with patrols and flankers. Today he simply wanted to get as many miles behind them as possible. As they cantered past the columns, each six abreast on the main track, no one cheered, but he did not expect that. They were going and that was that, the decision made for good or ill. Legio VIIII Hispana was on its way to Nicopolis. Only the gods knew what would await the legion once they got there.

Nicopolis
The same day, late afternoon

*T*HAT DAY WAS *a good day in the house of Simon because after two and a half long years his only son came home from his travels. The younger Simon was a burly man with a thick dark beard, bright eyes like his grandfather and sister, and a broad smile. His face was dark and lined from sun and wind, his gaze that of someone who had crossed through wilderness, always finding his way, and he wore a Parthian single-edged sword on his left hip. With him were two of the family's servants, who were welcomed almost as warmly, and two other men he had hired along the way. The last two were very short and stocky, with narrow eyes, who spoke few words and those with a strange accent, but who were accepted by the family because Simon trusted them. He had had a good trip, and between them they brought back eight camels and seventeen donkeys, half with panniers of silks and spices, and the rest with iron wrought by a craft unknown in Parthia, Osrhoene or Rome itself. They also brought a princess, although that was by accident.*

'It is more than time for this boy to marry,' John commented. Domitius had helped the old man keep steady in the crowd that had gathered as Princess Azátē had ridden into the city in her carriage, her escort of two dozen fully armoured cataphracts and as many archers going in front and behind. There were always plenty of people in any city happy to watch

any procession or sight, and the royal lady was well known and liked. Behind came the younger Simon and three or four other groups who had been graciously allowed to tag along and enjoy the protection of the royal party on the last stage of the journey to Nicopolis.

'Trust my brother to want a grand entrance,' Sara said. 'And the princess would never marry him – he's far too vain.'

Domitius had seen the princess at the window of her carriage, smiling at the crowd. Her hair was covered and she had a high, ornate headdress, but did not wear a veil. From what he had seen the face was a very pretty one, and the royal visitor could not have been much more than twenty years old.

The younger Simon pointed in reply. 'She knew you, sister, and when I said that I was Simon son of Simon of Nicopolis, she asked whether I was brother to you. Think of that? A man travels to the edge of the earth and back and the beautiful princess only wants to talk to him about his sister! There is no justice. Oh, and Father, she asked about the paintings in the synagogue because she remembered that you had thanked her for her gift. Is it finished?'

'Nearly. They have done the crossing of the Jordan, but not yet the fall of Jericho.'

John shook his head. 'It did not take so long in real life.'

'They are craftsmen.'

'They are lazy, Father,' Sara snapped. 'No matter. It must be finished before the princess makes her visit. While you were dallying, dear brother, did the lady happen to mention how long she planned to stay here?'

'It didn't come up, no. Maybe she is here for Passover?'

'Maybe,' Sara said, as if she did not believe a word. 'But now it is time for you to rest and cleanse yourself and then we can feast to celebrate. Oh, and by the way, the barbarian standing

over there is Domitius, a Roman who was of service to us and now works for Father. Can you paint, Domitius? No, then that is a pity. But that loom is still not fixed so I would be grateful if you could see what you can do.'

The younger Simon watched Domitius go. He was still smiling, but there was something harder in his gaze. Out in the streets, Domitius felt that he was being followed. Only in the last few days had the family trusted him to walk about on his own, and it was still an odd feeling. Most of the time he was in side streets, narrow, shadowed except when the sun was close to noon, and much like the back alleys of any city anywhere he had known. There was plenty of filth, and a wise man watched to see where the biggest piles and still more the traces of splashes were and then avoided those spots. It did not always work. Before he had gone far he was speckled by what he hoped was dirty water thrown off one of the flat roofs of a house. The best he could do was wipe his face with his cloak, which did not stop giggles from some of the women in the workshop. They were a friendly bunch, obviously devoted to Sara, who was firm, but paid and treated them well, so that nearly all of them had worked for her for quite a few years. She said that was important, because she wanted the best if their clothes and material were to fetch the highest prices.

'It's bust,' Nicaea assured him when he examined the loom. She was about the same age as Sara, a former slave who was in charge whenever the owner was not there. She was one of the smallest women Domitius had ever seen, the top of her head no higher than the middle of his chest. Her skin was very dark, her features delicate and pretty, if showing lines around her eyes and lips that spoke of a hard life. So did the scars on her wrists, on the rare occasions she did not wear long sleeves. Domitius did not know the details, but had heard hints and

sensed that the woman felt a deep gratitude to Simon and his family for giving her something better. More than that, she and Sara thought a lot alike and shared a deep pride in their work. Even though she was younger than most of the others, the rest respected and obeyed her. 'I'm not letting it be used,' she went on in a tone brooking no argument. 'You can take it to pieces and rebuild it, but be less fuss to get a new one. We won't need it for a month anyway. There's plenty to do, so better to spend your time buying or making a new one.'

Domitius nodded. There was worm in the frame so that more than half would need replacing otherwise it would keep on breaking. Even with lighter weights it would simply not take the strain.

'Well, now you are here, you can be useful. Go with Aphrodite to the dyers' shops and carry for her.' Nicaea turned to Aphrodite, the oldest woman there, whose white hair was thin and straggling, skin like old papyrus and bare arms heavy with loose skin. 'You know what I want?'

'Yes.'

'Good, then off you go and don't let them fob you off with anything but the best. Quick now – and this is work so no flirting.'

Domitius grinned. 'No promises.' Aphrodite had a cackle worthy of a crone in a play and the other women all laughed.

'I'm not that fickle, lad,' Aphrodite told him.

'Go on, the pair of you.' Nicaea sometimes even sounded like Sara.

The rest of the day was spent on errands for Sara's workshop and then, after he had returned to the house, for Simon. All the while he felt that someone was following him and once or twice he thought he spotted a man darting back into shadows before he could see him clearly. He did not think Ferox was seeking his *death, at least not yet, but if the centurion was able to find him then so could others. That night he slept fitfully, and dreamed of a loom, whose weights kept changing size so that he had to make all the others match and by the time he had done it another grew heavier or lighter. He had a dim memory of being told that such a dream foretold a journey, but the next day there were simply more errands for the family, pushing through the busy streets. John wanted a walk, and wanted a long one, because the Sabbath started tomorrow and there was rarely much time in the morning before it began.*

'My grandson tells me that there are rumours the Romans are coming,' the old man said as they sat on a stone bench watching people, mostly women, coming to draw water from a fountain. John liked coming here, because it was always busy, but not so busy as the main thoroughfares of the markets, and far less noisy than the markets. It was quieter and he liked watching people, especially women.

'There was talk of an expedition to Armenia,' Domitius said. 'The emperor was at Antioch at the start of the year and was massing a great army.'

'Everyone knows that,' the old man said dismissively. 'I mean here in Osrhoene. When Parthia is strong the Romans would not dare, but Parthia is weak as king turns against king and great empires like to flex their muscles. Rome is rarely subtle.'

'A famous Greek once wrote that the Romans instinctively turn to brute force to solve a problem.'

Simon nodded, running his fingers through his little beard. 'The Greeks write a lot of things, and much is nonsense or so clever that it amounts to the same thing. And then to spite us all they keep coming out with wisdom.

'This emperor of yours likes to be strong. He will see Parthia as a challenge – and best of all a challenge less strong than

*usual. I'm rambling as an old man will. What I meant to tell
you was that before my grandson met up with the princess and
her escort, he camped one night near to the entourage of her
brother, the prince. I know, I know, how is it my family hob-
nobs with royalty? I would not trust any king or prince further
than I could throw them, but I am old, so my wisdom does not
matter. The boy did not speak to the prince – his sister is unlike
the rest of her family in honouring the true God – but knew one
of the soldiers and spoke to him. They were on their way back
from visiting your emperor and watching the Romans show
off their might. The emperor wanted him to pledge loyalty on
behalf of Osrhoene. Those were not his instructions from King
Abgarus, and the emperor was angry about this and because
the king had not come but merely sent the prince.'*

'That does not sound a prelude to war,' Domitius said.

*'Men have fought over far less. But there was more if you
had not interrupted me! This princess is a fine young woman
in many ways, but she is a princess and ambitious and very
determined. Ha, I sometimes wonder if she should not have
been born Jewish! The court bickers and she defies her father
and will not marry the man he has chosen for her. Worse, she
talks to the Romans and, worse still, her brother and probably
father know that she does this. In the prince's case, it is because
he is also secretly sending messages to the Romans – and by all
accounts to two of the Parthian rivals.*

*'What this means is Princess Azátē's visit to our city may put
us all in danger. And if I know these things, then so must others.
A man has been following us today, have you seen him? A bald
man, big around the shoulders and wearing a drab cloak even
on a hot day like this? No?'*

'I have felt that someone was following me for a day or two.'

'Your senses are good, but not good enough. I think there

may be more than one. The bald one I have never seen before. Still, even I do not know everyone in the city. You are a Roman, claim to be an army deserter, but turn up at a time when war clouds gather. You can see how that might arouse suspicion.'

'Will the people here want to fight Rome?' The city felt so peaceful that Domitius could not really imagine its men marching off to war.

'Life is not what you want, but what you must do. If the whole kingdom submits then so shall we, as long as the Romans do not demand too much of us. If the kingdom fights then I expect so shall we. And if these people are attacked then they will fight, even if they fight alone. This is our home.

'At times likes that strangers are hard to trust.'

'Do you think the magistrates are watching me?' Domitius searched the street and could not see anyone paying them particular attention. Nor could he see any bald men. 'What should I do?'

'Yes, you are being watched, unless the strategoi are fools – and they are, but not in that way. As to what you should do, it depends a lot on whether or not you are a spy. And whether the other one watching you is from the city or from outside.'

'And what do you think, for you are wise?'

'I trust you, Domitius, former optio ad spem. You strike me as an honest man and a good one. Of course, my head tells me that any spy who did not strike others as an honest and good man probably would not last very long, so what do I know? It would be wise of you to think hard about what you will do. If it comes to it, will you fight against your old comrades to help this city? Or should you leave before you have to make that choice and go far away, beyond even the reach of Rome. From what I hear the legions are none too kind when they

catch deserters, and cruel indeed if they believe that such men had helped their enemies... Ah well, I do not think that she is coming today.' Often when they had sat in this spot they had seen a young mother arrive, with three little children trailing behind. She was pretty and smiled and talked to John, which the old man liked, but more than that the children chuckled, played with him and made him laugh. 'We should go, and you should think. Huh, I remember telling you that before. To tell a Roman and a soldier to think and make wise choices! Now that is the wisdom of a fool!'

They went home – and to his surprise Domitius realised that he thought of the house of Simon as home so that there was not really any more to consider, though there were more tasks and chores for him to do. Now that young Simon had returned, the family were busy, preparing to use what they could of his cargo, and working out how best to sell the rest at profit. There was silk of a quality Sara had rarely seen before, and she and Nicaea spent hours discussing how best to employ it. Domitius carried bales to the workshop, took apart the broken loom and carried the pieces back to a side room next to the stable in the house. He accompanied Simon, for once without Sara, to speak to some ironworkers who might be interested in the ingots, and while they discussed prices nothing was agreed, just as Sara had insisted. So Domitius lugged the sample ingot back with them. It was certainly the finest he had ever seen, and he had spent some time at the forge in the fabricae. Still, to buy it a man had to have some special work in mind to make the cost worthwhile.

'My son says that the wealthiest Parthian warriors make their arrow- and spear-heads from this Margianian iron,' Simon told the potential buyers. 'The princes have swords and armour from it.'

Domitius wondered again at talk of war, but then men needed weapons and armour whether there was war or the mere chance of war and it might mean nothing. He was still wondering when he was sent to take another bale of material to the workshop. The sun had almost set, which made the back streets almost dark, for unless a house kept a window open and let light escape, the only lamps were at each crossroads. A man had to be a good deal more careful where he trod, not to mention paying attention to the roofs above. A lot of people emptied chamber pots once it was dark. There were still enough folk abroad to make theft unlikely, although not impossible, and he had tucked a dagger into his belt.

Part of him did not want to believe that the Romans – his people – would attack Osrhoene or this city for no other reason than that they could. He was happy with Simon and his family, at least for the moment, and did not want to leave. Yet he was not sure whether he could fight, still less kill, even to protect them. The problem had bothered him ever since he had found Christ – or as Pausanias the preacher assured him, Christ had found him. Killing was a sin, but also might be a soldier's duty and Christians were supposed to obey the laws and keep their promises. He was not sure whether his arrest and desertion meant that he could break that oath. Would it matter if other legions came here instead of his own? He had killed the slaver, and that had not really bothered him at all. It was the right thing to do, for the sake of good people.

'Soldier!' The voice was in Latin and that made him start when otherwise he would have ignored it. 'Soldier!' the man hissed. 'Come on, we both know who you are.'

Suddenly the street was empty. Old John was right to say Domitius was not careful enough. The voice was coming from around the corner of a junction. He headed towards it, wondering whether he could throw the bale and then fall on the man with his knife.

'Close enough, soldier.'

Domitius stopped. He did not know what the man wanted or what he really knew. Conscience told him he could not attack so readily.

'Who are you?'

'Wrong question, soldier boy.' There was a shadow on the far side of the alley. Perhaps it was just the lamplight, but the man looked large and burly. 'You are Caius Domitius Clemens, late of Legio VI Ferrata. You don't need my name, but I can help you if you help me.'

'I know nothing important.'

'We both know that's a lie,' the voice said. 'Thought you Christians were supposed to tell the truth. Guess that's another lie.'

Two drunken voices were raised in song from further up the street.

'Think on it, soldier boy. I'll find you again.' The shadow vanished as a group of four or five merrymakers lurched towards him. Domitius ignored them and ran for the corner, but there was no sign of anyone apart from a little old woman struggling along with an amphora under her arm.

'Did you see a man?' he asked. There was no sign that she understood any Greek, and his halting Aramaic did no better. The old woman ignored him and went on past to be greeted by whistles and laughter from the drunks. It seemed good natured, and she ignored it, so Domitius did not intervene and went about his task.

The next morning, he woke to hear someone pounding on the main door into the courtyard. A servant opened it to admit a tall warrior in scale armour, though bareheaded and the sword at his belt his only weapon. Behind were three unarmoured men, with scabbarded swords, and then four bearers carrying a curtained sedan chair. The warriors all wore Parthian-style trousers and long-sleeved tunics. Domitius had only seen a few sedan chairs in the streets of Nicopolis, although they were common enough in the bigger Roman cities. It suggested someone of considerable wealth.

Domitius watched from the window and could see no sign of threat, although it was obvious that the leader was used to being obeyed, if only because of the name of his mistress.

'We come from the Lady Azátē,' the man announced, loud enough to be heard all around the courtyard. He had a slim face that would have been handsome had his mouth not been locked into a permanent sneer. 'She sends greetings to her friend, Sara, and begs that she come to her at the palace.' Old John had told Domitius that there was a grand house in the citadel that was usually occupied by the magistrates for official duties, although nominally kept for whenever the king or one of his family visited.

Simon appeared, hatless and with his hair rather wild. 'It is early, my lord. Perhaps…'

'My mistress apologises profusely for the inconvenience.' The officer's expression suggested that speaking the words pained him. 'She wishes to speak with your noblest of daughters, and is aware that this is a Holy Day for you and your kin, so would speak to her now, so that she can return before the morning is out.' Again, the expression suggested that the officer viewed the gesture as foolish indulgence of worthless people. 'We have brought the chair to carry her, and my men are escort. You surely do not wish to keep the Lady Azátē waiting?' There was more than a hint of threat about the last words.

For some reason Domitius remembered Caecilius assuring

him that a woman would always make a man wait, but in this case the veteran centurion was wrong, for Sara appeared, elegantly dressed, head covered and veiled. A servant followed carrying a bundle, and when Sara bade the officer to get one of his men to take these samples with them, the man obeyed. Domitius wondered what it must be like to have such charm, for not only did the officer do what he was told, but his sneer almost vanished.

Domitius smiled to himself, poured water into a basin, washed, shaved, brushed his caligae and then dressed. All was done mechanically, the habit of all those mornings waking to the trumpet calls. The same routine saw him check the blade of his gladius, before adding a little oil and sliding it back into the scabbard.

Then there was fresh pounding on the gate. This time Simon was relatively tidy, at least by his standards, although he was surprised to see more armed men. These were city guards, four of them altogether, and one with a plume on his high bronze helmet. This mark and his inclination to shout loudest suggested that he was in charge.

'There is a Roman here! We have come to arrest him! Bring him out!' His speech was short and abrupt. Domitius had seen plenty of his type in the legions. The man was old, his beard dyed black and dyed badly, face round, skin pockmarked and nose red from drink. An old sweat, but one without the brains or just too prone to going on drunks and breaking rules to rise very high.

'I am sure there is a mistake,' Simon said. His son appeared, and Domitius could see that for all that he was unarmed and eating a peach, the younger Simon made the guards wary.

'What is going on?' he asked.

'They want Domitius,' Simon explained.

'The Strategos Athenodorus wants the Roman! We are here to take him!' The leader still shouted, but was less confident.

'Why?' the younger Simon asked.

'Orders, sir!'

Domitius grinned. Yes, he knew the type.

Father and son whispered together, before the younger Simon called. 'Come on out, Domitius! I am sure that we can soon sort out this misunderstanding, but these men want to take you to the magistrates.'

'Athenodorus is a good, just man,' his father said, without sounding too certain.

Domitius looked down at his sword propped against the frame of his bed. Yet what could he do? Apart from the main gate, there was a back door to the side street from the stables, but he could not get there without going through the courtyard. He could climb up to the roof, and probably escape by jumping across the alleys and then... Then he would be on his own in a foreign city and his flight was sure to be seen as proof of guilt. He did not even know guilt of what as yet. It might be nothing, and he owed a lot to the family.

'Are you sure this is necessary?' The older Simon sounded nervous. 'We could bring him. There is no need for armed men.'

'Orders!' The leader's tone was stronger again.

Domitius left the sword where it was and came out. There was nowhere to go, because the only door from his room led into the courtyard. Nor did he want to abandon the family who had taken him in.

'What's this about?' he asked.

'You need to come with us,' the leader said. Up close Domitius could see that he was forty or more, that the dye on his beard left a lot of mottled hair, and there was a dent or two in his helmet. 'Best if you don't make any trouble.'

The younger Simon patted Domitius on the shoulder. 'We will sort this out.' The warmth in his tone was surprising. Domitius had got the impression that the pride of the family was none too fond of him.

'Very well.' Domitius held his arms out together. He had spotted the rope in one of the men's belts.

'Is that necessary?' the older Simon asked as the guard tied Domitius' wrists.

'Orders!' the leader barked. He added a 'Sir!' when he noticed the younger Simon watching him closely. 'Come on then, boy! Let's get going.' He clearly wanted to leave.

Domitius let them lead him away and wondered what was in store. The guards had their job to do, so they did it. As far as they were concerned it was simply a job and they did it as well as they did any other job. Domitius could not help noticing that there was rust on more than one spearhead, and fittings missing on two of the cuirasses. It was hard not to bawl the men out for this. These men were soldiers of a sort, even if not very good ones. So they did their job without particular malice and only hit him a few times on the way to the prison.

IX

Outside Nicopolis
Eighth Day before the Ides of April

THEY WERE MAKING good time, with the bright half-moon high in an endless field of stars, so that the land was silver. Only a fool could lose his way on a night like this, but since the army always had a fair few of these, Ferox had been careful to keep the column together. They were four abreast, each turma only a horse's length behind the one in front. The hardest thing was to keep to a steady, almost slow pace. They wanted to cover the ground quickly, but if you let the leading turmae lose their heads and canter or even trot too fast, then the column would start to spread and the ones at the back would soon be galloping to keep up – that is if they could. This was a beautiful night, the land rolled gently ahead of them and with so many horses together the urge to ride free and fast called out to everyone. A Sarmatian would have galloped and rejoiced in the feel of the wind and would somehow have found his kindred again the next day. From all Ferox had heard, the true Parthians were much the same, and the best of their warriors came from bands much like the Roxolani and Iasyges that he knew from the Danube. Brigantes were good horsemen, but not like that, and soldiers were soldiers, trained rather than raised to ride. So, he kept the column together and kept the pace slow, and knew the men were impatient to be off, but would not loosen his rein on them. This way it would be very hard for anyone to straggle, although every unit had a few men who could be ingenious in their clumsiness and might well find a way. Hopefully they would be picked up by the infantry column following behind at its own pace.

'Will we make it in time?' Flavius Cerialis asked, breaking the long and companionable silence.

'We can be outside the city soon after the sun rises,' Ferox confirmed. 'Assuming no one tries to stop us. Anything else, then my lads can always gallop ahead. After all, it's not really about numbers.'

'Let us hope that is unnecessary. Your men are a little – how shall I say – irregular. We don't want to frighten anyone after all.'

'And your six hundred armed and armoured riders?'

'A gesture of sincere respect to an ally.' Cerialis laughed. Back when Crispinus had served as tribune in Britannia, Flavius Cerialis had commanded the cohort stationed at Vindolanda while Ferox was the local regionarius, the centurion tasked with keeping the peace in the area. Like the aristocratic tribune, this had been Cerialis' first posting to the army, as prefect in charge of a cohort of Batavians, tough warriors from the Rhineland. Unusually, Cerialis was a Batavian himself, from the tribe's royal line, his father having managed to change sides early enough during the great revolt more than a generation ago. He was very ambitious, a little vain, but Ferox had come to respect him, for he was willing to learn and in time became a good soldier. 'This is all about respect, old fellow, about how much Rome values the friendship of Nicopolis and their princess.'

'By invading their country?'

'Visiting, my dear Ferox, visiting. And visiting in answer to an invitation.' Batavian royalty – his men often said king – or not, Cerialis had always acted the part of a suave Roman gentleman. Ferox had not seen him for many years, but if his hair was a little paler, the hint of redness in it almost gone, he had otherwise aged little. He was still tall and athletic, with the same ready smile and enthusiasm. Since Vindolanda he had taken his cohort to Dacia, served as narrow-stripe tribune under Hadrian himself, commanded an ala of Batavian horsemen, before coming from the Danube with this latest command. 'We are guests and it would be rude to be late.'

'Quite so.' Arrian had kicked his horse to come level with them as they rode at the head of the column. He was junior to Cerialis, who held overall command, and his place was really with the cohort of VIIII Hispana and other foot soldiers following on behind. His enthusiasm to come with them had been so great that Cerialis had accepted his plea that he needed to be on the spot, so that he could ride back and hurry his men forward if necessary. Ferox could not see any likely situation where the infantry would make a difference. Either Nicopolis opened its gates to them or they could stare at those walls for as long as they liked, for Arrian's eight hundred men with just ten ladders between them were not going to storm the place. The tribune had seen some service on the Danube, but Ferox got the impression this was the first time he had ridden so deep into what could prove hostile territory. Arrian seemed to be loving every minute of it and Ferox could not blame him. There was something very soothing about the rhythm of hoofbeats, the jingle of harness and the thump of shields and other equipment. Each cavalryman had two sacks of fodder fastened with rope, tied to the saddle horn and draped over the horse's back. If things did not work out, they would need this as well as the hard tack and salted bacon issued to the men because it could be several days before they met up with the main force and its baggage train.

'How many know we are coming?' Arrian asked after a while. Ferox sensed that the tribune was growing nervous.

'No idea,' Cerialis said. 'The princess, of course, her advisors, and the city magistrates must know by now. Whether "rumour, the swiftest of all evils" spreads the news as we speak I cannot say.' Ferox remembered how Cerialis always liked to parade his learning, even though it tended to sound rehearsed. 'Still, I suppose a civilised man like yourself, who is as Greek as he is Roman, may find Virgil no more than a poor man's Homer.'

'"Small at first through fear, soon she mounts to the very heavens",' Arrian quoted. 'No, no, not at all. Virgil was a great artist. Perhaps the barbarian's Homer would be better.'

Cerialis laughed so loud that he startled the horses.

'I think they know we're coming now,' Ferox said. In truth they had encountered no one and that made him wonder a little, although the presence of so many troopers riding in close column was hard to miss. The locals had enough reason to be wary of any bands of men riding in the darkness, given the slavers and the nomads who might just decide that a bit of robbery with violence would be profitable and entertaining. Vindex and several parties of Brigantes were scouting ahead of the column and he could trust them to spot any threat. His instincts told him that no armed men were out there, waiting in ambush, but it was wiser to assume the worst. For all the excitement of the night ride, which brought back childhood memories of hot winter fires and bards telling of raids and murder, he did not like this business. He did not expect the plan to succeed, which meant a siege which might or might not capture the city, and if it did, most likely meant slaughter and rape, for men who stormed a fortress boiled over with rage and hate. He did not know the people of Nicopolis well enough to dislike them and think that they deserved any of that. Not that it was up to him. He had orders and must obey.

'Strange to meet up so far from home,' Cerialis said after they had ridden for a while in silence. 'Makes you marvel at the sheer size of the empire, and an army that can pluck men up from one place and send them off thousands of miles. When you consider it, it is amazing what we have built.' Ferox wondered whether the true genius of Rome was to make a Batavian king think of himself as Roman.

'How do you find your Britons?' Arrian asked, using Greek on the assumption that none of the closest troopers would understand. Flavius Cerialis commanded ala I Flavia Augusta Britannica milliaria civium Romanorum torquata ob virtutem – and Ferox wondered how long it must take to start morning orders if they used the full name. Raised over thirty years ago in Britannia, mostly from the southern and eastern tribes, that first generation of soldiers had done very well on the Danube under Domitian and then won particular distinction during Trajan's Dacian victories. Their yellow shields – now protected by calfskin covers – bore a painted green wreath as a battle honour and all the men in service under Trajan had been granted Roman citizenship, which normally was a prize for their retirement. Perhaps a quarter of the men still serving had that honour, and the rest were dead or discharged.

'Rogues, every man of them,' Cerialis said happily. 'And all the better soldiers for that.' His Greek was clear and correct, with an overemphasis on each word typical of a man from the north west of the empire. It lacked the almost liquid flow of anyone who had grown up with it as his first language. 'We're not as wild as Ferox's bandits, of course.'

'Praise be to Zeus for his mercy,' Arrian intoned. 'Are they still mainly Britons?'

'About half,' Cerialis told him. 'When we can, we send recruiting parties there. We have some Durotriges – though they will slump in the saddle whatever you do. Coritani, who are decent soldiers as long as you hound them, and a lot of Iceni and Trinovantes, who ride like centaurs and fight and drink like that as well!'

Arrian grinned. 'No wedding feasts on this campaign then.' Senior officers loved to show their wit about the old stories.

'Best not. Those lads can get wild. Well, their grandfathers sacked three cities and wiped out half a legion – Crispinus' famous Hispana in fact!'

'Best not to mention that,' Arrian suggested, as a tribune of the same legion.

Cerialis laughed again. 'Probably not.'

'Your lads will, whatever you say,' Ferox told them.

'Aye, they will at that. Even the Pannonians and Thracians and all the rest we have picked up along the way. There's even a couple of Mauretanians we found somewhere – one carrying the vexillum of his turma and likely to rise further.' As with most units, it was easier to draw new recruits from the closest source, which meant that the title of Gauls or Spaniards or Britons often meant very little. Cerialis' ala was pretty unusual in keeping a core of men from its home province. 'Aye, they will. Probably be a few fights.' Cerialis sounded as if he quite relished the prospect. His own people, the Batavians, were widely admired as some of the toughest fighters in the army, but no one liked them very much and when there was no campaigning they quickly grew bored and tended to make trouble.

'Speaking of Britannia and Britons, my dear Ferox,' Cerialis said switching back to Latin and perhaps changing the subject as an excuse for this. 'My wife and the younger children have travelled there to stay with the delightful Claudia Enica. They did not want to stay in Pannonia on their own, did not fancy Antioch – an unhealthy place if ever there was one – and could not come on campaign, so instead Sulpicia announced that she was off to visit her friend. Well, after all these years, I had enough sense not to argue. And even if you would have thought she'd had enough of wild places after our time at Vindolanda, she had decided and that was that. Women...' Cerialis shook his head.

Sulpicia Lepidina was the prefect's second wife, a woman of rare beauty and truly remarkable intelligence. She was *clarissima femina*, the daughter of a senator and former consul, if one who had then squandered the family fortune, aided by the lady's brother, who as far as Ferox could see would have done the empire a great service if he had drowned himself when he was a boy. Cerialis' ambition, the considerable wealth of his family, his favour with Trajan, combined with her family's desperation had helped secure what was a remarkable match for him. The couple were happy, even though Cerialis was so keen to ape the behaviour of aristocratic Romans that he treated her like an ally instead of a lover. At Vindolanda he had bounced his numerous slave girls and frequented the brothel, and largely let his wife sleep alone.

'You married, tribune?' Cerialis asked.

'No. Perhaps in a year of two.' Arrian did not sound especially keen. 'I like the freedom.'

Cerialis was sympathetic. 'Well, that's duty for you. But being a father is wonderful. I've four children, you know. Three boys and the eldest almost a man now and looking to his career.'

Ferox knew that Cerialis was a good as well as a proud father. He also knew that the third boy was not the prefect's child, but his own. He had met Sulpicia Lepidina in strange circumstances, saved her life, rescued her from pirates in a series of adventures that sounded as if they had come from one of those ridiculous Greek novels. He had also fallen in love, and more to his amazement so had she. Their affair was brief, and Cerialis never seemed to guess what was happening, accepting the boy as his own and loving him as much as the others. The more Ferox came to know the man, the more it all bothered him, even if the few moments with Sulpicia were sweet memories. For her, for his son, and because he had wronged Cerialis, he would always do anything he could to protect them all. That was another reason why he had to obey Hadrian and go where he was sent. Somehow Crispinus had guessed and Hadrian had learned and used the information. Ferox did not doubt that the man would not hesitate to make the story public and that meant exile for Sulpicia Lepidina – and for him, but he was pretty much living that in the first place. Cerialis would be disgraced and humiliated, his children suffering, and young Marcus becoming an outcast if he was not killed.

'A man should marry,' Cerialis assured Arrian. 'Freedom is all very well, but when you have children everything you achieve feels like it is for them. With a princeps like Trajan, they can become anything – anything at all. Hmm, I am off again. Never let a proud father start talking about his children or there will be no end to it!

'Marry, my dear Arrian, that is my advice. Women like marrying soldiers, even if they never think about what that means. So we all secure beauties we'd never get otherwise – I mean, look at Ferox!'

'I'd rather not.'

'Don't blame you. But you should meet his wife! Stylish,

elegant, well-educated and as fair of form as he is – how shall I put it – distinctive? A queen as well.'

'This is indeed an age of wonders,' Arrian declared. 'A queen? Well bless me.'

Ferox did not bother to say that Rome was still to approve the rank. Sulpicia Lepidina and Claudia Enica were old and dear friends, with no secrets, so his wife knew all about the affair – in surprisingly great detail – as well as young Marcus.

'I said it is a wonder that you are all the way out here rather than back home,' Arrian repeated after Ferox ignored him.

The centurion held up a hand. 'Halt!' Lulled by hours of steady progress and the peace of the night, the response to the order was a little ragged. Arrian muttered something about discipline in Hispana. 'Riders coming in!' Ferox said just at the moment Cerialis spotted them.

'Brigantia!' Vindex called out the password agreed for the night. He and another three riders came at a walking pace because between them were two men on foot. They were shepherds, one an old man with a long straggling beard, and the other middle aged with a harelip.

'Found 'em a mile or so ahead,' Vindex explained. 'There's a boy as well. Left him to keep an eye on their sheep. A couple of the lads are watching him, but none of them gave any trouble. Can't understand what they're saying though.'

Ferox tried Greek, which prompted a stream of words, none of which he understood. Arrian ventured a little Aramaic, but admitted that he could not make out the reply.

'Do we keep them under arrest?' he asked. 'Or...' he trailed off.

'Kill them?' Cerialis used Latin, although he suspected that the shepherds were as baffled as they were. 'We are supposed to be coming as friends, aren't we? Reckon they can do any harm

if we let them go?' This was to Ferox, and it reminded him of
the old days at Vindolanda.

'Not really. They might spread the word, but I'll bet that's
been out for hours. Folk like this tend to know when strangers
are abroad, and the news passes faster than you'd think.'

'You would not think it could travel faster than we are going
on horseback,' Arrian said. 'And reach the city ahead of us, I
mean.'

Cerialis smiled. 'We're back to "rumour"' again. No,' he
added, making up his mind. 'I don't want to be slowed by
captives, don't want to leave anyone to watch them and I cannot
see them as a threat. So I'm not about to turn the country folk
against us by slitting their throats. Let 'em go.'

Arrian spoke to them in Aramaic. The reply was briefer this
time. 'I asked whether this was the right path to Nicopolis,' he
explained. 'They might have said yes.'

'Well, they know where we are going, so let's hope we can
trust them.' Cerialis' tone was arch, until he forced himself to
smile. 'Expect they knew that already.' Ferox nodded. They
were so close now that the destination must be obvious to
anyone. 'Quite so. Vindex, take these peasants back to the boy
and let them go. We need to move.'

X

Near Nicopolis
A little later

THE MOON WAS down, the stars fading with the approaching day. Cerialis ordered the column to dismount and lead their horses for half an hour, and by the time they climbed back into the saddle a great orange glow filled the sky ahead of them.

Ferox shrugged. 'Quickest path is due east.' He wished that he was wearing one of his old straw hats, so that he could pull the wide brim down and shield his eyes. Philo had never considered the headgear at all fitting for a centurion, and Ferox was not sure where he had hidden them all this time. Like the other officers, he was bareheaded. His helmet with its tall, transverse crest of black feathers, was slung behind his saddle. Cerialis and Arrian had their orderlies carrying their far more ornate plumed helmets. They would want them soon.

Bran appeared on the crest of the low rise ahead of them.

'Halt!' This time Cerialis gave the order.

Bran galloped towards them, stopping his horse with a skid of dust alongside the officers. He, like the Brigantes, was eager to show off his horsemanship in front of the regular auxiliaries, especially once they discovered that there were men from the southern tribes among them.

'The city's still there, chief,' he told Ferox. His Latin was good these days, but sticking to the language of the tribes was another way of showing their difference. 'Just where we left it.'

'We will see Nicopolis once we reach the brow,' Ferox told the others. 'Barely a mile away.'

'Gates open or closed?' Cerialis asked Bran. He had picked up a fair bit of the language during his years at Vindolanda and was finding it useful in his new command.

'Shut, lord.'

'Well, any city would have its gates closed at night,' Cerialis said in Latin, but there was doubt in his words. 'We may as well make a show of it. Decurions to me!'

The prefect was determined to make a dramatic appearance. His men dismounted, checked girths, drew their shields out from their covers, and once mounted again formed up five turmae abreast, with four lines of men. The Brigantes sauntered in while this was going on, and Ferox had them make up their own line on the left flank.

'Try to look honest and respectable,' he told them. They all turned to stare at Vindex, who raised his chin high as if above such mockery.

'At a walk. In line, march!' the senior decurion shouted. Ala I Britannica advanced, and Ferox had to admit that they made a fine show. When he had heard that he was to join them he had wondered why such a prestigious unit was not with the main army under Trajan. There were not many double-strength alae in the entire empire, and in normal times never more than one in a province. That the Britons were relegated to watching Syria had surprised him and he suspected that there was something wrong with them, like the sickly VIIII Hispana. Yet as far as he could tell, the only reason why Trajan had not selected them for higher things was that Cerialis and his men were late in arriving, delayed by a long succession of problems over orders and transport. Part of him wondered whether Hadrian had arranged that. Either way, the ala was well drilled, the horses in very good condition, as well as big by army standards, as were the men.

Even his Brigantes were impressed.

'Not bad,' one said.

'Iceni, some of them. Big bastards. Ugly though.'

'You know what they say. The Iceni love their horses so much that these days you can see the family resemblance.' They all looked at Vindex again.

They came over the brow of the hill, the lines still neat, and Cerialis ordered the trumpets to blare. Ahead of them lay Nicopolis, the walls high, white and casting long shadows ahead of them. The gates were still closed, even though most cities opened up at dawn.

Light twinkled on the ramparts as the sun caught helmets or weapons. There seemed to be more men up there than he would expect.

Ala I Britannica walked on.

'Don't look good,' Vindex said.

'Perhaps we should put a sack over your face,' Bran suggested. 'Be less frightening.'

'Cheeky bugger. Let me in before, didn't they?'

'Probably learned from their mistake.'

At a walk, the approach seemed to take an age, but going faster might seem hostile. They were close enough now for Ferox to see helmeted faces staring out from the battlements. There were a lot of them up there.

'Gates still shut,' Vindex said.

'I know,' Ferox told him.

'Halt!' The senior decurion ordered. There was shuffling as riders nudged their mounts into better lines.

'That means stop,' Vindex explained and the Brigantes laughed as they halted.

Cerialis spurred forward accompanied by Arrian, a standard bearer and trumpeter who sounded a series of notes, only slightly ragged as his horse cantered. The ala and the Brigantes were two hundred paces short of the ditch, as their commander headed for the bridge.

Trumpets blared from the towers. Something flashed as it caught the sun and slammed into the ground ahead of Cerialis and his tall stallion. The animal reared, and pulled back, doing a full circle before the rider brought him under control.

'Who comes armed for war to the gates of Nicopolis?' The voice boomed out from the walls. 'Speak, strangers, or the next one will sting you!'

They had agreed that Arrian should speak, for his accent was the clearest. 'We are friends!' he shouted, his voice impressively steady. 'We are allies, sent by the Lord Trajan Sebastos, King of Rome and guardian of peace.' Arrian had insisted that ideas like princeps meant little in this part of the world. 'Here the only title they understand is king.'

'Friends you may be, for we wish no quarrel with Rome or its king, but why do you come here?' a voice shouted down.

'We come in answer to the Princess Azátē, our friend, and the Lord Trajan's royal cousin, who asks for help and protection!'

There was a pause. 'Do you think they're going to say, sorry try the next city along,' Vindex said softly. The man must have picked up more Greek than Ferox realised, unless he simply guessed the exchange.

Still no answer came. Cerialis' stallion flicked its tail and tried to back away from the ballista bolt sticking firmly into the dirt. Closer to Ferox, Bran's mount decided to urinate and the sound of splashing was loud in the silence.

'We come in peace and to help our friends,' Arrian shouted when still no response came. 'If you wish, I will come in to you, alone and unarmed, to make clear our intentions and assuage any doubts.' Ferox had not liked the idea, but had at least managed to persuade Cerialis to remain with the force.

'This is Nicopolis!' Another voice shouted.

Vindex explained the shout to Bran.

'That's a relief. Thought we might have come to the wrong place.'

'This is Nicopolis!' the first voice called. 'And I am Athenodorus, Strategos, and I speak for the high council of the city. You are not welcome here! Go!'

'May we speak to the princess?' Arrian shouted up.

'Her highness is indisposed. This is our city, and I speak for it. Leave our lands! Go in peace and the friendship between us and Syria and Rome itself will remain unsullied!'

'We are but the first. Many thousands come behind us. A whole army is on its way in answer to the call of the Princess Azátē, friend to the Lord Trajan. My king will wish to be assured that her highness is safe. Only if we hear from her, will we know that this is true.'

'Go!'

'Let me come in and speak with you!'

'Leave. If you do not then we will treat you as enemies. Nicopolis is a free city. It is free because its citizens rule themselves and do not give way to force. Go!'

Cerialis walked his horse forward to talk to Arrian. A moment later they both wheeled around and went back to the ala. That was always hard, keeping to a slow pace and showing no trace of fear when a man was bound to wonder whether he was about to be spitted by a bolt.

'Oh well,' Vindex said. 'We're humped again.'

They withdrew back beyond the low ridge, leaving only a few of the Brigantes in plain sight to show that they had not gone further. Riders came out from the city, but none came closer than half a mile. For all their defiance, the Nicopolitans did not appear eager to start a war. Arrian, escorted by Vindex and a dozen Brigantes, went back to find the infantry column.

The morning passed slowly. Cerialis always kept a quarter of his men fully equipped and either standing beside their mounts or riding them, but gave orders that all in turn were to care for their horses, check their own equipment, take some food and rest. The sky was clear and the sun grew bakingly hot. Men burned their hands when they touched a helmet or anything else metal that had been left to lie. It was too hot even for the men to spend time watching the little lizards standing so still and then scurrying about.

There was some thin woodland to the north and Cerialis ordered the troops who were resting to move there. A little before noon he summoned Ferox to him.

'What are the chances of an escalade?'

'Next to none. You've seen the walls. Arrian's fellows will be tired when they get here. If the night's clear,' he said, glancing up, 'and all the odds say it will be, then there won't be much cover from darkness. Unless they're dumber than philosophers then they're bound to realise that we are hanging on for a reason, so they will keep a close watch. There aren't enough ladders or enough men to threaten at so many points that we strike a weak spot.'

'My lads are good,' Cerialis said, 'and can fight as well on foot as on horseback.'

'Say we use everyone. Say the Nicopolitans are half asleep, and say, because some god loves you, we get over the walls, what then? That's a fair-sized city. I've seen it. Main streets are broad, but the rest is a maze of alleys. Houses are high, flat roofed, so anyone can lob bricks down at us, but it's hard to get at them. That's not to mention the citadel, with its own walls. So if we get in, we die one by one, because Crispinus isn't going to get here anytime soon. But we'll never get in.'

Cerialis had nodded as Ferox spoke. 'Yes, that is what I think. No point to it at all. We'll lose good men for nothing. Worse, we will start a war and, worse still, start it by giving the enemy a victory. Maybe they'll see sense when Hispana and the rest parade outside their walls.'

Ferox stared at him.

'No, I don't believe that either,' Cerialis admitted. 'But it seems we must try.' He wiped his brow. 'Hercules' balls it's hot.'

'This is just the spring,' Ferox said. 'Be summer soon and then these plains will be like a furnace.'

'Huh, makes me wish I was back in Britannia with Lepidina.' Cerialis leaned over, and poked his index finger into the soil. Then he lifted it to his mouth and tried to spit, but was so dry he had to lick his lips before he could manage. 'My people say that brings good luck,' he said. It was a rare moment when he spoke as a Batavian. Ferox was tempted to say that he could not remember what it felt like to have that sort of luck.

'That's that then,' Cerialis concluded. 'For the present anyway. No sense lingering here. The fodder won't last long enough for us to wait for Crispinus. I don't believe his two days and reckon it will be more like four. If we start taking from the locals then the last chance for diplomacy will be gone. So we ride back to meet Arrian and then all march towards Crispinus and Hispana. The route is easy, you say?'

Ferox nodded.

'Good. I need another hour so that everyone gets some rest and time out of the saddle. We'll go then.'

It was nearly dark by the time they met the infantry, four or five miles back from where Cerialis had hoped that they would be. The men, especially the legionaries from VIIII Hispana were visibly struggling.

'It's the heat,' Arrian said in explanation. 'We have had to leave dozens behind because they could not keep up at all.'

They were close to a stream, so Cerialis decided to camp where they were and give time for the stragglers to come in. Judging the legionaries too exhausted to entrench the position, he ordered spears thrust into the ground to mark where the ramparts should be. Tent lines were laid out for each century and turma, not that they had brought any tents with them, and standing pickets established to watch the non-existent gates. The only digging was a straight, rather shallow trench to act as a latrine, placed away from the stream and downwind from the camp; Cerialis had the sense not to let every regulation slip. Sadly the horses were less fussy, so the camp soon smelled like a stable. Cavalrymen were better paid and had more slaves than ordinary soldiers, with three or four men often owning a groom. None had come on the expedition, but the troopers set to caring for their horses with a will. Everything he saw about the ala continued to impress Ferox.

Once the sun had gone down, the heat of the day fled and it was soon bitterly cold. Riding through the previous night, that had not mattered, but for men with only a single blanket or cloak as covering and trying to sleep, the cold seeped into their bones. Before long, most were huddling together to share what little warmth they had left, and many, even of the exhausted, slept only fitfully. Ferox and his men got less rest than most, for they patrolled around the camp throughout the night. Bran spotted some riders who watched them for a while from a distance, before vanishing into the gloom. They might have been from the city or they might have been nomads about their own business, and were not seen again.

At dawn the trumpets sounded, and officers reported to Cerialis for the day's password and orders, while the soldiers stamped to bring life back to numbed limbs. All of the stragglers had turned up, most within a few hours, and they set off at the infantry's pace. If anyone fell out of the ranks, then Cerialis' orders were for a trooper to dismount and lead the horse while the weary man rode. This prompted a wave of men staggering and falling, until the auxiliaries started to jeer them. From then on, it became a point of pride for each century not to lose a man. Comrades took their pila, helmets, and in a few cases even their shields to help the footsore keep going. Arrian set an example by going on foot and carrying a legionary's equipment for him, which meant that all the centurions had to do the same.

By the end of the day they had gone seventeen miles, which Ferox felt was good with so many unfit men in that heat. Before the sun set he saw a cloud of dust in the distance ahead of them, which surely meant Crispinus was on his way, unless things were taking a decided turn for the worse. The news spread and for all the cold there was a more cheerful mood in their camp that night. There was a faint glow to the north, but not enough cloud for them to see the reflection of campfires. Bran saw riders again, as did Vindex. Ferox tried to loop around behind them with a handful of men. He did not catch them, regretting that there was no time to stalk them on foot and even more that he had no Silures under command. However, he got close enough to think that they were Arabs, which meant little since he had seen more than a few of those warriors among the guards at Nicopolis.

Ferox suggested that he ride off the next morning and make contact with Crispinus, while the rest waited for them to arrive.

'No,' Cerialis told him. 'Better we arrive together. The lads want to be back with the army. Makes them feel more secure, I suppose, apart from better food.'

As they rode on, Ferox could sense that Cerialis was right. There was more chatter as they went and the mood was more cheerful than before. He could not share it. It was freer off away from the main force, and joining them, like going back to a camp, made him feel that the army's – and Hadrian's – cold hand was squeezing him tighter once again. He also did not like the thought of what was about to happen.

XI

In the plain in front of Nicopolis
The Ides of April

THERE WAS POWER behind the advance, and anyone
with eyes to see could spot the confidence of even the
outposts of pairs of horsemen who stayed just within
sight of the turma strength supports. A quarter of a mile back
from them, ala I Flavia Britannica rode in close formation as
the main advance guard. They went slowly, trotting now and
again to reach one of the low ridges, and stopping regularly. No
one could miss the confidence and determination in the way the
column came on. It was a glimpse of the might of Rome, but it
did not move quickly, so the cavalry in the lead spent as much
time waiting and watching as they did going forward.

The same was true of the leading infantry units, cohors II
Ulpia Galatarum, raised just five years ago from the province
of Galatia and with no honours on its standards, and cohors
II Flavia Commagenorum, a veteran unit of archers brought
over from the Danube in the same convoys as Cerialis and his
men. They were to act as a solid support to the cavalry, the
archers forming to shoot over the heads of a couple of ranks of
spearmen. A bowman on foot, if he and his bow were any good,
and the soldiers from Commagene were very good, always
outranged horse archers. It was a hard lesson of wars beyond

the Euphrates that the Romans needed to take a good balance
of different troops and make sure that they worked together.
Anything else risked disaster, at least against the Parthians,
and the kingdom of Osrhoene was more Parthian than it was
anything else.

'There they are again, sir.' The senior decurion pointed
towards the crest of a gentle rise about three-quarters of a mile
away.

'I see them, Clemens.' Cerialis was shading his eyes from
the sun. They were with the turma providing close support to
the outposts. Since daybreak several bands, each of around a
hundred horse archers, had watched the Romans. Cerialis still
was not quite sure whether there were four or five bands. Only
rarely was more than one visible at a time, and this was the
closest any had come. When he sent a couple of riders ahead,
the enemy – if that was what they were – trotted away. At first
it was exciting, like the moments of waiting, heavy spear in
hand, for a boar to be flushed from a thicket, but as the hours
passed it became routine, even dull. Cerialis chivvied his men
to make sure that the mood did not lead to carelessness. He
was in command of the cavalry screen as well as his own men,
so he visited the outriders along each flank of the column and
found that they had seen no one. A messenger from the prefect
in charge of the rearguard made the same report. Given how
many miles the column stretched, that was not too surprising,
at least if there were no more than four or five hundred horse
archers out there. Crispinus had visited about an hour ago,
taken a look, sent a centurion and interpreter riding forward
and watched as the closest band cantered away from them.

'They do not seem to be in a sociable mood,' he said. The
advance continued, and the need to watch the mounted bowmen
did not make any real difference to its progress, which was slow

because of the road, if the word could be used for a track left by caravans and farmers taking goods to market. None of them had much use for carts, let alone big four-wheeled waggons laden with timber for building, siege engines carried whole or in sections depending on their size, sacks, barrels and amphorae of provisions, bolts and well-shaped stones as ammunition, and all the myriad of other things felt essential. The soil was sandy, drying out as the spring advanced inexorably towards the truly hot season, and iron-rimmed wheels drove deep furrows into it and broke it up, so that the vehicles coming behind bogged down, and men sweated and cursed as they pushed to free them. Many ridges cut across their path, and none of them were high or difficult for a man or animal, but some of the little slopes were steep, which meant that teams had to be taken from several waggons simply to get one to the top, when the draft teams were sent back to repeat the exercise with the next one.

Five hundred men followed the advance guard and these wore no armour and carried tools rather than weapons, for their task was to improve the track as well as they could. They were mostly legionaries, apart from four score sailors – and the gods alone knew where Hadrian had found them. The men of the fleet had a good reputation for this sort of work, for long hours rowing or hauling ropes made them strong and the need to solve their own problems when at sea taught uncommon ingenuity. Yet there was only so much anyone could do. Gullies were filled or bridged, planks laid as a track where the path was especially soft, and gentler routes cut at an angle up some slopes. It helped a little, but still moving the vehicles was a struggle, and animals started to die as they were flogged too hard to make them move. Three carts were now hauled by relays of men.

After he had seen the horse archers shadowing them,

Crispinus returned with his escort to take his position, riding past the men carrying marker flags to lay out the evening's camp, and then the labourers working to improve the track. His place as commander was behind them, with his senior officers not otherwise engaged, all escorted by the Hispana's little force of cavalry.

'Any trouble, my lord?' Arrian asked when Crispinus joined his staff.

'No. Some fellows are watching, but not trying any mischief. So, gentlemen, we must make sure that all they see is discipline and strength.'

Next came the eagle and the other standards, followed by the first cohort of the legion and then the rest in their order of precedence for the day. All marched in a cloud of dust from the boots of those ahead, and the further back in the column the worse the dust, which was the reason for rotating the order and giving everyone the best and the worst positions in turn. Even more dust was churned up by the baggage train following behind, with a cohors equitata on either side to act as a heavy screen. Crispinus remembered how that damned fool Mark Antony had pressed ahead and let his entire siege train follow at its own pace, only to have it snapped up by the Parthians which doomed his entire campaign. He was not about to make the same mistake. It was hard work helping the train along, but more pleasant than it was for the two auxiliary cohorts following behind, who had to stop and wait each time something got bogged down, all the while eating dust and treading their way through the inevitable dung dropped by thousands of animals, many not in the best of health. There were cavalry bringing up the rear, mostly ala III Thracum who had been stationed in Syria for so long that the only Thracian was their commander, who was also a Roman and an eques. Like the vanguard they sent out outposts as a screen, and behind them all came Ferox and the Brigantes because Crispinus wanted good scouts watching the rear, because if there were enemy out there then they would mainly be horsemen and they might come from any direction.

'They make a fuss of everything, don't they?' Vindex commented after a long bout of coughing. They were able to hang back and avoid the worst of the dust, but every now and then the wind gusted, driving the muck into their faces. 'Not going to take anyone by surprise are we?'

'They might wonder why a cloud of dust is attacking them?' Brennus suggested. He was as old as Vindex and had served as a scout and then with the irregular band of Brigantes for as long as Ferox could remember. The man had lost his left eye, and now lifted the patch and scratched at the scar beneath. 'Taranis, it gets everywhere,' he added. It bothered Ferox that he could no longer remember when the man had taken the wound. 'No, think about it,' Brennus continued. 'You see this duststorm coming and you might think the gods are angry.'

Bran glanced at Vindex. 'Don't think any god looks like that.'

'Some are ugly,' Brennus said. 'That goddess back on the coast was just a lump of rock.'

'Her face was like stone, but she had a kind heart,' Vindex said. 'Plenty of lasses like that.'

Ferox was no longer listening. 'Come on!' he shouted as he headed off. They were passing one of the many farms and small settlements dotted around the plains and he had heard shouting. Crispinus had issued strict orders that there was to be no looting and no molestation of the locals until he gave the order. Yet the army was the army, and men always found an excuse to straggle off from the column and see what they could find. Every unit had its incorrigible foragers, so one of the other reasons for putting the Brigantes at the rear was to keep an eye out for trouble. 'Your fellows know a lot about robbery,' Crispinus had assured him, 'so they ought to know how to catch thieves.'

They found a pair of auxiliary troopers trying to make off with a couple of month-old lambs. An old woman was screaming at them and an old man was stretched on the ground, his head bloodied. Ferox's crested helmet marked him as a centurion, which made them hesitate, and when Bran, Vindex and three others galloped up, the troopers gave up.

'Names?' Ferox demanded.

'Longus, sir, ala Thracum,' the young one replied

'Comus, sir.' That was the older one, and there was at least a chance that this was his real name.

'Where are you supposed to be?'

'Outriders, sir.'

'Then get back to your station. I catch you again and it's a flogging.' Ferox doubted that the threat would deter them for he and his men could not be everywhere. He dismounted and had a look at the old man, who was sitting up. The cut was messy, but not deep and he helped bind it before they rode away. All the while he wondered what his men had stolen, not that he had seen them at it.

By this time the head of the column had already halted, the camp and tent-lines marked out, but it took three more hours before the baggage train came in and the best part of another for the rearguard units to arrive. The Brigantes led their horses to their patch, where servants had already started setting up tents. Beyond them the rampart was finished, for no one expected barbarian irregulars to have the skill for even this simple task. Philo and Indike had set up Ferox's larger tent at the end of the line. The lad had insisted on coming and also insisted on bringing his wife, and she was one of at least a hundred women in the camp. Outside the ramparts, among the tents and stalls hastily erected by the sutlers, there were as many more. Philo had prepared him a good, solid meal, and he might have enjoyed it even more if the air was not soon filled with the scent of chickens roasting on spits. The farmers were no doubt poorer, but since it could have been a lot worse and it was too late to do anything about it, he did not mind accepting a leg when he did his rounds.

The next day the vanguard and rearguard exchanged places, so the Brigantes were in the lead and no longer eating everyone's dust. Warned about the horse archers, they saw only pairs of them rather than the larger bands.

'Someone's worked out that one can see as well as a hundred,' Ferox told Crispinus when he came forward. 'And a second can carry the news.'

The legatus pursed his lips. 'Still not sure what they intend.'

'Maybe they're not either, sir.'

Late in the day, as the men were marking out the camp, Crispinus joined them again and Ferox took him up to a round hill on the left.

'So there it is,' Crispinus said. 'Nicopolis.' The city was about four miles away, its pale walls reddening as the sun set. 'You would not think so obscure a place could matter so much,' he added under his breath. 'Yet, I suppose over the ages plenty of men have died for much less.'

'Or for nothing at all,' Ferox said.

'Well, we have our duty, centurion. And yours will be with Cerialis and the advance guard tomorrow. I'll camp half a mile from the walls. Cannot expect them to accept all these men into their city.'

'That's if they're willing, sir.'

'Indeed. Well, we shall find out tomorrow.'

It rained in the night, the first rain for many, many days, and perhaps the last for even longer. Caecilius was awake and ran about getting men to catch what they could in any barrel or vessel already empty.

Next morning as they prepared to set out before dawn, there were soon patches of mud along the most frequently trodden paths. Crispinus summoned his officers to a consilium, and explained that the order of march would be different.

'While I hope that the city's leaders will see sense, prudence dictates that we prepare to meet resistance. We are not going far, so the advance guard will form as usual, but the legion will depart in two columns, each of which will wheel into a line to follow. After that we shall see.' There were many more details, questions, answers and discussion, and Ferox stood at the back and listened because it all really depended on whether they were in for a fight before they even reached the city.

The earth in each gateway of the camp was churned to mud as the vanguard left by the front gate and a legionary column through each of the side ones. Since there was a chance of fighting, the standards were no longer concentrated, save that each cohort put them at the head of its column. Shields were uncovered, crests mounted on helmets, and equipment polished as bright as was possible.

'If there is a fight, let's put on a good show,' Crispinus had urged his officers.

The Brigantes were among the first to leave, although to Ferox's surprise Cerialis instructed him to form his men to the left of the main body of the ala. 'Don't want you frightening anyone, do we! And you are the fastest riders I have because you don't care so much about keeping ranks. Might be a surprise if we need to unleash you.'

The advance guard was in position by dawn, with the two cohorts in close order behind the cavalry. Six *caroballistae*, the light artillery known as *scorpiones* mounted on and able to shoot from the back of a two-wheeled cart, were with them. Most of the labourers had returned to their units and only the sailors stood ready to help clear a path. Half an hour later the two lines of legionaries had deployed, the first line longer because it included cohors I on the right flank, and after some shuffling and dressing of ranks they were ready. There was a fifty-pace gap between each cohort's line, with the one in the line behind stationed to cover it. Two scorpiones, ones on ordinary mountings this time, were in each gap, for these were light enough for the crews to carry and keep pace with infantry, at least until the cohorts charged. The remainder of the army was to protect the baggage train as it advanced and then start laying out the new camp.

Crispinus and a few of his staff joined Cerialis and Ferox as the advance began. No longer having to worry about the pace of the baggage, they went steadily, stopping less often and only for a little while to keep the formation together. As they came to the rise, each unit stuttered in its advance and men talked as they saw the city.

'I fear that does not look much like a welcome,' Crispinus said dryly. 'At least not a friendly one.'

There were bands of horsemen dotted across the plain ahead of them. Ferox counted eight, and reckoned each numbered a little over a hundred. At the rear was a denser formation, half as big again as the others and sparkling as the sunlight glanced off helmets and armour. Between the city walls and the ditch were thousands of men. Although the distance made it hard to make out their equipment, there was some sense of organised formations.

'We keep going,' Crispinus said in answer to his officers' looks. 'Cerialis, send out skirmishers, but tell them not to throw or strike unless they are attacked first.'

'Archers, sir?' Along with his own ala, Cerialis had brought a couple of vexillations of cavalry from other units stationed in Pannonia. Fifty were horse archers.

'No. I want them in reserve.'

Four turmae rode ahead, each splitting into half, so that the decurion stayed with a formed group while the rest pushed on in pairs. The waiting Osrhoenes watched and made no move. They were still over a mile away. As the advance continued, the closest bands of horse archers similarly broke up, with files of riders trotting ahead.

'We must not strike the first blow,' Crispinus said, half to himself. 'Not while there is still a chance of avoiding it.' Ferox noticed that the legatus' cheek was twitching. The foremost bands of the Osrhoenes were barely half a mile away, the one going ahead even closer to the Roman skirmishers.

Suddenly, first one and then another file of the horse archers galloped straight for the nearest auxiliaries.

'Good lads,' Cerialis muttered in approval as his men halted. The horse archers kept coming, closer, closer, until they were no more than forty paces away when the leading ones spun their mounts sharply to the right, without slowing, galloping parallel with the dispersed Roman line. Each rider coming behind in turn peeled off and followed.

'Are they shooting?' Rufus asked. The man was squinting as he tried to see.

'No,' Crispinus said, lips tight as he forced himself to control the twitch.

'They're showing off.' Cerialis laughed.

'Press on!' Crispinus ordered. As the skirmishers closest to the galloping horse archers had stopped, so had everyone else, even though there had been no order.

Cerialis gestured to his trumpeter to sound the advance.

'Arrian, my dear fellow.' Crispinus was making such an effort to control his speech that the words were almost stilted. 'I realise that this is a lot to ask, but would you mind riding forward and suggesting to whoever is in charge that we ought to talk, and assuring them of our good intentions.'

'Of course, sir.' Arrian beckoned to a trooper with laurel leaves tied around his spear shaft, the traditional mark of a herald.

'See the one on the grey?' Cerialis interrupted. He pointed to a lone rider some way ahead of the sparkling cataphracts. 'I am sure that is Prince Arbandes. Saw him in the Lord Trajan's camp a month or so ago.'

Crispinus shaded his eyes and stared, although since he had never seen the likeness of the prince, let alone his actual person, he would have to take Cerialis' word for it.

'It's a young man,' Ferox said. 'Good rider, sits well. Riding a stallion. Bit too excited for his own good.'

'The horse or the prince?' Cerialis asked.

Crispinus frowned. 'Holy Juno, you have good eyesight. The princess' brother, then, not that kinship necessarily means *concordia*. Hmm. He might be less keen on our aid, but then again, he was at Trajan's camp so might simply wish to make a deal of his own. Either way, he is clearly the man to reach. Don't take any chances, my dear Arrian, but see what you can do.'

'My lord.'

'Wait!' Ferox shouted. Another file of riders was galloping towards a pair of skirmishers from the ala, but this time as they closed an arrow flicked through the air and slammed into a trooper's shield. The leading rider had turned away and sent another missile which went wide, but the man behind him was better or luckier and an arrow buried itself into the eye of the soldier's horse, which reared in agony and threw him.

'Bastards,' Cerialis gasped.

More arrows followed and other files of archers were charging forward and shooting. Another horse was down, and a rider reeling back, an arrow in his thigh. Some troopers threw light javelins in response, but none found a target.

'Is it a mistake?' Rufus asked. Ferox could see that the prince was sitting on his horse, making no effort to ride forward and control his men.

Crispinus did not bother to answer the question. 'Right, let's drive these impudent bastards off. Push on, Cerialis, but keep close to the infantry. When we are closer to the walls, we charge. Let's see those cowardly buggers try to dance out of the way of that. I'll be with the legion if you need me.'

'Skirmishers advance,' Cerialis said to the trumpeter, who sounded the command. The men responded eagerly. Pairs of riders shot forward, and the abrupt attack surprised the closest horse archers. A couple went down under the javelins before the rest galloped back, turning round to shoot as they fled and a few of those arrows found marks. Cerialis ordered the horse archers forward. 'Back them up, Ferox.'

'Sir.' Ferox trotted over to his men and waited for the auxiliary horse archers to pass before moving behind them. 'We only charge to protect them,' he ordered. 'They have the range and we don't.'

First blood had been drawn on each side, and it seemed to bring caution. The bands of Osrhoenes hung back, especially from the mounted auxiliary archers. One group looped wide and came at the infantry behind, until a volley of arrows brought a horse down and scared the rest off. As they fled, a scorpio from one of the carts spat its bolt and pitched a rider into the dust.

The Romans pushed forward steadily, and the Osrhoenes launched only tentative attacks, galloping towards the enemy, but peeling off while still at long bowshot. A lot of arrows were in the air, and a fair few javelins whenever there was a chance; few hit a target, and fewer still did damage. Some of the troopers had half a dozen or more shafts sticking from their shields without any harm done.

When the leading skirmishers were barely five hundred paces from the ditch, Cerialis had the trumpets sound and the main body of ala I Flavia Britannica went from a walk into a trot. The Roman skirmishers and supports wheeled to get out of their way, and at the same time the bands of horse archers sped away, half going to the right and half to the left. The cataphracts turned about and trotted back across the bridge. Before the trumpets sounded for the leading turmae of the ala to go into a canter, the field ahead of them had cleared.

Ferox could not help grinning. It was almost like an exercise choreographed to impress a senior officer. Yet it was well managed on both sides. A mounted charge could rarely catch horse archers who did not care about their formation and would flee and flee for as long as they had to in order to escape. In time the charge would lose momentum, ranks scattered and horses blown, making them easy prey when the archers wheeled back around and came for them. It was the way the Parthians fought, and many Sarmatians as well, but it needed plenty of space and there was none if they were driven against the ditch around the city.

'Is that it?' Vindex asked.

'Yes and no,' Ferox said. He could not see which way the

prince had gone. He called on his men to reform, as trumpets also halted the ala and then ordered it to pull back. Much further and they risked coming within range of any bows with the infantry behind the ditch, let alone any archers or artillery on the ramparts. Closer now, he could see that there were a few ordered and fairly uniform blocks of men standing between ditch and walls, and far more who jostled and bumped each other, carrying spears and all kinds of shields. Still, they were not a problem for the moment.

'Are we humped?'

'You must know the answer to that.'

'Aye, reckon I do.'

A little later some of the horse archers probed the Romans' flanks, but never pressed too hard and quickly retreated whenever shot at, especially by scorpiones. As the day passed, the Romans built their camp. Half of the men behind the ditch sat down as they watched, and eventually more and more drifted back inside the city, for there was no sign that much else was going to happen.

Arrian dutifully went forward to ask that a Roman force be admitted to the city, or at least that discussions begin. The answer was the same as before.

'We'll see tomorrow,' Crispinus told his officers that evening.

Nicopolis
The same night

D OMITIUS SAT IN *the darkness. There was no window*
to the cell, no light at all apart from the thin line of
torchlight under the locked door. He did not know
how many days he had been there, his legs in shackles, an iron
collar around his neck with a chain attached to a ring on the
wall. There were two others in the cell, both chained, and they
spoke little and in words he did not understand. Now and then,
probably at morning and in the evening, or at least so he had
thought in the beginning, a guard opened the door and they
brought a cup of cheap, highly watered wine, and a bowl of
thin gruel.

His guards had taken him directly to the prison, where
others put on the shackles and took him to the cell. He never
saw the Strategos, or anyone else for that matter, and no one
asked him any questions about why he was in the city or
anything at all. Apart from the ones who brought the food,
everyone else seemed to have forgotten his existence. The
other two prisoners said less and less, and one was breathing
with difficulty. The chain was just long enough to allow him
to lie down on the filthy straw so long as he did not move.
The inhabitants of the straw did enough moving for everyone,
and he could feel the lice crawling across his skin and fleas
biting. Sleep did not come easily, but after a while the heavy
breathing grew softer and then there was silence. The next

time the guard came with a meal he prodded the one prisoner,
before giving a short laugh.

'We've got a dead 'un!' he called. 'You hear that, Aristonicus?
That's three drachma you owe me!'

Another guard appeared. 'Next week, when we get paid,' he
yelled.

'Tight-fisted bastard. Come on, get the key and we'll drag
him out.'

Domitius felt himself tensing, wondering whether there was
some chance to surprise them, unlock his bonds and escape.
There was not, so he watched, blinking in the flood of torchlight
through the open door, as they pulled the corpse out by its feet.

'You two still alive?' Aristonicus joked before he slammed
the door shut. Domitius could hear their muffled conversation
for a while before it faded. There was a glow in his eyes from
the torchlight, and that took even longer to fade. He felt for his
meal, cursed as he spilled some of the wine, and ate the gruel.

Time passed and it could have been day or night. The other
man began muttering, the same phrase over and over again,
and Domitius wondered whether it was a prayer or a curse.
After a while, it took on the form of a conversation, as the man
seemed to argue with himself, at times becoming heated and
even yelling. Domitius was not sure who was winning.

Domitius tried to pray, but found the ongoing altercation
distracting. He tried repeating the prayer taught by the Lord
to his disciples out loud. This only made the madman louder
in his dispute and Domitius gave up, and even as he said the
words in his head somehow it felt as if the man's voice was
breaking into his thoughts. He wanted to shout, but felt this
was un-Christian, even if it was his instinct as a soldier. Apart
from that, the chains meant that he could not get close enough
to back up any threats with violence.

There were stories of martyrs spending weeks, months, even years in prison, often tortured and knowing that they would be executed with savage ingenuity as an example. Perhaps it was easier for them, knowing the prize awaiting them. Pausanias did not go into detail, but he had heard other preachers speak of golden crowns and other honours waiting in Heaven. Yet he was not a martyr to his faith in any direct way, so lacked that consolation that surely gave them strength. He had been arrested for refusing to recant his beliefs, and deserted because his prospects were not good. The Nicopolitan authorities were not likely to care about that. He told himself that he had stayed in the city because he liked Simon and his family and had nowhere else to go. The truth was as simple as it was absurd; he had fallen in love with Sara, a woman whom he barely knew and whom he would never be permitted to marry. She had such lovely eyes, such beauty of face – and his imagination assured him beauty of everything else. For the absurd dream of being with her, he had stayed and now was in prison, most likely suspected of being a spy, and no one was ever very pleasant to a suspect in those circumstances. The odds were strong that they would kill him at the very least and Domitius doubted anyone would repeat his tale in the way they recounted the last deeds and dreams of martyrs, without explaining how they knew so much of the story.

No one had the power to change the past, so he was here and that was all there was to it. At least the army taught you to put up with what you could not change, even if it was easier when there were comrades around so that you could moan about it all. On balance the cells back at base were a good deal more comfortable than this one, although he was not sure whether or not that should make him proud to be Roman. Domitius laughed out loud at the thought, and the realisation that he was here out of love for a woman who had surely never thought of him in that way, and once he started he could not stop, until the sound echoed around the room. The madman broke off from his debate, and when Domitius got control of himself there was silence for the rest of the night.

The next morning the guard who brought his food and drink laid it down carefully on the floor beside Domitius. Then, just as carefully, he spat into both vessels.

'Bastard,' he said. When he returned a few moments later with food for the other captive, he simply placed them beside the man, without comment or additional seasoning. Clearly madness commanded better treatment.

Domitius lifted the bowl of gruel to his lips, since food, after all, was food. The guard stepped over and kicked him hard in the stomach. Domitius doubled up, the bowl and its contents flying everywhere as he spat out the mouthful he had taken. A second kick slammed into his leg, followed by a third, which seemed to satisfy the man for the moment.

The day, assuming it was day, passed slowly, and Domitius felt hungrier than he ought to have done though missing one meagre meal. His beard was growing ever thicker, adding to the sense of filth all around him. To keep his mind occupied, he tried to remember stories of Christ and his ministry. Once, just over a year ago, Pausanias had shown him a borrowed scroll of the book written by Matthew, one of the disciples, and a few other times he had heard men read or quote from other books, some of them the ancient Jewish Scriptures. Domitius tried to remember all the stories, and put them in order, but the madman was disputing with himself once more, far louder this time, and laughing out loud no longer dissuaded him. Wishing the man would hold his peace or do the decent thing and die, Domitius decided that he had better pray for the man instead.

Once he had done that he began to think back over his years in the army. He repeated out loud drills learned by rote, half remembered rollcalls and orders. After a while he ran through the commands for marching, changing formation, and fighting, bawling them out at the top of his voice. It felt good, so he kept on, repeating anything he could remember. Try as the madman might, he could not match the power of someone who had made a centuria of legionaries sweat on the parade ground, and eventually gave up.

That evening, assuming it was evening, a different guard brought their food. He spoke to the madman in what was probably Aramaic and got no response.

'How are you?' he asked Domitius in Greek. It seemed a strange question to ask a man in prison, so he struggled for an answer.

'Hoarse,' Domitius said at last.

'Hmm. Yes, I heard some shouting when I came on duty.' The man glanced at the half-open door. No one seemed to be there. 'Take heart, brother,' he whispered. 'We are praying for you.'

'Oh.' Domitius saw the man frown as he passed him a bowl. There was the slightest hint of bacon in the aroma, and when he drank there was far more substance and taste to it. Domitius used his hand as a spoon to scoop it into his mouth. The bright light vanished as the door was closed.

'Thank you,' Domitius said, but the man had gone.

XII

In front of Nicopolis
Eighteenth day before the Kalends of May
First day of the siege

'SHE'S A BITCH,' Caecilius concluded. 'No doubt about it.' He chewed his lip for a moment. Every inch the soldier when on foot, the primus pilus of Legio VIIII Hispana almost slumped in the saddle as if to show that he was an infantryman at heart. 'A bitch.'

Crispinus felt his cheek threatening to twitch, so turned away to face back towards the main camp. The Nicopolitans were quieter now, the chanting dropped to a low buzz of noise. For the second day running, thousands of defenders had formed up between the ditch and wall, with a few score even going beyond the ditch and spreading out as a skirmish line. The cavalry were keeping their distance, just visible to the north. He had sent the Thracians to watch them and was pleased to see that their prefect was keeping his men well in hand. For the moment, he wanted to fight only if the enemy gave them no other choice. Four legionary cohorts, each three deep with an extra rank at the rear provided by the auxiliary archers, and with scorpiones in the gaps between units, formed a screen facing the city. They stood three hundred paces back from the ditch, and if the enemy had any engines on their walls capable of reaching so far then they had not yet chosen to use them. A few skirmishers who had pressed forward had run even more smartly back when the Romans sent a bolt into the ground at their feet. Crispinus' orders were the same everywhere; be wary and keep them at a distance, but only fight if provoked.

'It reminds me of Pergamon,' Rufus ventured.

Caecilius sniffed, then yanked hard on the reins as his gelding started. 'Peace, you mongrel,' he muttered. 'Aye, lad, there's something in what you say. Not seen walls and towers like that in this part of the world. Old fashioned, more like Caria or Bithynia, than anything down this way.'

'The reports we gathered were accurate?' Crispinus asked, for to his eyes the city was exactly as he had expected.

'Aye, well enough. Those openings halfway up the wall are for artillery. That makes the walls as thick as your spies said.'

'Well done, Ferox,' Crispinus said, ignoring the grunt of displeasure from Caecilius when he mentioned the name and the pointed use of the word spies rather than scouts. He was still unsure why the primus pilus did not care for Ferox, not that the centurion seemed to mind, and simply rode near the back of the group, his face wooden.

'Means they're hollow though,' Rufus suggested. The young officer was steadily gaining in confidence. 'At least for part of the way.'

'It does, but also means they can pack the space tight with rubble quicker than we can get a ram against it.' Caecilius glared around him. 'Never forget that they can think too and act. It's never just about what we plan to do. We have to out-fight, out-fox and out-last them, and they'll try to do the same to us.'

Crispinus knew the truth of this. Arrian had ridden close to the gateway soon after dawn, making the same request and getting the same answer. The Nicopolitans were not about to admit them, at least not yet, so they had become the enemy. As Caecilius said, this was now a question of matching wits and wills against each other. Hadrian had made it clear. One way or another, the city must be in Roman hands and there was not that much time. Two months was all he could promise Crispinus, for after that Hadrian might be replaced and at the very least the news of any siege would reach Trajan and give him time to respond. Hadrian was preparing a despatch justifying his actions, but could not be sure how the princeps would react.

All of that meant that every single day, almost every hour, was precious, for as Caecilius' said, the city was a bitch of place to take, with strong walls and defenders who appeared numerous and determined. There were more men outside the walls than Crispinus had expected. Still, they had seen so many abandoned or half-empty farms and villages on their march that it was obvious plenty of people had fled into Nicopolis. That meant more mouths for the defenders to feed as well as more hands to hold a spear or hurl a rock. Like everything else, it cut both ways. This morning Crispinus could have attacked to drive the enemy back behind their walls. It needed to be done, because until it was, the Romans would not be able to build any siege works, and the ramps he would need could not be constructed quickly. A mere glance at the high walls had confirmed his guess that there was not the slightest prospect of taking the place by an immediate attack with ladders, so the business would have to be done properly, which meant slowly. Caecilius would advise – it would be hard to stop the man even if he tried – as would others, but it all came down to Crispinus to make the decisions and spend his limited time well.

Today, he had decided that he wanted to make the

Nicopolitans realise that he was serious and that their best way out was to talk. To this end, Cerialis and the bulk of his ala, along with the remaining four cohorts of Hispana and two cohorts of auxiliaries, were marching in a big loop around the south of the city. A few small bands of horsemen watched them, but none of the men formed outside the walls moved away from the western gate and there were none waiting outside the city on the far side.

Caecilius whistled through his teeth. 'A bitch and no mistake.' He was staring at the ground as it rose, turning into bluffs that doubled the height of the walls. There was a ditch at their foot, albeit far shallower than everywhere else. 'That's the citadel then.'

The Roman column continued, screened by cavalry, not that there was much of a threat at present. Crispinus wanted a second camp on this eastern side of Nicopolis.

'Be an even tougher nut from this side,' Caecilius assured him.

'Impossible?' Crispinus asked.

'Not much is impossible if you're willing to put in the time, the material, the labour, and the sheer sweat. But's it's a bugger and no mistake. Take much longer.'

'All that matters is that they think we are launching – or we might launch – a big assault from this side as well as the west. Make them look two ways at once. And make them feel surrounded. We're coming for them and if it takes all year we'll get in, so they either die or they make peace. That's what we want them to see.' The legatus grinned because that helped him control his face.

'Sir.' Caecilius did not show any emotion. Rufus was keen, Arrian mixing enthusiasm with nervousness, and there was no point glancing back to see Ferox.

A cohort of legionaries and the auxiliaries formed a line
in front of the campsite facing towards the eastern gate. The
cavalry watched the northern flank. After an hour, a couple of
hundred horse archers came and sniffed at them for a while,
without pressing their interest any further. In the meantime, the
other legionaries marked out the camp, and started digging a
ditch and piling up the spoil into a rampart, while lixae and
other slaves and followers unpacked tents and other equipment.
A little later a stone was shot from one of the towers, lobbing
high into the air, but still thumping down a good sixty paces in
front of the infantry screen.

'I hear you did better,' Crispinus said to Ferox. That was
another flash of the dashing young tribune, who could never
resist parading his knowledge. Back in Dacia, Ferox had held
up an enemy column besieging his fort, by using a powerful one-
armed catapult with a far greater range than most machines.
It worked well, until one of the cords snapped and the thing
shook itself to pieces.

'If they have sense, they'll keep quiet about anything with a
longer reach,' Ferox said. 'Why kill a couple when you can wait
and kill far more – and give us a scare.'

'The lad's right.' Caecilius' praise was gruff, but it was the
first he had given to Ferox. 'Don't just see what they want us
to see, my lord. See what's really there, and think about what
you cannot see.'

'Sage advice, I am sure.' Crispinus smiled. 'Let's try to make
sure they only see what we want them to see then, shall we?
Well, we have our other big camp. Let's settle for three small
ones at the moment – one to the south and two covering the
north. That's better cavalry country so let's make life more
difficult for them. We can build those tomorrow if there is time
– today is busy enough. Do you need a closer look, primus?'

'Seen all I need, my lord.'

'Good, then I shall not detain you any longer as you have so much to do. Draw up your lists and orders. There is no need to tell you how important this is or urge you to do your best. You have first call on everything... Well then. Is there anything else you need now? No. Consilium in the principia in my camp at the start of the second hour of the night.'

No more stones came from the wall as the morning drew to an end. They could see faces peering down at them from the ramparts and the high towers, and sometimes there were more riders watching from the north and sometimes fewer. The camp's defences took shape quickly, which was a relief.

'At least it isn't too hard to dig over here,' Crispinus commented to Cerialis when he came back to report. In the main camp, they had struck a stony level after going down no more than three feet, and had eventually given up on making the ditch any deeper, which meant adding more obstacles outside to secure the defences. Here it was far easier, and soon they had a V-shaped ditch where a tall man could only just see out, and a good rampart behind it. There were not enough stones to hand to build low walls and make huts rather than tents, so the soldiers in both camps would have to make do with sleeping under leather, at least for the moment.

'I'll want reports from you every hour, night and day,' the legatus told Cerialis, who was to command the eastern camp. 'We cannot see each other, and until we have the small camps we cannot rely on a relay of signals.' Three legionary cohorts, one and a half of auxiliaries and his own ala were to be stationed here. 'And I'm giving you Ferox and his rogues.'

'Put all your Britons in one place, eh? Best way to keep an eye on them.'

'Yes, you cannot be too careful. I'll want them tomorrow and probably again, but they're hillfolk, so could come in handy when you go up those cliffs.' Crispinus glanced at Ferox. 'Look at him, not saying a thing. Bet he's itching to say that I'm talking nonsense or that no one could ride a horse up those rocks.'

'I leave such wisdom to Vindex, my lord.'

Crispinus sighed. 'You really do not change, do you? As if I did not have enough burdens to carry as it is. That's why I'm leaving him to mope around your camp instead of mine, dear Cerialis.'

'I have children, my lord, after that a sullen centurion is no great thing! And I'm fond of this one – like an old hound past his best, but still a little life in him.'

'There had better be!' Crispinus snapped. 'The primus pilus, who for some unaccountable reason, does not care much for you, Ferox'—the legatus ignored Cerialis' "why think of that"—'knows what he is talking about when it comes to sieges. We need to outwit the people in there.' He jerked a thumb up at the walls. 'You, Ferox, are of the Silures, and they say the Silures are most devious of all the Britons, and everyone knows you cannot trust a Briton, so I need that warped mind and soul of yours, and I need you to speak up with every twisted thought that comes into your mind.'

'The noble legatus is quite fond of you as well,' Cerialis said drily. 'But then, they say he is a man of strange tastes.'

Crispinus shook his head. 'I'm glad the city will be between me and the two of you. But we all need to work, so time to stop dawdling.'

'Sir.' Both Cerialis and Ferox spoke at the same time. The legatus shook his head again and rode back to the main camp, his escort trailing behind.

'Reminds me a little of Dacia, although those were mountains not piddling little hills like this.' Cerialis shaded his eyes as he stared up at the city above them. 'Well,' he said after a long pause, 'when I was at Sarmizegethusa, it did not help us that we had the high ground and strong walls. Bastards cut us to ribbons anyway.'

'Don't think we're going to persuade them to come on out though, are we, sir?'

'No. You say there is a spring in the city, giving them plenty of fresh water? Decent storage for food, although if refugees have fled inside the walls, that should make it harder, shouldn't it? Still, that won't be quick, and we have to feed ourselves out here and stop the horses from going to waste.' Cerialis knew the answers already, and was simply thinking aloud, so Ferox said nothing. Whichever way you looked at it, the odds were not on their side. 'He really is relying on you, my friend, to find us a way to win.' The prefect glanced back. 'I guess I am too.' His head went back and he roared with laughter. 'Perhaps we should have got our wives locked up in there! You're so good at rescuing ladies!'

'I'm glad they're thousands of miles away,' Ferox said.

'Aye, so am I. And I am keeping you from your duties. Let's make a start. We can worry about how it will all work when we have spare time, if we get any spare time. Your men won't labour, so I'll keep them busier than they've ever been with other duties... Chin up, Ferox, a wise centurion once told a young prefect in his first command that it isn't up to soldiers to decide whether something is a good idea or not – their job is simply to do it well. Isn't that right?'

'Something like that, sir.'

'Then let's get on with it. Send half your men to reinforce the screen to the north and you take the rest on a ride to the south. I don't think anything is happening down there, but let us not assume anything. Off you go.'

'My lord.'

XIII

Outside Nicopolis
Seventeenth day before the Kalends of May
Second day of the siege

THE ROMANS FORMED up as the sun rose. Ferox and most of his Brigantes had marched in the night to the main camp. Their horses stayed with Cerialis and his men in the other camp, although they would be released to graze during the morning. They were tired, having been ridden all of the previous day, and it was good that they were to get some rest, but that was not why Ferox had suggested that his men serve on foot. The Brigantes moaned, even though they had often served as infantry in the past. Originally the unit had consisted of both foot and horse, like the regular cohortes equitatae, until so many men had been lost that there were enough mounts for everyone. There had been no more than a handful of replacements sent to them over the years, and Ferox could not help wondering whether there would be any unit left at all after the siege.

'You got a plan?' Vindex asked, as they were issued with a couple of light javelins per man in the main camp.

'Only an idea,' Ferox told him. Half a dozen legionaries arrived, bringing three of the lightest of all the army's engines, so small that they could be held and shot by one man, while another carried the bolts and helped to spot targets. 'Something I learned from the Dacians back at Piroboridava.'

'Oh bugger. Remember they lost their war.'

'So did my folk, and I haven't noticed the Carvetii rising to take over the empire.'

'Biding our time, lad, just biding our time.'

The nearest Brigantes roared with laughter, and were soon chattering away as they moved out to take up their position, and still talking as they waited for things to start. Crispinus was planning to drive the enemy inside the city walls today. On the far side, Cerialis had instructions to do the same, that is if anyone came out to face him and the defenders did not simply rely on the strength of their position. If he got the opportunity, the prefect was to begin work on the first of the smaller camps.

On the western side, three legionary cohorts along with cohors II Galatarum formed the first line. Once again they were three ranks deep, backed by a fourth rank of archers, but today each century deployed separately with a wide gap on either side of its formation. Half of the centuries were held back thirty paces and positioned in the gap. As before, there were scorpiones in support and carroballistae were behind the formations, tasked with shooting over the men's heads.

'Is this not how the legions fought in the old days? Against Hannibal and King Philip?' Arrian asked Ferox. The tribune sounded excited. Crispinus had put him in charge of the four cohorts in the first line.

'Couldn't say, sir. Wasn't around then.'

The Brigantes were under Arrian's command, along with a couple of centuries from other auxiliary cohorts ordered to fight in open order. On the main track the first cohort of the Hispana was formed in a column, with turmae from ala III

Thracum on either side. For today, the task of screening any enemy horsemen was left to the cavalry of the cohorts. There were also a hundred men from each legionary cohort along with the sailors waiting behind everyone else and carrying tools and equipment instead of weapons. Next to them were Crispinus and the cavalry of the legion, as the true armed reserve.

Trumpets sounded the advance.

'Right, lads, here we go,' Arrian's voice had grown louder with his excitement. 'The line will advance. Listen for orders, keep silent, forward march!'

The first line stepped out, slightly ragged because it was harder to keep the dressing along such a large frontage, especially when they were acting as individual centuries, something rarely practised on this scale.

Trumpets and horns blasted from in front of Nicopolis, giving a harsher sound than the familiar calls of the legions.

'At least our hosts are expecting us,' Arrian whispered, leaning down in the saddle to talk to Ferox. 'Be such a shame if we had come on the wrong day.'

If anything there seemed to be more men outside the walls than on the days before, although as the rising sun was in their eyes it was hard to be sure. Ferox could see a dense block of men on the bridge itself and hundreds of individuals and little groups in front of the ditch. He wondered whether the Nicopolitans had thought to put ladders or ropes on the inner side to make it easier for these men to retreat if the Romans pressed them.

'Holy Isis, is that what I think it is?' Arrian was almost bouncing in the saddle in sheer exuberance. He had looped the reins around his arm and was shading his eyes with both hands. 'It is, it truly is! Look, Ferox, look!' The closest Brigantes were grinning at the sight of an officer acting like an excited little boy. 'Do you see, Ferox, do you see? It's a phalanx, as I live and breathe, a real phalanx!' The defenders on the bridge carried immensely long spears. Ferox guessed that they were almost twenty foot long.

'Sarissae! Ferox, can you see them? What a thing this is!'

'All well, tribune?' In his sheer joy Arrian had not noticed Crispinus trotting up or Ferox's expressions of warning. 'You seem happy?'

'I am, my lord, I really am. To see such a thing. A Macedonian phalanx! Alexander conquered the world with men like that.' More and more heads were turning, even from the rear ranks of the closest centuries. The optiones stationed behind each formation barked at men to face front.

'As I recall, the legions then chopped those same phalanxes into bloody ruin.' Crispinus was making use of his orator's training to make his words carry. 'Just as we shall today.'

'Of course, of course, my lord, no doubt about it – but it is a wonder,' Arrian added wistfully. 'Still, give the order and we can sweep them away. Should not have any trouble until we reach the ditch.'

'Perhaps, but that is not our aim for the moment. Remember, the more we kill or take on these plains, then the fewer left to fight from those walls. So there is no sense in rushing things.'

'Of course, my lord. But it is so tempting. They don't look much like a proper army.'

Crispinus leaned over theatrically, but made sure that his whisper carried. 'Don't let these Britons corrupt you. There is more to battle than getting drunk and then charging.'

Vindex stood by Ferox and gave one of his terrifying grins. 'Now that's the way to fight a battle! Saves everyone time.'

'Barbarians!' Crispinus told Arrian. 'Still, I am glad they are on our side today!' Once again the words carried well.

An arrow, arching high into the air, dropped past the head of the legatus' horse.

'Halt here,' Crispinus told Arrian. 'And then we can start.'

Arrian gestured to the cornicines standing behind him and, once they had sounded the three rising notes to warn of an order, he bawled out the command. 'Halt!' As soon as the signal had been given, men from the work party marked out the lines of three redoubts and the rest began to dig, piling up the spoil to make ramparts and raised platforms for the artillery.

A handful of enemy skirmishers were about two hundred paces away, including the bowman who sent another missile to land close to the Roman officers. More men waited a little further back.

'Wait for the order,' Arrian shouted to his own archers. 'Front ranks, testudo!' The legionaries in the first rank knelt behind their big rectangular shields. The ones behind held their own shields at an angle to cover themselves and the first rank's heads. It was not a formal testudo, but was a good protection for the legionaries and the archers behind. 'Wonder if they'll think we're frightened?' Arrian asked cheerily.

'That's the idea, tribune,' Crispinus told him. 'And Ferox, time for you to earn your pay.'

'Technically, my lord, I'm still under arrest so not receiving any pay.'

'Good, I hate to see the res publica waste its money. Now get on with it.'

'Sir.'

'And remember, captives if you can, corpses if you can't.'

'Vindex frowned. 'Is that what Romans call poetry?' he asked in the language of the tribes. 'Don't think much of it.'

'Then compose your own,' Bran suggested. 'There must be plenty of words that rhyme with tits.'

'Brigantes!' Ferox shouted. 'Follow me!' He jogged forward, weaving through a gap in the second and then the first line. There was no sense going too fast as this was likely to be a long day as well as a hot one. He had wondered whether to order his men to dispense with armour, before deciding against it. Bran and a few other younger ones had laid aside cuirasses and would rely on just shield and helmet. Ferox suspected that the rest felt that a true warrior fought with the best available weapons and armour. They were also nervous of the enemy's arrows, not that any of them would admit it.

Bran ran to the left and Vindex to the right, taking the warriors assigned to them, all of them shaking out into a loose swarm. Behind Ferox, half a dozen warriors formed a line of shields to protect the legionaries with the light ballistae until the time was right. Shouts came from the enemy ahead, and a few dozen advanced a little way towards the Brigantes. An arrow flicked the crest of Ferox's helmet.

'I think you've upset them!' Vindex shouted at him.

'Then let's really upset them.'

'I'd rather keep my trousers on!' Vindex yelled. Ferox ignored him and jogged forward on his own. An arrow came, straighter now as he was getting closer to the bowman, barely one hundred paces, and he caught it on his oval shield, one of the light ones usually issued to cavalry. The head thunked against the board before dropping away, lacking the power to break through even the fairly thin layers of wood. Ferox could hear Vindex's rather flat-footed run and though he could not hear Bran knew that the lad was also going forward on his other side. He kept his eyes to the front, watching the bowman as the man fumbled his next arrow. This was no warrior or soldier, but a townsman or farmer having a go with a light and rarely used bow. A couple of others were coming forward past the man, each carrying a bundle of javelins and a small round buckler. Another arrow flicked past him.

Ferox stopped. He guessed the two javelinmen were still sixty paces away, and just then one of them pulled his arm back and sent a shaft humming through the air. The aim was good, but the distance too long and it hit the earth and skidded towards him harmlessly.

'Come on, you mongrels!' Vindex screamed in Latin at the enemy. 'Let's see what you can do!'

'I am Bran, brother of the sword and servant of the Mother.' On the other side the younger warrior spoke his challenge in the language of the tribes. 'I stand here. Come and fight me with honour or flee!'

Ferox contented himself with stepping to one side and spitting on the javelin. The second man ran closer and threw with more strength, the point glinting as it came towards him. He raised his shield and felt the hard thump as the missile struck. Hefting one of his own javelins, he ran a few paces forward and threw. The javelinman timed it well, jumping to the side so that it passed.

Vindex whistled in derision. 'You're getting old, granddad!' he shouted. 'Oh shit!' The exclamation was prompted as he barely caught another light spear on his own shield. 'Now that's unfriendly!' He sprinted forward and flung one of his own back, aiming at the bowman, who had edged forward, but now ran away, going straight instead of dodging. The man flung himself into the dirt a moment after the javelin fell short. Vindex roared with laughter.

'Does any dare fight with me?' Bran had gone further forward than anyone else and then thrust one javelin point down into the earth. He spread his arms wide, lifting the other javelin and his shield high in the air. If the enemy could not understand the words then there could be no mistaking the gesture. Ferox wondered whether Arrian was saying something about the *Iliad* sprung to life before their eyes. For a short while this was war the old way, the way of the tribes throughout much of the world. More of the enemy were daring to come closer. An arrow came from the side, and he had to jerk the shield to his right to block it. It took a moment to spot the archer, a fellow in a pale yellow tunic and wearing an old-fashioned helmet shaped like a Phrygian cap. He had stuck a row of arrows into the ground and was reaching for another. Beside the bowman was another man holding a javelin in one hand and in the other a big round shield of the old Greek type, the ones you saw on monuments. He was sheltering the archer behind him, and if Arrian had spotted this then the tribune ought to be in ecstasy. Ferox tried to force such thoughts from his head and sprinted towards them. His remaining spear was in his hand and he held it up ready. The man with the round hoplon shield stepped away to let the archer shoot, and the arrow slammed into Ferox's shield, the tip bursting through the back. Then the man spun as a javelin came at the archer and he just managed to deflect it as Vindex cursed. Ferox flung his own and, before the man could heft his shield round to face the new threat or dodge, the point struck him in the face, driving through his cheek.

Ferox saw or sensed movement to his left, and spun the shield, catching a javelin which crunched into the dome-like boss, denting it, and making his hand numb where it held the grip. His right hand grabbed the handle of his sword and the long, beautifully balanced gladius slid free. He was shouting, yelling at the archer and two more men who had appeared around him, and he heard Vindex's bellow as well. The bowman fumbled as he tried to nock the next arrow, and should have run, but these were not experienced men. One of the javelinmen came at him, jabbing it as if it was a spear, and Ferox pushed it aside with his shield, stamped forward and thrust, so that the long, triangular tip of his gladius went past his opponent's buckler and into his throat. Blood seeped out, then turned into a fountain as Ferox twisted the blade and dragged it free. The javelinman dropped to his knees, trying desperately to stem the flow with his hands, as Ferox went past, and only now did the archer drop the arrow and turn to run. The other skirmisher shrieked as Vindex cut under the man's little shield and almost carved right through his thigh. Ferox caught up with the archer and slashed down from behind at the man's neck. The Nicopolitan staggered, Ferox struck again and the man was down. A javelin came at him from the side, and he only just deflected it at the last instant by bringing up the rim of his shield. The rest of the enemy had drawn back a little, but he could see one haranguing a knot of six or seven and knew that they would soon charge.

'Back!' he shouted to Vindex, who had finished off the man he had wounded. Over on the left a man had come forward to meet Bran's challenge and now his headless corpse lay stretched in the dust as the young warrior waved his trophy at the enemy.

'What did himself say about prisoners?' Vindex asked, taking in the four dead enemies.

'Let him take 'em himself. Now get back.' The one who had been yelling at the others had only persuaded them to come forward half a dozen paces before they hesitated and threw a couple of javelins at far too long a range. The leader, or would-be leader, decided to set an example and with a shout came running forward. He was young, with a wispy beard just visible between the cheek pieces of his bronze helmet, and with a well-polished scale cuirass. He had an oval shield and a curved sword. 'Go!' Ferox yelled to Vindex and walked towards the boy.

'You don't have to do this, lad!' he called in Greek, which prompted only a hissed obscenity in reply. Ferox stopped, shook his shield without managing to make the arrow fall out and braced himself. The lad kept on charging, trying to shout, although his voice cracked and it came out as more of a screech. Ferox waited, judging the moment and then stepped to the side an instant before the youngster tried to slam his shield forward and knock over the centurion. The boy kept going and Ferox thrust his foot out to send him sprawling, letting go of both shield and sword.

Ferox watched to see whether anyone else was following, but no one was close. An arrow whipped through the air and he parried it with his shield. The boy was pushing himself up, so Ferox stepped up beside him and raised his sword, then slammed down with the globe-shaped wooden weight beneath the handle. There was clang as it struck the bronze helmet, and the young warrior dropped flat on his face. Keeping an eye out for threats, Ferox wiped his blade on his trousers and thrust it back into the scabbard. He grabbed the boy's shoulder, felt dead weight when he started to lift him, and began to drag him back. Vindex appeared and took the lad's other arm.

'Captive,' Ferox said to him.

'Himself will be pleased.'

The morning wore on, and over time more and more of the defenders ventured across the ditch to confront the Romans. Some of the ones already there drifted back because they were tired or thirsty or had run out of missiles. Crispinus did not send more men to reinforce the Brigantes and the auxiliaries ordered to skirmish, but even so, they all got the chance to drop back a little, nearer the formed centuriae and rest. Slaves carried skins of water to relieve parched throats. Hundreds, perhaps thousands of javelins were thrown and arrows shot. Many of the light spears were flung more than once, back and forth between the two sides. There were a few more duels or little combats among the enthusiasts. Having set an example, Ferox was not inclined to push his luck any further, and Vindex was the same. Bran issued several more challenges, without finding any enemies willing to meet him. Later he dashed forward and flung a spear that spitted an enemy skirmisher who was distracted by another threat. That was one of the few men to die. More were injured and carried back by their comrades to safety. The Romans lost no dead and fewer injured than the enemy, because they had armour, apart from a few of the Brigantes who had laid it aside. More auxiliaries were hit than Brigantes, and Ferox felt that the regulars moved more clumsily than his men and were less skilled at watching out for each other.

Crispinus all the while restrained his archers and artillery from shooting, wanting to lure as many of the enemy forward as he could. A little before noon, he decided that the time was right, and rode up to Arrian.

'If you would be so good, tribune.'

'My lord.' Arrian, who as Ferox had predicted had spent much of the time waxing lyrical over the similarity to the *Iliad*, licked his lips and gestured to the cornicines. 'Sound the recall!'

'That's us,' Ferox croaked to Vindex. 'Time to go back. Come on, lads, back we go!'

'Such a fuss,' Vindex muttered. 'Wish we had just got drunk and charged.'

Auxiliaries and Brigantes jogged stiffly back through the

gaps in the line. A cheer went up from the Nicopolitans. Behind the cloud of skirmishers there were several dense blocks of fifty or so men.

The cornu horns sounded the three notes again. 'Prepare to advance!' Arrian called, his voice cracking. He coughed and spat. 'Archers, three shots if you please.' The men in the fourth rank flexed their arms, then lifted their bows and reached for an arrow. 'In your own time!' The men nocked. 'Loose!' Almost all the archers released at the same moment, so that hundreds of arrows flew into the air at the same time with a sound like a strong wind whipping through a field of wheat. The cheering stuttered, men looking up. Already the second arrows were following the first as men shot at their own pace. Most had sent the third before the first volley struck. It was not aimed, other than to guess range, but some of the skirmishers panicked and ran in any direction. Dodging one missile at a time was easy for an alert, moderately agile man, as long as he kept his head. The cloud of arrows was a shock, and some found a mark. Arrian saw a man who happened to raise his empty right hand and took an arrow through the palm, then gaped at it, more baffled than anything else, until another shot drove into his eye. Perhaps half a dozen fell, with more nicked and able to hobble away.

'Forward!' Arrian shouted. A good few of the legionaries in the front rank had sat down during the long wait and were eager to do something.

'Stay in line!' a centurion shouted. 'Keep formation!' The advance was a little ragged after spending so long as observers. 'Straighten the ranks! Watch your dressing there!'

Stunned by the arrows, the Nicopolitans were silent, each man wondering what to do. An arrow went through the centurion's mouth just as he opened it to shout again. He made a choking sound, his shield clattered as it fell and he sank to his knees. The line wobbled and bent as men stepped around him.

'Leave him! The optio yelled, barging his way through to the front rank.

Suddenly, sooner than Crispinus would have liked, trumpets sounded and turmae of ala III Thracum raced around the flanks of the line, eager to ride down the scattered and wavering enemy. Ferox saw one tall decurion riding a big black horse leading the men to the left.

The Nicopolitans broke, dashing back to the ditch because on the bridge the pikemen who had been resting for so long, once again took formation and lowered their sarissae.

'Come on!' a legionary yelled and ran ahead of the men on either side. They hesitated for only a moment before surging after him and then the entire centuria was haring after the fleeing enemy. The rest of the line followed, leaving some of the archers and all the scorpiones behind. Formations fell apart as one crowd chased another looser crowd.

'Form up, lads!' Ferox shouted at his tired Brigantes. Most obeyed, although a few had gone off with the soldiers. Others were back looking for food or helping the wounded. He reckoned he had some forty still with him. 'You too, lads,' he said to the legionaries with the hand-held ballistae. 'All of you, come with me.'

Deciding that there was nothing else for it, Crispinus rode up to the first cohort. 'Sweep those fellows off the bridge for me!' he told the centurion at the head of the column. Caecilius was not in command, for he was too valuable to risk.

'Sir!' The man saluted and gave a wicked grin. 'At the double!' he shouted and led his men in a jog down the road, armour clinking in time as they went.

Romans were falling, as archers on the far side of the ditch lobbed missiles high, hoping to clear their own fugitives. Some of the legionaries were too excited to be careful and dropped, hit in the face or beneath the knees where the shield did not reach. Even more felt arrows clang against their helmets or the reinforced armour on their shoulders.

Ferox kept his men together as he crossed the trackway, sprinting because the head of the first cohort was bearing down on them. He wanted to get past them and over to the left side of the bridge because most of his men had fallen back in that direction.

'Out the way!' the centurion leading the column screamed at them.

The last of the Brigantes was across as the elite of the legion, the tallest men and many of the most experienced, pounded along the track. On the bridge, the phalanx stood ready, pikes of the first five ranks lowered and braced in both hands, and the ones behind holding the shafts at an angle.

'This way!' Ferox shouted, for the noise had redoubled, the pursuing Romans still cheering, but shouts and horn blasts meeting them from the defenders on the far side of the ditch. He ran, taking his men to the bank twenty paces or so from the bridge. An arrow whisked through the air and buried itself in the chest of one of the young warriors who had not worn his cuirass. 'Shields! Form a line here!' The others clustered either side of him, forming a wall of shields. Another man yelped as an arrow grazed his leg. Then one was flung bodily backwards as a bolt from an engine drove through shield, mail shirt and flesh, sending him flying and knocking two others off their feet.

'Shit!' Vindex yelled.

'Down there!' Ferox pointed into the ditch and half ran, half jumped down the slope. This was one of the patches where travellers too impatient to wait for the bridge to be clear had worn down a rough track. 'Come on!' There were other Romans dotted along the ditch, men whose enthusiasm had carried them this far. The last of the defenders were scrambling up the far side, either using one of the paths or rope ladders put there for this purpose.

'That way!' Ferox swept his arm across the far side of the ditch.

Vindex nodded. 'With me! Shields.' The danger was that the enemy would line the bank and shoot them down where they stood.

'Engines, where are you?' Ferox searched around, then saw the first of the legionaries with the light ballista slipping and sliding down to join them. Behind came another clutching a sack filled with bolts. Ferox looked up at the bridge to check the angle. This would do.

On the track the first cohort was fifty paces from the phalanx, coming on steadily, hobnailed boots crunching on the ground and armour rattling and bumping.

'Come on, boys!' the centurion called, then his head jerked back as a bolt drove through his iron helmet with such force that the point came out of the back. He fell, tripping a man in the front rank.

'On, lads, on!' The cohort's five signifers were jogging alongside the column, for it was not their job to lead in the last moments of the charge. Today, the aquila remained in camp, but the signa were important, and the men who carried them carefully chosen. 'Go on!'

Another centurion ran to catch up with the men in the lead. 'Steady the First! Keep going!'

They were forty paces away. A stone came throbbing through the air, pale white and big as an orange. It came from the left, from a slit in one of the towers, and knocked the crests from the helmets of half a dozen men in the column.

'Pila!' the centurion shouted. Legionaries in the first rank raised their heavy javelins ready to throw. The formation was a little ragged as they had doubled down the track, and a man in the second rank cursed as the butt of a pilum knocked his shoulder.

Another stone-throwing engine shot, this time from a tower on the other side. The missile hit the ground, just short, before bouncing up to take the leg off a signifer.

'Wait for the order!' the centurion, the *princeps posterior* of the cohort, was running just beside the front rank now. They were thirty paces away. Arrows flew from the far side and the walls, pattering against shields. No one fell.

Down in the ditch Ferox ducked to dodge an arrow that had come over the line of shields held up by Vindex and his men. 'Come on, quickly now.' He pointed up at the bridge. The side wall hid the pikemen from the waist down, but their chests, shoulders and heads were exposed. Ferox had gone to the left, because that meant that he and his men would be on the right of the phalanx, the unshielded side. 'You!' He tapped one of the legionaries on the shoulder. The man's face was pale and one hand stroked the side of his machine. 'Kill the man in the front rank. You, the one behind and you, start at the back. Then work your way along. Got it?' They nodded and one grinned.

As the first cohort closed, the leading ranks were shielded from most missiles by the phalanx. The stone throwers switched their aim, and one shot cut a swathe through the middle of the formation, smashing the heads of seven men in turn. Those around were sprayed with blood, brains and fragments of helmet and bone. One bled to death after the ragged edge of a torn-off cheek piece slashed into his neck.

'Front rank!' the centurion called. The six men lobbed their pila, arcing them up because the range was still fairly long. There was a rattling as most hit the shafts of the pikes held up by the men in the rear of the phalanx. One slipped through and struck the forehead of a pikeman, just below the brim of his helmet. He staggered, then fell forward, and the man behind stepped onto his body to take his place.

'Second rank!' Six more pila came at the phalanx. One hit a pikeman in the chest, another punched through a shield and miraculously did not strike the man's arm or body, and simply stuck there, weighing the shield down. The others bounced off sarissa shafts, apart from one that did not even land on the bridge.

'No more! Keep going, keep going,' the princeps posterior screamed at his men. There was always a tendency to slow, even stop when each rank threw its pila in turn and he did not want to lose momentum. 'Just kill the bastards!' he bellowed and then just shouted, urging them all on.

The first cohort obeyed, running forward towards the bridge and the serried pike-heads. They stopped just before they would drive themselves onto the points, for the phalanx had not moved. Some of the men behind did not see and barged into the ones in front. A legionary in the front rank screamed as he was driven forward and the sarissa punched through his shield and armour. On the flank, the centurion slashed with his gladius just behind the head of one of the pikes, throwing off a big splinter, then parried with his shield as the pikeman tried to jab at him.

At that moment the pikeman on the right of the front rank shook as a bolt struck the side of his helmet. It dented the bronze, without penetrating, and made the man sway. The one standing behind him turned to see and another bolt sprouted from his right eye.

'That's it!' Ferox said encouragingly, as the legionaries cranked their weapons.

'Third rank, pila!' the princeps posterior yelled, but the head of the column was too tightly packed for anyone to have room to raise and throw a pilum. Other men were doing their best to chop at the shafts of the enemy's pikes. One slashed right through, breaking off the head, then slammed his shield to push the shaft aside and step forward. The head of a sarissa from the second rank thrust at him and he only just managed to parry.

Ferox's men shot for the second time, but only one struck home, killing a man at the rear of the phalanx. 'Take your time, boys,' he said. 'Don't waste them.' The one hit on the helmet suddenly dropped his pike, swayed, and fell over the side of the bridge to land with a thump on the floor of the ditch. He did not move.

The nervous legionary chuckled, then gasped as an arrow went through one of the plates of his cuirass.

'You shoot, I'll load,' Ferox said to the man's comrade, who was staring wide eyed as the wounded man clutched at the shaft of the arrow. 'Now!'

'Sir!' The soldier passed him the bag and picked up the fallen ballista and began to crank back the arms. Ferox felt for a bolt. Another arrow flicked past far too close for comfort and then another, until the air was filled by a volley of missiles coming from the Roman side of the ditch.

'Thank Taranis,' Vindex said.

Ferox glanced up and saw a line of auxiliary archers. Behind them Arrian, still on horseback, gave him a thumbs up. He hoped the tribune would not regret making himself such a tempting target.

One of the hand-held engines cracked like a whip as it shot. The sound was higher pitched than the bigger engines, but still spoke of formidable power. Another pikeman fell, then another and a third as the man he was loading for shot. Arrows slammed into them as Arrian must have ordered some of his men to switch target.

The phalanx broke. Men at the front, helpless against the shots coming from the side, dropped their sarissae and turned, trying to run. The men at the back hesitated, unsure, and did not begin to flee for a long moment.

'Kill the bastards!' the princeps posterior yelled at his men and led them on, bounding over the mass of fallen pikes to drive his gladius into the back of a man with feathers on either side of his helmet.

'Kill them!' There was an animal quality about the roar as the men of the first cohort surged forward. Confused, packed together on the bridge, the pikemen were helpless. Some men thrust, but most cut and slashed, the drill book forgotten as they hacked, fear and anger blending into rage. The sound was like a crowd of butchers chopping meat, and men were covered with blood.

'Prisoners!' Arrian shouted at them. 'We want prisoners!'

Only the legionaries at the rear of the column listened, and they could do nothing.

'Bastards! Bastards!' a legionary grunted each time he cut.

'We want prisoners!' Crispinus had ridden up.

'Bastards!' Another pikeman fell, this one with his neck almost cut through. Men slipped in pools of blood and tripped over the corpses or moaning wounded. Half the phalanx died before the press relaxed and the rest fled. Shooting from the walls redoubled. A stone, twice as large as the others, skimmed across the bridge, killing or maiming a dozen Romans.

'We're going!' Ferox called to Vindex.

'Bout time.'

'Back, lads, that way!' Ferox pointed to the path they had followed down. Holding the sack with one hand, he scooped up his shield to cover them. Vindex came to stand on one side and Bran on the other.

'Shit!' Vindex spat out the word as an arrowhead burst through the back of his shield before stopping. He glanced past the edge to stare up at the walls. 'Let's go home!'

'Wish we could,' Bran said.

A stone, one thrown by hand or sling, banged on the front of Ferox's shield.

'You can go, if you like,' Ferox told Bran.

'No I can't. Not until you two go.'

'We really are humped, aren't we?' Vindex said.

Ferox peered back over his shoulder. His men were all up. 'Slowly back,' he said. They took one step, then another. Dirt flicked up onto Ferox's foot as another stone just missed. 'Right, run for it!' All three men turned and fled, and happily their archers shot another volley at that moment, which helped them all scramble up the bank and reach safety.

One-eyed Brennus was waiting for them. 'Glad that's over,' he said.

'You reckon?' Vindex said and strode off. 'I need a drink,' he called back over his shoulder.

XIV

Outside Nicopolis
Fifteenth day before the Kalends of May
The fourth day of the siege

'WE COULD CRUCIFY the little bugger,' Caecilius suggested, 'and the rest of them. Make a big show of it, setting up the posts in plain view and letting them watch. That's not nice for anyone, especially the family and friends.' His face was impassive, the tone the same as when he spoke of quantities of timber and how much a hundred men could be expected to build or dig in an hour. There was a hint of bitterness, but that was nothing unusual. The primus pilus always sounded more than a little sour, and gave the impression of absolute belief in his superiority over all those around him. On the whole, men of his rank had fairly good reason to think that way, and this was accepted as how the army was.

An hour after dawn, Arrian had once again asked to negotiate, and this time had taken along the young man Ferox had captured. His name was Heraclides, and he claimed that his father was a councillor and one of the leading and most popular men in the city.

'He did his best,' Arrian told the rest of the consilium. 'Told them of our strength and how we really did not want to fight

217

them at all, but wished friendship. He was more eloquent than I expected.'

'Did not work though, did it?' Caecilius spoke as if pointing out an error in a calculation.

'Well, he does admit that he has three brothers, all older than he is. But...' Arrian searched around the room for support. 'But that only makes his loss less fatal. Even the father might not sacrifice his city for a younger son, that's assuming that he has the influence to sway the rest.' The tribune felt that logic was the best way to counter the suggestion.

'I remember reading of Corbulo's campaigns.' Rufus' confidence continued to blossom, and even Caecilius admitted that the young centurion was good at planning and calculation. 'They came to a city and had to fight to get close, just like us. He ordered the heads cut off the enemy dead and shot them over the walls. One came through the roof at a meeting of the elders and turned out to be one of their sons. They surrendered straightaway.'

Arrian tried to lighten the mood. 'Well, my dear fellow, if you can tell us precisely where the council of Nicopolis meets, the time of their meeting, and calculate the angle and force needed to strike such a target with precision... And frankly if you know all that, I would have to wonder whether you are a spy for the other side!'

Rufus stared down at his lap, blushing, but laughed with the others, and even Caecilius smiled.

'Save your bright ideas for the real work, lad,' he said with some fondness.

'And we can all save our more savage instincts for the moment,' Crispinus declared, bringing the meeting back to order. 'I do not believe executions – or the adoption of body parts as missiles'—there was more laughter—'to be useful at present. There is rarely utility in savagery for the mere sake of it, and as well as creating fear you can stiffen their resolve. I want all our prisoners treated well. And let's make sure they are visible. Show the citizens that we can be very kind when we choose, even to people who have raised their hands against us. Later, then we shall see, but for the moment that is the message. We wish to be friends and allies, not enemies, and fight only because we have no other choice.' Something made him search for Ferox's face, expecting to find him offensively expressionless somewhere near the back. Then the legatus remembered that he had sent the Brigantes off on a special task. They would not return for a few days. Oddly enough, he was disappointed not to be annoyed by the man. Crispinus reached for his cup and drank. He liked his evening consilium to be a relaxed affair, feeling that more was done that way. The temperature would soon drop overnight, but in here, one of the few stone-walled rooms with a tent as roof, it was still stuffy because they needed plenty of lamps to see the maps, plans and tables in front of them. Rufus had even brought some models to show what they were constructing.

'In addition, I want you to keep reminding your men that any citizens or others who come from the city unarmed and in peace are to be allowed through our lines. They may stay with us, if they wish – we can set up tents by the sutlers' camp – or go on their way.'

Caecilius sucked in through his teeth. 'That's a fine judgement for a sentry to make on a dark night, sir. You see shapes out there and the instinct is to shoot.'

'I understand and know the risks, primus. But this is important. These people are not rebels, and are enemies only because they do not yet have the sense to accept us as allies. I want them to come out and show the rest that they are safer out here than behind those walls. They need to trust us. My hope is that once they realise that, then more and more will come, especially the men of wealth and their families. So they must not be killed, molested or even robbed. We need them. Every one of them who leaves weakens the resolve of those inside. That may make the rest see sense, and even if it does not and we storm the place, then at least we have some well-disposed men to take over the reins of government in the aftermath. We need to make all ranks understand that.' The legatus lifted his cup and drank some more of the wine, grimacing because it had not travelled well.

'All in all we have made a good start, but it is only a start,' Crispinus announced and managed to hold back a cough, for coughing too often made his cheek start twitching. Odd how taking a drink when thirsty made him want to cough. 'As the primus reminds us – and will no doubt continue to remind us...'

'No doubt whatsoever, sir,' Caecilius chipped in and there was more laughter. 'More haste, less speed.'

'As you say, and if it was good enough for the divine Augustus, then who are we to argue. We cannot rush and let ourselves make mistakes. Everything must be done with care, and everything must be done properly. That is the only way in the long run, and sieges tend to be about the long run. As importantly, it sends a message. The other thing the good citizens of Nicopolis need to understand is that we are determined to come into their city. If they will not admit us as friends then we shall force our way in as enemies. So we show our utter determination. One way or another, we are coming.' Crispinus tried to fight down the thought that anything one said about a siege and assault had a sexual air about it. The idea grew, spreading like leaven through bread, until he was struggling for words. It worried him, less because of the thing itself, than the fear that he no longer found it easy to concentrate.

'One way or another, we are coming,' he repeated, making himself go on. There was no hint that anyone else found this remotely amusing. 'We must show them that not only are we determined, but that we are fully capable of breaching'—just stopped himself from saying penetrating—'their walls. Once they realise that this will happen whatever they do, then they may be willing to talk.

'Think about it and try to imagine their feelings. Each morning our works come closer, our ramps will grow higher.' He tapped his finger hard on the table. 'The next morning closer again,' another tap, 'and the next still closer,' he tapped again. 'On and on, day after day. They must know that there is no escape. They may just as well surrender their virtue to us first as last.' There were puzzled frowns around the table. Crispinus took another drink and stood so that it would be easier to gesture at the plan.

'We have the two main and the three small forts – so Cerialis is no longer cut off from my signals and free to wage his own war!'

'It is a burden, I'll not deny,' the prefect told them.

'We have redoubts and other positions facing the main gateways. And soon the little gates in the city walls?'

'Tomorrow, sir,' Caecilius confirmed. 'And their ditch is a help wherever it runs. Hard for them to attack us across that and even harder to escape if we repulse them.' In the last two days, few defenders had come outside the walls to fight, and only the archers among them posed much of a threat. A bigger danger was the artillery in the towers and inside the walls, so the Romans built ramparts and redoubts to give cover to men and their own ballistae. Once one was built and secure, they could start on another a bit closer to the enemy. 'The first musculi were brought forward this morning, and another dozen will be ready tomorrow. Eight of those are the ones in the prefect's camp.'

'Little mice?' Arrian was frowning, then realised he had spoken his thought out loud. Musculi were sheds, the frames mounted on wheels and covered with hides as protection. They allowed soldiers to get closer to the enemy in spite of missiles so that they could work. 'Sorry,' the tribune said, 'I'm a mere Greek, and I'd never thought about it before. Why are they called that?'

'Because they creep up on the enemy,' Rufus suggested. 'You know the way women are frightened mice will run up their legs.'

'To be honest, no,' Cerialis said.

Crispinus raised his hand as a gesture for the others to be silent. 'Such matters are surely of interest, but let us save them for another day. We have done a lot, and must keep up a steady pace. You are content with the allocation of work, primus?'

'Yes,' Caecilius grunted and nudged Rufus.

'Each cohort divided into four teams,' the young centurion explained. 'Deducting men assigned to the engines, to guard duty, administration and other tasks, that gives some sixty to seventy in each team. Each will alternate between a day on outpost duty, a day with the work parties, a day in reserve and another day half as work parties and half standing guard during the night. Cavalry get a day on outposts, a day in reserve, a day with the horses, and a day as camp guards. None of that includes the cohortes equitatae, who will mainly be concerned with foraging and escorting the supply columns to the river and back. Ideally it's two days there, two days back, and a column sets out every fourth day.'

'That sounds admirable,' Crispinus told them. 'I leave it to you, primus, to assign each group with its task. So, show me the main projects.'

Caecilius stood up. 'By your leave, sir.' He had a wooden ruler of the sort engineers used, and pointed at the map. 'The gates on both sides are death traps. The gates themselves can be burned or smashed, but the towers and walls around them are the strongest parts of the defences, and it would take years to knock them down. If we smash the gates any assaulting party is trapped in a courtyard, with no way out and no real way of getting a battering ram against the inner gate, so they die where they stand.'

'So we don't go that way,' Crispinus said.

'No, sir, we don't. These walls are sandstone. Not the strongest. It's harder than mud brick, but crumbles more easily if you can prise it apart. If you look at this plan, you can see that they have towers at regular intervals along the wall.' The officers rose, even though they had all seen the real defences plenty of times. 'Those towers stick out in front of the walls – project is the fancy term technical engineers like Rufus here use.' Caecilius tussled his colleague's hair as if he was a small boy. 'Whatever you call them it means that they can shoot sideways along the line of the wall. So to make their life as hard as possible, we go for the corners. Here in the north west.' He pointed with the ruler. 'And here in the south east, over on the prefect's side. There isn't a real corner, but we go as close as we dare to the tower where the walls curve off on the far side.

'That means we fill in the ditch here and here.' Caecilius indicated the spots. 'Over the top goes a ramp, twenty paces wide, because we'll need that width to carry an assault tower that will be higher than the top of their towers by a good fifteen feet. Each tower has a ram, at a height to strike the curtain wall just halfway up. Once we get that far, the musculi can scamper towards the lady's legs, and will see if men with crowbars cannot start to pull some blocks out!'

'She'll scream, I warn you,' Cerialis said. He was standing, peering closely at the attack planned from his side of the city.

Crispinus was doing some very quick calculations in his head about how much earth would need to be shifted. He did not care much for the answers. 'So these are the priority?'

'Yes, but we can run them alongside each other. No hurry with the towers themselves. That's more skilled work, but does not need to be finished until the ramps are ready. The slog will be filling in the ditch and making the ramps. Not so skilled, but hard, hard labour. It will also take a lot of timber, although doesn't have to be prime stuff. There's not a lot of good woodland around here, but before we're done there will be none.'

'Will we have to bring more from across the Euphrates?' Crispinus had seen few trees of any real size within ten miles of the city. There were pines on some of the slopes further back, but he wished he had paid more attention. There was always so much to do and so much to consider. The fear grew that he was no longer capable of understanding and doing everything.

'Perhaps. I hope not, my lord, but I don't know. Depends a lot on how active the lads inside are. The ditch holds them back, but at some point they'll find a way to hit us, maybe at night when it's easier to sneak across and get back. Don't think they'll just sit and watch us as we work.'

'Their engines are accurate, and some are powerful,' Rufus pointed out.

'You're right, lad, but what I fear – what any besieger really fears – are men who come out to burn what we make and steal our tools.' There were bemused frowns, and a few sniggers. 'Think about it, noble lords'—Crispinus could not help thinking of Ferox's knack of injecting so much scorn into his courtesy—'wood is the hardest thing to replace apart from saws, spades and axes. We lose those and how do we keep working, no matter how keen we might be?'

'Battles are won with the *dolabra*,' Crispinus said. 'So said our friend Corbulo, at least.'

'And he knew a thing or two, sir. We have to be on our guard all the time, and that's hard, just plain hard because as the days pass you start thinking only about getting the work done and forget the murderous buggers – beg your pardons, sirs – that are waiting, watching our every move, and ready to pounce. I know a few of you have seen a little siege work, haven't you?' A couple of the centurions and one tribune nodded. 'Well it's like a marriage. You and the defenders get to know each other better than you know anyone else in the world. The one who is better at guessing what the other one is about to do, and can sense their weakness and how to exploit it, is the one who is still standing at the end.'

'Are you married, noble Caecilius?' Cerialis asked.

'No.'

'That may be as well.'

Caecilius gave a rare grin. 'Yes, but for me or the lass?'

'I am not sure any man has claimed true victory in wedlock,' Crispinus told them, 'but again we drift into philosophy and I don't want to permit Arrian to share some of his cheerful thoughts. Save that for when we are inside. So these are the main projects for the moment – the main ways of getting through or over the walls. Will they be enough?'

Caecilius nodded approval. 'Once they're well under way, we'll see about a couple more mobile towers, without rams this time, but high enough to drop bridges onto the wall. They should not need such big ramps, and we can fill in the ditch later. Depends on having the spare timber to do it, though. And ladders of course, but those are to spread the defence when we launch a full assault, or to help climb a breach.'

'You judge twenty-one days sufficient for the towers and main ramps?' the legatus asked.

'No, my lord, I don't. If you remember I said that with fit and skilled soldiers we could do it in that time. Hispana doesn't have enough of those.' There were murmurs of dissent around the room, so Caecilius raised his voice. 'If we ignore the truth we won't get anywhere. I know I'm new to the legion and some of you are old hands, but there is no sense in pretending. There are a lot of young soldiers, and a fair few that are too old. A lot of them are sickly, and with the best will in the world and plenty of doses of a centurion's cane, they cannot do the work as fast as strong men. A blind man could see it. Things just take longer than they should.'

Crispinus rubbed his jaw because he felt that his cheek wanted to twitch. 'Then how long do you reckon?'

'I'll give you a better answer in a day or two when I can measure progress. Twenty-six days, maybe even thirty? We will do our best.'

'I am sure you will, primus, and I am sure we all will.' Crispinus propped his elbow against his chest so that he could cup his chin. 'Finally, there is the other project, which I am equally sure that I do not need to remind everyone must remain a secret.'

'They are starting tonight – and I'll go and take a look after we are dismissed. The redoubt should mask it from view, and if we are right the soil should be easy to dig.' Beside one of the small camps on the southern side, Caecilius proposed digging a mine to reach under the enemy's walls.

'Do they have enough men?'

'They need the right sort, rather than just numbers, my lord, but I think I have picked men who can do it. There are even a few former slaves among the sailors, who used to be miners. The problem will be timber.'

'Again.'

'Yes, my lord, again. There's just no way around it. After that we may have to watch where the earth goes.'

'The earth?' Arrian was once again puzzled.

'If you were up on those walls and saw mounds of fresh earth piling up, wouldn't you be suspicious?'

'I just might,' Arrian conceded. 'I suppose I just might.'

'On that admission, and if there is nothing else?' Crispinus stared around the room. 'Then you are dismissed. Those of you who do not have duties, I suggest you get as much rest as you can – and look forward to the day when we shall all feast up in their citadel, whether as conquerors or new allies. Goodnight to you all.'

Nicopolis
The sixth day of the siege

D OMITIUS KEPT TRACK *of time only through the meals.
In what seemed to be the morning, his food was
spilled or spat upon, and the guard hit him harder
and more often each day. He was sure one of his teeth was
loose, and suspected that the last kick had broken a rib. In the
evening, the Christian, whose name was Apollodorus, brought
him much better food as well as a kind word. His companion
in the cell no longer spoke, and did not seem to sleep either.
Whenever Domitius was awake, the hunched figure was there,
eyes gleaming faintly from the crack of light coming under the
door. Then one morning, two men came with the usual guard,
unlocked the prisoner's chain and led him away, shackles
clinking. The guard did not pay much attention to Domitius,
apart from a half-hearted kick.*

*Left alone, Domitius wondered for a while whether he would
miss the company, before deciding that he would not. He prayed
for a while, and found himself thinking of the family who had
taken him in. He prayed for Sara most of all, because he had
heard enough of sieges to know that women suffered the most
when soldiers broke through the walls and ran amok. It would
be cruel if he had rescued her from slavery and degradation
only for her to be raped and sold or even killed, and most likely
to see her family cut down. So Domitius prayed for her safety,
and it seemed natural to ask such a boon for one of God's*

chosen people. Passover must have come and gone while he was in prison. Would this new horror pass by his friends' house? He wondered whether old John was up on the walls doing his weak best to fight off the enemies of his youth, and found himself laughing when he thought of Simon, whose eyesight was so poor that if he threw a stone he was as likely to strike friend as foe.

Somewhere above, the sun trod its path across the sky. The legion – he wondered which legion and whether he knew anyone out there or whether it was even his own VI Ferrata, sent this way instead of to the north – would be toiling at the siege works. A deserter found in an enemy city could not look forward to much that was good, although perhaps it would help that the enemy had locked him up. Domitius wondered whether he could pretend to have been a spy all along, at least for long enough to slip away. For some reason he did not think his story would end here. It was not faith, and some said a true believer should welcome death since it meant a blessed life in the presence of the Lord. 'In my Father's house are many mansions.' The words kept going through his mind, although he could not remember whether he had read them or heard them.

Death was not to be feared. The army tried to convince its soldiers of that, and so did half the philosophers whether they sat in their great Schools in Athens or other cities, or were the wild-eyed, ragged-arsed vagrants hanging around market-places. Odd how everyone wanted you to stop being afraid. Domitius chuckled to himself in the darkness. Meant they knew that deep down everyone was afraid, whether of judgement or empty darkness. He chuckled again. Well, he was in the empty darkness now and it was not so bad.

Domitius was sure that he was not going to Heaven yet

and that somehow he would come through this. He could not understand why, but the feeling was growing stronger and stronger, and with it came worry, for he would loathe himself if he could not save Sara – the angel who had tended him back to life. It would also be nice to show old John that not all Romans were bad, and protect bumbling Simon from the worst of the world. The younger Simon had not seemed to like him too much, so he might have to save him out of spite. Hard to be indebted to someone you do not like. That would teach the bastard, he thought, the language of the barracks coming naturally to his mind.

That evening the guard did not bring food, but just a drink. 'Quickly, brother,' he whispered to Domitius, leaning close. 'Our prayers have been answered, but you must have a care. Do what they ask of you.'

Two men appeared through the door. Domitius thought that they were the same guards who had taken the other prisoner, although he could not be sure. One went to the wall and unhooked the chain. The other held a torch, the firelight dazzling.

He slapped the Roman hard on his cheek. 'Head up!' The other guard fiddled with the neck collar and unlocked it. After that he did the same with the shackles on Domitius' ankles.

'Get up!' The one with the torch slapped him again. Domitius stood, and felt his legs weak beneath him. His knees shook and there was a pain in his feet, and he slumped down.

The next blow knocked him over. 'Up!' The Christian guard grabbed his shoulders and helped haul him up. He squeezed the Roman's arm presumably in a gesture of reassurance. Domitius wondered what the believers in Nicopolis had been praying for on his behalf, but his belief that he would live through all of this was only going stronger. Then he wondered whether prisoners

about to be thrown to the lions had the same foolish thoughts.
This cannot possibly happen to me. He must have smiled, and
the guard noticed it in spite of his unkempt beard, for another
blow followed.

'Come with us.'

It was agony to walk, and he blinked to shield his eyes
from the torchlight, as he was half led, half dragged along the
corridor, up some stairs, around a corner and up some more
stairs and out into a courtyard. The sun was setting, the sky to
the west above the courtyard walls a blaze of red and orange, so
that even with his eyes shut he saw a great ball of light.

'Ah, there he is.' The voice sounded familiar, but he could not
quite place it. He swayed when the guards let go of his elbows,
only just managing to stay upright. Life was slowly returning
to his limbs. 'Look at the state of him?' the voice went on.
Domitius opened his eyes, and for a moment saw only a dark
shape before the ball of light in his eyes faded. The man wore a
conical helmet with cheek pieces, a long-sleeved mail shirt, and
had a sword at his belt. Behind him were two spearman, with
similar equipment and round shields.

'Get him cleaned up!' the leader barked and at last Domitius
realised that it was the younger Simon.

'Why not wait until the decision?' one of the guards asked.

Simon strolled across and then slapped the man so hard
across the face that he staggered. 'Do not dare to speak to me
like that!' His two spearman lowered their weapons.

'Apologies, my lord. Please forgive me.'

'I'll forgive you if you show yourself brave against armed
enemies and not helpless captives. Send for slaves. I want him
shaved, fed, and cleaned up. Only then will he be fit to present
to the strategoi. Get on with it! My men can watch him for you.
Go!'

The guards went, and smartly. Domitius remembered being bawled at by senior officers and doing the same himself.

'I think it is best if you walk around,' Simon told him. 'Gets the blood flowing again.'

Domitius did as he was told, walking in a circle, and only then realised that the words were in Latin. He had not known that the man knew the language. Then other thoughts fell away as he glanced up and saw a body hanging from a gibbet. He was pretty sure that it was his former cellmate, still filthy, but now stinking from more than dirt.

'Get moving!' Simon barked, before coming over to walk beside the Roman. 'Now, Domitius, there is not much time and a good deal to explain. I am taking you to the leaders of our city. Blame my grandfather, if you like, for it is his idea. He tells me that you know about engines and sieges. Well, Nicopolis has a Roman army outside our walls, and the old boy thought that your knowledge might help us to keep them out.'

'I cannot fight my own kind,' Domitius whispered, and surprised himself by his certainty.

'Hush. They will not ask that, at least not yet, so do not say anything until you understand your choices. The other reason that I am doing this is because my fool of a grandfather says that you are a true friend of our family, and that you care a good deal about my sister.'

'Sara?'

'How many sisters do you think I have? Well, shut up and listen. All our lives, but especially Sara's may depend on you. Do you remember the Princess Azátē who came to our city? Just nod. Good. She is well liked here, and a good friend to my people. But it turns out that she has been negotiating with the Romans. Ambition, no doubt, and something about marriage plans she did not like. So she promised the Romans that she

would come here and charm the magistrates and citizens into opening their gates to a Roman force.' Simon sniffed. 'She is used to getting her way that one, and who can blame her, for her charm is considerable. She's tiny, you know – I doubt you realised when you saw her in the carriage, but she is little and still one of the most perfect women you will ever see. So if she had asked almost anything else, and glanced down demurely with those great dark eyes, then magistrates would have been falling over themselves to please her. She's so little any man with spirit wants to protect her, and any with lust wants to... well, you're old enough to take my meaning.

'But not handing over the city! Not to Rome, not to anyone – even the Parthians, and they are close enough to fear in normal times. Nicopolis is free, from ancient times, even if that means voluntarily paying taxes to Edessa and obeying the king most of the time. And it's free inside the walls, so that we Jews have our synagogue and our arguments, others have their own temples, and you Galileans can dip each other in a pool in the basement of one rich fool's house. It is a good city. A good place to raise children, if I had time to have children.

'No matter. The magistrates refused Azátē's request – and would have had a riot if they had done anything else or if they had harmed her. But they won't risk letting her go, since she is a friend of the Romans. So there she lives, in the old palace just up the hill a little way, and she is attended by her ladies and eunuchs and guarded by a dozen of her own guards, while the rest have been sent from the city. And outside the palace, at a polite distance, her guards are in turn heavily guarded by men set there by the magistrates. We wouldn't want anyone taking a night-time stroll and opening a side gate to admit the enemy, now, would we? You follow me so far?'

Domitius nodded. He was feeling better and started to drag off his filthy tunic.

Simon wrinkled his nose in disgust. 'Your people are strange folk. Do you also remember that Sara was summoned to the princess who wished to speak to her and purchase clothing? Yes? Just before they dragged you away. There was nothing strange in the request, nothing at all, but then we did not know Azátē's plans. Sara remains in the palace. The magistrates probably think she could carry messages out from the princess – and perhaps they are right – and in turn maybe the princess thinks that there is no harm in having a hostage or just likes having a nice Jewish girl trying to run her life for her. Who knows how someone else's mind works? What it means is that our family is under suspicion. I am appointed as an officer, because I have seen more of the world than most here, and I can be sure that there will be eyes watching me, even from among my own men. To keep Sara safe, I must fight well and be utterly loyal to the city. They probably won't harm a princess, whatever happens, but a nice Jewish girl…'

'What can I do?'

'Good, you can see clearly. What I need you to do is explain to me and the magistrates what the Romans are doing. You don't have to strike a blow, but will you tell us what they are up to and help us work out ways to stop them?'

'Yes,' Domitius said, as sure as he had been that he would not fight. 'I can do that. And I owe Sara and your family.'

Simon nodded. 'Good. That is what I thought and I did not want to add the threat that if you don't then you will surely be executed. Hard to trust a man after threatening him. And I think you are smart enough to know that they will watch you even closer than they watch me, and if they don't like anything they see …'

'Thetatus.'

'I don't understand. Well, I don't care and there is no more time.' There was the sound of the gate into the street opening.

'Know that matters are still more complicated because the princess' brother came to the city with hundreds of warriors. The council refused to let him within our walls or to see his sister, for they do not wish to take sides in a family argument. He does not quite have his sister's charm, but can make himself pleasant enough in his way, and he craves a reputation as a warrior like most men crave riches. His warriors helped fight against the Romans on the first day and now are somewhere out there – sometimes in sight and sometimes not. The leaders of Nicopolis will not want to offend him, and will try to make use of him without committing themselves to his cause or making themselves vulnerable to him.'

'Can he raise a bigger army? One to break the siege?'

A shake of the head was the only answer Simon gave, for the guards reappeared, one jostling a slave, and the Christian carrying a bowl of food. 'Get him shaved, cleaned and fed!' Simon commanded, switching back to Greek. 'Try to make him look human. And be quick about it, I am to take him to the strategoi at the start of the second hour.'

Domitius soon felt fuller than he had for a long while, and to be clean was even more of a pleasure. The slave had shaved him in that wonderful, immaculate way that removed every hair without once cutting the skin. It was a secret that seemed known only to slave barbers and was all the more remarkable given his wild beard. The boy had looked positively distressed by the sight, whether from the thought of the scale of his task or from sheer offence such neglect caused to his sensibilities.

As Simon and his guards led Domitius to a large house just outside the walls of the citadel, he felt a lot better. The *tunic was rough, and even if it would take time to free himself of all the vermin, quite a few had gone with his old one. He would have felt even better with thoroughly cleaned boots – one of the guards had waved a rag at them – and better yet a proper belt and a sword in its scabbard, but in spite of that this was good. He found that his shoulders went back as they walked, and realised that he was going already unconsciously in step with Simon's stride. When they were admitted to the big house, he was marching, stamping his feet, head high as he went across the courtyard. If they wanted a Roman soldier then they could have one.*

'This is Domitius, noble lords,' Simon said as they were let into a side hall, where three men sat on high-backed chairs at the far end. Domitius marched up and stamped to attention. He recognised Athenodorus, with his round face and small nose that gave the impression of an owl. Beside him was a taller, thinner man much more of a vulture than anything else. Both men had eyes as cold as any flesh-eating fowl, and the third man, the leader of the council, was little better. Memnon did not resemble any bird or beast, and might have been handsome when he was younger, if his expression did not suggest that he did not really see people and instead only their value to him.

'You have explained what we want?' The vulture had a surprisingly soft, musical voice.

'Yes, my lords.'

'Is he capable of speech?'

'I am, my lords,' Domitius said. 'I shall do my best to serve you.'

'You had better.' Athenodorus' head even moved like an owl's. 'Tomorrow shall be the first test. At dawn, you will accompany us to the walls and tell us what you see from them. Answer our

*questions well and you will live, at least for the moment. You
will have to earn any more than that. Is that understood?'*

'Yes, my lords.'

*'Then confine him tonight. He need not be chained or abused,
but the watch must be secure. The guards can lock him in the
storeroom. Until tomorrow then.'*

*Simon said nothing as they went back to the prison and
Domitius was not inclined to break the silence. The guards
must have been given time to prepare for there was a cot and
food and water in the storeroom. Domitius undressed and lay
down, thinking that he had too many thoughts for sleep, and
then someone was shaking him awake and saying that it was a
bright dawn. He barely had time to eat and dress before Simon
and some of his men arrived. As they walked towards the walls,
Simon told him that the Romans had arrived just over a week
ago, and after a moment's thought Domitius realised that he
meant seven days – or just over seven days. That seemed about
right for the work done so far.*

*'The commander will be in one of the two big camps,' he
explained to Athenodorus and Memnon, the two strategoi. It
was an old title, and in many cities had long ceased to mean
anything like commander, but the Nicopolitans seemed an old-
fashioned bunch in many ways. 'My guess would be the one to
the west. There are more workshops behind it and an unwalled
camp for traders and the like. You can see plainly that they plan
a ramp down there, he pointed. Are there similar signs near the
eastern camp?'*

'Yes,' Simon answered.

*'They'll try to reduce the number of towers able to shoot at
them. The three other camps are to make it harder for attacks
out of the city, and for people and supplies to get in and out. If
they get really worried they'll connect them all with a rampart*

and ditch.' None of what he had said so far was not obvious to anyone who thought about it. 'They're the Ninth,' he added, for he had spotted the device on their shields. 'I don't know them.' That was a relief, he had to admit. 'They came to Syria last year. Been in the far north west for generations. The legions there lack discipline, and half of them are barbarians so they are fierce, but lazy.' Domitius knew that the soldiers in the west denigrated men like him stationed in the east in much the same way. In fact he had rarely heard legionaries with much good to say about any other legion in the army. 'Do you know the name of its commander?' Domitius asked.

'Atilius Crispinus,' Memnon said, pronouncing the name as if it was wildly outlandish.

'Oh yes, heard of him. Rumour is that he's mad or used to be, and how many really shake that off? He's old certainly, so probably desperate to make a name. He will be determined, but might hurry and make mistakes.'

The strategoi asked questions about ramparts, redoubts and the power and numbers of artillery. Domitius answered them as well as he could. Once again, there was nothing really secret in any of this.

'How do we slow them down?' It was Simon who asked the question, after they had gone to a tower on the far side of the city and studied the eastern camp. 'Cannot just let them keep on working day after day.'

'Our catapults keep their heads down,' Memnon pointed out, but he was not dismissive. 'Still a sally might do more.'

Domitius rubbed his chin. The barber had come again this morning, not that there had been much growth, and there was pleasure in touching the smooth skin. 'They think your ditch makes them safe. Truth is that it does mean that it's harder to charge out and dash back before their reserves come up. So go at night. Get men to creep into the ditch and wait. Others come behind with torches, hidden as well as you can because you don't want to give the game away. Then rush them, scream, blow trumpets, cause chaos and have the men coming behind burn everything they can't smash or steal. Even have some with shovels to dig up as much of their ramps as you can. But you have to go in fast and then quit before they get organised. Then do it again the next night and the next night, until they're always on edge, and then you wait a night or two before you do it again.' His enthusiasm grew as he spoke, and in his mind's eye he saw soldiers fleeing and ballistae and anything else of wood going up in flames. There was a joy in outsmarting people.

'It could work,' Memnon conceded.

'Give me and my lads a chance and we'll prove it,' Simon told them. 'They're itching to go. Tonight if you want? There's plenty of time to organise. Why wait.'

Athenodorus' owl's head rolled as he looked at each man in turn. 'What do you think, Roman?'

'I'd wait. Go tomorrow or maybe the next day.' He sensed their suspicions growing, and wondered why they could not see the obvious. 'They've really only started on the works and, as I say, they reckon they're safe. Let 'em build some more, raise the ramps a little higher, then it will be worse when you destroy them – and more of a shock that you can. Make the most of this first surprise. Be harder to catch them really off guard later, but each quiet day and night they have now will make them relax. They'll be told not to, but soldiers get bored easily, so let them keep on thinking they are safe. Then torch all they've built.'

'You would target the ramps?' Memnon asked.

'This time, yes. They're what's most important. After that maybe the camps. A small one if you want to hit them where

they are weak, or one of the big ones if you want to shock them even more. Then vary your targets to keep them guessing.'

Memnon and his colleague exchanged glances. 'We shall see. Tomorrow morning we will do this again. Otherwise you will return to your confinement.'

'And if I need him?' Simon asked.

'Go to the prison whenever you like,' Athenodorus told him. 'But he does not leave those walls without our permission.'

'Of course.' Simon turned to Domitius. 'Seen something else?'

Domitius was gripping the parapet, knuckles white. It was a good half a mile away, and he could not be sure, except that he was. No one else rode quite like that or gestured in that way. Caecilius was with the besiegers.

'No,' he lied. 'Thought that there was some digging over there, but it's just shadows. I wondered whether they were starting another fort or even connecting them with a wall as I mentioned. It's nothing though.'

Simon stared at the spot where the Roman had pointed. The earth seemed to have been turned, but that was all he could make out. A party of Roman officers were riding past it. 'Then time to be off.'

Domitius went with him. Sorry, old friend, he thought to himself as he wondered whether the Nicopolitans would guess that the Romans were most likely mining. His old friend would surely be involved and he did not want to provoke an attack on the works. Still, he could not keep Caecilius safe all the time and just had to hope that the old man would not be in the wrong place at the wrong moment.

XV

Up country
Thirteenth day before the Kalends of May
The eighth day of the siege

THERE WERE SIXTY carts and waggons in the convoy and hundreds of pack animals. On the way to the river most of them had been empty, the rest carrying no more than enough food for the animals and the soldiers of the escort. The return trip was different, after a day spent at the ferry crossing, loading up with supplies from the great stockpile on the far bank guarded by a cohort of VIIII Hispana and other detachments. On the way back, wheels cut deep ruts in the trackway and all the slog of getting the army to Nicopolis had to be repeated. They were better prepared this time, for the workshops had made little wooden ramps to lay in front of wheels and make it easier to haul the waggons out of each patch of soft sand. Yet the work was still hard, and there were fewer hands to do it.

Ferox had watched the dust approaching from the north west, the thin, straggling clouds churned up by vehicles. There was no way of hiding the movement of a convoy like this, unless it travelled at night, and the chaos of that did not bear contemplation. Oxen were dim beasts, and had a nasty habit of walking into the cart in front. Apart from that, it would be all too easy for a few raiders to sweep in and kill or steal. So the convoys had to travel in daylight, and everyone for many miles around would see them coming, which, given that there was only one path they could take without going many miles out of the way, did not really matter. This was the lifeline of Crispinus' army, the link with the empire and its bounteous supplies, and it was perilously thin and horribly vulnerable. Crispinus hoped that their enemies would not realise this, at least not yet, and would keep their gaze fixed on his army and the siege works. A man might as well hope to leave his purse on a bench in the bathhouse and find it still there and still full an hour later.

They were close now, the track three-quarters of a mile away or near enough. Ferox was keeping low, and looking through a dried-up bush as he lay on the sloping side of the gulley. Whenever there was a storm, water would flow through here like a torrent, but today it was dry as a bone, so they had to keep the horses as still as possible to prevent them stirring up dust, apart from making any noise. It was nearly noon, and they had come here during the night and thought to bring plenty of water because otherwise the animals would have been parched and suffering by now. In another country he would have hunted for some woodland, to give them shade, but the only patch here was a long bowshot ahead and to his right, and he had good reason not to go there. This was the spot, the spot he would choose if he were in the enemy's place.

The leading outposts had already passed. At the front were the usual pairs of riders, spread out in a wide screen, almost half a mile ahead. A dozen men riding together and led by a decurion were a few hundred yards back, and an entire turma the same distance behind them. More pairs of men acted as screen on either flank, and made up the rearguard. The prefect Caius Gellius Exoratus was in charge, and from what Ferox had seen was a man who understood his job, even though this was his first posting to the army. He was a Spaniard, in charge of cohorts IIII Callaececorum Lucensium equitata, which had been raised in Iberia by the divine Augustus, probably as much as anything to employ the warriors who had fought with such determination against his armies. Nothing much changed, thought the Silurian prince turned centurion. Augustus had also sent the cohort off to Syria, keeping them far away from home and the temptation to use their newfound discipline, drill and weaponry on their new masters. They had stayed there ever since, and Ferox would lay good money to bet that Exoratus was the only man from the Iberian Peninsula in the entire unit. The men would be Syrians and Cilicians, half-starved waifs from the slums of the cities, or the burlier, barely better fed sons of farmers and tenants. No one else tended to be that keen on joining the army.

Ferox could see Exoratus riding up to check on the advance guard. He rode well, head forward as Iberians tended to from the habit of hunting. The man was barely twenty, and both keen and well connected to hold this responsibility so young, for he had been in the post for at least two years. Everything he did was careful and controlled, and with his curly black hair and watchful eyes Ferox could understand why some Romans believed that the Silures were kin to the Spanish. As well as the bulk of his own cohort, apart from detachments left with the main force, Exoratus had cohors III Augusta Thracum equitata, another outfit that had been in and around Syria for nearly a century. There might be some Thracians in the ranks, since after all, the province was closer than Iberia, but the bulk of the men were from the same places as the other cohort. All told, Exoratus had some two hundred horsemen and three hundred and fifty infantry, along with a hundred or so army slaves, some of them armed *galearii*, and he was using them as well as he could. The cohortes equitatae usually got the dullest, most difficult jobs and this was no exception.

'See anything?' Bran crawled up beside him. Vindex was with the other group, a little further back so that he could see what happened and decide whether or not to join in.

Ferox gave a slight nod towards the wood to their right and kept watching.

'Guess it's the obvious spot,' Bran agreed. The wood was a mix of pines and firs, none of them very high, but tended by the local farmers because they needed timber. 'Don't see anyone though.'

'You're not supposed to. But can you see the ground from there back to the hills?'

Bran stared for a while. 'Yes,' he conceded with the tone of someone suspicious of the question. He waited, for he was used to Ferox after all these years. After a long silence, he gave in. 'Afraid I don't see anything.'

'Again, that's the point.' Ferox turned and saw Bran frowning. 'It's been swept with branches. Someone's come through, then cleared up behind them. See how it's different to the land either side?'

'Not really. Looks the same to me, but then I am not one of the Silures, am I.'

'It's an old Sarmatian trick. Too wet in my country to be worthwhile! But I've seen the Roxolani do it, and the Iasyges. They tell me that some of the finest warriors serving Parthian noblemen are Dahae and Saka, and the Sarmatians see them as kin. Maybe this prince or whoever is out there has some of those lads with him. Not too many, I hope, otherwise we're in real trouble.

'Look – there we go!' Ferox hissed, keeping low, but pointing past the convoy to a ridge on the far side. A couple of horsemen were silhouetted on top, and a moment later dozens more rode up to join them. 'Show 'em one threat first – then another!' A second band of horse archers had appeared on another low rise, nearer the rear of the column this time and further back. 'Make 'em look in the wrong direction.'

'You sound pleased,' Bran whispered.

'You sound like my wife,' Ferox replied before he could stop himself.

The younger man tapped him on the shoulder. 'You really have been on your own too long!'

'And you should spend less time with Vindex. There!' He gestured. 'Another band, although smaller I'll warrant.' This group was even more distant, and all Bran could see were a few horsemen and a dust cloud behind them.

'More branches dragged behind horses?'

'That would be my guess. Good, you are learning. Exoratus' men are watching.' He could see the prefect galloping across to his outposts on the far side of the column. 'He's got the sense not to stop, not yet, but he'll start shifting men to face that way in a moment.' A dozen or so archers from the first group galloped towards the nearest pairs of riders from the flank screen. 'That's right, tease them.' Arrows flew, but the range was long and the auxiliaries dodged out of the way and cantered back towards their supports.

'I'm never quite sure whose side you are on?' Bran muttered. 'You sound as if you are enjoying this.'

Ferox did not want to think about that, in case the lad was right. His eyes scanned the convoy and the land on either side. As predicted, Exoratus began to move some of his formed cavalry over to face the threat. 'Why don't you go home?' he asked, not looking at Bran. 'You've more than paid your debt to me.' It must be fifteen years or more since the boy had pledged to follow Ferox for three years. 'You could be a big man in your tribe, or an honoured one in the queen's household if you prefer.' He tried to lighten his tone. 'Has she set you to watch me?'

'To watch out for you, yes. She is my sister and I owe her that and more. But my home is not in her household or back with my own kin, not yet. There are things I must do first, one day.'

'Sosius?'

'And others. There is plenty of time for all of them. In the meantime, I have found being with you and with Vindex and these Brigantes to be interesting. Life away from you all would be far more dull.'

'Might be longer though?'

'Not so far.'

Ferox had always found that Bran would rarely talk seriously unless it was just before a fight and there was seldom the opportunity then. His eyes kept scanning the plains ahead of them. More and more Roman horsemen had gone to the far side of the track and even the formed turma on this side of the track had dropped back to cover the rear. Exoratus and his men had seen what they were meant to see, and done the natural thing. All that was left this side were infantry marching alongside the waggons and pack animals, and the thin outer screen of riders.

'Get everyone ready. Mount when I raise my arm. You all know what to do.'

'Aye.' Bran slithered back into the gully. He was not one to waste words.

Ferox glanced at the wood. He could not see a stretch of the outpost line beyond it, but noticed the pair who were closest to it and still in sight stop. One reined his horse back so savagely that the animal reared in protest. The cohortes equitatae got the dirty jobs, and their horsemen got less pay and smaller and poorer horses than the flashier cavalry of the alae. Most were good though, and he could see the rider giving the warning signal of enemies in sight. Ferox raised his arm.

There were whooping cries as another band of horse archers appeared, these ones half a mile away, beyond the wood and coming from behind another gentle rise. They were using the folds in the land just like the Sarmatians and surging forward, while the bulk of the Roman horsemen faced the wrong way.

Ferox heard the horses rush up the slope of the gully.

'Here!' Bran called. He had Ferox's mare by the reins, and the centurion ran alongside and jumped into the saddle. That was one technique even the Romans had sense enough to practise and easy enough with a small pony like this.

'Come on!' Ferox called. His men were not in ranks, for this was not that sort of a fight, and went as a swarm, almost like geese flying, with Bran just behind and the others spreading back on either side as soon he was at the head. He took them towards the wood. Bran gave him a questioning look, but there was not time to explain that the trees would shield them from the band of archers he knew was surging out of the front of the wood. Others were bound to see them, but not in time to send a warning.

One of the auxiliaries was down, horse and rider both peppered with arrows. His comrade and the rest rode back, turning in the saddle so that they could hold a shield to cover the horse's back and be ready to throw a lancea if they got a chance. Steering the horses with knees and seat and with reins looped over their arm, they fled, for the enemy had numbers as they charged, shooting ahead. A horse was hit in the rump, for the shield could not give full protection, and the beast staggered, the rider almost falling, before it lurched back into a canter and kept going. Ahead, a cornu was blowing, some of the infantry were forming up in a dense block, while a couple of smaller carts clattered off from the main column, drivers whipping their mules.

Ferox led his men around the wood, for going through would take too long. Apart from Bran he had thirty-four men. Vindex had about forty, and he hoped they would be getting ready behind them, using the far side of the ridge to keep out of sight. Coming round the trees, Ferox saw the first of the enemy, a fellow riding a sand-coloured pony with dark legs, and wearing a fur cap and drab tunic and trousers. His bow was in his hand and an arrow ready, but it tended to be the less enthusiastic who hung back and made noise and a great show of eagerness without taking too many risks. The rider had not seen them, but that could not last.

The Roman screen was back, galloping behind the block of infantry for shelter, but the foot soldiers had spears rather than bows and the horse archers rushed towards them. Arrows rattled against the large oval shields as the auxiliaries clustered together. The two mule-drawn carts slewed to a halt and men yanked the covers off the carroballistae in them.

Ferox could see the rest of the horse archers now, some sixty or seventy in a swarm. The one in the drab clothes heard the noise, glanced back over his shoulder and his jaw dropped.

'Charge!' Ferox screamed and kicked his pony on. The Brigantes whooped as they followed.

A couple of auxiliaries fell, shields dropping, and it took a moment for their comrades to pull them back under cover. With a crack like a whip, the first ballista spat out a bolt which drove deep into a horse's head. The animal's front legs collapsed and the rider was flung forward through the air. The second engine shot, but missed as an archer swayed down from his saddle so that he was almost clinging to the side of his horse. From behind the infantry, a dozen or so of the auxiliary cavalry galloped forward, raising a strange ululating cry as they did. Caught from two sides, the horse archers scattered, some going left and some going right. One of the carroballistae sent another dart, which struck a rider squarely in the back and pitched him out of the saddle. His horse galloped on with the others.

The drab-clothed rider headed away from the Brigantes, twisting round to shoot back at them. The first arrow went high, the second was short, flicking through the thin grass just ahead of Ferox. Then the man realised that the auxiliaries were pressing from the other side and spun around to escape to the right. Bran threw a javelin and hit him in the small of the back. He slumped forward, dark blood spreading from the wound, and managed to cling onto the neck of his horse. Ferox saw a brightly dressed rider wearing a cuirass of mixed silvered and gilded scales on a tall black horse, but the man was already too far away for there to be much chance of catching him, so he swerved left, kicking his horse onwards, and the beast stuttered into a faster gallop, hoofs pounding across the hard earth. The archer and another were crossing his path, and the nearest saw him, flicking his bow around to shoot. Ferox felt a blow on his shoulder as the arrow nicked his mail before skidding off. The distance closed very, very fast, and the archer half-cowered because there was no time to draw his sword. Ferox's horse barged with his shoulder against the other man's mount, and he cut down and to the right, feeling the blade hit bone high just below the shoulder. The rider fell, his horse swerved into his companion, who checked, before speeding away. Ferox slapped his horse with the flat of his blade. 'Come on!' he urged her, and he leaned forward, knowing that there would be just one chance before the second archer's pony hit its stride and left him behind. Aiming carefully he lunged into the small of the man's back, heard him scream as he tried to arch away from the pain, and Ferox almost lost his balance, falling hard with his weight against the saddle horns. His mare gave in, slowing and then stopping, and that gave him the chance to pull himself up.

A few of his men and some of the auxiliaries were still chasing after the horse archers, but already the gap was widening. The enemy were good, or at least quite good. He doubted that a band wholly of Roxolani or, from all he had heard, of Dahae or Saka, would have been ambushed so easily. The brightly dressed leader was still with them, his strong horse carrying him to the front of the swarm of fleeing men, and Ferox thought it was the prince they had seen outside Nicopolis, although at this distance he could not be sure.

'Rally on me!' Ferox shouted at the top of his voice. It was a big mistake to chase horsemen like this too far, because once they felt safer they were apt to turn around, especially as there was the other band close by.

Ox-horn trumpets blared, the tone more rasping than any army trumpet, and he hoped that meant Vindex was playing his part. Ferox searched behind him, and saw a puff of dust on a ridge that must be behind the other band of archers. A few of the Brigantes appeared. Hopefully more would bob up at other points, enough to make the enemy fear that there were several bands of riders out hunting them. Again it was the sort of trick the peoples of the Steppes would see through, but might work here.

'Rally!' he called. An auxiliary tubicen began to blow the recall signal and, with some reluctance, troopers and his own men slowed, then stopped. He could hear the closest Brigantes chattering in excitement.

'Get one?'

'Nah, bastards were too quick.'

'Must have smelled you coming.'

'This one won't be smelling much,' another said. He was on foot, holding up a head he had just taken from one of the corpses. Ferox sometimes wondered what it would take to stop Brigantes from talking.

Three of the horse archers were dead, with four or five more bleeding out their lifeblood on the grass. Two of the prisoners were hurt, but would live, and a third – the man whose horse had been shot by the carroballista – had broken his nose in the fall without taking any more serious injury. At least a couple of the ones who had escaped were wounded, perhaps badly. None of the Brigantes were hurt, although a couple of horses had taken arrow wounds.

'It was well done,' Bran decided.

'We'll see,' Ferox told him. 'They might come back.'

They did not, or at least did not again press close. Vindex and his men made several appearances, always pulling out of sight before the enemy dared to investigate, and brought all his men back to the main column after a couple of hours.

'Hot work,' he said.

'Is that all of you? Exoratus asked, running his eyes along the little band of Brigantes. He had been drinking from a skin and handed it over to Vindex. He and all his men were covered in dust so pale that it almost looked like flour.

'Every single one,' Vindex said, before taking a long swig from the wineskin. 'Ah, that's good.'

The convoy kept going, the oxen trudging along as they always did, until the drivers declared that they could go no

further today just as they always did. Exoratus ordered his
men to camp for the night. The enemy had shadowed them,
keeping well outside bow range, presumably guessing that the
carroballistae could shoot much further. Just before sunset, two
hundred men from the ala III Thracum arrived to escort them
on the last, short stage of the journey in the morning.

'Think we're all right now,' Exoratus told his officers once
the camp was settled for the night. 'Reckon so, Ferox?' He
searched the faces around him. 'Where is the centurion?'

'Gone, my lord.' Vindex made a great effort to be polite,
dipping his head a little. A true chieftain should not expect
a warrior to do this, but he had spent many years among the
Romans and knew them to be queer folk. This one seemed one
of the decent ones, who did not shout too much and seemed
well liked by his men, which was always a good sign. Still, you
could never be sure and Ferox had urged him to be as tactful
as he could, which had not prevented his friend clearing
off with Bran into the night and leaving Vindex to explain.
'Said to tell you that it should all be fine the rest of the way
– especially now these lads have joined us.' He nodded at the
decurions from ala Thracum. 'The problem won't be now, but
next time.'

'Where has he gone?'

'Not rightly sure, my lord. Said he had an idea.'

Exoratus grinned. 'An idea? Really? What is this army
coming too!' Vindex laughed with the rest of them. 'My
thanks again to you and your men,' the prefect continued. 'Do
they have everything they need? I know you came without
baggage.'

'The wine was much appreciated, my lord.'

'Least we could do. Tell your fellows to rest. We will provide
all the guards and pickets.' Exoratus frowned, as if worried

that might imply that he did not wholly trust the discipline of the irregulars. 'But we will want you scouting ahead in the morning.'

Vindex gave one of his leering smiles. 'A pleasure, my lord.'

XVI

Zeugma
That same night

A HUGE MOTH fluttered around the lamp, casting monstrous, flickering shadows on the painted walls. Hadrian was alone for the first time since waking. The assizes had finished yesterday, with all the cases that could not wait for the new governor to arrive resolved, which in some cases meant referring it back to local courts or up to the princeps himself. Today had been spent reading letters and dictating replies, sometimes with a covering note if the letter was to be passed to the authorities in a city, or forwarded to the princeps. Citizens could always appeal to the emperor, even if the shrewder ones hoped to get what they wanted faster and more certainly by influencing decision makers closer to home. Trajan had a strong sense of duty and did his best to be fair, so he would answer all petitions as soon as he was able, which might mean months or even years. A fair outcome was not something all petitioners genuinely wanted, and Hadrian had taken care to hint to several men that pushing the matter higher up was unlikely to help them. Not everyone listened, and sometimes the case could only be settled by the princeps, but all in all Hadrian felt that he had kept to the 'spirit of the age' promoted by an emperor keen to be seen as approachable and also avoided sending too many petitions to Trajan when his mind was on other matters.

Hadrian guessed that the imperial party should still be making their way north. News had come of a second embassy from the king of Armenia, asking this time that the legatus of Cappadocia be permitted to arbitrate on his claim to the kingdom. Trajan had rejected this as he had rejected the first approach. An army of the size being mustered around Satala was not about to disperse without taking the field. Hadrian had heard that Lusius Quietus was to receive one of two or three major field commands, and no doubt would perform his duties with his usual skill and good fortune. That was no surprise, even if it was frustrating. Trajan was not going to stop with Armenia. He wanted glory, which probably meant war, since it was doubtful that everyone would submit at his approach, whatever the might of his army.

Soon, Hadrian must write and inform the emperor that he had ordered an intervention in Osrhoene rather than permit civil strife within its royal house and risk Parthian involvement. This would take very careful wording, but it was important that the first news of this come to Trajan from him, rather than anyone else. The day after tomorrow was the longest he could leave it, and he would write the draft in his own hand, before letting one of his own slaves produce the neat version.

Nicopolis had not welcomed the Romans and accepted close alliance and a garrison. That was disappointing if not really surprising. Sosius had written days earlier suggesting that the princess had exaggerated her influence over the civic leaders. He had also – and so had other sources – spoken of the eagerness of Prince Arbandes to prevent his sister from creating a base for herself and winning over the Romans. Showing more intelligence than Hadrian had felt the young man possessed, he was none too fussy how he did this, thus willing to fight with the citizens against the Romans, while also happy to discuss the matter with Hadrian in the hope of making himself Rome's favourite. His father had other children, but the prince and princess were the oldest and by far the favourites. Arbandes, like anyone else who paid attention, realised that the Romans were happier with male rather than female rulers. It was not an attitude Hadrian understood, for he would prefer his servants to be capable and reliable more than anything else. Time and considerable thought would tell whether either of the siblings were worth promoting. For the moment Hadrian – like their father King Abgarus – did not need to commit firmly to either of them.

Hadrian clapped his hands, crushing the moth, before absent-mindedly wiping the residue on a napkin and then reaching for Crispinus' brief despatch. There was little to say, other than that the attempt to seize the city had failed and that the siege had begun. The legatus stressed his repeated attempts to convince the authorities to seek peace. That was the right thing to do, for it saved time, but all Sosius' reports suggested that it was extremely unlikely. Only one letter had arrived since the start of the siege, and Hadrian wondered whether his agent would be able to reach him in future, as the blockade around the city tightened. Yet it was best not to underestimate Sosius.

Crispinus did not know about Hadrian's spy, and would not, unless Sosius found a way to get the army inside the walls and had to reveal himself in order to pass the information to the besiegers. That was a risk, for there was a chance that he might be arrested or even killed trying to reach Crispinus. Well, that was his risk, and Sosius understood. The man was hard to kill, and knew enough to convince Crispinus of his identity. Ferox and some of his men knew Sosius as well, and, even if there was no love lost between them, they could be relied upon to do their duty. None of this was without risk, but Trajan would be delighted with the capture of Nicopolis, if it could be accomplished and presented not as a breach of Roman faith, but a bold enterprise in the best interest of the empire.

From his brief account Crispinus was setting about the siege methodically. There was praise for the diligence and insights of Caecilius in his planning, without repeating unnecessary praise for Hadrian's selection of the man. Arbandes had brought no more than four or five hundred warriors to assist the defenders, harry the besiegers, or do whatever he felt was best. While the prince had taken part in the fighting, he had not tried to deal with Crispinus in any formal way, which meant that it would be easier to deny, or at least play down, his involvement if that proved convenient in the future. What mattered was that he had not come at the head of an army. Abgarus could easily raise ten times as many soldiers if he wanted, but all the sources from Osrhoene were certain that the call had not gone out. As long as that was the case, then the siege remained practical. Hadrian had managed to find another eighty cavalry and two hundred infantry by combing the detachments that were always dotted through any province, especially one like Syria with a large garrison. The men were on their way to assist Crispinus, with the suggestion that they be employed to escort the supply convoys. Arbandes and his men were one thing, and a serious enough problem, but if it became known that the convoys were vulnerable and worth plundering then it would not be long before freebooters gathered from all the neighbouring kingdoms.

King Abgarus was remaining aloof, not committing to Trajan's war plans, havering in his loyalty to the rivals for the Parthian throne, yet not reacting to the expedition as an invasion of his realm. For the moment, he appeared content to behave as if this were a local problem for the Nicopolitans. Sources – and sources that Sosius swore were reliable – in Edessa and the royal court insisted that the king and his councillors had not sent word or embassy to Trajan to ask his intentions. Instead, a man had been chosen to go to Syria, but the terms of his mission were vague and there was a deliberate lack of urgency about his departure.

Distant trumpets sounded the second watch of the night. There were not too many men left here at Zeugma, although there were plenty of women and children belonging to the legion which meant that some areas, like the big bath house, remained busy and boisterous, and still the trumpets sounded and all the rituals were performed. The men who were left included all those men good at working the system, at setting down such deep roots in any camp that they were far too indispensable to be sent on campaign, or kept with the eagles because disease or injury rendered them unfit while sentiment ensured that they were given light tasks. Men like that tended to be even stricter about the regulations and routine of the army's day than everyone else. Neat, and brightly whitewashed stones now lined the parade ground, while anything visible that could be polished was polished with such vigour that they must be starting to wear away.

Hadrian enjoyed the relative peace of a half-empty principia, and had settled into the lavish praetorium, finding shelter in its calm after days spent in the basilica of the city itself. He should move on, for assizes were due elsewhere, and he was wondering how long the excuse of not wishing to pre-empt the formally appointed governor would last. A letter said that the new man expected to arrive in Antioch by the Kalends of July, given fair weather. It would be better to be there to meet him, for that was the custom, at least for properly appointed governors. Still, if the siege was not quite done, or there was a need to ensure that he took credit for its success or provided explanations for a failure, Hadrian could probably justify absence by the requirements of state. Crispinus had more than two months, and that ought to be enough one way or another. It would be hard indeed to keep his army supplied during the height of the summer, and long before then Trajan would be aware and able to intervene.

Hadrian considered what he had written so far, beginning with an explanation of the messages from Princess Azátē, and emphasising the precarious condition of Osrhoene, and the dangers posed should the king make close alliance with the Parthians.

Considering the security of the province, in this region where the Euphrates can be crossed with some ease, action to secure it against any possible threat seemed wise.

Hadrian toyed again with the idea of mentioning past invasions and the ease of the route to Antioch, before discarding them. The princeps was not only a shrewd soldier, but hated statements of the obvious.

Believing that this opportunity for assisting an ally, who is eager for our cause and hostile to that of the Parthians, was one that ought to be seized upon forthwith, I committed to aiding Azátē and despatched Legio VIIII Hispana supported by auxiliaries. Their commander, Atilius Crispinus, although fresh to his command, has experience and is eager to prove that he and his men are capable of performing any task in service to their princeps and the res publica.

No, most of that would have to go. Best not mention the Parthians directly, for the inference ought to be obvious. The style was also difficult. Trajan hated too much rhetoric in an official letter, and was fondest of something akin to the divine Julius' *Commentarii* when it came to style, and that was not something which came naturally to Hadrian. Crispinus needed to be mentioned, for he deserved credit if there was enough to go around, and could prove a convenient scapegoat if not. Still, this reminder of his eagerness to prove his loyalty was too strong.

This legion will assist our ally in every possible way. While it is to be hoped that the operation will prove bloodless, it is important to support our friends appropriately, and should the conspiracies of a faction threaten the princess' position in Nicopolis, then our men can deal with them.

Any good Roman – and Trajan saw himself as a very good and decently old-fashioned Roman – would feel a shudder at words like conspiracy and faction, which was a little odd given how many of both figured in Rome's past. It was a pity that Azátē was a woman, and Hadrian wondered how to make this less obvious. Her name was suitably outlandish that perhaps it was better to use it instead of the word princess.

To protect our friends and defeat rebels, it may be necessary to capture Nicopolis, which will then prove a valuable ally, which controls one of the main routes to the great river.

The emperor ought to reach his army sometime in the second half of May. If Hadrian sent his letter the day after tomorrow then it ought to catch up with the imperial party not long before they arrived. Trajan would be in a good mood, eager to review his great host and embark on operations. The letter would inform him of the expedition, without stating that the city was resisting and a siege underway. That could wait for the next letter, which ideally would include encouraging news. Perhaps then, or later, he might mention Arbandes, but he would have to wait and see.

Hadrian sighed, laid the draft letter down and took a fresh sheet of papyrus. It was not of the highest quality, being stained near one edge, but it would do for his purpose and there was no sense in wasting the best on his rough copy. He stared at the blank page. No need to write the introduction as the scribe would know what to do. Call her Azátē, not princess, he thought to himself as he tapped the stylus and accidentally flicked ink across the table. There must have been more left on the nib than he had thought. The same napkin stained with dead moth was there, so he rubbed it and seemed to make things worse. There were two more insects flapping around the lamp, so killing the first had achieved little in the long run. Hadrian could not help thinking back to Athens, and wondering how a philosopher would embroider the story to speak of the futility of life or of ambition, or of how one death did not matter in the great scheme of things.

'It mattered to the moth, though,' he said aloud.

Azátē of Edessa, child of King Abgarus appealed to me by letter to prevent the kingdom aligning itself more closely with Parthia.

That was better. After that, stick to the name and never say princess or daughter unless there was no other way. Women were a problem, especially in politics, and if the gods had had more sense the world might have done without them. Trajan had said as much himself more than once, even though he was a dutiful husband. Hadrian doubted that the emperor had ever loved any woman, or perhaps even anyone at all, but he treated his womenfolk with respect and some affection. He even talked to them, at least when there were no rugged military men or boisterous lads to provide him with his favourite company.

Trajan's wife, Plotina, and niece Matidia, along with a gaggle of aristocratic women were supporting the emperor by having a prolonged holiday near Antioch. The emperor was devoted to both of them, treating them like beloved sisters or even his dear departed mother. Both of them were fond of Hadrian, laughing as he playfully flirted with them when they met or at his letters filled with salacious gossip. It was wise to cultivate them, but in truth Hadrian enjoyed it, for their devotion to him was encouraging. All in all, he had more pleasure chatting or corresponding with Matidia than he did with her daughter and his wife, Sabina. He was glad the latter had chosen to stay in Italy, leaving her as happy in her country estates as he was out here.

Plotina and Matidia wrote to him almost as often as he sent letters to them, and that was useful, for they spoke of the emperor's moods, his likes and dislikes for those around him, as well as useful titbits concerning the women of the court and their husbands. They loved him like a son, and were pained that Trajan did not. The emperor's attitude was harsher than it had been, and in the last year they had told of trying to mollify him when he ranted about Hadrian as a dangerous, unreliable schemer. They could both be persuasive, and were certainly persistent, and had done enough to convince Trajan to give Hadrian his current post, which was at least something, since it gave him this opportunity. It might well prove the last. Trajan had given in, limited the post to a temporary one, and spent more time with Hadrian earlier in the year as a sop to his womenfolk. After all that, he had still sworn not to give the 'little shit' another job – the women had not written the words, but Hadrian was very familiar with the emperor's manner of speaking about him. News like that was always worth having, even though it was bad, so Hadrian was grateful for the letters; an ambitious man could never know too much.

So all was well, at least as well as it could be, and he had created the chance for glory denied to him when the emperor did not choose to take him on campaign. In many ways it was better. Being around Trajan only ever seemed to remind the princeps that he loathed Hadrian. Distance gave freedom to act and a chance to present the emperor with such good news that he would forget his animosity.

Then some of the letters went missing. At first it seemed a mistake, when a pretty slave in the house where Hadrian was staying offered to help clear one of his rooms, and his own fool of a freedman was too busy flirting to think. Partly that was Hadrian's fault, for he usually burned anything dangerous as soon as he had read it, but on that occasion he had been called to the stables where one of his finest hunters was sick. That was sentiment for you, it always caused trouble. The host was apologetic, nervous when told that there was official correspondence among the missing letters – and there was, albeit a report on the sources of grain for the chief bases in southern Syria. The girl was put to torture, eventually admitting that a nice man in the agora had offered her money for any scrap papyrus, because he wanted to scrape it clean for resale. That might or might not be true, but the man was not to be found, and Hadrian was suspicious of chance. His agents were investigating the corruption in the provincial army at that time, which alone made him suspicious. Ferox knew nothing of all this, but Sosius had searched the property of the tribune he had killed and found one of the letters. In it, the criticism was mild, but there were others where Trajan's mistrust of Hadrian was obvious, making clear that he was unfit for high office. Those were out there somewhere, and he had to suspect that they were in the hands of the men behind the corruption, waiting to be used at some point. Yet no one had approached him or threatened in any way. Sosius did not believe that the deserter

Domitius had them, but had not been able to confirm this before the man was arrested. Even if he did not, then he might know more. Then there was Caecilius, bluff, very military Caecilius, who just might be one of the leaders or might just be too simple a soldier to have noticed the peculation going on under his very nose. Like everything else, this problem seemed to focus on Nicopolis.

Hadrian's mind had wandered, and after a moment he realised that he had written the city's name four times and then the word trust. He did not think Sosius had much to gain by betraying him, but then the man was such a good agent because he did not think in straight lines and had no scruples. Ferox was different, but experience suggested that it was unwise to assume the man only knew what he was supposed to know. Both men might just be coming to the end of their usefulness. Hadrian lifted the page to the lamp's flame, waved it gently to speed the fire and watched it burn. One of the moths collided with the papyrus, scorching its wings and dropping onto the table.

'Your own fault,' Hadrian said out loud, and crushed it with the napkin.

XVII

The siege lines outside Nicopolis
Eleventh day before the Kalends of May
The tenth day of the siege

'**B**EST BE CAREFUL, sir!' The soldier was missing his front teeth, so that there was a whistle when he spoke. 'They take a shot now and then just on the off chance.'

'They'd love to bag a centurion!' his comrade added. He had a very deep voice, so that it was a shock to see it coming from a boy with legs like sticks and a face so thin that the cheek pieces of his helmet hung loose.

'I'll be careful,' Rufus replied. He was getting to know more of the legionaries as he did the rounds of all the work sites and other parties. Caecilius had warned him that he would be surprised by how many little detachments and groups with special duties would get created in the first few days, and it was truly amazing. As the primus pilus kept reminding him, all his book learning of siegecraft did not fully prepare him for actual operations. That was true, and Rufus was revelling in learning more of the reality, of realising that he had simply not thought of so many of the problems involved. Solutions had to be found for each one, which often created new problems and new demands for men to labour making or carrying, and more calculations to be made of angles, weight and force.

'You'll work hard and sleep little,' Caecilius had told him and he was right. Rufus had never enjoyed himself so much in his entire life. This was engineering with a purpose and not mere theory, and no matter how beautiful a concept might seem it was no good at all if it could not be made to work on the ground. He enjoyed being part of something bigger than himself, of seeing the high walls of Nicopolis as a challenge to his wits and knowing that he and the rest of them would meet that challenge and win. For the very first time, he felt as if he belonged in the legion and he was surprised how much he enjoyed that. Even Caecilius was a good deal less gruff, approving of his enthusiasm and impressed by his ability to make complex calculations in his head.

Rufus had stepped beyond the covered shed so that he could measure the angle of the ramp's surface. It had looked wrong earlier today, and although Caecilius had dismissed his concern, he wanted to check. Even a slight shift changed the force needed to push a tower up once the ramp was finished, and altered the way its weight pressed down.

'Do you want a shield, sir?' the first legionary asked. Rufus knew that he had heard the man's name earlier on, but could not bring it to mind.

'Thank you, but no – I need both hands.'

'Cover him, Lucius.'

'You do it,' the deep voice said in what it must have thought was a whisper.

'Hush, both of you, or you will start some trouble,' Rufus hissed. 'I'm fine. Just give a shout if you see anyone moving up there!' There was still some shelter from the screen ahead of him, but that would not block a missile coming high from one of the towers. The centurion was hoping that the shadows would conceal him, for it must be hard looking down, even on a bright night like this. He had been up at the works on the western side of the city for more than an hour since sunset and no missiles had come, so perhaps the defenders were having a good rest.

A legionary had been killed this morning, hit square in the face by the bolt from a ballista. The man had peeked just a little too high and for too long over one of the screens and no one was quite sure why and whether it was curiosity or simple carelessness. A dozen or so soldiers had been wounded during the course of the day, most lightly, and that was about average. The defenders had shot well on the day that the legion had driven them inside their walls, but for a while it had seemed that this was no more than luck. For the next morning their aim was poor, missiles usually going too high or thumping down short. They were improving, slowly and steadily, and yesterday had even got a man as he dashed between a gap in the entrenchments, something that had seemed safe until then.

It was harder to tell how much injury the attackers were causing. Now and then, when some bold fool made a good target of himself on the parapet, they could see a head shattered by a stone or a body flung back by an arrow or bolt – a sight that always prompted a cheer from the besiegers. Mostly the Romans shot and hit the wall, or went through a gap in the crenulations or over without any sign that it had struck home. Both sides flung hundreds of missiles at each other for every definite hit, and Rufus wondered how many times some arrows had been shot, then shot back and so on. Anything not broken was reused, and the fabricae set up behind the camps were turning out scores of arrows and bolts every hour. They had also found a patch of rocky ground not far away, and a detachment was kept busy prising pieces up and chipping them to shape.

Rufus had mentioned to Caecilius that manuals recommended a constant onslaught, including attacks by escalade, to wear down the defenders. Outnumbered, they would have to keep manning the walls and suffering a trickle of casualties, whereas the more numerous besiegers could swap men around so that they all had plenty of rest between making each attack.

Caecilius had sniffed, although with less scorn than in the past. 'Good way of wasting your own men's lives as well – and some of your best and boldest too. Oh, I dare say in the old days they did not have much choice. Techniques weren't so advanced. We can break their walls, given time and care, and that takes sweat. No sense in fighting more than we have to. I'd prefer the lads to be worn out from slog than attacks with no hope of succeeding. That way at least we've got something to show for it. It's started well, lad, it really has, so let's get on with it and see it done.'

That had been days ago, and once again Rufus was now convinced that the primus pilus was right. Fighting was messy, whereas making something was reassuringly predictable, at least if care was taken to spot any mistake while it was easier to put right.

Rufus ran the palm of his hand across the hard-packed surface of the ramp. He could not see well in the far distance, and sensed that Caecilius had noticed it, but other than that he felt his sight was good, at least in daylight. There was a change, he was sure of it. He had brought a stick, five feet long and painted white and red in blocks to show a carefully measured 12 inches, not that he needed to use that. Instead he laid it down, stretching the rod back so that it lay flat against the surface at the bottom of the ramp. It lay flush, which meant that the angle was consistent, and given all the care he had taken to measure it at the start, he was confident that it was also correct. Crouching, he moved the long ruler up its whole length, and still it touched the surface everywhere. He did it again, and this time it would not lie flat and flush. He was right, the angle had increased, and if it kept doing that then the slope would be steeper and all the harder to raise the tower and stop it from rolling back. Rufus lay flat on the ground to make absolutely sure.

'Lucius,' he hissed back. 'Come and hold this for me.'

He heard a snigger from the darkness back in the shed, before light glinted off the top of a helmet and the legionary came towards him.

'I want you to hold the stick as it is now,' he whispered before the man boomed out a question. 'Keep low and hold it steady.' The soldier did as he was told, and Rufus reached into his pouch for a compass to measure the change of angle. It was less than he had expected, a mere one degree, but then things always felt and looked worse than they were.

'What are you doing, sir?' Lucius asked as the centurion crawled over to the edge of the ramp.

'Hush!' Rufus wanted to take a look down at the side of the ramp. 'Go back to the shelter!' He was at the edge before he decided that it would be hard to see while lying down and easier to kneel. He pushed up and leaned out to study the timber supports. Pale faces peered back up at him, dozens of them.

'What are you doing?' Rufus asked, his mind so full of the issue at hand that he surprised even himself by his stupidity. He gaped. The ditch to the side of the ramp was full of armed men, sitting and waiting.

'Alarm! Sound the alarm!' Lucius' powerful voice was good for something. The man stood behind Rufus, and then raised the ruler and flung it down into the mass of enemy warriors. An arrow came back, making a dull clang as it broke through a plate on his cuirass, and then a bolt from the wall flicked the top of the parapet and slammed into his back, and he fell, pushing Rufus aside and tumbling off the side of the ramp.

The ditch was like a disturbed ants' nest, a teaming mass of bodies getting up, and there were ladders against the side of the ditch. Men's mouths opened as they shouted, an angry roar rather than any words, and already some were rushing up the ladders.

Rufus sprang to his feet and ran.

'Alarm!' The legionary with the missing teeth gave an odd, hissing shout. Other voices were shouting, then a cornu began to sound. A stone slammed into the roof of the shed and the legionary flinched. Rufus went past him before he turned to look back. There was no one else in the long shed. He reached for his sword, before remembering that he had left it behind because it was bound to get in the way when he had to measure the ramp.

'Oh shit!' the legionary gasped, crouching behind his shield. He fumbled to draw his own sword. 'Oh shit!' The blade would not come free.

'Run, man! Run!' Rufus tried to call, but his voice was no more than a rasp. His throat felt parched. The legionary glanced back at him, uncertain, then staggered as a spear struck his scutum. He spun, reeling for balance, and another spear was driven through his armour and into his stomach. A big man put a foot on the Roman, who screamed as the spear point was ripped free. Others were crowding behind him.

Rufus ran, fleeing down the shed and out into the nearest redoubt. He saw the startled faces of two soldiers waiting to man the scorpio. They gaped at him and he wanted to say something, but could not find the words. Nor could he stop himself. Instead he bounded past them and out of the gap in the rear rampart. The two men followed the centurion, but Rufus did not look to see what was happening and all he heard were pursuers close behind him, so he forced himself to go faster. There were more men ahead, dozens of them, from a huddle of men on outpost duty to thirty or forty who had carried up timber and wicker screens to add to the defences.

Horns blew, and there were shouts of triumph from behind him.

'The enemy!' a voice shouted.

'Save yourselves!' came another voice.

Men dropped what they were carrying, unsure what was happening and where to go. Ahead was the main camp, and Rufus headed for it because it was in his path and perhaps because he felt that it was the safest place to be.

A stone came whizzing out of the darkness, striking a knot of the men on guard and flinging two aside like rag dolls. Another of the men started shrieking, and suddenly all of them began to run. Someone barged into Rufus, almost knocking him over, but he kept going until his boot caught on something and he tripped, slamming into the ground. His leg screamed in agony as someone trod on him and someone else stood on his hand. He tried to push up, there was blow to the back of his head and then only blackness.

Crispinus was taking a light meal when the trumpets began to sound. He was alone, glad for once not to have people expecting him to listen or tell them what to do, and as an indulgence he had taken off his shoes. He leaped up from the couch, slid his gladius from its scabbard and hurried to the door, his ungirt tunic hanging almost down to his ankles. His chamber led to a larger room, where two slaves sprang to their feet. Crispinus ignored them, as the trumpets kept calling. A helmeted head appeared through the flap forming the main entrance.

'Alarm, sir! Sounds like an attack!'

Crispinus went past him. There was the glow of flames beyond the front rampart, bathing the top of the city wall with red light. Men were talking excitedly, emerging from the tent lines, running about, sometimes even to the places where they were supposed to form up. A centurion emerged from the principia.

'Turn out! Turn out!' the man bellowed. 'Get a move on!' He saw the legatus and dashed over.

'A sally, my lord! Looks like they're after the ramp!'

'Yes. Form them up as quick as you can and bring them on. You and you,' he pointed to two of the guards still outside his tent, 'follow me!'

'My lord?' the centurion called after him, but the legatus was running for the main gate, barefoot and armed only with a sword, the two legionaries struggling to keep up. 'Oh bugger,' the centurion added under his breath. 'Stand to arms!' he yelled. 'Form up!'

Crispinus reached the gate as a crowd of fugitives surged to come in through the sheltered entrance, pushing aside the sentries.

'Stop, you mongrels!' The legatus bawled at them.

'Halt, you bastards!' Caecilius had appeared, and if he lacked the skill of a trained orator his voice had the power of someone well used to giving orders. Two more centurions rushed up to join them as they stood in the middle of the road.

Crispinus wondered what he would do if they did not stop,

then felt a wave of sheer relief as the men slowed to a walk, then stopped and began to look sheepish.

'Who is in charge here?' Caecilius bellowed. 'You. Longus, isn't it? Then get a grip, lad! Sort these buggers out.'

'Stay here, Caecilius,' the legatus told him. 'Out of my way.' He strode into the crowd.

'Clear a path for the legatus!' one of the centurions yelled as both followed him.

'Greeks! Hundreds of the bastards!' a sentry called down from the top of the narrow tower built to the left of the gateway. It was a clavicula, the wall on the right curving out so that no one could rush straight into the camp, which at the moment meant that Crispinus could not see past it. He ran forward, pushing stragglers out of the way, until he was clear because he wanted to see if anyone was still resisting.

'Praise be to holy Isis,' a centurion said as he came up beside him. The picket was still there, fifty paces in front of the gate according to regulations. There were forty of them and Crispinus was glad that he had listened to Caecilius and doubled the number of men even at night, for there they stood, solid as a wall and tall as towers, facing off a mass of enemies some thirty or forty paces beyond them. Behind them fires were spreading, and he guessed that the Nicopolitans had done a lot of damage, but at least they had not broken into the camp.

'Come on!' Crispinus knew that his duty was to go back and make sure that his men were forming up and then direct them to fight in an organised manner. Yet every moment he waited, more would burn, and besides he did not want to wait. He sprinted up behind the picket, saw Sentius, a centurion in the third cohort, standing stolidly beside his men.

'Caius, I'm glad it is you,' Crispinus told him, ignoring the officer's surprise at seeing a barefoot and unbelted legatus. In truth he was pleased. Sentius was an unimaginative fellow, lacking in initiative, but he had a doglike stubbornness and loyalty about him.

'They're holding back for the moment, sir,' Sentius reported.

'Then let's drive them off.'

Sentius blinked, then obeyed. 'Prepare to advance. Hey there! Silence in the ranks!' he bawled as men muttered in surprise.

'Come on, boys!' Crispinus called out. 'These cheeky buggers are burning what we have made. Let's show them that they don't mess with Hispana!'

They cheered. Crispinus could not really believe it, but they cheered him.

'Forward march!' Sentius called, and they went, almost as neatly as on parade, four ranks each of ten men walking towards two or three times their number – it was hard to tell in the gloom, but there were at least that many dark shapes against the flamelight behind them.

'Steady there!' Sentius told his men. 'Watch the dressing.'

One of the warriors ran forward a few yards and threw a javelin, which dropped short. No one followed him and after a moment he drifted back to join the rest.

'Pila!' Sentius shouted. The legionaries got ready to throw.

'No, keep going!' Crispinus called and was not quite sure why. 'On to them.'

Sentius realised that the legatus was next to him, as he stood just to the side of the right-hand corner of the formation. He blinked once again, and again obeyed.

'Ready to charge.' The legionaries shifted their grip slightly to wield the pila as spears instead of throwing them as missiles.

'Charge!' Crispinus yelled, raising his sword high as he ran, his loose tunic billowing like a woman's dress with the motion.

'Kill the bastards!' Sentius screamed as the legionaries charged, shouting defiance at the enemy, most of whom faded into the night. A few raised shields, and one flung a javelin which bounced off the boss on a legionary's scutum. At the last moment they turned to escape. One was knocked over as a shield slammed into his back, and the pila jabbed forward, the little pyramid-shaped heads driving deep through armour and clothes and into flesh. The man on the ground screamed as he was stabbed again and again.

'Keep going!' Crispinus shouted, for the legionaries had halted as they finished the men off.

'Stand fast!' Sentius yelled. 'Look!' A row of men were coming towards them, weapons glinting. Arrows came, clattering against shields or clanging off helmets. 'Steady there! Front rank, pila!' Men shuffled back into formation, and changed their grip. 'Now!' Ten men flung the heavy javelins into the night. The enemy stopped, and there were grunts and cries of pain as a couple fell. Slim javelins hissed as they came back, banging louder into shields than the arrows.

'Get behind me!' Sentius shoved the legatus back so that he could protect them both with his own scutum. 'Second rank, now!' An arrow hit the centurion's shield, the head just breaking through. 'Third and fourth ranks, now!' A couple of the pila clattered together and fell harmlessly, but most kept going. 'Follow me!' Sentius called. 'Charge!'

A legionary was struck in the face by a javelin as he ran and his head snapped back, before he fell, tripping the man behind. Some of the Nicopolitans came on to meet them as both formations broke apart. A stocky, bearded man deflected the thrust of a heavy scutum on his shield, and managed to slip his own blade low, past the Roman's defence and drive it into his groin, making the man squeal in sheer agony. Sentius saw a tall warrior, punched with all his weight behind the boss of his shield, driving the man back without knocking him over. Behind him, Crispinus dodged a cut, counter attacked, taking a lump of bronze edging from his opponent's shield, then jumped back to avoid another slash. There seemed to be more and more enemies coming out of the shadows and closing on the legionaries. Sentius rammed the point of his gladius through his opponent's teeth, then slammed his shield forward to push the corpse free from his blade. The one facing Crispinus saw a chance, slashing hard to the side, slicing through the centurion's crest and denting his helmet, before the legatus cut with all his strength and sheared off the man's arm. Blood pumped, and the warrior stared disbelievingly at the stump, until Crispinus drove his blade into the man's throat.

The legionaries were holding on, but only just and half a dozen were down, two more felled by the stocky bearded man, who was yelling in a language that was not Greek. Still more enemy were coming. Crispinus heard horses' hoofs pounding on the ground, and saw the tall shapes of cavalrymen coming from the right, but could not tell whose they were. Sentius was staggering, his helmet knocked askew by the blow and blood pouring from his forehead into his eyes. A warrior appeared, spear ready to throw. Somehow Crispinus just managed to swing his blade to deflect the missile, but a horseman was galloping towards them, then he was past, his long spatha sweeping in an awkward cross-bodied arc, but the rider must have had great strength and the blade a keen edge because the blow beheaded the warrior facing him. Crispinus just had time to see the wreath shield blazon of ala Britannica before the rider was past, hacking down to the right. More troopers followed, among them a decurion with a high plume to his helmet, and the enemy fled once again. Trumpets were sounding behind them, which hopefully meant that men were coming from the camp.

Sentius had ripped off his helmet and was scrabbling at his eyes. 'I can't see!' Crispinus leaned down, yanking the cloak from one of the corpses and spat onto the edge of it before wiping the centurion's eyes. As he did he noticed that a Roman corpse was just a few yards away. It was one of the centurions who had followed him from the camp, the one who had thanked Isis, and now the man was dead, lying over the corpse of a warrior. Presumably he had killed the man, and then someone else killed him, but although it had gone on so close to him, Crispinus had not realised that the centurion was there, let alone what he was doing.

Sentius breathed a sigh of relief. 'Beg pardon, sir, but you look terrible.'

Crispinus realised that his tunic was drenched in blood already turning sticky, and his feet hurt and might be cut or bruised, but none of that mattered because the enemy were retreating and he felt that the attack was over for the night. Apart from the horsemen there were men appearing from all sides, and officers shouting, but this time they gave a sense of control rather than shambles.

'You all right, sir?' Caecilius had appeared.

Crispinus grinned. 'You should see the other fellow – oh, there he is!' He pointed to the corpse.

'They fooled us, my lord. Made us think they didn't have the guts to attack.'

'We won't make that mistake again, primus.'

'No, sir, we won't. But why don't you get cleaned up while I make sure everything is secure and take a look at the damage.'

'I'll come with you. You, man,' he pointed to one of the

legionaries. 'Run to the praetorium and tell my boys to bring me fresh clothes, and especially boots.'

'Sir.' The man turned to go.

'Oh, and the rest of my dinner! The bastards interrupted me.' The closest men laughed. 'Right, let's go, primus.'

XVIII

The large camp to the east of Nicopolis
Tenth day before the Kalends of May
The eleventh day of the siege

THE THREE LEGIONARIES stood rigidly to attention,
helmets clasped under their left arm, and right arm
pressed firmly against their side. All three were bearded,
although in the case of the youngest, Julius Felix, this was a
generous description of the wisps of hair on his chin. The main
chamber of the praetorium in Cerialis' camp had gone quiet,
for the soldiers were deeply uncomfortable at being summoned
before not simply their centurion and one of the tribunes, but
the prefect in charge of this camp and even the legatus himself.
This was not how they had wanted their morning to begin.

Cerialis and the other officers stared at them for a while,
before the prefect sighed. He knew what had gone on – or at
least most of it – but Crispinus said that he wanted to hear it
from the men themselves so they must go through it again.

'So you were on guard?' Cerialis asked the spokesman, with
an encouraging smile.

'Yes, sir!' Clodius Secundus had been with VIIII Hispana
for fifteen years, a lazy, unreliable man with a long record of
facing charges, usually of drunken and disorderly conduct,
with periodic forays into theft and abuse of civilians. The gods

alone knew where he was from, but the record showed that he had enlisted in Londinium. Privately his centurion suggested that this had probably been in an advanced state of inebriation and that it was rumoured the man wanted to hide in the legions after upsetting several of the gangs in the city.

'With these two, Felix and Priscus? At the far end of the outpost line, where the rocky outcrop faces the highest part of the cliff? Before the mounted pickets take over and link us to the northern fort.'

'Sir.'

Crispinus interrupted. 'You have not done anything wrong, Secundus – or at least nothing we chose to notice this time. It's Lucius, is it not?'

'Sir.' The soldier's tone suggested that he was wary of admitting this, but could not see another way.

'And you were on the alert because you heard the commotion and saw the light from the sally on the western side of the city.'

'Yes, sir, we were on the alert, sir.'

Crispinus rolled his eyes in frustration, prompting Cerialis to pick up the report in front of him. 'Perhaps it is easiest for the moment if the tesserarius tells us again what you told him.'

'Sir!' Duccius stepped forward and stamped to attention. He was one of those men who liked to shout. He also cared for precision, and produced a writing tablet from the pouch on his belt. 'Yes, sir! On the eleventh day before the Kalends of May, I came on duty at the start of the second hour of the night and began to inspect the outpost line. All was in order at picket one, and picket two, after which I spoke to the *duplicarius* Acer, from the ala Britannica, because his men were providing a dozen troopers for guard duty for each watch. He observed that it was a fine night, and I replied that—'

'Perhaps we could skip this part and get to your encounter with these three men,' Cerialis suggested.

Duccius nodded, then began to scan his tablet, his lips moving as he read his own account.

'The last outpost in the line is much further ahead than the rest, is it not?' Cerialis prompted. 'And can you explain to us why that is?'

Duccius' eyes flicked from one face to another. His written version had not covered this and surely the prefect knew full well about all of this. 'It's further forward, sir.' He affirmed. 'So in advance of the rest and nearer the city.'

Cerialis' pity and impatience got the better of him, and he turned to Crispinus. 'There is a cluster of rocks. Getting to and from them in daylight is risky, because they have engines able to cover the ground, so the men who take over at the end of the night have to stay there all day. They've stretched cloaks across a few poles driven into the ground to give themselves shelter, and take food and drink to last their shift. Three men spend the whole night there, one on guard at all times, and then another three take over for the day. Isn't that right, Duccius?'

'Yes, sir! There is a cluster of rocks. Getting to and from them in daylight...' Duccius' brow furrowed as he tried to recall the prefect's words. 'So that it is risky...'

'I believe I understand, tesserarius,' Crispinus said, interrupting the recital. 'I believe what matters is when you came to inspect them. That was unusual I understand?' Seeing the panic in the man's eyes, he quickly went on. 'I mean to say that you arrived earlier than usual.'

'Yes, sir, I arrived earlier than usual. The reason I arrived earlier than usual was that...' Relief flooded across the man's dark tanned face as he found his place. 'The duplicarius explained that one of his outposts had reported strange noises coming from the city. Agreeing that we ought to check on this, the two of us went to see the decurion in charge of those outposts. He informed us that the noises had ceased and that there was no other cause for concern, but that he would keep close watch and told us to do the same.' Duccius sniffed his displeasure. He was a *principalis* in a legion, and the seniority of such a man to a decurion in an ala was unclear and a most delicate subject.

'After that, the duplicarius went back to his men, but now that I was at the far end of the outpost line, I decided to check the closest position first and then move down the line in the opposite direction than usual.' Duccius again appeared nervous, even though Cerialis had assured him that he had acted sensibly. Everyone knew the risks of surprising a nervous sentry in the dark, but someone walking past behind the outposts might well cause an unnecessary alarm.

'That was sensible, Duccius,' Crispinus told the man. 'I like initiative in my officers.' It was a moot point whether the most junior of the *principales* counted as an officer, but the man needed encouragement. 'Which meant that you first went to the outpost performed by these three men?'

The legionaries stared at the edge of the tent as if the mere intensity of their gaze could bore a hole in it and let them fly away to freedom.

'Yes, sir. These three men, sir.'

'And this was what, a good half an hour before you would reach them in the normal routine?' the prefect asked.

'Give or take, sir.' It clearly pained Duccius to be imprecise.

'And tell us what you found.' Cerialis' face was so rigid that it must have taken considerable effort. Unlike Crispinus, he had heard this testimony before.

The tesserarius licked his finger and found his place. 'As I approached the outpost, I took care to stand tall and walk in as plain sight as possible. I called out "Venus" because that was the password for the night. In response there were low noises and I heard someone say, "Go on, my son!" in an encouraging manner. Coming closer I observed Priscus standing guard, his pilum propped up against his shield.' This time the sniff was one of disapproval. 'In the shadow of the rocks, Secundus was crouching, while Felix lay on his front beneath the shelter of a cloak. On approaching closer I observed that a woman lay underneath the legionary. They were humping.' This produced far less scorn than a man standing guard and not holding shield and weapon.

'I approached and said, "What is all this?" Secundus said, "Oh shit!" and sprang to his feet. "Omnes ad stercus!' said Priscus, while legionary Felix continued to hump, while the woman moaned. "Get up you fool!" Secundus told him. "We're humped!" Legionary Priscus grabbed for his pilum and knocked this over with his shield and said, "Oh bugger, oh bugger!"'

Cerialis bit his lip to keep a straight face, and was relieved when Crispinus cut in.

'This was a woman from the camp, I presume?' the legatus asked.

'No, sir, once they were finished'—the two older legionaries exchanged brief glances at the expense of their younger comrade—'she said that her name was Artemis and that the price was a half drachma for playing my flute and a full drachma for more. She was from the city, my lord. A professional,' he added.

'Jupiter's holy toga,' Crispinus said, shaking his head in sheer wonder. It was a traditional oath of the legions, more of a joke now than anything else. 'You, Secundus, how often has this happened? Every time you went on outpost duty.'

'Sir,' the legionary acknowledged.

'And what about the nights when others were on duty?'

'Don't know, sir,' Secundus lied.

Crispinus chuckled. 'Then Venus was the right password, wasn't it?'

'Sir.'

'The centurion Germanus had mentioned that he wondered why there were so many volunteers for outpost duty during the night. Sounds as if this whore appeared the first night, and they told her to come back the next night at a set time. Judged right, all three could enjoy her before someone came to check on them.'

Crispinus barked his laugh. 'Well, I did say I wanted to see initiative in my men. And where is this Artemis now?'

'May be best to let Duccius finish his story.' Cerialis knew that he was on the verge of breaking down. 'It is, uh... interesting.'

Duccius stamped to attention again, in spite of Crispinus' effort to wave him down. 'I stepped towards them and said, "Well, my lads, what have we here? You are in trouble now and no mistake." At which point the woman, Artemis, came towards me and knelt down, lifting my tunic.'

Arrian choked back a snigger.

Crispinus glared at him. 'Go on.'

'At that moment, legionary Priscus shouted, "Hey, there are more of them tonight!" and as I pushed the woman away I saw that two more whores had appeared, one of whom said that she was Princess Azátē, daughter of King Abgarus of Osrhoene.'

'Hercules' balls, man, you cannot call a princess a whore!' Crispinus gasped. Cerialis covered his mouth with his hand so as not to betray himself.

'Sorry, sir, forgetting myself. Two women came into the outpost – Princess Azátē, daughter of King Abgarus of

Osrhoene, and another whore.' Arrian was shaking with silent laughter, and the angry expression of the legatus only made it worse. 'Priscus clapped his hands,' Duccius went on, 'and took the princess by the arm and said, "I don't care who you are, lass, let's see your tits!" At this point Secundus said, "Oh shit! Shut up, you fool!" and young Felix stood up, adjusting his breeches and said, "What is going on?" He sounded very cheerful.'

'I bet he did,' Crispinus conceded.

'At this point the princess shook herself free and stepped back. "Take me to your commander," she told me, but I was busy pushing away the whore in front of me. "Oh yes, my girl," I told her, "and how do I know you are who you say you are and not just another whore."' There was sweat on Duccius' brow, but he was a man of resolution and continued to read. 'Priscus lunged forward, saying, "Fancy name or not, I'm first!" and the princess pushed the other whore at him and he began to tear at her clothes. She screamed and tried to fight him off, and the princess started to run, until young Felix grabbed her around the waist and used his other hand to rip her dress down in front before kissing her.'

Crispinus stared at the soldiers. Young Felix was blushing a bright red and his right leg was quivering. 'Disgraceful,' he said, shaking his head. 'But the princess was not harmed otherwise?'

'Her dress fell away, along with her under tunics, but she still had her cloak, and she was screaming in a hearty voice that she would have us all killed. But then the trumpets sounded from the far side of the city and I told her to shut up, and sent Secundus to give the alarm, and told Felix to let go and Priscus to pull himself together and stand to arms. Artemis vanished in all of this, and I told the princess to be silent again or she would feel the back of my hand, because we had to listen out to see if the enemy were attacking over here as well. And she would not keep quiet, so I hit her and she bit me, and... and it was not long after that that your lordship rode up with the reserves.'

'Indeed I did,' Cerialis said, because there was nothing else of importance to recount. 'And the enemy did not attack us in this area, launching their main sallies to the west and against our fort to the north, although that one appears half-hearted at best.'

'And we threw them back, in no small part thanks to the men sent to our aid from your ala.' Crispinus smiled at the prefect.

'Merely following standing orders – your standing orders, my lord.'

'Then aren't we both clever. There is damage and loss, but it could all have been far worse. And thanks to the unorthodox conduct of these three soldiers, we also have an exalted and useful guest in our camp – albeit one who has been treated in a style that no royalty would expect. We cannot undo that, and on balance I am willing to overlook your conduct. Nothing will go on your records, but I shall keep my eye on you and expect you to prove your worth when the time comes to storm the city. Is that understood?'

'Sir,' the three men chorused.

'You will not be placed on outpost duty, but I am sure your centurion can find something suitable for your unusual qualities.' The centurion grinned broadly. 'Good. Then dismissed.' The men marched out, their relief palpable.

'Do you want me to make sure there are no more commercial assignations?' Cerialis asked.

'No. But do make sure there is an intelligent officer at that outpost. See if he can find out anything useful about the mood in the city. He has discretion to do this in whatever way seems appropriate for the good of the res publica.'

'That's an order you don't find in any manual,' Cerialis said happily.

'And what of this princess? Are we sure that it is Azátē? When can I see her?'

'She is asleep, my lord, and her girl says that she cannot be disturbed until she has recovered from all her perils. She is in the praetorium.' Cerialis gave a theatrical cough. 'And of course I have vacated the place. While her identity cannot be proven, her manner is sufficiently commanding to suggest high birth, and I believe her.'

'Indeed, why would anyone take the risk merely to claim to be a princess. Though why has she come out at all? It is puzzling, is it not? Hmm. Have we been able to find suitable raiment, at least for the moment?'

'Arrian has generously donated several dresses.'

Crispinus arched his eyebrows.

'They are presents for my mother,' the tribune assured him. 'Finest silk from Antioch.'

'They are being let in at the moment, by some of the camp women handy with a needle. The good tribune's mother has a more imposing figure than the princess. And for my part I do not doubt that that is who she says. She knew your name, and that of the noble Hadrian, and spoke with some familiarity of our purpose here. I wondered whether we should ask around the traders to see whether any have been to Edessa and seen the princess, before deciding that we might wish to keep her presence hidden, at least for the moment.'

'Very wise, very wise indeed,' Crispinus said. 'Yes, you did the right thing, and we must give every honour to our guest, but ensure that only the barest minimum know that she is with us. She is not badly hurt?'

'Pride, more than anything else. Just as well Duccius was there though or it might have been a good deal worse – and the Nicopolitans helped by launching their attack. We got off lightly, all told.'

'If by that you mean that our royal guest was not actually raped then I suppose that is true.' Crispinus shook his head. 'The surprises of military life continue to baffle me. Let us hope the experience has not soured her view of us.'

'She's determined, and very ambitious. I could tell that from the start. If we can give her what she wants then I reckon she will be as well-disposed as you wish.'

'We shall see. Once darkness falls, send her to my camp. Make sure the escort is composed of reliable men and send enough to make sure that she is safe. I'll have suitable quarters prepared and then can see what she wants. Understood? Good, then we had best take a look at your positions before I return to the far side of the city.'

Crispinus was impressed with what he saw, with the redoubts being strengthened.

'We will have double the men on duty and armed day and night,' Cerialis assured him. This second ramp was the obvious next target, and as he studied it Crispinus realised the true extent of the damage to the western one. The attackers had poured pitch over the timber supports on both sides and then set torches to it. On the left the fire had not really taken, but on the right the timbers had almost all burned through and the earth spoil subsided into the ditch. Caecilius was not sure that they could repair it, and favoured starting afresh, which meant that they had lost the work of a good ten days. The primus pilus also wanted an increase in the number of men ready to fight rather than in the work parties, which meant that the labourers would have to do more for longer or the progress would slow. We got off lightly, the prefect had said, and it could indeed have been a lot worse; could have been a lot better though as well.

Crispinus could not help thinking of Cleopatra as the hooded and cloaked figure was ushered into the dining area of the praetorium. The maid appeared for the moment, the one her mistress had flung into the grasp of her attackers, and then they were alone. A meal was set on the table, half in Greek style and half according to Jewish custom, since Hadrian had told him that the princess favoured Hebrew practices. Crispinus was not sure whether these would permit a shared meal, assuming that she was ardent in her adherence to their rules. She could refuse if she wanted, and at the very least the offer was a mark of hospitality. In deference, and in case the alarm went up again, he had on well brushed shoes, a bleached tunic and a muscled cuirass. His sword hung from a stand, ready for him to slip the belt over his shoulder.

'Welcome,' he said, inclining his head the tiniest of fractions. Roman senators bowed to no one, save emperors whose memory would be damned as soon as they were dead and it was safe to insult them. 'May I offer you some light refreshments. There is wine from one of my own estates.' That was not actually true, but it came from vineyards nearby and she was not likely to notice the difference.

The princess stood in front of him, her hood so deep that he could not see her face. She said nothing.

'I know dear Cerialis has already apologised for the

misbehaviour of our men last night, but I too must beg your forgiveness. You will not see those men again.' Cerialis had strict instructions to ensure that, and let her think what she chose.

Still the princess stood, like a small statue being delivered for a garden and still covered to protect it. When she moved, it was fluid, and if not Cleopatra and her laundry bag, the hooded cloak fell away behind her, and Crispinus had to wonder a good deal about Arrian's mother, for the silk dress was almost transparent. Presumably the respectable matron wore other layers underneath.

Azátē let him take a good look, then dropped to her knees, hands clasped in front of her. 'Please, lord, help me,' she begged, her Greek with a heavy accent yet clear in every word. 'I beg you to save me and save my people.' The performance was a good one, making him wonder whether royal ladies were taught this sort of thing as children or by instinct knew how to do it. Crispinus tried to remember what age the divine Julius had been when Cleopatra came to his room and stirred his pity, lust and interest. This girl was a similar age, but he reckoned that he was a decade or so younger than the dictator. So much the better.

The legatus reached down and took hold of her arms. Azátē looked up, the faintest of bruises on her cheek and he suspected that she could have concealed that if she had wanted.

'I am sent here to help you, your highness, so will do all in my power. Now stand, for you are the daughter and granddaughter of great kings.' He lifted, as gently as he could, and she rose. Crispinus was a short man, yet even so the top of her head barely touched his chin. Her hair was soft and lightly perfumed. Presumably her maid had brought the essentials with her, or somehow obtained them in the unlikely setting of a camp.

'I was a prisoner,' she whispered and her voice now was husky. 'I came to free my people and the magistrates locked me up in the palace.'

'Then they will be disappointed.'

She moved her head, eyes large in that small, delicate face as she stared up at him. 'They do not know. I left a girl to pretend to be me, and a household to give all appearances that I am still in the palace.' She gave a thin smile at her own cleverness. 'The same girl learned of the way out used by the women of the night, so I came out in disguise, while they were all distracted planning their attack. They do not suspect a thing.' Her chuckle was that of a small child, very pleased with herself.

Crispinus wanted to know whether she brought any word of weaknesses in the defences, and whether they might sneak men in through this side door, but concentration was not easy as her eyes widened even more and her lips parted, moist and welcoming. He kissed her, and just had time to hope that those bastards from the city did not attack tonight.

Nicopolis
Late on the fourteenth night of the siege

D OMITIUS WRESTLED WITH *his soul. He had killed another man – at least almost certainly, for his aim was true and the bolt had struck the face and flung the soldier back behind the wicker barricade. They said that Philip of Macedon, Alexander's father, had lost an eye to an arrow shot by an engine, and yet had lived on for twenty years, leading his army and fighting on foot and horseback. Domitius had always wondered about the story ever since he had first seen a ballista operated on the practice range and driving its bolts through thick planks to burst out the other side. Those were modern machines of course, and the instructors liked to show off so chose targets whose destruction would prove most spectacular – there was not much practical purpose to shooting at a melon, for instance. Perhaps in Philip's day, the early ballistae had far less power, being little more than glorified bows, or the king was at long range or the missile bounced first on cover and lost a lot of its force. People could be lucky, but he did not think that was true of his target; that man was dead or perhaps worse dying a slow and painful death.*

Whatever had happened, it was done and nothing could undo it. Most days, Domitius was taken around the walls to advise about the use of the artillery, and to repair engines when there were problems. The Nicopolitans were keen, but most of the engines were old and there was no one who had any experience of shooting them at real targets. Domitius knew the theory, and it had not really bothered him to instruct these men just as in the past he had learned and then instructed legionaries. Pride, his sense of what virtue meant, far more than the threats, made him do the job to the best of his ability, and his pupils were improving, not least because they got plenty of practice. They were still poorer at hitting a moving target, or the briefly appearing head bobbing up from cover. It was always a hard thing to drum into anyone's head, that the trick was to guess where the enemy would be and aim there, not at where he was.

'So think,' he had told the men working a light bolt shooter in the tower closest to the Roman siegeworks to the west. Several shots later, all of them missing, and he had taken over and aimed the machine himself. 'Now wait, wait,' he had told them, leaning over the machine, watching a gap of no more than a foot where the wicker screen was lower as two 'mice' were joined together, so that a man's head was visible as he passed. A moment before that, men coming from up the slope cast a shadow plain enough to see even at this distance. It would be a lie to say that he did not think anything at the time, that the habits of instruction had taken over, for he knew that curiosity was stronger. After years spent working with all kinds of artillery, this was the first time he had ever been offered a live target and the temptation was so strong to find out whether he really was as good at his job as he thought. The shadow appeared and he pulled the lever without the slightest hesitation, felt it was a good shot and then the sheer thrill of success flooded over him as the helmeted head appeared, the bolt struck and the man was flung down.

'That's how it is done,' he had told the grinning men. Some

of them were too young or too old to be in the legions, but in so many ways they reminded him of the soldiers he had known and he felt close to them.

There ought to have been remorse. He had had hours and hours to think about it, but instead of sorrow or guilt there was only the guilt that he did not feel any regret at all. Blame the engineers for leaving that gap – probably for light to help work and save having to use lamps or torches – and blame the damned fool himself for not ducking or at least rushing past an opening. The men nearby did not seem to have learned the lesson, or at least had forgotten it quickly and blamed the strike on bad luck, because when he came back to the tower later in the day the crew was excited because they reckoned that they had hit another man in just the same spot. Domitius had congratulated the bald old man who had aimed and shot the dart, patting him on the shoulder.

Domitius had felt more divided the morning after the first sally, although even then it had been easy to share Simon's excitement when he spoke of leading one of the groups. One of the guards helping to escort him had chipped in to say that the merchant's son had cut down four or five Romans as he led the charge. Simon had shrugged and assured him that it was only three and then the other man had joked that a trader like him ought to know better how to sell something.

'All right, make it ten, if you like,' Simon had agreed.

That morning all the men he passed were happy, most of them talking and few really listening. They had hit the enemy hard, and it made them feel good. Domitius had seen something of the damage, and reckoned the western ramp was severely, even fatally, compromised.

As usual, Simon was shrewder than most. 'We lost a few. Going too far rather than pulling back. Their cavalry came up and caught a good few.' He gestured at the row of severed heads mounted on spears atop the nearest redoubts. 'Reckon they captured some as well,' he added grimly. 'Don't know what has happened to them.'

The next morning Simon was far more subdued than he had been since the earliest days of the siege, although he would not say why.

'Have you seen, Sara?' Domitius asked. 'And the rest of the family.'

Simon nodded, but would not be drawn. However, John met them up in one of the galleries inside the curtain wall, helped there by the servants. Once there, he sat, and chipped away at stone shot waiting to be used by the engines.

'I thought that they might like to benefit from my experience,' he said. 'I was once quite good with those things when I was young.' He pointed to his face. 'Hands not so steady or so strong now, but I can still help them prepare – and tell them how best to aim.'

'Just remember to shoot only at the enemy, old man,' Simon chided him, cheering up for the first time that day.

There was a shout, and men fully raised the hatch so that the light stone thrower close by could fling a missile down at the Romans. An observer watching through a narrow slit shouted excitedly, prompting a cheer.

'You see how much they are learning from me,' John assured them.

'I should go back to my cell and leave the work to you,' Domitius said.

'No.' John's face was serious. 'Better not. Show yourself to be useful.'

A runner came from one of the strategoi, and Domitius was summoned to fix a broken mechanism in an engine in another *tower, so saw no more of the old man that day, and was kept busy until after sunset before being taken back to his cell.*

The next day was the same, for the repeated use of the city's catapults meant that breakages became more and more common, and tended to get more serious. Craftsmen, including some he knew from the elder Simon's workshop, were tasked with fixing the problems, but no one else had as much knowledge as he did, and he was always in demand. He saw less of the younger Simon, although his men still acted as custodians whenever he was away from the prison, and they were friendly, and even more devoted to their commander than they had been from the start.

'Got to be careful,' one whispered. 'You know his sister is with the princess? Yes? Well, her royal highness is inclined to play games. He won't say, but I know our lad is worried.'

That night Domitius was woken by distant shouts. There was a tiny window, high up on the wall of his cell, and through it the light was tinged with red. He wondered whether the Nicopolitans were launching another sally to burn the siege works, and figured that it was about time. The ramp to the east was very high now, which at least meant that it was easier for the artillery in the wall and towers to aim at the Romans there; earlier on, the enemy were so much lower down that the angle was too steep to let them strike that close to the walls.

In the morning Simon was grim faced. 'Be on your guard more than ever,' he said when they were out of earshot of anyone else for a short moment. 'There was a fire last night, houses burned and people dead, food stores destroyed. It does not look like an accident.'

'I was locked in. What do they think I am, a magician?'

'They might not think clearly. Frightened people rarely do.'

There were some bitter glances, men who stood in his path

glaring, only moving to let him by at the last minute, but they were just a few and most of those doing the fighting, including all of the crews he saw that day, welcomed him as enthusiastically as ever. As in the past, they shared fruit and wine with him. Afterwards, on the way to the workshop set up for major repairs to springs and anything else needing retooling, an urchin dodged past Simon and spat at Domitius. A guard swung his open hand at the boy, who ducked and escaped. Before he had gone he had pressed something into Domitius' hand.

'Are you all right?' Simon asked.

Domitius kept his fist clenched to hold the rough object as he wiped his face. He grinned. 'Never happier.'

The craftsmen showed not the slightest change in their attitude. Most were careful, precise men, and they dealt with life as a series of little problems to be solved, and of improvements to make. For the moment, this meant ensuring washers fitted precisely so that sinews could be twisted and the power stored in the springs until released. Mainly they got on with their jobs quietly, only dimly aware of each other's presence, although now and then they would joke and laugh. There was a lot of amusement when someone said that he had heard from someone else that the magistrates were considering asking women to cut their hair short so that it could be used to make ropes for the artillery.

'Be more use if they let them talk the Romans to death,' one said.

'No, if you've ever seen my wife in a rage, you would be more frightened of her than any warrior!'

'Well, she's angry, poor lass – after all, she has to put up with you every day!'

As soon as he had taken a proper look, Domitius had crushed under his boot the little ostracon passed to him by the boy, and as they laughed he happened to be nearby and ground down the last fragment into dust. The flatter fragments of a broken amphora were a good substitute for paper when a man did not want to waste money.

That night he did not sleep well, even before there was more noise and once again the glow of flames. Domitius stared up at the bare ceiling and thought about the note scrawled on the shard of pottery.

'Which side are you on?'

The truth was that he no longer knew.

XIX

Before Nicopolis
Fifth day before the Kalends of April
Sixteenth day of the siege

'G ET LOST, DID we?' Vindex asked as Ferox and Bran rode towards Crispinus' main camp.
'Something like that,' Ferox told him.
There were compounds and work areas spreading for more than a mile behind the main position, mostly occupied by parties of soldiers, although a few had been set down by the traders and other followers, or were housing the animals. Vindex was with a dozen of the Brigantes watching their horses graze and get some exercise, having moved back to the western camp in the last few days. The sound of sawing wood and hammering nails filled the air, and closest to them was one of the siege towers, already some forty feet high and still not finished. A second stood several hundred paces to the right. They must have been plain to see from the walls of the fortress, and Ferox knew that the army usually liked to keep machines like this secret until they were ready. Still, there was not really a suitable ridge to conceal them that was also close enough to make it worthwhile and not mean dragging the things for more than a mile. The one meant for the eastern assault ramp would have a long enough journey as it was.

Vindex nodded at the nearest one. 'Big, isn't it?'

'It is.'

'Taller than the ones at Piroboridava,' Bran noted.

'And look what happened to them!' Vindex reminded them. They had all been besieged in the Roman fort and the Dacians had attacked with two towers. One had bogged down on its way to the wall and been smashed by stones flung from their engines. Ferox, Bran and some others had burned the second one. The young warrior stared up at the tower for a long while.

'Anything new?' Ferox asked Vindex.

'Not much. The convoy has gone back, but I was told we weren't wanted this time. So we help out with the patrols and pickets, and try to look busy the rest of the time so no one asks us to work... Oh, and it sounds like the big chief has found himself a woman. All a secret, and she lives quiet in a compound that's heavily guarded and fenced off from the rest of the camp. Rumour is that it's the princess – the bint you said started all this. He's certainly happy – right ray of sunshine whenever you see him.'

'How many know?'

Vindex shrugged. 'I got chatting to a lass, turned out she was fetching water for another lass who serves the princess. Not sure many know, but you can't really keep a secret like that.'

Ferox gave up wondering just how Vindex had managed to understand and be understood by the woman in question. For all his sinister appearance, the warrior got on well with a lot of people, and especially women, and somehow managed to communicate.

'How is the siege going?' Ferox asked instead of exploring that mystery.

'They came out once in a big way, burned some stuff,

killed a few, got chased back. Reckon they did better than us though. Since then, only a couple of little attacks. Been fires in the city though, the last few nights. Plain enough to see from here, and I reckon one not far back from the main gates and to the left. Not sure otherwise from out here. Made me think back though, like the lad.' He nodded towards Bran, who had walked his horse across to the foot of the tower. 'Remember?'

'Yes.' Ferox said. Before the siege had begun, someone had started a fire in the fort, burning granaries along with vital supplies. Ferox had never quite found out who had done it, although he had his suspicions. Hadrian's man Sosius was there that night, and if he had not started the fire, he had used the distraction to attempt a murder, and now the fellow was inside Nicopolis. 'Makes you wonder,' he said.

Vindex glanced at Bran and sighed. 'You think he still blames himself?'

Ferox did not need to say anything.

'Aye, course he does, poor little sod.' One of the others who had attacked and burned the siege tower was a young woman, a fierce warrior whom Bran had loved, but who had been killed when the Dacians swarmed into the fort. 'I'll keep an eye on him.'

'Thanks. Get him some food and rest now. I'd better report.'

'Are we off again?'

'Maybe.'

'That means yes, and that it'll be another bastard of a fight.'

'Better than working, isn't it?'

'Maybe,' Vindex grunted as Ferox trotted away. 'But then no one's ever called me smart.'

★ ★ ★

A lot had changed since Ferox had been away. Not only had the activity sprawled over a wider area, but there were all the signs of an army settled down. Alongside the sounds of men working was a constant buzzing of flies. His horse was twitching its tail, obviously bothered, and there must already have been a dozen climbing on her face. He leaned forward and flicked with his hand, brushing them off. She had known him long enough to trust him so did not react, but a moment later half of them were back. The wind shifted slightly and the scent rising from row after row of piled manure, each mound twice as high a man, filled his nostrils. That was the army way, just as in a properly regulated camp the latrines were dug, used for ten days, then filled in with earth and a new one dug fifty paces further out, and upwind if they were sensible. The longer the army stayed in one place, the further a man walked to relieve himself. The old joke was of a soldier holding a sponge as he came to report to his centurion, asking for a three-day furlough and permission to shit.

As far as Ferox could see, the camp was in good order and the Hispana and the rest were maintaining good discipline, stacking refuse neatly in set places rather than tipping it anywhere handy, and following all the other regulations. The change came on the outskirts, where the mix of civilians and followers were less fussy about themselves and their animals. All in all, combined with so many people and animals to bite, food and other things to investigate, the plains around Nicopolis had become a sheer paradise for flies, which must make it hard to sleep. If Vindex was right, that was not bothering the legatus too much, and for all his dirty mind, the old scout had a nose for these things.

Crispinus was not in camp when he reported at the praetorium, so Ferox left his mare with one of the orderlies, and made his way on foot forward to the siege lines. The picket in front of the gate were at ease, leaning on shields and chatting. Ahead, paths were marked by numbers, and the steady passage of so many feet and heavy loads had worn away the ground so that they were like very shallow trenches left by some enormous plough. Ferox saw a party carrying baskets of stones on their shoulders heading for a route marked II, and since they were going towards the city, decided to tag along behind. Soon the furrow grew deeper and led into a shed covered on sides and roof with animal hides.

'Out of the way! Out of the way!' a legionary shouted as he pushed men towards the wall. 'Clear a path there! They've hit Serenus.'

The carrying party did their best, struggling to push tight up against the side because the roof sloped down to meet the walls and there was not much room for their baskets. One let his load slip, spilling stones onto the ground.

'Daft bugger, Faber!' an optio yelled at him, but there was no time to pick them up, for more men appeared, carrying a stretcher. They had to slow to squeeze past, then were through. Ferox saw a centurion he knew by sight being carried past, his right arm at a weird angle and his cuirass covered in blood.

'Get those damned flies off!' the one in front called back, and the man was on the brink of tears.

Slowly, as men shifted burdens back to a better carrying position, and the clumsy Faber began scooping up the fallen stones, they prepared to go forward. Ferox went to help the man, and, after a flash of surprise and resentment, the optio came back to do the same.

'Get a move on!' A man came towards them, but the shadowy interior of the shed meant that Ferox only recognised Rufus at the last minute.

'Oh, it's you,' the young centurion said in surprise. He had no helmet and a bandage was tied around his forehead. 'Get a move on, you're clogging things up!' he barked at the optio.

'Sir.'

'Come on, lads, get moving.' The legionaries shuffled off with their burdens.

'Looking for someone?' Rufus asked. 'Thought you were off with the convoy?'

'Supposed to report to the legatus,' Ferox told him. 'They said he was inspecting the siege lines.'

Rufus nodded. 'You might be able to catch him. Now let me see – yes, it's better to keep going and then head across. I'll show you.'

'You've been in the wars, I see,' Ferox said as they walked, because he knew that most Romans did not care much for silence.

'Oh, it's nothing.' There was an edge to Rufus' voice which made this seem more than decent modesty. Reaching a junction between this and other sheds, they went out through a side door to the right, past one of the redoubts, which now sported a tower some sixty feet high. Rufus glanced up. 'Thought the legatus and his party might be up there,' he said. 'He'd mentioned going back to get a better view of it all, but there's only the usual watch up top.'

Ferox was glad, his legs were still stiff from the long ride and he did not fancy climbing all those ladders. They kept going, into another row of sheds, dashing across a gap to reach another. There were no shots or any real sense of danger, but he guessed that Rufus ought to know the risks well, so copied what he did. They moved to the side as a dozen soldiers with empty baskets passed them on their way back to camp, and then again as another group, heavily covered in dust and carrying tools, followed them. From then on there were men everywhere, working, watching through narrow embrasures in the redoubts or heavy screens, waiting beside scorpiones and all the range of larger ballistae, or coming on duty or going off after a shift. The faces were sometimes tired, often bored, and there was a little less of the chatter and joking usual for soldiers. Ferox could not quite sense the mood, but at least did not feel that it was bad.

Rufus led him to one of the redoubts, built on the very edge of the ditch and with a roof protecting it from missiles coming down from the city walls.

'I'd like a tower to match theirs,' Rufus explained, his face more animated than before. 'But there isn't the spare timber yet, or the labour to make it, apart from the trouble we will have from the Nics.' He grinned. 'That's what the fellows are calling the Nicopolitans. You've been away for quite a while so I guess you haven't heard.'

'Where are we in relation to the assault ramp?' Ferox asked. It was always wise to know as much about what was happening as possible, even though he hoped he and his men would not be called upon to play too much of a part in the storming – if it came to that.

Rufus beckoned for him to follow. 'You have to be a bit careful, as the buggers are getting better and better at shooting. Stand just there, hard against the side.' He pointed to a spot beside one of the embrasures. It was closed by a shutter, the bottom pulled back a few inches. Ferox obeyed and squinted through the gap.

'That's the new ramp,' Rufus said, 'or will be.' Ferox could see that the ditch was wholly filled in, and on top of it, stretching to within ten feet or so of the wall was a wide shed with an angled roof rising up in the centre. As he watched, a stone smacked hard against it, throwing up a plume of dust, and then slid off to the side.

'The Nics burned the old ramp, wrecking the whole right-hand side and tumbling it into the ditch. Too hard to repair and we were going to start again, when the thought came that we could use the left-hand side and built a new one out from it. So that's what we've done.' Rufus' pride was obvious, and Ferox suspected that he had had a lot to do with this bright idea. 'And Caecilius wants to make the most of the rest of the ramp in timber, hence the wide sheds. We'll do as much as we can under cover. We're also adding an extra storey to the tower to save us time building here.'

Again, Ferox could not help thinking that 'we' meant Rufus had thought of it. He glanced towards the wall itself and saw that along one section at its foot were the ruins of some mobile sheds. There were corpses among the debris, the flesh bloated and the skin turned such a dark red that it was almost black. He could see chips around the wall's stonework, and a few fragments broken away where they had been attacked with crowbars and picks. There were also far bigger chunks of pale stone among the ruin, far more than had been prised away, so he crouched a little to see up. A long section of parapet was missing from the wall just above, and the gap was covered with sacks filled with sand and bits of timber.

'Ah, you've seen where they tipped their own wall down?' Rufus said. 'Not one of our best plans, at least in hindsight. Lost some good men, and we haven't been able to get the bodies back, which is hard on the men. Still, shows how desperate the Nics are becoming, doesn't it?'

'How long until the ramp and tower are ready?' Ferox asked, not wishing to give his opinion on that.

'These ones? Fifteen days for both? Might shave a half a day or even a day off that, but then we might not. The eastern one wasn't attacked, so has made good progress. It's higher that side though. Be ready in eleven or twelve days.'

'You making that tower taller as well?'

There was silence for such a long time that Ferox turned around. Rufus had his hands over his face, like a child who has just realised that a baffling mystery was simple after all.

'No,' he said sheepishly. 'I don't think anyone has thought of that. Still, have to be careful, don't want it to become unstable. No sign of the legatus. We'll check the sheds on the ramp itself, but I suspect he has moved on from there. May have to leave you to it after that, old fellow. Think I've got some calculations to make.' He grinned.

Crispinus was not at the other sheds, and Ferox found himself walking around behind the two small southern forts and the picket line to reach the eastern camp. The sun was baking, but he preferred being on his own than in all that bustle. If Crispinus wanted him to stay in and around Nicopolis for a while, then he ought to make the most of what little solitude was possible, so he put up with the heat, exchanged the minimum of pleasantries with anyone he encountered and walked on, his own personal cloud of flies buzzing over his head. At least he had acquired a decent broad-brimmed hat – that was decent by his standards even if no doubt unable to meet Philo's. Ferox wondered how the boy and his wife were doing, especially when the Brigantes were away. Vindex had had the sense to make sure that one or two of his warriors were always nearby and ready to accompany Indike if she went far on her own. The pretext would be a lame horse or horses, and as the rigours of the campaign grew, that was unlikely to be a pretence.

Ferox had not heard Rufus or anyone else saying anything

about the city being convinced to surrender. The siege lines and the men in them had a purposeful air about them. That was necessary if the threat was to be convincing, but men readily fell in love with the works of their hands and wanted to know that they did what they were supposed to do. A lot had changed while he was away, and the most visible mark was the severed heads, all crawling with flies, facing the enemy walls. He had passed the prison compound as he rode in, and seen the subdued, dirty men sitting in what little shade had been provided, and wondered what the legatus might decide to do next to prove that his determination was to be feared.

By the time he reached the works on the eastern side, Crispinus had inspected and moved on, but Cerialis was as welcoming as ever, and Ferox was grateful for a short rest and even more for a long drink of watered wine. He could see that Rufus had been right and the ramp this side was much higher. The redoubts, artillery platforms and ramparts to protect it were equally impressive.

'They're bound to try a sally here,' Cerialis told him. 'Surprised they haven't already.'

'Guess they want to wait and do more damage.'

'Probably, but we'll not make it easy for them. If you and your rogues aren't needed elsewhere, I'll be glad to have you over here again. When they do come out, I want to hit them so hard that they don't try it again, and a few more Britons will help scare anybody!'

Ferox thanked him and went on his way. His flies, or possibly their relatives, found him again when he came out of the shelter of the tent and they all resumed their stroll. More than an hour later he at last caught up with Crispinus.

'Where by all that's sacred have you been?' the legatus

shouted cheerfully. 'Loafing somewhere, I suppose? What can you expect from a barbarian, eh?'

Vindex had been right, the aristocrat was certainly cheerful. The sight reminded Ferox very much of the restless, capable and highly conceited young tribune he had known all those years ago, a man in love with intrigue and with himself. Part of him was glad to see the change; the other part remembered just where the eager tribune's schemes had tended to lead in the past.

Ferox had found the bulk of the legatus' party waiting in the hollow by the entrance to the mine workings, only moments before the commander emerged, brushing non-existent dirt from the skirt of his tunic.

'You'd think it would be cool down there, but it's almost warmer than up here,' Crispinus told them. 'Splendid, splendid.' He noticed a trail of dark earth spilled from one of the sacks carrying away the spoil. 'We'll have to switch to doing that only at night from now on. And take it further. No sign that the Nicopolitans know what we're doing and it would be nice to keep it that way. Well, let's be on our way.' He gestured for Ferox to walk beside him. Caecilius showed surprise, but he and the others understood to drop back a little.

'Any of your fellows know anything about mining?' the legatus asked after a while. 'Weren't some sent to the mines?'

'None of the ones left.' Ferox knew that a couple of the former rebels had been condemned to hard labour, but thought that they had all worked on the salt beds and not underground. He did not like closed spaces, even caves, and had no wish to encourage the legatus to send any of his men there.

'Only a thought. They are finding it very good going, so even though it is such a long, long way, it might be ready in time. Hopefully won't need it, but should hate to decide that we do when it is too late. You should take a look – make a nice change to see you bent double when I can stride tall and straight! So did you find what you wanted?' The question was abrupt, and that was also like the legatus' younger self, always playing games and treating a conversation like a fencing bout.

'Yes.'

'You think it will work?'

'One way or another, given luck.'

'That means you don't know. Still, for once your laconic thrift with words does save us all time, and there is so much to do. Alive would be better, but is not essential.' Crispinus glanced back over his shoulder and raised his voice to call back, 'Caecilius, consilium at the seventh hour. Let me see your calculations again and ponder whether we are making best use of all our men. And make sure the miners are on course. We have some numbers for you from their records.'

'Sir.'

'What's that!' Arrian shouted and was pointing. They were in front of the city, walking along the outpost line, so comfortably out of range. The great gateway was near them and something dark had been dropped on a rope from the right-hand tower.

'What's it supposed to be?' someone said.

Ferox found it puzzling that the answer was not obvious, even at this distance. 'It's a man,' he said. 'Or at least it was.'

'One of ours?' Crispinus asked.

'No one missing, my lord, unless it has happened in the last few hours,' Arrian replied.

'Someone from inside then.' He glanced at Ferox, but said nothing. From this distance it was hard to say much, other than that the dangling body could have been Sosius.

'Think there is a sign hung on him,' Ferox said, pulling the brim of his hat down to shade his eyes.

'Make sure we check,' Crispinus told his officers. 'If it is one of our lads then ten of the prisoners get their turn before sunset... And send someone to tell me what the placard says.'

'When?' he said softly to Ferox.

'See how this convoy fares on the way back. Probably when the next one is due or the one after that.'

'Alive is better,' Crispinus told him. 'But if you cannot, then dead will do.'

XX

CRISPINUS WOKE WITH a start from a nightmare, just as the stitching on a section of the tent serving as a roof ripped open and the whole covering shook. Azátē stirred, but did not wake, until another section tore loose and cracked like a whip as it blew in the gale. Hailstones came through, just a few of them, and there was a sound like a falling cliff as more thumped into the roof.

'What is it?' Azátē clung tightly to him, eyes wide and frightened like a child's.

'Get something around you!' he said and shouted for his body slave.

The boy appeared, dressed and well awake. 'There is a storm, my lord!'

'I know that! Attend to the princess.' Crispinus leaned back and kissed her. 'I must go.' He had to force her off before scrabbling for boots and clothes. Someone started to sound the alarm, which was as well, even if it ought to be pretty obvious to anyone. There were shouts as well, and with a great rent half of the roof of his chamber tore away. 'I'll be back,' he said, breeches on, tunic slipped over the top and his sword belt over his shoulder.

Outside was chaos, animals and men running everywhere, the great sheets of tents flying through the air, hail turning to driving rain and anything that could be lifted blowing over. Crispinus stared around him, wanting to do something, but not knowing what it was. He saw the nearest of the siege towers quivering in the gale, then the one beyond it, the taller one, closest to completion and half covered in great iron scales, began to lean and kept on leaning at more and more of an angle until it crashed down onto the ground.

'Oh bugger,' one the guards to the principia said. The man had come to stand behind the legatus, ready to protect him.

Caecilius ran past, bellowing at men to get covers over all the artillery. Rufus trailed after him, echoing the shouts, but with less sense of purpose. Someone yelled a warning and then Crispinus was smothered by damp leather, beaten to the ground as a tent ripped free from one of the huts, and the legionary with him gasped as a spiked peg drove into his arm. They rolled on the ground, and there seemed so much of the great sheet that Crispinus could not fight his way out until help arrived.

'You all right, sir?' Arrian's face was filled with concern.

'Yes, but get help for that man.'

A horseman appeared, somehow weaving his way through the chaos and managing to keep his mount from bolting. He skidded to a halt, and there was no mistaking that gaunt, leering face.

'They're attacking on the eastern side!' Vindex shouted to be heard over the wind. 'The chief says to watch out over here as well, and that they're holding, but could do with whatever help you can spare.' He nodded affably, and did not bother to explain whether the chief was Ferox or Cerialis.

'Fetch me a horse!' Crispinus shouted. 'Now!'

Vindex's gelding tried to run, felt the pressure of the bit in his mouth and contented himself with a crablike shuffle to the side.

'I'm coming with you,' Crispinus told him. 'Once they bring a horse.' They did, very quickly, as well as a couple of legionary cavalrymen, which was the most escort to be found in all the confusion. Rufus came jogging back. 'Tell the primus he is in charge!' Crispinus shouted to him, then jumped into the saddle. 'Whoa, boy, whoa,' he added, smoothing the stallion's neck. 'Tell him I am going to see what is happening on the far side and that he is to stand to arms here and be ready to send reinforcements when I call or he feels he can spare them.'

Rufus nodded, face nervous, but then he always seemed nervous whenever anything happened suddenly.

'Come on, let's go!' Crispinus called to Vindex, who probably could not hear as another tent noisily tore itself apart nearby, but kicked his horse on to follow the legatus as he sped away. One of the legionaries' horses bucked, kicking out and almost hitting Rufus. The rider was flung up, bounced hard back in the saddle, bounced again and somehow stayed on. He let go of his spear, and clung on to the mane as the beast half ran, half hopped after the others.

'Come on!' Ferox shouted. 'We can hold them.' He had a dozen or so of his Brigantes, and almost twice as many others, with a mix of legionaries, auxiliary infantry and cavalry. All of them were on foot, and they were in a ragged line, just two ranks deep. No one had a pilum, few even a spear or javelin, and half a dozen in the second rank lacked shields and were wielding dolabrae as weapons rather than entrenching tools. All stood with their back to Nicopolis, and closer still the huts covering the approaches to the assault ramp. Ferox saw a glow along the horizon, knew that dawn was close and hoped that the dust swirled up by the storm would make it harder for them to be seen from the walls of the city, because he knew that they must be in range. A mob of attackers faced them, trying to build up the courage to sweep them away and then get among the siege works. No torch would keep burning in this gale, but they were bound to have fire pots and tar and could do a lot of harm in a short time. If there were other Romans around then he could not see them. The picket outside the camp ought to have been close, but he had seen no trace of them when he had ridden with all the Brigantes he could find because this was the vulnerable spot. The Nicopolitans had come out in force, and most were attacking the front of the position, well entrenched by Cerialis' men, who by the sound of it were fighting hard and holding them. That would not matter if the hundred or so attackers facing him got through.

Ferox started to bang the flat of his sword against the edge of his shield. 'Let them hear you!' he shouted, and men started to take up the rhythm. The Nicopolitans ought to have come on already, but they were hesitating and anything he could do to make them keep on hesitating was worth it.

A leader appeared from the mass of enemies, urging the rest on, waving a Greek-style kopis in one hand and an oval shield in the other. The sun started to rise, its light giving an odd glow to the dust in the air. A helmet clattered as it rolled in front of Ferox and he had no idea how it had got there. The Nicopolitans began a chant of their own, almost a song with the same angry word repeated over and over again.

'Ready lads!' Ferox called, and braced his shield, gladius held back, elbow bent so that the point was ready to jab forward at eye level. He spat dirt from his mouth, and it still seemed full of muck.

The Nicopolitans charged, the leader and a few others jogging, the rest at little more than a walk, but they came forward and they did not stop at the last minute. The man next to Ferox on the right was flung back as an arrow struck him in the face, and for the moment Ferox faced two enemies. One was the leader, who cut, caught his blade in the top of Ferox's shield, and pulled back when the gladius speared forward at him. Ferox glanced to see if there was a chance to slash at the man on his right, then did not have to, because a legionary with a dolabra stepped into the open space and brought the pickaxe down with a great scything slash that gouged wood from the Nicopolitan's shield. The leader stamped forward, cutting at Ferox, who managed to parry the blow and punched with his shield, driving the man back a pace. Ferox followed, pounding with the shield again, once, twice, before slashing back into the neck of the warrior facing the legionary. That man slumped forward, and the legionary pushed him aside and slashed with his axe again, grunting with effort as he drove the rear spike deep into the forehead of the warrior behind. The other Romans were pushing forward along the line, and suddenly the Nicopolitans went back a few paces.

Both sides stared at each other, all of them gasping for breath. The sun's light was blinding, right in the eyes of the Romans, making them blink. Ferox glanced as best he could to either side, saw that he had several men down, but that the line was still holding for the moment.

The legionary beside him held his dolabra ready and spat

noisily. He had a gladius on his belt and there were shields to pick up from the ground, but the man did not seem interested. Shaking the axe at the enemy he screamed something that was not Latin or Greek or any tongue that Ferox understood. His features were heavy, his arms thick and heavily muscled, and his bare head fringed with grey around a bald centre. Then his entire head disintegrated, shattered by a stone that whipped on and smashed the leg of one of the Nicopolitans ahead of them. Ferox was sprayed with blood and brains, and had to spit because some was in his mouth. The headless body stood for a moment, then sank down.

'Charge!' Ferox shouted, because he had to do something or stand there in horror and because the enemy were as horrified as the Romans. He ran forward, slammed the boss of his shield against the leader, making the man stagger and his shield drop just a little. Ferox stabbed, under the cheek pieces and into the neck above the man's cuirass, twisting the long triangular point free, and more blood was spraying. The other Romans were coming on, shields thudding together, blades sparking as they met other blades or armour, or thudding into flesh and bone. Another catapult stone came, to the left this time and carved a bloody furrow through Roman and Nicopolitans alike. There were shouts, and as Ferox blocked the jab of a short spear, he saw riders, no more than silhouettes, coming from behind the enemy. The warrior facing him jabbed again, and suddenly Ferox's helmet yanked forward, throwing him off balance as the tie snapped and it fell off. His opponent was snarling hatred one moment and then his face collapsed and there was only a bloody mess between the cheek pieces of his helmet as a stone the size of an apple smashed into it.

Both sides broke, and men fled any way they could. A rider, one of the legionaries escorting Crispinus, was plucked from his horse and flung to the ground by another stone, a Nicopolitan fell with a bolt deep in his back, and a Brigantian had his knee shattered by a stone before the missiles stopped as abruptly as they had started. Ferox staggered, his head throbbing, and saw Bran, Vindex, with half a dozen of their men and the remaining legionary horsemen with Crispinus, all struggling to control their panicking horses.

The enemy had gone, and he doubted that they would come back because from the gate of the camp a column of legionaries was doubling forward. Then he realised that the wind had died away, and that would have been a relief had his head not hurt so much. Propping his shield against his leg, he rubbed his forehead and his fingers came away bloody. His helmet lay in the dirt, the crest-holder twisted into a weird shape and half the horsehair crest ripped away, and he guessed that the metal had gouged his skin as it was ripped off.

Crispinus waved to him. 'What a shambles!' he shouted, and then spurred off.

'Keep an eye on him!' Ferox called to Vindex and then decided that he had better get into some shelter in case the people up on the walls tried to do better than the grazing hit that had ruined his helmet and come within a whisker of doing the same to his head.

Thirty-five men stood in two ranks, parading without armour and helmets, without even their belts, so that the issue tunics went down well past their knees. It was the middle of the afternoon, there was no shade and they had stood rigidly at attention for more than an hour. Five of their comrades lay on the ground, left where they had fainted. Three hundred men, as many as could be spared from the clean-up and all the usual work parties and guard posts, formed three sides of a hollow square around them. There were representatives from all the parent units of the men waiting for judgement.

'An oath is sacred!' Crispinus began, standing on a makeshift podium that was really just a neat pile of pack saddles. There was a proper commander's platform behind his camp on the western side, but he wanted this ceremony to occur in the same place as the crime. 'Each man who joins the army swears to serve the princeps and the res publica, to give his strength and his very life to protect them. This is the duty of the soldier of Rome. This is the *virtus* of a man.' He paused for breath and effect. Ferox could see that another of the beltless men was swaying a little, his eyes beginning to flicker.

'Some men are called upon to perform special tasks and take even greater responsibility. Since the days of the kings, eight hundred years ago, the soldiers standing guard in front of a camp of the legions are bound by the most solemn duty to stand their ground at all costs. To fail in this duty is to forfeit life!'

The soldier Ferox had been watching fainted with perfect timing.

'Many famous commanders have imposed that punishment in its sternest form.'

Arrian was standing on the opposite side of the square to Ferox, and the tribune seemed to mouth the word, 'decimation'.

'Our ancestors taught us virtue, they taught us duty, and they taught us justice. Manlius killed his own son for disobeying an order, even though the youth had challenged an enemy and cut him down in single combat. That is justice.'

Ferox felt that the legatus was losing his thread, lost in an aristocrat's love of rhetoric.

'What justice should I give you?' That was better, and had their attention as the legatus waited and ran his eyes over the men. 'What will cleanse this stain on your honour and the even greater honour of your centuriae and of your legion?

'The sentence is decimation!' The legatus' voice thundered across the lines of men. The accused were silent, although several hung their heads, but there was something between a sigh and a groan from the watching soldiers.

'But that sentence is postponed and may be reversed!' Heads went up, eyes were nervous, disbelieving. 'Your names are marked, but you will return to your units and your duties. Serve well and I will consider at the end of the campaign whether or not the judgement can be forgotten. Prove yourselves heroes and the stain to your honour and your unit's honour will be expunged forever!'

The parade cheered the commander.

'He had me worried,' another centurion said to Ferox after the men had been dismissed.

'I guess that was the idea.'

'Never heard of a decimation, not for generations,' the man went on. 'Better to inspire than waste men and terrify the rest. Reckon that lot will give their all.'

Or desert, Ferox thought. They were still a long way from breaching the defences and even that did not mean that the city would fall. As far as he could see there had been no significant damage to the assault ramp or any of the other siege works during the latest sally. The havoc caused by the storm was harder to judge, especially as it sounded as if the western camps were hit worse, and he had not been over there to see.

'He tries to be a good chief, doesn't he?' Vindex said a little later. The Brigantes rode behind Crispinus on his way back round to the western camp. After several days reinforcing

Cerialis, they were to have a day off and rest their horses back at the main camp. 'Scares 'em, then holds out mercy with his judgement.'

'He looks happy anyway,' Ferox conceded. Whether or not it was simply a brave face, the legatus exuded confidence.

'Of course, he looks happy. He's on his way back to camp and you won't see him going short or without his comforts whatever was destroyed. And a cute princess to hump all night! Give me that and I'll be as happy as you like.'

'Sorry,' Bran chipped in. 'When a man came round selling princesses, we thought you wouldn't want one so sent him packing. Were we wrong?'

XXI

Before Nicopolis
The day before the Nones of May
The twenty-sixth day of the siege

THE EASTERN RAMP was ready, and at dawn the one siege tower repaired and ready to work was drawn by two dozen pairs of oxen and pushed by relays of men as it made its slow and stately progress along a carefully prepared trackway. There were six wheels, three on either side, and each was almost as tall as a man and rimmed with iron. Its base was forty feet square, its height almost seventy feet, and the front was covered in big iron plates, which flickered and shone red as the sun rose behind the city. The sides were protected by animal hides stretched taut, and padded behind with rags, all fixed to the structure itself. About a third of the way up, a long ram was mounted, the beam tied fast so that it did not start swinging as the tower moved. The tower kept out of range of anything the enemy could shoot from the walls and now and then stopped as men made sure that the track was solid enough to support its weight. On the walls, rows and rows of people watched, for Crispinus had ordered his artillery and archers not to shoot unless the enemy first shot at them, and the Nicopolitans were too transfixed to bother.

Arrian was sent and once again made an impassioned speech

appealing to the city leaders and citizens to accept the friendship of Rome and open their gates. He stood on the western ramp, some of the barricade at its top pulled back, so that he could be seen clearly, and was close enough for his face and its honesty to be apparent. For half an hour he spoke, pleading with them, and reading to them the words of a letter he assured them had been sent to the Romans by Princess Azátē.

'This jewel of Osrhoene, this pearl of your kingdom wrote to the Lord Trajan pleading for his help to protect her and the loyal subjects of Osrhoene against those who would enslave them. Such an appeal, such a simple, brave and humble appeal, could not help move the Lord Trajan. That is why we have come to Nicopolis, as strong friends in answer to this noble call. You can see the power of Rome before you this day, yet we are a tiny fraction of its true might. You see one legion before you – one of thirty. Many of the others will come soon as the Lord Trajan sets right the kingdoms of the east, stripping power from usurpers and making sure the rule of the just and rightful monarchs. Is it not better to be on his side?'

The Nicopolitans listened politely, although anyone could see that even Arrian did not quite believe that they would give in. He ended with a threat.

'By ancient law and custom, when the Romans prepare to assault a fortress they are willing – nay, eager – to welcome the surrender of the defenders with generosity and mercy, even with reward. That changes when the ram touches the wall for the first time. For when that happens, mercy must be locked away for another season, and all that is left is implacable determination to take and sack the place no matter what its strength. See that great tower!' He pointed. 'And see the great battering ram mounted in it. Before the day is out that ram will strike your walls and begin to pound them into dust – unless you heed the advice and pleas of your princess, look to the welfare of your wives, your children, your aged parents, who wordlessly beg you, and accept the verdict of your own heads and hearts to end this war. Rome is your friend. The Lord Trajan is your friend – and we are your friends, your true friends, who would shield you from enemies who come only to destroy. For centuries Romans have been known throughout the wide world for their good faith. Trust that faith, trust the evidence of your eyes, trust your sense of reason. I beg you this last time, to let me come into your city and talk to your leaders – or have them come outside and talk to my commander, the noble Atilius Crispinus. Talk now, before it is too late. You have until the tower is in place and the ram swings to strike!'

There was no answer, just silence from the faces on the wall, and no arrow or bolt came to show defiance. Yet nor was there any sign of capitulation, as the siege tower trundled slowly around the southern side of the city.

'They're not about to give in,' Arrian said to Ferox as they watched men unhitching the teams pulling it. The tower was as close to the foot of the ramp as it was safe to bring it without risking the defenders shooting at the oxen, which might cause a stampede and risk overturning it after all this labour. 'They're proud, and proud men often refuse to see a fact they do not like even when it stands before them.'

'Bit surprised the princess did not appeal in person,' Ferox said quietly.

Arrian's face betrayed no surprise that the centurion knew of Azátē's presence. 'She wouldn't. And the legatus would not let her anyway. Says he wants to hold her back and make one last roll of the die – maybe when we have a breach.'

'That bit about the ram touching the wall and ancient

tradition, is that true?' Ferox had a dim memory of reading something in Caesar's *Commentarii*, but he had been in a fair few sieges during his time in the army and never remembered hearing about such a law or even a custom.

Arrian shrugged. 'I don't know. Pretty sure I read it somewhere or other. Seemed like a nice touch though, and might help concentrate their minds.'

Ferox said nothing, for the love Romans and Greeks had for rhetoric and argument still seemed strange to him after all these years. It was a greedy, possessive love, making words and ideas serve the need of the moment regardless of truth. The bards of his people told many lies, as what bards did not? Yet they had a joy in the words and verses themselves and their themes were brave heroes and beautiful women, battles and feasts. They loved life and honoured death more than they loved their own cleverness.

Rufus was shouting to men as they looped cables through the first of a series of pulleys designed so that they could haul the tower up the slope while other teams pushed. They were not far from where Ferox and his thin line had faced the attackers, yet no shot or arrow came from the wall and towers above, and he wondered for a moment whether the Nicopolitans were considering giving in. If so, then they were leaving it very late. More probably they wanted the targets to come closer before they began their bombardment. Either side of the ramp, and on platforms raised beside it, Roman crews waited beside their large and small ballistae. There were a couple of scorpiones on the central floor of the siege tower itself and auxiliary archers on the open top, but none were shooting. Instead, everyone waited and watched.

The ropes were in place and the teams began to haul, stretching the cables taut until the tower gave the slightest of quivers and then began to inch forward, until the wheels turned readily as it went over the flat ground before the slope began. Someone had thought to oil the wheels, so that they made no noise, and that was a pleasant change, because the transport drivers always swore blind that the creaks and squeals of unoiled axles frightened away evil forces. The tower reached the incline of the ramp, hesitated and began to creep up the slope, ever so slowly.

'Sisyphos,' Arrian whispered and Ferox hoped that that was not bad luck, and that the damned thing would not reach near the top only to roll back every time. So slow was the progress of the tower, that the walls and the cliff on which they stood seemed higher than ever. After a while there was a pause, the tower braced and held in place, while the cables were taken to the next set of pulleys, and the ascent resumed.

The first stone hummed through the air, missed the side of the tower by a good six feet and kept going to fall harmlessly in one of the few open spaces.

'Ah,' Arrian said. 'Well, I cannot say I am surprised.'

More stones and bolts followed, and some clanged against the iron plates on the front of the tower or now and then thumped into the padded sides. The Roman artillery responded, aiming at anyone they saw on the top of the wall, or waiting for the hatches to open so that a catapult could shoot.

The noise grew, punctuated by cheers when a hit was scored. Arrian, Ferox and a couple of other officers crouched behind a stretch of earth rampart to watch as the tower continued its climb. After a while, when the ropes had shifted to the final set of pulleys, Rufus came in to join them.

'Nearly there,' he gasped nervously. Crispinus, along with Cerialis and other senior staff were in an observation tower built some way back, but the centurion did not seem eager to join them. The primus pilus had remained on the western side, in charge both from his rank and as the chief engineer of the siege works there in case the Nicopolitans saw an opportunity to attack while everyone was focused on the opposite side of the city.

'Come on, girl, easy does it.' Rufus had a tight grip on the top of the parapet, his head higher than it needed to be, so intent was he on watching the progress of the ladder. He was the senior engineer here and now, and also the man who had designed the tower and supervised the repairs and rebuilding after the storm. The siege tower crept up the ramp.

'You can do it, go on, go on.'

By now the top of the siege tower was higher than the rampart of the curtain wall, although still a little beneath the towers. A few of the archers dared a shot, bobbing up, loosing an arrow and then ducking down. One of the scorpiones spat out its bolt and skill or blind chance sent the missile through a slit in one of the towers. Someone cheered from inside, and the shouting spread, so that for a moment even the men hauling the ropes hesitated.

'No, go on, go on,' Rufus begged them. The tower crawled the last few yards stopping almost at the edge of the ramp, which did not reach to the wall itself. 'That's it, that's it!'

'How far is it to the wall?' Arrian asked.

'Sixteen feet and seven inches,' Rufus replied. 'At least that's what casting a plumb line told me last night. Give it that much cord and you hear the lead tinkle against the stone. Any less and it didn't.'

'Fascinating,' Arrian said. 'You know I had never really thought about how you judge the distance in a case like this.'

'That's the theory anyway, and I—' Ferox had seen the stone coming from the right towards them and hauled Rufus under cover. The missile smashed into the earth rampart, flinging muck everywhere.

Rufus gulped. 'Thank you,' he said after a moment, and then peered back over the top, keeping lower this time. 'They need to tie off the tower itself and replace the hauling parties with the ram's crew. 'I just hope that I've—'

'It will be fine, I am sure, and if not, then that will also be fine,' Arrian assured him. 'There is no sense in worrying about things already done and which we cannot change.'

'Don't be a damned fool—' Rufus snapped before he could stop himself. He realised that he had just insulted a senior officer.

Arrian smiled. 'Well, I'll try, but it would break the habits of a lifetime.'

'What are they doing now?' Ferox asked, to distract them both. Rufus explained how the ram's crew had trained, swinging the heavy beam from a gantry rigged up in the workshop areas. Sixteen men operated the ram at any one time, and there were five teams to take over in turn. As he talked, his confidence grew, although his fingers still twitched nervously. In its final position the siege tower topped the fighting platforms of the towers on the wall by about the height of a man, and the archers were shooting much more often, making the most of the advantage.

'They're ready,' Rufus said at last. They saw a man on the artillery platform stand at the open back of the tower and wave a red flag. Rufus seemed to be muttering a prayer or even a spell as he glanced back at the observation tower. Crispinus waited for what seemed an age, then raised his right hand and brought it down to hammer against the palm of his left hand. A cornicen sounded, the brazen rasp carrying over the noise of missiles. On the siege tower, the soldier with the flag bobbed it down to acknowledge the order, and Ferox and the others heard the shouted, 'Begin!'

Rufus held his breath. In the tower, the sixteen men waited for the call and then pulled back as one and slammed forward. The ram was made from six beams, each seventy feet long and bound together all along their length. At the tip was the iron head, cast like the head of a horned ram, its face down as it charged. The tower creaked as the weight shifted.

There was a sharp crack as the ram struck the stone wall squarely. Rufus breathed out. Arrian smiled again, and patted him on the back.

'You see, no sense in worrying, was there?'

The ram struck again.

'Why do they hit the walls and not try for the gate?' Ferox asked, not because he did not know, but because he felt Rufus would enjoy telling him.

'Too hard to approach and too strongly defended. If we smashed them down, we probably wouldn't be able to get inside afterwards. There is plenty of wall so we can choose our spot. It's good that they're stone. Mud brick is softer, so the ram dents it rather than breaks it. Here we can try to loosen the individual stones, and break or prise them out.'

'How long will that take?' Arrian wondered.

'No idea until we try. Days probably.'

The ram struck again, the tone different this time, and the sound went on, hour after hour, pausing only when the crew was relieved and replaced by another. On and on it went, not stopping when the sun set, and throughout the night it went on, the creak of rope and wood and the crack or thump as the ram's head struck the stone. Team replaced team, and the relieved men ate, drank and rested until all the others had done their shift and it was their turn again.

Nicopolis
The next day
The twenty-seventh day of the siege

D OMITIUS HAD BEEN *working on a catapult when he heard the ram striking the wall for the first time. That was it then, the true assault had begun.*

'Never thought that I'd hear that again in my life,' John said. The old man had taken to sitting in the workshops now, and keeping him company.

'If they have any sense, they will lower bags of flax and try to block the blows,' Domitius said, for he had known that this was bound to happen and had combed his memory for tricks to help the defence. That was not something the legions thought about very much. As far as they were concerned, the Romans always did the attacking, and defending anywhere was a problem only for their enemies.

'I once saw a man hurl rocks at the shaft of the ram and break it off just behind the head,' John said. 'He was a big man. Brave too, for he jumped over the wall and grabbed the iron head before the Romans could retrieve it and brought it back to us. They shot him then, clear through the back so that the point came out of his belly in front. Took him a couple of hours to die and it wasn't pretty.'

'You volunteering, old man?' one of the craftsmen asked.

'No, I thought I'd shout encouragement as you do it.'

'I bet that grey hair is just a wig and you're really nineteen!'

John spread his hands apologetically. 'My secret's out at last!'
The door opened and Simon appeared, his face and armour
covered in dust. 'Hullo, reckon you are wanted.'

Simon nodded to Domitius. 'They'd like your opinion.'

There were four guards with him, two of them strangers
rather than his own men, and these ones did not smile or say
anything as they wove their way through the streets. The route
seemed unnecessarily long and tortuous, and he was surprised
when he was taken not to the tower closest to the Roman ramp,
but the next one to it. They went up to the open top, because
otherwise it would have been hard to see. Everything suggested
that his captors did not trust him at all, even if Domitius was
baffled as to what they thought he might do.

'They're frightened,' Simon whispered to him when no one
else was in earshot. 'And I can't blame them.'

The siege tower was big. Domitius had read about these
towers, been set exercises to design them and work out precise
dimensions and the amounts of material and labour required,
and made models of them, but he had never helped to make a
real one, or seen one so close up. Part of him was proud of the
legionaries who had made this ramp and machine, and who
now were driving the ram's head into the wall. The damage was
already obvious in a patch several feet square, and as he leaned
over the parapet and squinted he thought that one of the stones
had shifted so that one end poked out from the wall by an inch
or so. Given time, the ram would breach the wall.

A bolt from a scorpio clinked against the cap stone on the
raised section of the battlement just next to him and he jerked
back under cover.

'It's worse nearer their ram,' Simon assured him. 'Hard even
for our boys on our tower, because their one is higher and their
archers are good.'

'*Are they making the tower higher?*'

Simon frowned. *He was sweating, the rivulets making stripes in the dust on his face.* '*How do you mean? Can't rebuild the thing with the Romans shooting at us.*'

'*Doesn't need to be stone. Use timber and animal skins, planks or wicker screens for cover. You build up so that you are higher than they are and you shoot down on them.*'

Simon shook his head because it was obvious, and he could not understand how he had forgotten all the stories about cities doing this to fend off attackers. Domitius explained about lowering sacks to meet the ram's charge, and that was another idea so obvious that Simon grinned at his own stupidity. The strategoi appeared, and Domitius watched the young Jewish officer explain his thoughts, and saw the magistrates pass through the same series of expressions, from disinterest, even impatience, into enlightenment and amusement that no one else had thought of such obvious tactics. Men were despatched to find sacks and suitable ropes.

Simon was happier than he had been for a while. '*The building can wait until night, although they'll start making sections. Give 'em a nasty surprise tomorrow morning when we're looking down on them again!*

'*Oh, the strategos asks why they are still adding to their ramp? Won't they just come across that drawbridge from the tower?*'

'*They'll want to get more men forward if they can make a big breach. The idea is that the spoil from the wall falls down to make a ramp. I'm guessing they are already filling up the rooms inside that patch of wall with rubble.*' Simon frowned, before he gave a smile and nodded. Secrecy could be carried too far, and he was growing to like Domitius. '*So they extend the ramp to get close enough for that, and to put work parties at the foot of* the wall to see whether they can help. You'd be surprised what you can do with some crowbars and a lot of sweat.' Months – what seemed like an age ago – Caecilius had used the same words when instructing him. Domitius was almost certain that his old boss was among the officers watching from the observation tower. There was something about the way one of the tiny figures stood that was distinctive. At least he had not been killed.

In less than an hour, they lowered a filled woolsack off the rampart in front of the siege tower. Men with shields lifted them high to protect the ones with the rope. The ram struck, a foot or two below where they had put the sack. Trying again, they let it drop, only to go too far and have the ram's head slam into the wall above it.

'Come on, you can do better than that,' Domitius muttered. 'That's it!' At the third attempt the ram gave a dull thump as it drove into the cushion of the sack. 'What do you say to that, Caecilius?' he added in Latin. Simon gave him an odd look.

They stopped the fourth charge of the ram, then the Romans shifted their aim and struck the wall just to the right of the sack.

'How far can they move it?' Athenodorus had come up beside him.

'Hard to be precise,' Domitius admitted. 'A few feet either side at least. Less up and down, but it will be designed so that they can batter a wide area without moving the whole tower.'

'More sacks, then,' Athenodorus decided, as the men managed to catch the edge of the ram and take some of the force from the blow. 'Oh!' The mild exclamation came when a stone from a large ballista shattered the shields held above the men at the rope, flinging up fragments of wood and leather and limbs. Unsupported, the sack slipped down to the bottom of the wall. 'That's a shame.'

Domitius thought that it was more luck. Until they added platforms large enough for the bigger engines on either side of the ramp, anything that size was shooting up at its steepest angle and with its highest force, which rarely made for accuracy.

'Can we smash that tower?' Athenodorus asked him. 'Or burn it?'

'Perhaps, perhaps not. Always hard to know until you try. Try to hit the same spots again and again with stone throwers, or sally out with torches and set light to it.' Domitius watched as a bolt shooter sent a missile trailing black smoke to slam into the side of the tower. It smouldered for a while, but the flames from the tallow tied behind the head eventually faded without spreading onto the stretched hide. 'Begging your pardon, my lord, but do you want me to take a look at the other ramp. They were making quick progress with that, last time I was over that side.'

'No. This is the one that matters. Unless you have any more inspirations, then you had better get back to the workshop. There is plenty to keep you busy, I understand?'

'Yes, my lord.'

'Run along then.'

Simon and the guards took him away, weaving a different route through the streets this time, that seemed even more unnecessary than their earlier detour. They passed a street where a dozen or more buildings had burned out, and had to take care stepping past folk living on the street itself, under makeshift roofs supported by the shells of the houses. Faces were drawn, eyes worried, and a few of the children had the bloated bellies that mocked their hunger. His own rations had got steadily worse in the last days, and turning a corner they saw larger halls, no doubt once warehouses, also destroyed by fire.

'Bad luck,' he said to Simon. 'Is there still enough?'

'Not for everyone, or at least not for long and all staying healthy.'

'Bad luck.'

'Luck had nothing to do with it, although they reckon they caught the bugger who was behind it.' Simon lowered his voice. 'Said he had been paid by Prince Arbandes.'

'You don't sound convinced.'

'Well, his rotting corpse won't tell us any more and there have not been any fires since. A Roman would have made more sense though.'

Domitius spent the rest of the daylight hours and the first part of the night in the workshop, cursing the mechanism on a small stone thrower because it just would not pull back and go forward smoothly. There was a flaw somewhere, small perhaps, but enough, and he could not find it. The guards, without Simon this time, eventually insisted on taking him back to his cell. He thought about the problem, thought about Caecilius out there, and wondered how much the man had known about his arrest all that time ago. He also wondered about the western side, and had a nagging feeling that he was missing something important. Yet next morning when he suggested taking a walk to the walls on that side, Simon refused. 'They don't want you there. Reckon they have things sorted out.'

They took him to the eastern side instead. The higher platform on the tower was like the little turrets the navy used for battle. Apart from archers, a few slingers from among the shepherds who had come into the city, and javelinmen, there was enough room for a small bolt shooter. They could not quite sweep the Romans from the top of the siege tower, but they killed several and the auxiliary archers were reduced to bobbing up to take quick shots before they ducked down.

Yet *as if in answer to Domitius' challenge, Caecilius, or someone else among the besiegers, had come up with a counter to the woolsacks, three of which were lowered to protect the spot most marked by the ram's attack. A pole emerged from the level below the top one on the tower and wobbled as it went forward. On the end was a blade like a sickle, and the Romans tried to hook a rope supporting a sack. The men on the wall hauled it up, allowing the ram to strike hard against the wall itself. Down came the sack once more, heavily enough to snap the pole, leaving the blade hanging down and the defenders cheering. A second hook appeared, its advance slightly more confident and it caught another of the ropes and began to saw away. Pulling at the rope only made things worse, and as the cord weakened the sheer weight of the sack made the rope snap. Falling onto the edge of the cliff, the bag burst asunder in a cloud of white, and this time the Romans cheered.*

The ram kept striking the wall, but the rhythm was less certain now, the blows a little less frequent and sometimes blocked. Bolts and stones pounded the siege tower so that it shuddered, and there were more dark patches where incendiary missiles had struck and burned for just a little while. Yet still it stood, and still the ram nibbled at the wall.

XXII

North west of Nicopolis, some miles from the road
Fifth day before the Ides of May
The thirty-second day of the siege

A S THE SUN set, fires were lit and the scent of stewing and roasting goat meat drifted on the gentle breeze. A man sang, his voice strong and soft with the nasal tone of these lands and he must have been accounted good, for conversation died away as they listened. Afterwards someone played a flute and there was talk and laughter.

This was a good place for a camp, the little stream snaking gently through the middle. The water was low, and in a month or two might run altogether dry, but there was enough for the moment for man and beast alike, and the grass on its banks was higher and lusher than the grazing for a good distance in any direction.

No village was in sight, and only in part because the land formed a shallow bowl, the hills on either side rising so gently that they were scarcely worthy of the name, any more than this place could really be called a valley. Few people lived here, and although the shepherds came here in winter they tended to avoid it at this time of year. The crumbing walls of a dozen or so houses testified that once there had been a settlement, but who those people were, what they had called themselves and what gods they worshipped were all long since forgotten, buried with the dead in their cemetery up on a low rise behind the ruins. There were heaped remains of what had been tombs, a lot of broken pottery and shards of bone in the earth up there. When they first came here the riders had poked around a little, but seen nothing of value. No one wanted to sleep or eat too close to the dead, whoever they had been, but a man did not travel far in these lands if graves bothered him. So they poured a libation to their memory, and did not trouble if any of the horses wandered over to crop the thin grass.

There were half a dozen waggons in the camp, and twice that many tents, most of them big, and one a glorious bright red pavilion that stood out for its height and sheer splendour. Were it not for the row of Roman heads mounted on spears, and the other spoils of weapons and captured horses, the camp had the air of a hunting expedition and was not so very different from the camp of a Sarmatian band or one from any of their kin on the Steppes. The difference was that they did not keep coming back to the same spot during the spring and summer months, and kept a better guard. As night fell, the eating and drinking around the fires, the singing from the royal pavilion and the hubbub of conversation gradually tailed away and the riders and even their servants settled down for the night. There were only a dozen guards, and no outriders patrolling some way out.

One of the sentries was a young warrior, who had been sent to serve the king at the end of last year and was enjoying almost every moment of it. The older men kept saying that he must watch each night, since he could not sit still and probably would not sleep anyway. He did not really mind, for the Heavens above him were beautiful, and earlier today he had killed his first enemy. The man had been a Roman cavalryman, one of the outlying pickets from the convoy, and he and his comrade had strayed too far out. Up until now, every arrow the youth had shot had seemed cursed, missing marks that he would have hit every time in practice. It had begun to bother him, so that when he felt the arrow leave his bow he had doubted that it would strike, until the Roman had turned his head and the missile drove deep into his right eye. Other warriors dropped the man's companion and his horse, but only the youth had struck this man, and had ridden up to finish the job and claim his trophy. The Roman was moaning as he lay stretched on the ground, one hand plucking feebly at the shaft, and the youth had hesitated before bringing his sword down to end the man's life. It had not been fear or nervousness, he assured himself, but simple curiosity. He kept wondering who the man was, and one of the other warriors had shown him marks on the neck guard of the man's bronze helmet and told him that the scratches were the soldier's name and that of his clan chief. He would have to find someone who could read them.

The youth wore the helmet proudly for the rest of the day, and waited until everyone else had gone to sleep before taking it off, even though the cursed thing was heavy and uncomfortable. His task was to watch, until someone came to take over, so he wandered on the edge of the camp, nearest the old ruins, and listened to the soft noises of men sleeping, the louder sounds of horses breathing, stamping in the dust, or rolling over, and wondered whether the dead soldier had been a famous warrior. There had been a lot of grey in the man's beard, which oddly reminded the youth of his own father, himself a proven warrior, who had told him again and again that the only thing that really mattered apart from honour was being around to tell the tale.

He wandered out a little way from the camp, staring up at the stars. The moon was rising, and the rolling lands around were brightly lit. No one moved out there. Then he heard a scratching, the small sound of some creature scrabbling for food or to burrow. It did not seem reason to call out, but the noise continued, and he realised that it was coming from the old graveyard. Yesterday, just that thought might have frightened him, but today, buoyed with the thrill of ending a soldier's life and the proof that he could and would win as a warrior, he was too proud to be afraid. A man who had slain another could not let himself be timid. The youth walked up to the burial site, where there were two tombs larger than the rest, and near the centre an even bigger monument where the fallen stones still formed a rectangular pile standing proudly. The scrabbling was coming from somewhere close to them and was louder now.

Stones and dirt shifted, there was a grunt, another even louder, and then a soft crack as wood broke and more pebbles rolled away. The youth took his bow and strung it, his breath coming in gulps, for the deep shadows around the tombs were moving. A shape broke from them, turning itself into the dark figure of a man, who stepped forward and his face was white, pure white, the flesh gone and little more than a skull, with eyes shining.

The youth tried to put an arrow to the bow, but his hands shook and he dropped it. He realised that the figure had a helmet on, just like the man he had killed and his mind reeled as the thought came that this was his spirit. Instinct somehow took over, and he reached for another arrow, nocked and loosed. It flicked away into the night, straight at the ghostly shape, and missed or went through him, because the spirit kept coming, and steel glinted as it drew a blade.

A hand clamped hard across the youth's mouth, a great force pulling him back and then there was horrible pain as the knife stabbed up through his back and under his ribs. The ghost was coming closer, teeth even whiter than its pale face as it leered, and there were more shapes behind him, as the youth's eyes went dark.

Ferox wiped his blade on the dead warrior's tunic and stood up. Vindex nodded to him.

'Wasn't sure you were coming,' he whispered. He and the other three Brigantes were covered in pale dust and filthy from lying in the tiny chamber for a day and a half. It was an old tomb, sunk into the ground, and they had felt it wise to pile the bones neatly in one corner. Then Ferox and the others had covered them over with planks and dirt, leaving a narrow slit to see out. If the enemy had not come within another half day, then they would have dug them out and tried again later in the month, but the enemy had come, so they had waited for the moon to start rising and then broken out.

'This way,' Ferox hissed. There was no sign of another guard, but two ponies were wandering nearby, cropping at the grass whenever they had a mind. He went to the closest, speaking softly, smoothing its head and neck until the animal was willing to trust him. Vindex did the same with the other one, and you could trust the Brigantes to make friends with horses. Using them as cover, they walked in the animals' shadows, leading them slowly into the camp. Halfway to the stream, Ferox turned and tapped the Brigantian following him on the shoulder, making a sign for him to wait. The centurion vanished into the dark, and though Vindex had seen nothing, he did not doubt that there was some threat out there. Glancing up at the sky, he realised that they were running out of time, and still there was no sign of Ferox. Then there was a sigh, as peaceful as the wind in the grass, and the centurion reappeared, still holding his stubby pugio dagger.

They pushed on, letting the ponies go when they reached the stream, for the tents were beyond it and it would look odd if horses were loose among them. A man saw them as they splashed through the water, and raised a hand to wave. The camp seemed almost unnaturally still, as if this was a trap and they were walking right into it, and it took an effort to stroll through it all as if they had every right to be there. Weaving past clusters of sleeping men, piled saddles and equipment, and then between a few of the tents, they kept going, for time was pressing and they needed to get to the big tent before the alarm was given. A man stirred in his sleep, stared up at Ferox, smiled vaguely and rolled over, pulling his cloak about him more tightly.

Ferox led, and as he turned the corner of a tent, a man appeared, scratching his bare chest. The centurion punched with the dagger, driving into the warrior's throat, who gulped noisily as dark blood sprayed onto his chest. Ferox's hand slipped as he tried to lower the dead man gently to the ground and someone asked a question from within the tent.

'Go!' Ferox pointed at the big pavilion just ahead of them. There were two spearmen standing guard outside. 'Easy though.'

Vindex began to whistle through his teeth, and staggered slightly as he and the others walked towards the men. A Brigantian laughed drunkenly as one of the guards lowered his spear and rather than give a challenge told the men to clear off. There was no need to understand the language to judge his meaning. From inside the tent, the voice called, more urgently now. Ferox ignored it, and crouched, hoping that the tall Brigantes would shield him, as he switched his pugio to his left hand and drew his gladius.

The second challenge was formal. Vindex stopped, raised one hand apologetically, just as a trumpet sounded.

'Now!' Ferox shouted as he sprinted forward, pushing

through the Brigantes. He had hoped for a little more time, but there was none, and the trumpet sounded again, joined by another, and that meant both of the attacks were coming in, and that at least was good.

One spearman shouted something, sounding confused, but the other had his spear up, and Ferox managed to push it aside with his dagger and thrust the long point of the sword straight at the man's eyes. The guard retreated, only to trip and fall. Ferox left him to the Brigantes and jumped high over him, pushing through the loose flap of the tent. A woman screamed, but she was the only person in the outer chamber and he kept running, for filmy curtains showed that the main room was beyond and had a large bed.

A big man was in front of him, perhaps one of the Dahae for he had their narrow face, a conical helmet trimmed with fur, and a long, straight blade. Sparks flew as Ferox parried the man's attack on his own blade, but both weapons survived the impact and did not snap. He thrust with his dagger and hit only the little round shield the man had in his left hand. Another woman screamed, sitting up in bed, her chest naked, and a man was with her, but he simply stared in wide-eyed horror.

The warrior raised his sword and slashed, and Ferox ducked the blow, flinging himself at the man, so that both of them fell. His gladius was gone, so he felt for the man's throat and tried to stab him with the dagger. There was noise behind him and Vindex came into the room bellowing, another of the Brigantians following.

'The prince!' Ferox called, then gasped because the warrior had slammed the pommel of his sword against the top of the Roman's head. Ferox felt his knife strike against the scales of the man's armour and pushed, but did not have the force to break through.

'Up, laddie!' Vindex ordered the prince. The point of his sword was an inch from Arbandes' bare chest and apart from a nod and wink to the prince's bed companion, his gaze was fixed on him. The girl, little more than a child, kept on screaming.

The other Brigantian kicked the warrior in the head, making him roll away from Ferox. Following up, the scout slashed with his sword across the man's face. The warrior dropped shield and sword and clutched at the wound, and a second blow severed his right hand at the wrist. Ferox was gasping for breath, head throbbing, and slow to stop the almost frenzied attack, as without much skill, but plenty of rage and strength, the Brigantian kept slicing. There was so much blood that even the girl stopped screaming.

'Tie his hands!' Ferox ordered, and Vindex grabbed the prince by one wrist and hauled him out of bed.

'Hoy, Cunominus, the rope!' Vindex barked at the Brigantian, who was staring mutely at his handiwork. The trumpets were sounding, and there were shouts from outside. 'Move, you mongrel.'

Ferox picked up his gladius. 'I'm going to the front. Suspect we'll have company.'

'Aye, but remember this is a humping tent. A man with a blade can come in any way.'

'Do what you have to do,' Ferox told him. 'They'll be coming for us here, so we stay as long as we can.' He pushed the gauzy screen up to get past. Weapons rang from just outside. The young woman was silent, huddled to one side, clutching a sheet tightly to her chest. Shadows played on the material of the tent, and someone screamed in agony. Ferox went out just as one of the Brigantians dropped, his left leg sheared through below the knee and almost before he was down his opponents slashed again and again. There were two warriors already down and bleeding, another locked in combat with the remaining scout. One of the men hacking at the dead Brigantian saw the centurion coming and raised his sword, but Ferox hooked it aside with his dagger and thrust low into his belly. The man had no armour and the sword went deep as he groaned and fell, and Ferox let go rather than be pulled over with him for the gladius was stuck fast. That left only his dagger, and the remaining opponent gave a wicked grin as he came on. Behind him one of the tents burst into flame. Horses, some with riders, some without, were galloping in every direction, and a trumpet sounded, closer now.

Ferox went back, ducking as the man slashed across his body. The Brigantian and the other warrior exchanged blows and neither seemed to have the advantage. Ferox was back in the doorway to the tent, and threw his dagger, making the man fling up his sword to block the throw. It gave Ferox a second and he searched for a weapon, but saw none, so yanked the sheet from the cowering woman and whipped it towards the warrior. He flinched, stepping away, advanced again, so Ferox threw it over him and for a moment he was tangled.

'Here!' Vindex had lifted the screen and threw his sword. Ferox caught it as the man freed himself and was about to strike when the point of a spear burst through the warrior's tunic. His mouth was open, his eyes wide as he stared in disbelief, and the trooper from the ala Britannica grunted as he twisted the shaft and tried to pull it free. Arrian appeared behind him, his face flushed.

'By all the gods, Odysseus and Diomedes,' he gasped. 'Do you have him?'

Ferox turned to Vindex.

'Aye, safe and sound. Mostly anyway.' The warrior named Cunominus came through, leading the prince, who had his arms tied behind his back and a bruise swelling on his cheek. 'Got ideas,' Vindex explained. 'Do we take the lassies?'

'Only if they want to go,' Ferox replied before Arrian could intervene. 'If that is all right, sir.'

'I suppose so.' Arrian stared around him at the tent. Some of its furnishings more lavish than anything in the Roman camp. 'The horses are outside.'

'Then we had better sound the recall and get away from here.'

'What? Oh yes, of course.' Arrian had his sword out and prodded at the sheet on the floor. 'I'm sure this is silk. Sorry... but look at this place?'

'Rather look at the lasses,' Vindex said.

Arrian grinned nervously. The girl from the bed had a cloak around her, and not much else, and was clinging to the other. Together they could easily be sisters, with long, black hair and eyes that looked as dark in the flickering lamplight. 'She cannot ride like that...' Arrian was not really concentrating. 'But Herakles' balls, man, you did it.'

'*We* did it, sir,' Ferox said. 'And we need to go.'

'But they're running like sheep.' One hundred men from ala Britannica had attacked from the south, and Bran with forty Brigantes had come in from the north. Both had ridden by night and camped by day for the last four days, going far to the east before looping back. Fortune had been on their side, helped by the enemy's carelessness, for Sarmatians would never have been surprised so easily.

'Then we had better be away before they stop and realise how few of us there are, hadn't we?'

'Of course.' Arrian took a deep breath. 'Lord prince, my name is Flavius Arrian and I am a tribune of Legio Hispana. I would like you to come with us, and can assure you that your person will be respected and that you will be welcomed by my commander as a guest.' Arbandes was about to say something when Arrian cut him off. 'However, my men are in danger here, so if you refuse to come or give me any trouble on our journey then I will have not the slightest hesitation in ordering your execution. So will you come?'

'Yes,' Arbandes said, his voice like a child's.

'Splendid.'

It took a while to rally the men, for some had chased off into the night. The camp was in chaos, the tents collapsed or burned and two of the waggons tipped on their sides. There were corpses everywhere, scores of them, and other bodies still moaning.

'Leave them,' Arrian commanded, when a trooper went to one wounded man and raised his sword. 'We haven't the time, and it might delay any pursuit if they stop to care for them. If they don't, well, these men are their kin, not ours.'

Vindex nodded. 'Boy's learning,' he said to Bran in the language of the tribes.

Apart from the warrior killed defending the pavilion, none of the attackers had fallen and the few wounded were all able to ride. Less than an hour after Vindex and his men had pushed their way out of their hiding place, the whole column set off into the night. The prince was sullen and silent, hands still tied behind his back, although riding with ease, a trooper on either side. The two women were on a pony, the younger one clinging to the other.

'They're his slaves,' Arrian explained to Ferox. 'Bought 'em just a few months ago and could not bear to be parted from them, even though he was travelling light.'

'Think we're on the wrong side,' Vindex muttered.

The convoy was not due for half a day, so they rode directly back to camp. Some Arabs found them, just before noon, but kept their distance. About a hundred of the prince's men appeared late in the day and shadowed them. The horses needed a rest, even more than the men, so they camped that night, and kept a careful watch. The next morning there were twice as many horse archers ahead of them. Arrian kept the column together, and one of the troopers held a drawn sword by the prince's neck. When some riders approached, empty handed to show that their intentions were peaceful, Arbandes gestured to them to leave.

'That's right, lord prince. No need for trouble, is there?' Arrian said.

XXIII

In front of Nicopolis
The day before the Ides of May
The thirty-fifth day of the siege

P RINCE ARBANDES WAS very obliging, especially when he learned that his sister was already in the Roman camp. Crispinus would not permit them to meet, not yet, and installed the prince in Cerialis' camp, but informed him of Azátē's presence and hinted at his – and Rome's – sympathy to her cause, while making clear that this was not set firmly in stone. The legatus regretted the misunderstandings that had occurred so far, both between the Romans and the leaders of Nicopolis and the royal family of Osrhoene, and hoped that sensible men of good spirit could find common ground. Although guarded, the prince was granted every available comfort, in addition to his slaves to keep him company.

In the morning, Arbandes went with Arrian to the western siege ramp and showed himself to the defenders, asking to speak to the strategoi. They duly appeared, and the prince spoke at length about the need for friendship and hoped that they would admit a token Roman garrison.

'What of the fires?' Someone had shouted back.

'I do not understand.' Arbandes called up.

'Your agents have burned houses in our city and now you ask us to trust you.' There seemed to be a scuffle on the wall.

'Give us a day to consider,' a different, more educated voice carried down to them. 'A day of truce.'

'That is not possible,' Arrian cut in. 'Give us your answer now.' He lowered his voice to whisper to the prince. 'We are close to making a breach on the far side of the city, and this ramp is ready for use. Tell them their time is running short.'

Arbandes did as he was told, but no answer came from the walls.

'They are stubborn folk and disrespectful,' he said at last. 'They deserve all that they get.'

Arrian could not think of anything to say to that, so after a short while led the prince back through the sheds on the ramp.

'Down to us then?' Caecilius asked. He was supervising the men preparing for the second siege tower to be brought up in a few hours' time.

'Well, be a shame any other way after all this work,' Arrian replied. The primus pilus was not amused, but turned to bark orders at some legionaries.

There was less theatre about bringing the second tower up, at least at first. The defenders knew what to expect, and apart from anything else the tower did not have so far to go. Even so, care needed to be taken to prevent it from bogging down under its own weight. All those who did not have other duties paused and watched as it jerkily rolled along. More oxen were needed to pull it, for the animals were thinner than they had been, bones showing from a diet of poor grass, but eventually it reached the approach and they were taken away.

Crispinus watched, for as on the other side, they had set up a tower out of range of the walls, and, while they were preparing to haul the tower up the slope, he paced back and forth across the platform.

'Ah, the convoy,' he said to no one in particular as he saw the advance guard riding ahead of the straggling dust thrown up by the wheels. Something was odd, for there were surely more riders than he had sent, and as he watched, half a dozen broke away and galloped around the camp and towards him. It did not take him long to recognise Hadrian, streaking ahead of them. There had been no warning of this visit, and that was worrying. For a while he leaned on the parapet, clutching it tightly because he knew that his face must be twitching. By the time the acting legatus of Syria brought his horse to a skidding halt below them, he had calmed himself.

'Welcome, sir!' Crispinus called down and raised his arm in salute.

Hadrian jumped down from his horse, tossing the reins to a soldier standing close by. 'Think I have arrived at a perfect time! Don't come down – I'll join you!' He strode over to the ladder and almost bounded up it. For a man at the end of a long ride he did not seem at all tired or stiff.

'Was about to write to you when I thought that I might as well come in person! How did you know to put on such a show for me!' Crispinus half expected to be slapped on the back, but the acting governor contented himself with striding over to the front of the tower. 'So that is Nicopolis. Ferox wasn't kidding about those walls. But look what you have done. This is the new ramp, the western one, isn't it? Good work to have it ready so soon after the damage to the first one – yes, yes, I pay attention to your despatches you know. Oh, and your convoy is here, without losing a man or beast, although I don't think that had much to do with my escort coming along. Yes, I got your letter last night – saved the rider going the rest of the way. Arbandes is taken. Well done, young Arrian – although reading between your fulsome praise, may I take it that our friend Ferox had something to do with it?' Crispinus nodded. 'Yes, well, no need to spread that around.'

Crispinus explained that he was keeping brother and sister apart, and that the prince had obligingly gone up and addressed the defenders, pleading with them to surrender. 'They haven't, as you can see, but the young man has readily adapted to his change in fortunes.'

'He is ambitious,' Hadrian said, 'and it does no harm at all having brother and sister in our camp. Her presence remains a secret? Yes, no harm in that, although she may need to show herself. When they hear what the Lord Trajan has done in Armenia, they will be all the more eager to win our friendship. Oh, wonderful, they are starting.' Caecilius' voice carried from the ramp as he shouted out the orders for the men hauling on the ropes and the tower rolled forward.

'Has the princeps dealt with the king?' Crispinus asked.

'In a manner of speaking. The cocky fellow came in answer to his summons, then rode into camp, dismounted and threw his tiara at Trajan's feet, acting the part of a repentant and suppliant client.' It was an odd word to use of a king. Senators, indeed many wealthy and influential men, had clients who honoured them, respected them and offered services in return for favours. Crispinus was not sure whether he had ever heard it used of a monarch, although in truth it was apt.

'I take it the Lord Trajan was not impressed.'

Hadrian snorted with laughter. 'Not at all. It was months too late and could not make up for all his past insolence. So a praetorian is sent to pick up the crown, and the king left kneeling and ever more nervous. After a while Trajan informs him that he is not king, never was king, and never will be, although his life is spared. When it suits him, the princeps will choose the true king of Armenia.'

'Disappointing for the man who was a king a few moments before.'

'Such is life, I fear, but he was not fool enough to argue with nine legions. He waited for a day or two, hoping that the decision would change, which shows how little he knows of our princeps.'

'Without wishing in any way to criticise, it might not be wise to let him wander off?' Crispinus suggested.

'No longer a concern. I am unsure of the details, but there appears to have been some treachery on the part of the deposed king. He tried to make off, and some of the singulares Augusti caught him and killed him.'

'Ah well.'

'Quite. They are shifting the ropes to the next position, I see.' Hadrian's face was eager, for he dearly loved all aspects of engineering. 'Perhaps we could take a closer look?'

Such a request was, of course, an order, so Crispinus led the way, beckoning to a few officers and his escort to join them. Others led horses for when they were needed, since the acting governor was bound to want to tour all the camps and siege works. As they walked, Hadrian asked question after question, but interrupted himself whenever he saw something of interest.

'The men appear in fine fettle. Have you had much trouble with sickness? Sieges do tend to draw pestilence.'

'So far we have been fortunate,' Crispinus told him. There were over five hundred men in the hospitals, a mixture of the wounded, mostly from arrows, the more numerous victims of accidents, inevitable with so much construction, and various ailments. A dozen men in the eastern camp had gone down with dysentery since yesterday, which was worrying, but on the whole the numbers were not bad for a campaigning army, and especially one stuck in the same position for so long.

'Ah, Caecilius,' Hadrian greeted the primus pilus. 'See you have been busy.' Then he asked about how the new ramp was built, its strengths and weaknesses, and how they had calculated the angle of the ramp, the height of the tower and the positioning of the ram. Crispinus did not pay too close attention, since he had already gone through all these things with his officers and it was too late to change anything now. Hadrian was patient, letting the senior centurion break off to give orders, and laughing and joking with the men. When the ropes had been shifted to the next position, he insisted on taking his place in one of the gangs, which meant that Crispinus must do the same, so in turn half a dozen senior officers took their places on the cable and hauled when the primus pilus shouted at them.

'Go, on, put your backs into it!' Caecilius bellowed at them. Men grunted as they tugged. 'You can do better than that!'

'I think he means you,' Hadrian said to Crispinus before the next heave, and men grinned.

'How long to get it in place?' Hadrian asked Caecilius when they had got the tower to the next stage and were shifting the ropes.

'An hour – or just over.'

'Splendid. But though I would dearly like to stay, I think the work will be faster without my assistance!' Hadrian had raised his voice for the soldiers to hear, and smiled with them. 'So we will have to come back. Let's see a bit more, my dear Crispinus.'

They went back to the horses, and as they rode around past the southern camps, Hadrian gestured for the two of them to go a little ahead of the rest. 'How is the mining going?'

'Well, indeed very well, although it is a long way to dig. As far as we can tell they have no idea what we are doing. Shall we ride that way now?'

'No, let's look at the obvious things first and that should not create any suspicion. When will the mine be ready?'

'Six, seven days at least. The ground is getting harder, and it takes longer to bring out the spoil because the mine is so long. They use little carts.'

'I should like to see those. Now, my friend, you realise the implications of what the Lord Trajan has done? For us, in particular.'

'Crispinus glanced to his left, at the city walls. 'It suggests that his plans are considerably more extensive than who will rule Armenia, and that this city would be very useful in any operations to assert our control in this region.'

'Quite. Having both factions of the royal family with us should help.' Hadrian followed the legatus' gaze. 'Those are pretty walls, as well as formidable... But in the end it is only of use if the city falls. Will it?'

'Yes. One way or another, it is within our grasp.'

Hadrian showed his teeth in a broad smile. 'Good, that is what I came to hear, and to see whether there is any way I can help you to that end.'

'Your replacement?'

'Delayed, but only by a little. Nicopolis must fall by the end of this month, or...' Hadrian did not finish the thought and Crispinus had no need to ask. Yet as they rode towards the eastern side of the city, it bothered the legatus that he could not hear the pounding of the battering ram. When they arrived the news was worse than he had feared.

'They were not trying to block it today,' Rufus explained, stammering a little at being presented to the acting governor – and a relative of the emperor. 'We did not think much of it, as we had cut through all their sacks protecting the wall yesterday. Then suddenly they lassoed the shaft of the ram. Must have used leather or something strong, and had that tied to cables, because they hauled on them and made it hard to operate. We tried to cut their ropes, but could not. Then they got another rope around it and hauled, jerking first from one side then the other.'

'It pulled the ram out of its mounting, I suppose,' Hadrian said, and rubbed his beard. Rufus nodded, unable to conceal his surprise at a senator able to understand these things. 'You'll have to make a new mount, won't you?'

'If we can, my lord.' Rufus had been struggling to work out how ever since it had happened and had not cracked the problem so far. 'Would you like to see?'

Hadrian's smile was broader. 'No harm in taking a look.' They went inside the tower, empty for the moment apart from men shooting from the upper floors, and Hadrian discussed the problem with the young centurion, gently easing him towards a solution.

'It's a lot of work, my lord.' The only way was to take out the ram, put new bolts in the framework, fit ropes, and hang it again. 'Cannot do it quickly.'

'Then do it well.' Hadrian stood on his toes to peer through a crack in the timber front, one of the few not covered by the big iron plates. He stared at the damage done to the wall and could see that it was considerable, with more being done by the men working in covered gantries now that the ramp reached all the way to the far wall. 'You are so close,' he assured Rufus. 'And it will be better now that they are threatened from two sides at once... And success would not taste so sweet if the task was easy. We should never forget that even enemies can think and surprise us.'

'They have help,' Rufus said with some bitterness. 'There's a deserter up there, I am sure. We have seen him a few times – slim fellow watching all that we do.'

'You are smarter than he is, young Rufus,' Hadrian assured him. 'I can see that by the way you deal with this problem. All the good money is on you, not the terrified runaway up there.'

Crispinus added his encouragement, although it was oddly more difficult to feign enthusiasm and optimism when Hadrian was there, so that it was no longer his sole responsibility. Even the excellent reports from the men undermining the wall by hand failed to lift his spirits. Time was pouring away like the water in a clock, and there was so little he could do to speed things up.

As they rode to the northern camp, they caught the faint sound of a cheer, and then another much louder.

'The tower,' Hadrian said with some satisfaction. 'Is that the ram?' he asked, cupping a hand to his ear. 'Hard to tell.' By the time they approached the mineworks the steady pounding was unmistakeable. Crispinus waited nervously for an interruption, for surely the enemy would employ sacks and the other ploys used against the other tower. Yet the noise kept on, solid, determined and never missing a beat.

Hadrian was impressed with the mineworks. 'And you are sure the defenders are not responding by digging their own?'

'We have parties sitting and listening for any sound, my lord,' the centurion in change assured him. 'If they are countermining then they are a long way away or in the wrong place because we have not heard a thing.'

'Where are you now?'

'By our reckoning, almost at the point where the inner wall branches off from the main one.'

'That is their citadel,' Crispinus explained. 'We did not want to get inside one wall and still be shut out from the other so have aimed for the join.'

Hadrian nodded encouragingly, his features shadowed in the dim lamplight inside the tunnel. 'And how sure can you be of your reckoning?' He waved his hand in front of Crispinus because he wanted the centurion on the spot to speak. 'It must be hard to be precise.'

'We are confident, my lord. We know the angles and the distance. But as anyone will tell you, always best to add a tenth to your target. Better to go too long than come up short.'

'And better still not to waste time answering damned fool questions from nosy aristocrats, eh!' Hadrian grinned. 'You're doing wonderfully. Keep it up.'

'I am impressed,' Hadrian assured Crispinus as they went on their way, heading for the western ramp. They were close enough to hear a sharper noise of metal striking stone after the heavier thump of each blow. 'Everything is well in hand. I knew I was giving you a very tough nut to crack with only the barest minimum of resources, and yet here we are, on the brink of success. Ah, here is Ferox.' Hadrian had requested the presence of the centurion, who was now trotting towards them.

'Well met, Flavius Ferox – and well done!'

'My lord.'

'Ah, your usual garrulous self, I see. After all these years, you really ought to appear more Roman and forthcoming.'

'Sir.'

'Why did I want to see you?' Hadrian asked.

'As a reminder that some problems are insoluble, my lord,' Crispinus suggested, 'for some people never change.'

'True. They have their uses, though. Tell me, have you seen any sign of the errant Domitius?'

'Once or twice on the walls.'

'Can you really be sure. Faces up there seem so small.'

'It's him, my lord.'

There was little left of the corpse suspended from the walls when Crispinus drew their attention to it.

'Poor fellow,' Hadrian said. 'Wonder who he was?'

Crispinus dropped his voice even though the closest trooper was some way away. 'We did wonder about your man.'

'I doubt that it is him, but time will tell.' Hadrian reined in. They were out of range of the walls, but still a couple of hundred paces from the tower. Looking from the side, it meant that they could see the ram strike. The sun was setting, casting a long shadow in front of the tower and showing the puffs of dust each time the ram's head struck the wall. Artillery was shooting from both sides, the stones dark against the pale wall and bolts glinting when they caught the light.

The ram slammed into the wall again, and there was another puff of dust from the impact. A cloud shrouded the space between the tower and the wall, and drifted around the tower itself.

'It's quite beautiful, in its way,' Hadrian said, 'although I doubt any painter could capture that light.'

Crispinus frowned. 'There is so much dust.' He did not remember such a cloud around the ram on the other side.

A cornu sounded the alarm.

'That's not dust,' Ferox said. 'It's smoke.'

XXIV

T HE RAMP BURNED, and so did the tower. It started slowly, the air becoming hotter, and ever thicker smoke coming up from underneath and through the gaps in the timber supports. They had used a lot more wood to speed the construction, and that helped the blaze gain hold. No one had thought to protect the tower from fire coming from below, so its big wooden wheels and the beams of its floor soon began to burn.

'Can we haul it back?' Hadrian had asked, when he and the others galloped over to help organise the firefighting.

'Not designed that way,' Caecilius replied. 'No time to set up ropes to haul it back and if we let it roll it will smash itself to pieces.'

'Then let's get the flames under control!'

There was no water close enough to make this easy. Bucket chains were formed from the stream, but that was back beyond the camp, had very little water in it, and they probably lost half of what they carried in their hurry. Crispinus let some of the barrels in the camp be loaded onto waggons and brought forward, but it was not remotely enough.

'Like pissing into Etna!' Caecilius shouted. The blaze was raging, the noise so loud that it was hard to understand what anyone was saying. Stones came from the walls, smashing anyone in their path, while bolts and arrows knocked them down. Men died, achieving nothing, but they kept trying, for after toiling for so long it was hard to see the work consumed. In the end it took much shouting, and some blows from the troopers escorting Hadrian and Crispinus, to pull men back. The fire lit the night, burning on for hours, and the next morning a cloud of dirty smoke drifted across the city.

No one had died from the fire itself, for there had been time to pull everyone from the tower and the works around the ramp. A dozen had been killed by missiles and twice that many wounded, with a similar number burned more or less severely.

'It's gone,' Caecilius told them, 'all of it.' They were on the observation tower, Hadrian, Crispinus and ten officers crammed into the narrow platform.

'Can anything be salvaged?' Hadrian asked.

'No. It's gone – the tower, the ramp, more than a month's work... finished. Buggers must have been mining for a good while. Got right underneath, packed the tunnel with oil, tallow, pitch, anything that would burn. Once that's ablaze it's bound to go up and all that dry wood – poof!' Caecilius gave a thin smile. 'Well, you know what I mean. We were so busy feeling smart about our own mine that we never thought that they'd be burrowing away at the same time.'

'Do you think they are at it on the eastern side as well?'

'Doubt it. Very rocky over there. And if they had one why didn't they fire it at the same time?' The defenders had launched a sally during the night, and only heavy fighting by Cerialis and his men had protected the siege works and driven them back inside. 'Wouldn't make sense to waste men coming out if they had another mine to fire. So that should be all right.'

'We hope to have the ram remounted by tomorrow.' Rufus was trying and failing to sound optimistic. A beaten, exhausted mood had spread throughout the camps.

'And here?' Hadrian was leaning on the rail, staring at the ruin.

'If we want to start building from scratch, then I'll need a lot more timber... a lot.' Caecilius' voice was flat and even he did not sound convinced. 'There is nothing much left around here.'

'I shall see what I can do.'

The acting governor and the commander of the legion toured the camps and the siege lines, doing their best to rouse the men's spirits. It was easiest on the eastern side, where Cerialis' men felt pride in having repulsed another sally, and some satisfaction that their tower would soon be back in operation. Everywhere else, men's eyes were down, their movements stiff and lethargic. Everyone and everything seemed covered in a layer of dirty smuts and dust, making them old, almost decayed.

'Did Pliny ever tell you about the day Vesuvius spread ruin all around?' Hadrian asked Crispinus, as they sat down in the praetorium for a light meal. He flicked some dust from his couch. 'The stuff gets everywhere. Reminds me of when I went to Ferox's garrison in Moesia – the place caught fire within a couple of hours of my arrival.'

'Philosophers might begin to see a pattern,' Crispinus joked. He felt his cheek throbbing and had to concentrate to control it.

'We must take solace in the fact that it all turned out well in the end – more or less anyway. So we must make sure that the same happens now. Is it worth attempting an escalade? Ferox is good at making the most of darkness. Try to storm at night – on this side, when they think that we will be putting all efforts into the assault in the east. We're tired, but they must be more tired – and relaxing after this success. Could take them by surprise and break their spirit.'

'Shall we summon Ferox?'

'Holy Athena, no.' Hadrian chuckled. 'Don't think I could take more of his gloom at the moment... And I know that those are high walls and this is a big risk. Maybe start making some ladders, just in case.'

'Of course. And once the other ram is back working we have a chance.'

'And there is the mine. Yes, I know, I know, we still have a lot going for us before our time runs out. Be nice to give the men something though. You know soldiers. Love smashing things and burning things, hate labouring, but take a pride in what they have made and hate even more to see it destroyed. If we do attack up ladders we'll need 'em keen, and that's one thing they are not at the moment – oh, I know, this is Ninth Hispana and they'll do their duty. Storming a strong city takes more than duty. You know it and I know it. We need luck and we need—'

There was a dull rumble before a great rolling crash that seemed to go on and on. Hadrian sniffed the air. 'Strange, did not see any sign of a storm.' There was silence, no sound of rain on the tent stretched over their heads nor any more thunder. Outside, men began to shout and cheer.

'We may have our luck,' Crispinus said. Princess Azátē appeared, heavily veiled and in her finery to meet the acting governor. 'Apologies, lady, but we must go.' Hadrian stood, gave the slightest inclination of the head, for no more was appropriate, treated her to an encouraging smile and dashed outside with the legatus. Ahead of them, hovering over the city was a great cloud, almost a fog, thicker and paler than the smoke from the fires. Soldiers were lining the camp rampart, staring at it and talking excitedly.

Hadrian grinned at Crispinus. 'Let's take a closer look!'

There was no point climbing the observation tower, so they pressed on, into the redoubts and other works left after the fire. They found the primus pilus dancing, an odd, ungainly sight, and Crispinus could not remember ever seeing the man so excited or so cheerful. 'Got you, you bastards! Got you! Thought you'd won, didn't you? Yes, you did! Stupid bastards. Now look what you've done! Ha! Serves you right, you little buggers!'

'I take it there is good news,' Crispinus said, as suavely as he could. The primus pilus calmed a little, and stopped shouting, contenting himself with waving his fist at the city – or at least where the city should be through the thick cloud of dust. They were all coughing.

'We've a breach,' Caecilius shouted, and grabbing Rufus by the arms, whirled him around. 'A breach!' He let the young centurion go and started screaming at the city again. 'Didn't expect that, did you, you little sods!'

'The wall is down, sir,' Rufus explained. 'Part of the tower as well. They must have undermined them with their own tunnel. Maybe more collapsed than they expected or they just didn't think it through.'

'Not sensible then, like us,' Hadrian said, wooden faced, but the irony was weakened when he started to cough.

Slowly, the dust cloud thinned and cleared, although the air seemed so unnaturally still that it took hours. Thirty feet of curtain wall had collapsed altogether, and the corner tower was leaning outwards, a great crack running down from the top. A lot of spoil had dropped forward, piling around the remnants of the Roman ramp.

'Can we get up there?' Crispinus asked his consilium, once the officers had been summoned. Hadrian was present, but had begun by saying that he was not there to take over from such an able legatus. He was there to help as best he could.

'Not yet,' Caecilius said. It was hard now to remember his earlier enthusiasm.

'If we work all night, should be able to ready by noon tomorrow,' Rufus explained. 'We need to make a new ramp strong enough to take the weight of the attacking column. And get some ladders to help climb wherever there is still a slope.'

'And what are they doing?'

Rufus glanced at Caecilius who gestured for him to answer. 'Building a rampart. Mix of earth and timber, probably beams stripped from houses. They're trying to block the breach up.'

'And we're making it hard for them, I presume?' Crispinus asked.

'Much as we can.' Caecilius' gruffness had returned. 'Anyone and anything that can shoot is shooting. But the angle's wrong. They're still uphill and we don't have the advantage of the tower anymore.'

'So the longer we wait then the harder it will get?'

The primus pilus nodded.

'It's a race,' Rufus said. 'They'll never make it as strong as a real wall, but they can make it strong. And it takes us time to get the sheds back into place or bring new ones up, then to bring the earth and pack it down to complete the ramp.'

'Sacks!' Hadrian's interruption surprised everyone. 'My apologies. But I wonder whether work could be saved if we get a lot of sacks and pack them with fleeces or straw. This ramp does not need to last forever. Pile in a lot of sacks and you can fill up the gaps and get across much faster. Be a surprise to them as well.'

Caecilius drew breath. 'Maybe,' he conceded, then thought for a little longer. 'It could work.' Rufus picked up a tablet and began writing some figures.

'We go tonight,' Crispinus decided. He paid no visible attention to Hadrian, who was sitting slightly behind him, so did not see the acting governor nod in approval. 'Is midnight possible? Your honest opinion, primus?'

'No, sir. As late as we can.'

'Then two hours before dawn. Good. Now that is settled, we must make it happen.'

One hundred volunteers drawn from the entire army led by a centurion would lead the attack, backed by the first cohort, followed by the best men from two more, and as many auxiliaries. Ferox was more than a little surprised that his men were not involved, although shortly after receiving that news he was told that he and ten of them were to guide the men carrying the sacks, who inevitably had to precede everyone else.

'You are so good at finding your way in the dark,' Crispinus assured him. 'But I don't want to lose you, so once you have got the bags in place, get out of the way, and let the storming party do their job.'

'Where will we go, my lord?' Vindex asked, his face as innocent as he could make it. 'They'll be hundreds of big lads coming up behind us.'

'Oh, just slip off the side of the ramp. We can always fish you out of the ditch once it is all over, can't we?'

Vindex and Bran insisted on coming with him, and to his amazement all of his men volunteered and they had to draw lots to pick the remaining eight.

'Need to look after you,' Vindex assured him.

'Don't believe a word of it,' Bran said. 'He's been listening to stories of the royal harem inside the city.'

'They might need my protection,' Vindex announced.

'And me to protect them from you, you randy old goat.'

They were behind the main camp, tending to their horses. Everywhere men were busy, sewing up sacks, packing them with straw and anything else they could find, and checking equipment. Some men made wills, for the law allowed one soldier to witness another's provisions. Over everything else came the scraping sound as blades were honed to a fine edge.

XXV

The breach in the western wall
The eleventh hour of the night, the Ides of May
The thirty-sixth day of the siege

THE SOUND OF pick striking stone carried down from the city. There were other noises too: soft conversation, and the scraping of tools as the citizens laboured to make their new wall. Every once in a while, a ballista cracked and sent a missile into the darkness, and sometimes there was a thump or a scream to suggest that it had struck home.

Ferox and his party were where they should be. Kneeling down in one of the musculi, ready to rush out onto the ramp and use their sacks to fill up the remaining gaps in it. Brennus the Brigantian waited beside him, with another warrior beyond that, and behind each of them the fifteen men of each carrying party. The others waited in similar huts for the signal Caecilius would give when he was ready. The man was as surly as ever, his dislike of Ferox as obvious as it was unexplained, but he knew his job and it was reassuring to have him there.

Two legionaries waited to push aside the screen protecting the front of the hut, their faces hidden in the darkness. Someone tapped three times on the wall of the musculus.

'Go!' Ferox hissed, and the screen went down. He stood up and beckoned to the rest to follow. The air was fresher outside, the starlight bright, so that it felt as if everyone must see them. He went on, found the place, and pointed down. 'There!' The two Brigantes pulled off to the side, as the man at the head of each file came up and tipped his filled bag down. Beyond them the men from the second musculus were doing the same thing, and quickly the ground ahead was filled, so Ferox stepped forward. 'Down there.' The ground shifted only a little under his feet, which meant that the plan was working.

Caecilius appeared, jumping ahead. 'Here and here!' he called.

Something fell from the wall, something much like a straw-filled bag, but burning. A man shouted, another joined him and a horn sounded.

'Come on!' There was no point keeping quiet anymore. 'Get this filled in!' Ferox grabbed the next one and pushed it into place. Vindex was nearby, doing the same, and suddenly all the shouts were drowned out as massed cornu horns and the slim trumpets of the legion blared out in challenge. Thousands of men cheered.

'Shit!' Vindex spat the word. 'We're humped!' The last sacks were dropped into place.

'Down there!' There was no other choice, for they could already hear the storming party rushing through the covered sheds, so Ferox pointed down the side. 'Go!' He half pushed the carriers and watched as they slid down the bank into the shadows of the ditch. Soldiers – cavalrymen from their helmets – appeared holding a ladder and jogged forward, turning into a sprint as they got the tall ladder fully out of the hut. Vindex had already gone, so Ferox followed, slipping, almost losing all balance, and gripping the piled earth to ease his way down, until it gave way and he fell the last six or seven feet. Vindex broke his fall, so that both of them ended up sprawled in the ditch.

'Clumsy bastard,' Vindex shouted, but the words were lost as the trumpets sounded again. There was another shout, but it was less united, and individual cries came as the storming party made it across the ramp and reached the foot of the breach. Ferox saw the troopers raising their ladder against part of the wall where it sloped down, and beside them, men were climbing up the steep pile of rubble. Another burning carcase of straw fell, then another, bathing the figures in red light. Some fell, struck by arrows or stones hurled by hand. The centurion was clear in the flamelight, his transverse crest marking him out, and he was climbing the rubble, shield juddering as it was struck by arrow after arrow.

'We going or staying?' Vindex asked. The carrying party had already climbed up the bank to withdraw, and only Bran and four other Brigantes remained. The others must have gone down the far side of the ramp.

'Let's wait.'

Vindex grunted, then looked up as light flared brightly. 'Oh no!' A stream of oil cascaded down from the last section of solid wall next to the breach, and almost as soon as it fell, another carcase dropped and it erupted into a sheet of flame. Men screamed as they burned. A trooper grunted as he was knocked from the top of the ladder by a stone, and the ladder slipped, fell slowly back, men falling from its rungs. The centurion was still going, then was struck in the leg by an arrow, and kneeled. A bigger boulder rolled down the breach and swatted him aside.

Trumpets sounded again, and the head of the first cohort sprinted over the ramp, ranks ragged, but pressing on towards the wall. Closer to them, other men dropped and slid into the ditch near the Brigantes and they had a ladder. Ferox did not think that they had orders, but there was no harm in trying.

'Come on, lads, the third will beat everyone else inside!' their centurion shouted. Ferox recognised him, struggled to recall the name, but remembered a rather stolid, unimaginative man, so this seemed a surprising action. Then he noticed Hadrian, silhouetted against the top of the ditch and cheering them on. Part of him felt it was a shame no one on the wall had seen so important a target.

'Pity we haven't got a bow,' Vindex whispered, as if reading his mind. 'Or even a javelin.'

The legionaries were across the ditch and they had two ladders with them, high enough to make it easy to climb out. The centurion led them.

'We're going then,' Vindex said as Ferox watched. It was not a question.

'You don't have to come.' Ferox drew his gladius. They would need to find shields when they reached the top, but there were bound to be plenty.

'One day we won't,' Bran shouted, for the noise meant that it was the only way they could hear.

The centurion – Sentius, that was it, Sentius – had forty or so men with him, so most of his centuria, and they were nearly all up. Ferox and the Brigantes rushed over, for the legionaries had turned and were hauling one of the ladders up after them.

'Wait, lads!' Ferox shouted. The soldier gaped, but did as he was told, before pitching down and almost knocking Ferox aside. He glanced down, and Vindex shook his head. There was the shaft of a ballista bolt in the legionary's back. Ferox went up the ladder as fast as he could. The rest of the legionaries had gone forward, apart from one who sobbed as he clutched at his leg, which was nothing but a bloodied stump below the knee.

Ferox took the man's shield, and held it to protect the others as they climbed. 'The ladder!' he called back. 'Bring it with us!'

The ground was littered with bodies, worse even than those spots on a battlefield where a cohort broke and the enemy slaughtered them as they fled. By now a crowd of men was trying to climb the spoil heap of the breach. There did not seem to be any more oil, but the flames still burned and there was the ghastly smell of roasting meat to add to the stench of blood and entrails.

'That way!' Ferox shouted, now that they had the ladder up. He pointed to the left, nearer to the edge of the breach, because so many men were being drawn into the centre. 'Get shields.' More men were streaming across the ramp, tall men from the first cohort, who piled in behind the rest, going slowly once they reached the spoil because that was the only way a man could go and keep on his feet, and they were shouting, a great surge of rage without any words. Arrows, spears and stones drove into the press, and men dropped to be trampled underfoot.

Ferox and his men ran to the foot of the wall, as he looked for the best spot. There were legionaries there, Sentius' men, and someone grabbed Ferox on the shoulder.

'Centurion!' It was Caecilius. 'Oh, it's you,' he screamed in Ferox's ear. 'Would be. Now get men up there. Up the wall and inside! Understand?'

'Yes.' Ferox could see the jagged edge of the breach sloping upwards and the hollow space where one of the artillery chambers had been. Perhaps there was a way into the city through there. He gestured to the others and began to climb. The broken outer wall was a few feet thick, but crumbling, with the big stone blocks loose or missing altogether. He started to climb, dropping the shield because he needed both hands to pull himself up where there were four great blocks still in place on top of each other and the slope vertical. An arrow whipped past, but whether it was aimed or a wild shot into the darkness no more followed. He glanced back, saw Vindex hauling Bran up behind him, and beyond them the surge of legionaries climbing the breach and getting no further. The defender's wall was little more than eight feet high, but it was complete and lined with men throwing down javelins and stones. Fire flared up once more, as oil was set alight and the awful screams of the men caught by it carried even over the noise of battle.

Ferox had to concentrate to get any further. The wall, what was left of it, started to narrow because he had reached the level of one of the chambers, but most of the floor had gone.

'Taranis!' Vindex hissed.

'Copy me,' Ferox called and hoped that they heard. He stood up, arms spread wide for balance and started to walk along the top of the wall. The stone beneath his feet wobbled, slipped to the side an inch and then held, so he kept going, trying to keep steady, although the last few steps were faster and faster, and as another block gave way he leaped, felt himself falling, thought he was short and then slammed into the side of the floor and the fill beneath it. His elbows were on top, and breathing hard because he had winded himself, he managed to haul himself up.

'Daft bugger!' Vindex was squatting before the narrow strip of wall.

'Get the ladder!' Ferox shouted. 'We can use it as a bridge.' The jump was longer, now that the block had fallen away and taken some others with it, and he did not think anyone would make it.

Vindex stared at the gap, shook his head in dismay, but told Bran who was behind him and who in turn called back. Ferox saw an arched doorway beside the back wall, which must lead into the next chamber along. Otherwise there were broken fragments of a light ballista, a few bolts and not much else in what was left of the room. He went to the door, drawing his sword, but keeping to the side until the others came up. It gave him a clear view of the defenders' improvised rampart. As he watched, a legionary thrust to kill one of the Nicopolitans, then pulled himself over the parapet. Another man came to the top of his ladder, and the first one stamped forward, punching with his scutum to knock a defender off the walkway. The falling man screamed, even though the drop was not far. Another Nicopolitan came from the legionary's right side, hacked hard into the man's shoulder, knocking him to his knees whether or not he had broken through the armour. Then he spun and slashed at the one on the ladder, a huge blow that went under the cheek guards and sliced through the man's neck. The headless torso, blood pumping, clung to the top of the ladder, then dropped back, knocking down the legionary behind. By this time the one on the wall was surrounded, blocking only some of the blows raining down. His shield was shattered and soon he lay still, until they lifted the corpse and tipped it back off the walkway. Other ladders were up against the rampart, but Ferox could see no Roman on top, let alone any real sign of a breakthrough. Trumpets were sounding, as more legionaries came up to support the first cohort.

'Here!' Vindex had the ladder, and was reaching forward with it. Ferox went over, managed to catch the end, and took more of the weight as it was pushed towards him. They laid it down, and it spanned the gap well enough, even if it looked flimsy. Bran pushed past Vindex, and almost tipped them both off the wall, as Ferox stood on the end to weight it down. The young warrior licked his lips, then walked forward, crossing quickly.

'It's fine,' he called back.

Vindex appeared unconvinced, and lifted the wheel of Taranis slung around his neck and kissed it before he almost ran across, making the ladder shake. The rest of the Brigantes followed, and then Ferox was surprised to see Caecilius scrambling up, followed by a legionary.

'Why are you hanging around?' the primus pilus snarled, before breaking into a broad smile.

Ferox went back to the archway. He drew his sword, wished he still had the shield, but none of the Brigantes had managed to keep one during the climb, so they would have to make do. He glanced back, and still the defenders were clinging to the wall, killing or hurling back every legionary who climbed up. Taking a deep breath, he jumped into the doorway, just as a bolt shooter cracked like a whip to send a dart out into the darkness. A man was standing at the end of a long hallway, framed in an arch just like this one, with light behind him, and he must have been lazy or stupid, because it took a moment for him to react. Ferox sprinted towards him, gladius held low and trusting that the others would follow. The defender gaped at him, tried to shout, and then turned and fled.

Ferox screamed a challenge, the sound echoing along the corridor, and then burst into the light. A man slashed at him with the heavy bolt from a ballista, but he caught him by the wrist and stabbed once, twisting the blade to free it. Bran was behind him, and a burly man went for him, until Bran danced aside and severed his opponent's arm, before jumping the other way and spitting another of the crewmen. Vindex followed, shouting like a fury, and killed a fourth man. The rest fled, through another archway.

'After them!' Ferox shouted. Surprise and panic would only last so long, so they needed to keep going.

'Out the way!' Sentius had appeared, and the man held a scutum. Ferox stopped and let the centurion take the lead. Legionaries were spilling into the room, some with shields, some without, and Caecilius was among them.

'We need a way out!' he shouted.

There was no one in the next chamber, although the lamp was still lit and a machine much like a scorpio was cocked and ready to shoot. This time there was no arch in the far wall, but a door on what must be the inner wall. Sentius bellowed at a legionary to try it. It would not budge.

'Axes!' Caecilius shouted. He tossed a dolabra to one of the men. Ferox had not even noticed that the senior centurion had been holding one instead of a sword. The legionary began to attack the wood. Vindex grabbed a tool much like a crowbar and went to the door. The soldier understood, reversed his blade and slid the tip into the gap on the other side to the hinges. Vindex did the same with the end of the crowbar and they both strained, faces taut, grunting with the effort until the door sprang open. There were steps leading down from the wall.

Sentius went down them and Ferox followed. To his right were tall houses, and he could not see the breach or the defender's new rampart. The houses had flat roofs, so there might be a way across, although there was no sign of any stairs. In front were more houses, but there was an alley someway to the left, and if they went down there then maybe they could loop back around and get to the breach. Just a few men coming from behind might well be enough to open the way for the legionaries attacking from outside.

'Over there!' Ferox shouted and gestured. The men were streaming down the steps, a mix of Brigantes and legionaries and stopping to sort everyone out would waste precious time when the alarm was going out from the fleeing crewmen. 'That way! We can try to find our way around!'

'Do what he says!' Caecilius shouted.

The alley was narrow, and longer than Ferox had expected. It was empty, so he ran along it, leading the rest. There was no path heading off to the right, only another to the left, so he took that, came to a crossroads with a little fountain, and ahead could see the distant main street they had gone along all those months ago.

With a crash, a heavy tile struck a legionary, crushing his helmet. More missiles came from the high roofs above them.

'Keep going!' Caecilius shouted, for there was no point standing to face attackers they could not reach. Ferox ran on, turned right at the crossroads, headed up the narrow street, until he saw an opening on his right and took that. The sound of fighting at the breach was faint, but men appeared, three of them, with oval shields and javelins and they shouted in alarm. One threw a javelin, Ferox flung himself to the side, and it thumped into Sentius' shield.

'Kill the bastards!' the centurion shouted as he charged, and turned the last word into a scream. Ferox pushed himself off the wall and followed. One of the warriors was down, knocked off his feet by a blow from the shield's boss, and the centurion slashed at the unshielded right of the man next to him, snapping through the spear shaft as the Nicopolitan tried to parry. Ferox went for the other, pushing aside a feeble thrust and then stabbing into the man's stomach. He was not wearing armour, and up close he could see the lined face and white beard of an old man as he hissed in agony and fell. Sentius finished off his opponent, then slammed the edge of his scutum down to knock out the one on the ground.

'Which way?' he asked.

Not far ahead was another junction, leading off to either side, but some sort of high-walled shrine was in front of them and blocking the direction they wanted to go.

'Go left!' Vindex shouted, and since he had seen a little more of the city than Ferox it seemed as good a bet as any. He scooped up one of the oval shields, saw that the old man was still alive, but could not do anything for him, so ran on. There were shouts, more tiles, stones and heavy pots coming down at them from the rooftops and a woman's voice was screaming abuse at them in vilely accented Greek. One of the Brigantians crumpled, his head bleeding from the strike of a tile.

They ran on, around the corner, and fifty paces ahead was an open square, which must surely link to alleys going off in all directions, so they sprinted ahead. Men appeared, half a dozen of them, and they were archers and sent arrows whipping through the night. Ferox's new shield shuddered as one struck home, and behind him there was a deep sigh. Brennus the Brigantian had an arrow through his remaining eye, and a legionary was squealing because another arrow had struck him in the thigh. More men appeared, warriors with shields this time.

'Form up!' Ferox shouted, but there was not time and what with the darkness and men running in from all sides, the square became filled with a mix of men, stabbing, cutting, defending. One legionary turned with a start, and stabbed a comrade in the face before he could check the blow. He stared aghast, until a Nicopolitan rammed a spear through his segmented armour and out the far side. Ferox killed a man, chopping down into his skull, freed the blade, pushed on, used his shield to hook an opponent's aside, and then thrust into the man's throat. Sentius beat another man down through sheer brute force, and the training and rush of the attackers swept the square clear.

More arrows came in, this time from the rooftops. Caecilius

was struck in the shoulder, then took another through the leg. A legionary opened his mouth to shout a warning and was shot through the teeth instead. There was a dull clang, like the ringing of broken bell, as an arrowhead punched through a plate in another soldier's cuirass. He spun, was struck again and again, dropped his shield and sank to his knees. A rank of enemies appeared on the widest road coming into the square, and there were more behind them.

'Try that way!' Caecilius pointed in the opposite direction, hissing because of the pain from his wounds. Sentius was standing over him, covering the fallen primus pilus with his shield.

Ferox, Vindex and Bran ran off, followed by the last remaining Brigantian and a legionary, but the Roman was hit in the leg and stumbled, knocking the Briton over, and as he lay sprawled a stone slammed into the back of his head. They went around the corner, Vindex searching around for something familiar.

'There!' he said, before Ferox hauled him bodily into a side alley and Bran followed. There was the pounding of feet and a great crowd came running past them, dozens and dozens of men, some with weapons and some simply with clubs. The three men backed away into the shadows and no one noticed them. Ferox pointed in the opposite direction, so they went that way, turned and found themselves in an even narrower alley. It ended up in a blank end, but there were steps leading onto the roof of one of the buildings, so they went cautiously up.

No one was in sight. There was shouting, lots of it, from some way off, presumably from the square. Ferox went across the flat roof of the building to the far side and could see nothing. He climbed onto the low wall and jumped across the alleyway onto another roof. Bran came next, then Vindex, whose boot smashed through the mud roof. If anyone was below they either did not notice or were too frightened to investigate, and after a struggle and much cursing on Vindex's part, they freed him.

Ferox stood for a moment, listening.

'Poor bastards,' Vindex said, for there was no more shouting or any sound of fighting. 'Couldn't hold that many.'

'There's nothing coming from the assault either,' Bran whispered. From up here they could see the line of the outer wall and its towers, much further away than they would have expected. The leaning tower next to the breach was stark in the moonlight, and they could just see where the breach began.

'Reckon we'd know if they'd got in,' Vindex said.

'We'd know.' Ferox had seen stormings before, when men half wild with fear and rage spilled out into the streets.

'So what do we do?'

'Hey! Who are you?' The challenge came in Greek, from a tall man in armour down in the street.

'Back!' Ferox led them over the roof again. They vaulted across the alley, sped across the next roof, and jumped to another house. Ahead of them the sky was growing red, the sun about to rise. There were no stairs, so Ferox swung himself over, clung to the wall as he let himself slide down and then dropped, rolling as he landed. The others followed, Vindex cursing. There was no one in this narrow street, but torchlight flickered from a junction up ahead and they heard singing. They went the other way, around a corner. Hopefully any pursuers would have lost the trail, but that did not help them with what to do next.

'Come here!' The hissed command was in Latin and from the shadows. Ferox hesitated.

'Come here, you daft sods!'

'He's talking to you two,' Vindex told them.

'Quick.' There was a vague figure in the shadows ahead of them. 'Now or never. Follow me!' The shadows moved as a man ran off down an alley so narrow that a loaded mule would struggle to fit.

'I know that voice.' Bran's tone was bitter.

'We haven't got much choice.' Ferox said, and followed.

XXVI

Outside Nicopolis
Seventeenth day before the Kalends of June
The thirty-seventh day of the siege

C RISPINUS HAD READ the reports, but each time he
saw the breach and the debris of the failed assault, the
sheer scale of their losses horrified him. The dead were
everywhere, already swelling in the heat. When the Romans
had tried to recover them, and see how many were wounded,
the Nicopolitans shot them down. When the defenders started
to roll bodies down the slope and into the ditch, the Roman
artillery and archers had killed them until they gave up. There
were so many flies that you could hear a deep humming in the
air, as the corpses rotted and stank.

There was not any good news this morning. They still had
their breach, even if the Nicopolitans were working hard to
strengthen the rampart behind it. His own men had nearly
finished raising some platforms that ought to allow some of
the heavier ballistae to strike at these new defences. With luck
they might knock some of it down, since surely earth and
timber would prove flimsier than stone. At the very least it
would make the enemy's work harder. Rufus was cautious, still
shocked because with Caecilius gone missing, he was seen as the
most knowledgeable engineer they had. The man was nervous,

382

embarrassed because the remounting of the battering ram was proving harder than expected and would take at least another day. Worse still, the roof of the mine had fallen in, hundreds of paces back from the wall, and not stretching up to it as far as they could tell, which meant that it was not likely to do them any good. A dozen workers were buried, perhaps dead or trapped on the far side waiting for the evil spirits of the mine to take their lives. An attempt to reach them only brought down more of the roof, and it was clear that they needed far more supports to make the tunnel safe. Rufus was not sure whether they could make the mine work at all, and at the very least the job would take many days.

Rufus had good reason to be nervous, and there was a vulnerability about the man that helped Crispinus not to lose his own temper. He had not truly warmed to Caecilius, but the man had done his job well and spoken his mind. What the damned fool had been doing at the front of the assault was hard to tell, for up until then he had been so cautious. Yet he did care about the soldiers, and perhaps had hoped that he could get the job done at less cost if he was right in the thick of things. Men said that the primus pilus had led a party into the city, using the edge of the breach, but they had vanished and none of them had come back. Two other centurions were missing, although someone claimed to have seen one of them on the enemy rampart, fighting until he was cut down, so he was either dead or a wounded prisoner. Three more centurions were most certainly dead, along with one hundred and forty-three men. Some seventy wounded had got back on their own or been carried by comrades, and almost as many were missing, which meant dead or captured. Somehow staring at the piles of bodies in and around the breach, it was hard not to believe that the losses were even heavier. They were heavy enough, and this was a defeat, which made so much difference because the losses became waste instead of noble and necessary sacrifice. No one ever won an award for a defeat.

Ferox had also vanished. No one had seen him fall, and although the bodies of a couple of his Brigantes were clearly visible, the centurion was not among them. Crispinus hoped that he was not dead, for all the man's irritating habits. Now and again he had a wild thought of the Briton somehow at large in the city, and finding a way to open the gates to the Romans. He was a tough man, but everyone's luck ran out eventually, and the odds were that he was dead or a prisoner, which would be tough on his captors.

Crispinus gave a signal and a tubicen sounded a fanfare. Arrian strode out of the cover of a musculus on the ramp, his hands raised to show that he was open and wished to talk. Behind him came Arbandes and, for the first time, his sister. The stink of death was foul enough from this distance, so Crispinus could only imagine the reek up there, and picture that pretty little nose wrinkling in revulsion. No one would see, for she was wearing a veil, although she had offered to lower it if the Nicopolitans did not believe her when she told them who she was. Azáté had not been keen to go at all, and he could understand that, and some of that was fear for the people she had left inside, once it was known that she was not among them.

Hadrian had insisted. 'We need them both. Be good for the magistrates to see that both of the king's children – and the only two to matter, at least at the moment – are here with us and want them to surrender. Might just give them pause and make them willing to give in. After all, they've won honour enough already. Held us for nearly forty days, repulsed a major attack. Not many can boast of that. If they're smart they'll take it and save themselves, for they must know that they cannot win in the end.'

Crispinus was not so sure. The new rampart seemed so feeble compared to the old walls, but it would not be easy, and if they did get the ram working and make a breach on the other side, then who was to say another makeshift defence would not block them there as well. Food was running short, and they could not stay here forever. Worse than that the spirit of his men had gone. He could sense it, even if he could not put his finger on what it was. The excitement when the curtain wall collapsed had ebbed away to nothing after the failure of their attack. No one believed anymore, not deep down, and a little voice in his own mind kept whispering that it was hopeless and perhaps they would all die here. It might be for the best.

'Well...' Hadrian paused. 'We must not count on anything. Perhaps they will give in, perhaps not. Remember we have a breach, the prospect of another before long, and that we are far better soldiers. It really is only a matter of time.' Hadrian gave a rueful smile. 'Hasn't it always been that? Well time is getting short, but it has not run out on us yet. We do not lose anything by seeing whether they are now more amenable. More importantly, having brother and sister espouse our cause and show themselves before the city sends a message to Nicopolis and all the world. We are supported by the royal family of this kingdom. They are our friends and allies. Thus the people of Nicopolis are rebels opposing their rightful rulers. That becomes the essential, unarguable truth – we are not invaders, but allies helping to crush a rebellion. Thus we are in the right and the citizens are in the wrong.'

With the acting governor insisting, Crispinus had no choice and nor did Azátē. After Arrian had announced their intention, and the magistrates and other worthies had been summoned to the makeshift rampart, the formalities could begin. Crispinus had summoned Ferox's boy, Philo, to translate, for the princess had explained that she might well have to argue some of her case in Aramaic. At first they used Greek, and after Arrian had spoken, Arbandes gave a long, highly impassioned speech.

'Ambitious boy, that one,' Hadrian said. 'Got a frosty reception from the princeps last time, but Trajan always likes good-looking young lads when they have a hint of martial swagger.'

Arbandes talked for a long time, far longer than before, almost as if he enjoyed making his sister wait. The response was brief and in words neither Crispinus nor Hadrian understood.

'They are not impressed,' Philo explained.

Azátē took over, and Crispinus, who had never heard her speak louder than in a soft, slightly husky tone, was impressed by how well her voice carried.

'The lady is telling them who she is,' Philo told them, for Azátē was using Aramaic from the start. 'They say that they do not believe her, and now she addresses the two strategoi by name, and also calls out to several others she recognises and pays honour to their courage – and their wisdom.'

'Smart girl,' Hadrian commented as the discussion went on. 'That's good and bad. Trajan is too much the Roman to be comfortable around a smart woman.'

'They still have doubts, so she is saying that she, even she, princess of the blood, lady of Edessa, will prove it.' They saw her peel off her veil and throw off the covering of her head. Crispinus' heart pounded as he remembered her arrival in his tent.

'Cleopatra,' he said under his breath.

'They are arguing,' Philo went on. 'She assures them that if they harm any of her folk inside then she will have each and every one of them impaled.'

'Oh, not perhaps the best aid to diplomacy,' Hadrian noted.

'The lady tells them that they are defying her will, and the will of her father and brother. That the Romans came as friends and they rejected them, and fought them. That such a fight is hopeless and can only end in the burning of their city. The men will die, their wives and daughters will be raped and those who survive that enslaved along with their children.'

'Hercules' balls,' Hadrian muttered as the translation continued. Crispinus felt a pang of regret. Last night, coming back from the failed attack, he had gone to Azátē and he had not been as gentle as his wont.

'They have repulsed one attack, but more will come and in the end the Romans will have their city. That will be the end of Nicopolis – in the victory of others – unless they give in now. There will be no more chances.'

'Hey!' Hadrian said. 'Shut the bitch up!'

Philo frowned in disapproval, realised what he had done and swiftly went on. 'She has come to them because she loves them. They are her people and she wishes only the best for them, so that her heart breaks to see them on the path to utter ruin. Turn back now, and surrender within the hour or there will be no more mercy, and even she – the one who loves them more than she loves any other folk – will not weep, for they have only themselves to blame. It is they who will be cursed by their tearful women and children. That is all!'

Philo did not really need to translate her last words, because they saw the diminutive figure turn on her heels and stride back into the musculus.

Hadrian rubbed his eyes with both hands. 'Not quite what I expected. Still, if she hasn't frightened them, she's certainly given me a scare. Let's hope it works.'

An hour passed and no surrender came.

'Pity, but let's push them before they draw breath. We still have ladders. Let us storm the rampart and be done with it. Assemble two cohorts – and a dozen volunteers to lead the way. I'll speak to them first, get them going. We go at the seventh hour.'

Crispinus half expected a great oration from Hadrian, as the men paraded before moving up towards the ramp.

'Those bastards up there have killed our commilitones and are laughing at us!' Hadrian growled at them. 'They're cowards and scum. They've got a city behind them full of the prettiest women east of the Euphrates and more gems and gold than you can carry.' He stared at the ranks of soldiers. 'So go and take them!'

They cheered, although there was something odd about the sound. It was loud enough, but to Crispinus felt more like surprise than martial rage. As orders were shouted and the formations turned and marched up to their assault positions, the legionaries moved jerkily, like puppets. Only the twelve men chosen to lead the attack went with real enthusiasm. Three were the men who had been caught using a whore while on duty on the night Azátē came over to them, and the rest were also offenders of one sort or another.

There had not been much time for preparation. The new artillery platforms were ready, although they were still hauling the ballistae into place. Crispinus had all the artillery that could bear shooting, along with as many archers as they could get into place, making the best of what cover was available. More missiles went in than came back, which might only mean that the defenders were waiting. Most of the men on the rampart ducked down to avoid the barrage.

Trumpets sounded and the attack began, the dozen leaders dashing ahead, shaking themselves out into a thin line. The first fell to the bolt from a light ballista before the main column had started to come out from the sheds. Two more went down to arrows as defenders bobbed up all along the rampart, and a fourth had his kneecap shattered by a sling stone. A dozen large pots were flung from behind the rampart and shattered as they landed, thick liquid spraying up. The three men from the night picket, Secundus, Priscus and young Felix, kept together, and were still going forward. The boy slipped and fell, not on a body, but on the stones which were wet from the contents of the pots. Another dozen flew over the rampart and broke noisily

The head of the column quivered.

'Oil!' someone shouted. 'Bastards have oil!'

'Keep going!' a centurion yelled.

A cavalryman from one of the cohorts was thrown down by a bolt from an engine. His comrade went to help, saw that it was hopeless and as he turned back to the wall a stone slammed into his face and smashed it to bloody ruin. Arrows claimed more of the assault party and in a moment only the trio were left.

'Charge! Charge!' a centurion screamed. He stepped ahead of the men, turning his back to the enemy, and yelled at the legionaries to come on.

Crispinus moved to get down from the observation tower and Hadrian grabbed his arm and held him. 'No,' he said. 'Not today.'

Secundus reached the wall first. Priscus had a graze on the calf, just above his boot, and Felix helped him. Crispinus wondered whether they realised that the supports were not coming and suspected that they did not. He could see Secundus shouting, and the other two held one of the shields level, so that he could jump onto it. They heaved, he slashed, clearing a space on the parapet, and somehow managed to vault over. An archer leaned out, further on, and sent an arrow squarely into Priscus' back. He arched away from the pain, letting go of the shield and there was time for a second arrow to drive through his mail shirt before a bolt from a scorpio went into the archer's head and he vanished.

'Come on, you cowards, follow me!' the centurion shouted, almost pleading with his men. They did not move. A fire arrow arced through the sky to land on the spoil in front of the breach, and the legionaries ran. No one stopped to see that the flames went out almost immediately.

Felix drove his sword as far as the hilt into the rampart, reached down to take Priscus' sword and started to climb. Secundus' head and shoulders were visible above the parapet, and Crispinus saw his arm come back and thrust forward at eye level. He turned, punching with his shield, clearing space for the youngster to join him, and Felix was almost up when a stone dented the front of his iron helmet and he fell back. That left one man alone, facing the entire enemy army, and the man was not a hero, but a bad character who had skived his way through long years of service. Something of his training had rubbed off, for his balance was good, shield and sword working together, pushing men back, wounding them if they came close. Then he glanced back, saw his fallen comrades and no one else, swept his heavy scutum in a wild arc and hurled it at the enemy

'I think we can forget any charges about the past,' Hadrian said quietly, for Crispinus had told him about the men. They watched as Secundus jumped back down. Felix was up, staggering to the rear, so he leaned over and hauled Priscus onto his back. Arrows pursued them. The first ones missed, even though the range was short and the target so easy. Secundus had come twenty paces before an arrow drove into his thigh. He wavered, almost dropped his burden, then went on, blood streaming down his leg. The arrows stopped coming and the defenders watched the three bloodied legionaries weave their way through the corpses as they went down from the breach.

'They deserve decorations,' Crispinus said, his voice hoarse.

'They deserve a lot of things,' Hadrian replied. 'But like most people they won't get them. And no one gives *dona* for a defeat. How you choose to punish the cohorts who fled is up to you.'

'Yes, my lord, it is.' *Just as it should have been up to me to order the attack, or better yet to have waited*, he thought, but did not say. At least the ballistae on the new platforms were ready and they watched as the first stones struck the rampart. One knocked a great chunk from the wooden parapet, while the other threw up a puff of earth.

'Make sure they have all the stones they need,' Crispinus ordered, 'and keep shooting, day and night.'

Two messages arrived for the acting governor just after sunset. Hadrian was dining with Crispinus, several officers and the royal siblings, and excused himself for reading them, but explained that they might be urgent. He did not say any more, but afterwards asked Crispinus to walk with him to the outposts.

'I need to go,' he explained. 'I shall do my best to send anything that might aid you, but the new legatus will arrive sooner than expected and I ought to meet him. Best not to do anything that might appear suspicious.'

'The Lord Trajan has less enthusiasm for our initiative than we had hoped?' Crispinus had seen the seal on the imperial letter, and since Hadrian's face had remained stiff and unemotional while reading it, it did not seem to contain good news. On a day like this it was hard to expect anything else.

'He is cautious,' Hadrian said after a while. 'My letter clearly took him by surprise, for he did not expect any campaign here. He invites me to make absolutely certain that my actions are in the service of the res publica and efficiently managed. There is no open reprimand, still less any order to pull back to the province itself.'

Crispinus thought for a while. 'So we must win, and win quickly.'

'Yes.' Neither man sounded optimistic. 'That's about it. The dice will fall as they will. I cannot think of any stratagem to get you inside those walls any quicker. At least their new rampart is suffering. And they must be short of food, getting tired.'

So are we, Crispinus thought, without saying, but Hadrian's expression made clear that he knew how empty those words were. 'I'll leave before dawn,' the acting governor told him. 'I think you have twenty days. Maybe one or two more, but by then the new legatus will be in Antioch and have had time to send orders to you or even arrive himself – if he proves more active than his reputation.' Hadrian sighed. 'There is no magical way to win. Yet I will say this. The Lord Trajan can be hard, and he does not care too much for me – or for you, for that matter. But he is sentimental, and he admires bravery and determination over almost anything else. Impress him with your courage, and he will forgive a great deal.'

True to his word, Hadrian and his escort rode off before the sun rose. Crispinus was up to salute him as he departed, for ceremonies must always be observed. He was a little worried that fifty men was not enough to protect so important a man from ambush, for even though Arbandes' men had dispersed, the convoy escorts reported seeing quite large bands of Arab raiders. Well, Hadrian had made his choice and must take his chance like the rest of them. Crispinus watched the horsemen disappear into the darkness and wondered whether he was more relieved to be back in sole command or weighed down by the burden. Neither really seemed to matter.

A little later he heard the faint sound of the ram resuming its pounding of the eastern wall. Men on the rampart of the camp tilted their heads to be sure that they were not mistaken, and there was some talk. There were no cheers, and Crispinus did not blame them. Everyone knew that they must attack again, and perhaps again and again. If they did not take the city, then those who were left could slink away, leaving so many dead comrades behind them.

'So be it,' he said to himself.

Another message had already arrived during the night, but no one spotted it until the dawn and no one realised what it was until another day had passed.

The prison at Nicopolis
Three days later
The forty-first day of the siege

CAECILIUS WAS DYING, *his skin pale and clammy, his eyes red rimmed and weak. The arrow wound in his leg had turned bad, as wounds often did, especially in the warmer months. Two days ago they had taken the leg off below the knee, but the poison remained and spread. This morning they had gone higher, and amputated at the thigh. Both operations had been done by the same Jewish physician, who insisted that he treat prisoners as well as their own sick and wounded. The magistrates consented, if grudgingly, while insisting that he deal with the Romans in their cells. Domitius saw him briefly, saw resignation on his face, and when he was allowed to visit the primus pilus in his little cell he could see why.*

'Oh.' *Caecilius was propped up on a mattress made of straw, and the cell was better than the one Domitius had been given back at the start.* 'It is you. I thought I saw that ugly face up on the walls.'

What was he to say? How are you was absurd, even offensive when his condition was so obvious. He had been given a draught, so ought not to be feeling much at the moment, and might even think that this was all a dream.

'Is there anything I can do for you?' *Domitius asked after some time.*

'Open the gates and let our boys in? No? Pity.'

394

'I am sorry things have turned out the way they have done.'

'Huh.' Caecilius did not seem impressed. 'Thought you buggers believe everything is your god's will.'

'We do,' Domitius said. 'But that doesn't mean we have to like it all. You know – it's like army regulations.'

Caecilius laughed, then winced and had to cough. There was a big bandage tied around his chest. 'My chest hurts when I move suddenly,' he explained. 'And my toes are itching like buggery.'

'Do you want me to scratch them?'

'Only if you can find out what they did with the foot.' He hissed with pain. 'Damned stuff he gave me must be wearing off.'

'I have wine.' Domitius lifted a small amphora and poured out a cupful.

'Any food?'

'Not much. Everything is getting short.' He got out some grapes and scraped away the mould on them.

'We've done something right, then... What are you going do when the lads come over the wall next time and nothing stops them?'

'They've tried. Most of them legged it last time. We threw pots down and they thought it was oil so panicked. It wasn't. There isn't enough left and they're saving what they have to cook. It was some root called fenugreek – you mash it up and it turns into a liquid like oil.'

'Your idea?'

'No, an old man saw it done at a siege years ago. If it spreads, it makes the ground really slippery. It didn't, but given the panic, they were well pleased.'

Caecilius stared at him for a while. 'Can't make up your mind whether it's we or them, can you boy?' His breathing was *becoming laboured and noisy. 'So was it worth it? Running off like that?'*

'I did not see much of a choice.'

'Huh. Of course there was a choice. You could have lied and walked away.'

'No, I couldn't.'

'Then you'd no business joining the army if you couldn't lie to senior officers! ... Was it worth it?'

'Was what worth it?'

'All of this? Deserting, running off here, fighting against your own kind?'

'I have not really fought,' Domitius said, and knew that he was lying. 'Not really. But what else could I have done. This seemed a safe place, some people took me in, and how was I to know a legion was going to swan up out of nowhere and attack.'

'Damned Romans,' Caecilius agreed. 'Was it you behind that mine of theirs?'

'No, they don't trust me.'

'Don't blame 'em.'

'Didn't even tell me about it. I have...' He stopped even though the urge to boast was strong. He had always wanted Caecilius' approval, and seen him almost as a second father. 'In truth I've mostly helped them repair ballistae. The family who took me in are in trouble, partly because they had taken me in. I had to protect them any way I could.'

'A woman?'

Domitius nodded.

Caecilius grinned, winced again and rubbed his chest. 'At least you're not quite as stupid as you look... So maybe it is and maybe it isn't worth it all, but where do you run next? It isn't going to be long. The legatus is a ponce, but he's Roman *at heart, and you know the Romans don't give in. This city will fall and soon, so what does that mean for you, and these people?'*

'I don't know.' Domitius was not sure that Nicopolis was doomed, although part of him wanted to believe that Caecilius was right, because part of him still thought of himself as a soldier of the legions. The new rampart was being savaged by the Roman ballistae quicker than it could be rebuilt, but what the attackers did not know was that a new, much stronger line had been made behind it, using the nearest houses as strongpoints and joining them together with a stone wall. They were doing the same to close off any breach made in the eastern wall, now that the ram was pounding away once more.

Caecilius pushed himself up a little straighter, moaning because it hurt him, but refusing any help. 'I am going to tell you something. Might not matter, not ever, but it might give you a chance, someday or other. Reckon I owe you that.'

'You don't owe me anything, sir. It's the other way around. You taught me so much.'

'Not enough though. And you're wrong, but it does not matter. You were dumb not to lie, dumber still to have let that bastard Ferox talk you into telling him things.'

Domitius frowned. 'I don't understand.'

'Thick, as I've always said. Who in all of Hades do you think turned you in as a Christian? You did not give me much choice. Others wanted you dead, but I came up with a way to let you live, but make sure you didn't say anything else ever again, because the old charge could easily come back. All made sense, until you buggered it all up.

'Hate me if you like – if you folk are allowed to hate, that is. Doesn't matter now. Nothing much matters now, but come

*close and I'll tell you a few things that might just save your life
– or not, but it will help me to die easy at least.'*

*Domitius did as he was asked, even though his mind was
reeling and he even wondered whether the dying man had a
dagger hidden under his blanket and was about to stab him. He
listened for a long time, pausing now and then to help Caecilius
take a drink.*

'Got all that?' the primus pilus said at last.

'Yes.'

*'Good. Might be a chance. Gives you something else to
bugger up, at least. Now clear off. I'll happily see you tomorrow
if I haven't escaped!'*

*Domitius had tears in his eyes as he left, and was not sure
how much was sorrow and how much was rage. Even hearing
the Roman voices talking, when he passed the hatch in the door
to one of the bigger cells, brought back so many memories of
his old life.*

*Sleep did not come readily, although he must have drifted
off at some point, because he jerked awake when he heard a
woman screaming. He was locked in, and his shouts prompted
no more response than one of the guards pounding on his door
and telling him to be silent.*

*Next morning Simon came to fetch him. 'Get dressed, and
be quick about it!' He would not say any more, and vanished
leaving two of his soldiers waiting outside. They were almost
in the street before he reappeared, and even then he said little
other than they were going to the eastern wall because it seemed
bound to collapse very soon and they wanted ideas to help stop
the Romans.*

'Isn't there the second wall?'

*'No. It's not finished, so we need either to speed that up
or stop them before they get there. This is important, so you*

must find a way.' At a nod, the soldiers dropped back a little. 'They have taken Sara to the prison, along with all the Princess Azátē's little court.' Domitius remembered the screaming in the night and prayed that it had not been Sara. Word had spread days ago that the princess was with the Romans, along with her brother, but at first the magistrates had left her household alone, beyond the guard maintained since the start.

'Why now?' Domitius asked.

'Does it matter? To save her and the family, I need to prove myself, which means so do you – or I'll kill you myself.'

There was only so much he could do. Big cracks were visible in the back of the curtain wall, and a glance from one of the towers showed that the front was worse, both where the ram had hit and where the men were undermining it. The whole thing looked ready to fall at the next thump of the ram, and he was almost surprised when it did not.

'Artillery,' Domitius said after he had thought a while. He pointed from the wall at the flat tops of the houses they were trying to make into an inner wall. 'There at the far end and opposite it. The range will be close, but you shoot at an angle at where the breach is going to be. Pound them with stones as they come across it. And bolt shooters there, there and there. Same thing. Don't aim straight ahead because it will go high. Shoot along and across them.'

The strategoi appeared, and Simon explained the ideas to them.

'They need more. You can see how many gaps there are. We've barely built across one of the alleys and the two widest are open.'

'Stakes.' Simon frowned, so Domitius used his fingers to show what he meant. 'Lots of stakes, driven into the ground and sticking up diagonally.'

'There won't be enough to block the alleys.'

'Doesn't have to. What we want is enough to slow them down, make them stop and try to push them aside or weave their way through. While they're stopped we are hitting them with everything we can throw. The last of the oil can pour down on them.'

'How do we drive stakes into paved roads?'

'Rip the stones up. Put them on the roofs and we have more to drop on them as they come in.'

'Makes sense,' Simon conceded, and eventually the strategoi agreed. 'You'll have to stay close and direct them.'

'Fine. I don't have anywhere else to go.' Domitius wondered whether he had found out which side he was on.

He spent the whole day working hard, every now and then glancing over his shoulder in amazement because the wall had not fallen yet. They hauled artillery onto the roofs, using ropes, cranes and a lot of sweat, and put up the rows of stakes to cover the alleys.

The shadows were long, when a stone fell from the front of the wall, followed by another, then another and with a great rumbling slide a wide stretch of the curtain.

Simon appeared. 'How long before they come?'

'An hour, perhaps a bit more. Take them that long to form the assault columns.'

'Then go.' He gestured to two of his men to form the escort. 'They won't trust you here, so best get out of the way.'

'What about you?'

'This is my city – my home.'

Domitius went with the men, only to stop when he heard a call.

'Thank you!' Simon waved to him.

The alleys were already dark, and the guards took him away

*from the main routes because they were filling with men, moving
towards the new breach or the old. They were thin, tired, quite
a few already bandaged or limping, but there was something
inspiring about their determination, of men with grey hairs and
beardless youths going to defend their home.*

*Less inspiring was the pair of soldiers in one of the alleys,
obviously drunk, for one was leaning against the wall, talking
half to himself, while the other crawled on all fours, his shield
and spear lying in the dust.*

*'I tell you, there's no gold down there,' the one just on his feet
assured the other, every word slurred. 'It's just stone and mud,
like all the other streets.' His companion muttered something
incoherent in reply.*

*'What are you playing at?' one of the escorts yelled. 'The
bastards are coming for us. They need you, now!' He moved
to grip his spear with his left hand, still holding his shield, and
reached down to pull up the crawling drunk, who sprang up
and thrust with a sword no one had seen until then. There
was movement behind, a hand grasped the other guard's head,
pulled it back, so that a knife blade could slice through his
throat.*

*'Remember me, boy?' The drunk snarled, but he was not
drunk at all, even if his clothes reeked of wine. He was Ferox.*

*'Oh shit,' Domitius said before he could stop himself. Two
men were behind him, and apart from Ferox the other one had
pushed himself off the wall and was striding towards him.*

*'You have a choice and must make it now.' The voice was
familiar and it took a moment to remember the shadowy figure
who had tracked him all those nights ago.*

*Ferox interrupted. 'The legion is coming. Better for everyone
if it's over quickly and they take the whole city, including the
citadel. We want you to take us to the prison. There are Roman*

prisoners there, a couple of centurions and a dozen or so men. Once we are there, we are going to let them out and together we'll seize the gate by the market, the one that leads into the citadel. So take us to the prison, help us get in, and it's up to you what you do after that. If you want to stay, then I'll do my best for you, but you know how the law stands. If you want to go, then take our goodwill and whatever else you can carry and go fast. There will be a way out of the city in all the confusion, and it should be possible to slip through the outposts without too much trouble.'

'If I don't help?'

'You die,' the other man said, quite matter of fact in his tone.

'You would not really give us much choice, boy,' Ferox said.

'There is a condition,' Domitius told them, feeling certain at last. The other man moved to say something, but Ferox held up his hand to silence him and listened to what Domitius had to say.

'Agreed,' Ferox said. 'Now we must move.'

XXVII

The citadel at Nicopolis
The last hours of the fourteenth day before the
Kalends of June
The forty-first day of the siege

G ETTING TO THE prison was easier than Ferox had
feared. He, Bran and Vindex were dressed in the
manner of the soldiers of the city, a mixture of
equipment and clothes provided by Sosius, and the rest stripped
from the two corpses. The dead men were hidden as best they
could in the shadows, and from there they marched, to all
intents and purposes escorting Domitius back to his cell, even
if in an undertone he was giving them directions. Ferox led,
speaking only when essential, and then using Greek. Nods and
smiles, or a stern look as seemed appropriate, were the only
ways he could deal with other calls, and their luck held and no
one treated them with suspicion. It was dark, save on the main
streets where there were torches and some lamps, and it was a
big enough city for there to be plenty of unfamiliar faces.

Sosius had gone off on his own. The man had found them
on the night of the assault, and hidden them since, in the back
of a warehouse not far from the wall, where he had made a
little compartment behind great piles of sacks full of grain
someone was hoarding in secret until the prices reached a peak.

Hadrian's freedman had some sort of arrangement either with the owner, or perhaps a foreman who was cheating the owner, and they were not bothered. Given the contents of the place, visitors were not encouraged, so they saw no one apart from Sosius who came and went. The food he brought was meagre, made worse because they were living next to an abundance of wheat and barley, without having any means of grinding it or cooking the flour. Sosius explained that he was doing his best, and that nearly everyone in the city was going short.

'Some of the poor are dying,' he told them. 'Especially the ones who came in from the farms and do not have friends here. There are rumours that they are eating the corpses, and even killing anyone who strays too far into the back alleys.'

Ferox had heard rumours like that before and usually they were not true. Sosius spoke Greek to them, because he knew that the other two did not understand the language. Both made clear their loathing for him, but he showed no sign of caring. He told Ferox about Domitius, and explained his plan. The only thing that could be trusted about Sosius was his ruthless determination to serve his master at any cost, and apart from that, there was not much choice other than to go along with his plans. Sosius had gone off to start some distractions, and inevitably there was the nagging fear that they were walking into a trap to make just such a distraction. It still made sense to try. Sosius claimed to have sent messages to Crispinus tied to arrow shafts. Ferox was not sure how reliable that was, but the eastern wall was breached, so the attackers were coming and there was no reason to think that they would wait for longer than it took to organise the attack.

He was surprised at how lightly guarded the prison was. There was no one on the gates into the courtyard. On the far side, the main door was bolted shut. Domitius told him that the guards knocked three times and called out the name of whoever they thought was on duty inside. He did not have a clue who that would be from one day to the next.

'Try Callisthenes,' he suggested.

'Nah, Callisthenes is no good,' Vindex said under his breath. 'Ask for blonde Venus.'

Ferox ignored him, knocked on the door, and did not say anything. When nothing happened, he tried again, much louder, and this time shouted, 'Hey!'

A voice came from inside, the lock clicked, bolts were drawn back and the door opened inwards.

'Oh, you're back,' the guard said, recognising Domitius and not paying much attention to the others. 'Later than I expected.' He stepped away, beckoning them to come in. As he turned his back, Vindex hit him with a club and the man dropped. Another man was sitting on a stool in the corner, and gaped, letting fall the spoon and bowl he was holding into his lap, the hot liquid scorching him.

'Brother?' he said. It was the Christian. Bran had his sword out, and was ready to thrust.

'No!' Domitius yelled. 'You are my prisoner now! Drop your sword.' The guard's sword was in its scabbard, while the tip of Bran's blade was inches from his chest. He blinked, confused, and defiance and fear struggled with each other until he gave up, raising his hands.

'He's got the keys,' Domitius said. Vindex gave a wicked grin, enough to terrify anyone, and took them.

'How many more of them?' Ferox asked.

'A couple at most. Call them and no one needs to get hurt!' Domitius said to their captive.

The man shook his head. Bran edged the blade forward, but still the guard refused. Domitius shouted, 'Hey, there's trouble.'

Vindex and Ferox went to either side of the doorway leading off from the main chamber. The scout ducked, and as feet came running he swung the club low. His feet knocked from under him, a guard flew forward to slam onto the floor. The next came shouting, sword in hand, and gave a feeble cut at Ferox, who beat the blade aside and killed the man with a thrust through the neck. As he fell, Domitius realised that it was the one who had beaten him, and grinned, before wondering whether as a Christian it was wrong to enjoy revenge.

'Where are the Romans?' Ferox shouted. The captive did not mind showing them, and there was no time to ponder the rules men made, for they needed to hurry. Sentius and his men were in chains, and it took a while to free them. Sometimes, lack of imagination was an advantage, so Ferox gave the centurion orders rather than trying to explain what was going on.

'We're ready, sir,' Sentius said, rubbing his wrists where the shackles had cut. He had ten men fit enough to move and fight. The others could stay and watch the prisoners, locking themselves into the jail because the rest needed every weapon they could scavenge. 'What about the primus?' the centurion asked. 'They say he is down the hall.'

Domitius had already been to see his old mentor. He came out, eyes glassy and shook his head. 'He's dead.' He almost felt cheated that his old mentor had not lived on just these few hours, so that he could have seen Domitius helping the legion, but there was too much to do. He climbed the stairs to the higher cells, and peered through the little hatches in each one. The first along the corridor held several men, the second, two women, but neither were Sara. He thought that the third cell was empty, until the bundle of blankets or rags stirred.

'Sara?' he hissed. 'It's me, Domitius.' The shape moved, and he opened the door. 'You're safe,' he said. 'It's me.'

Sara sat up and began to weep. Her hair was dishevelled, her clothes torn to rags, and there were bruises on her face and arms. 'It's all right,' he said, as he held her. 'It is all right.'

Ferox appeared. 'We need to go. Lady, you are safe,' he said as soothingly as he could, and hoped that it was true. 'Here, have my cloak.' He unclasped the brooch and handed it over. Sara stopped weeping, freed herself from Domitius and stood, taking it. She could not or would not speak, but her face was determined.

As they left, the guard who had been tripped stared wide eyed at them, and especially the woman. Sara saw him, went over and spat in his face. Bran's eyes went from her to the man, and back again. The guard was cowering as the young warrior walked over and stabbed him in the belly, twisting the blade to widen the wound before wrenching it free. Sobbing in agony, the man slumped onto his side, blood spreading in a pool onto the flagstones. He started to scream, so Bran thrust again, finishing the job.

'Lock up behind us, and if you have any trouble with them, then kill them,' Ferox told the wounded and weak men they were leaving behind.

Out in the street, there was no one about, nor any sign that the dying guard's scream had caused an alarm. Distantly, trumpets sounded, surely heralding the attack. Then in the lower city, flames suddenly sprang up, burning brightly.

'Sosius,' Vindex said. 'Bastard,' he added after a moment's thought.

Ferox and Bran walked in front of and behind Domitius, hoping that anyone who saw would assume that the prisoner was wanted for some task. Sentius and his men came behind, and Ferox had ordered them to stick to the shadows as much as possible and be quiet. Instead they were chattering excitedly, stopping only for a moment whenever the centurion hissed them to silence. Thankfully the streets were empty. Behind them all, Vindex escorted Sara, with orders to save her and leave them if anything happened.

A man came running down the street towards them. 'Have you seen the strategoi?' he asked.

'Far side of the Agora,' Ferox replied, glad that the question was in Greek and thinking of the only landmark he could remember.

'Thanks.' The messenger ran on, going past Sentius and his men without stopping. They were in tunics, boots and not much else, and some carried weapons, and he must have seen them, but did not seem to notice anything suspicious. In the same way the escaped legionaries watched him pass and did nothing. Domitius stared in bafflement at Ferox, who could only shrug.

The inner wall was less high than the outer curtain, because in front of the gate it sloped sharply upwards, and the inner wall stood on a ridge, which meant that its walkway led directly into a tower on the outer wall. Its gate was flanked by another tower on either side, narrower than the ones on the main wall, but again for anyone approaching from the outside, they were made larger by the slope. Coming from within, they were a good deal less daunting, hexagonal in shape, three storeys high, and each entered by a door at ground level. They did not look big enough to mount any artillery, save perhaps the lightest of bolt shooters, which made Ferox worry about their plan. Ahead of them the gates were closed and barred, and the only sentries were on the tops of the towers. They were shouting to each other, looking out ahead, and another glow in the sky suggested that Sosius was at work again.

Before Ferox could bang on the door of the right-hand tower, it opened, and a soldier appeared, with a high-crested, antique bronze helmet that would have seemed fitting on a statue of Athena.

'Who are you?' he demanded.

'The Strategos Athenodorus sent me,' Domitius announced. 'Want's that bolt shooter of yours fixed.'

'Nothing wrong with it,' the man replied belligerently. 'Piss off and bother someone else!'

Ferox had not drawn his gladius, not wishing to appear suspicious, so bunched his fist and swung, catching the soldier under the chin, knocking him back.

'Hispana!' he shouted, but Bran was through the door ahead of him, sliding his sword from his scabbard as he went. A man thrust a spear at him, striking the wall instead. Bran cut, snapping the spear shaft, and the man was shouting. Ferox had his gladius, stabbed the first man as he was pushing himself up and went for the second, who backed towards stairs going up. A legionary appeared in the doorway, saw a man coming down and flung a spear over their heads. It missed, clattering into the stairs, but made the soldier retreat up them. Bran pushed aside the stub of the other soldier's spear, and swept back to open his throat to the bone. He fell, blood gushing, and Ferox charged up the stairs bellowing. A man was at the top and he hit him with his shield, but the blow only knocked him back a little because this was a light shield made in the city and not one of the solid ones used by the army. Ferox lunged with his gladius, nicked the man on the leg, staggered as a blow came onto his shield, then slashed upwards. The soldier keened a high-pitched squeal and fell.

Ferox was in a chamber, empty save for an engine about the size of a scorpio – presumably the one that was working properly. Another stair led off at an angle, so he went up, Bran close behind and a legionary following him. He had to hope that Sentius was doing as he was told and clearing the other tower, but there was no time to check and he went up the other stairs taking them two at time because he knew that if he slowed down he would not want to go at all. His mind conjured images of spearmen waiting by the opening, ready to thrust, but when his head came up into the next level he saw that it was empty. A ladder went to the top, and a man was coming down it slowly, and without any sign of urgency, still talking to someone up above.

Ferox dashed up into the room. The man saw him, jumped the last few steps and started to fumble with his sword, which jammed as he tried to draw it. Ferox sprang at him, gladius reaching forward.

'Prisoner!' he hissed, hoping the man knew the Greek word or could guess. The soldier was round faced, and he nodded nervously. Ferox pointed Bran to the ladder, then when the legionary came up pointed at the captive. 'Watch him!' Then he followed Bran.

There were two men on the roof, and the shout of their comrade must have warned them, but in the few moments it took Ferox to get up the ladder, Bran killed one, and left the other crouched on the floor, hands bloody as they clutched at his chest. On the far tower, men were shouting, then Sentius appeared, roaring with rage, and as he drove the guards back more of his men followed him up and the Nicopolitans were overwhelmed. Sentius turned to Ferox and waved his bloody sword in triumph.

'Get the gates open and jam them that way!' Ferox shouted across. 'Get them off the hinges if you can!'

'Yes, sir!'

An arrow flicked the top of the parapet. On the nearest tower of the main wall, an archer had seen them and was shooting. There did not seem to be anyone with him.

'Head down, lad,' Ferox told the legionary, 'but keep a good watch.'

He led Bran back down to the ground floor. Domitius was outside, helping three legionaries lift the bar from the gate.

'In the alley over there!' Ferox pointed. 'Dump it there!' The men nodded and staggered as they carried the stout beam away. There was not time to hide it properly or destroy it, so the most that could be done was to make it a little harder for anyone to find. There were catches on the wall, and with Domitius they pushed one gate open and fastened it back, and then did the other. Sentius arrived, and one of the men with him had a crowbar.

'We'll see what we can do,' he told Ferox. Ahead of them, a great swathe of the city seemed to be on fire, for the wind had picked up and was blowing hot air towards them.

'Hold as long as you can,' Ferox said. 'Keep the gate open for our boys. They know you're here and some will come straight up the cardo to relieve you.' That is what Sosius claimed had been arranged, assuming his messages had got through.

'Are you going, sir?'

'Yes. I have a promise to keep.' Ferox gestured to Bran. 'Show us the way, Domitius.'

Sentius watched them vanish down into the city and wondered when the first attack would come.

'Well done, boys,' the centurion told his men. 'Now let's get ready for when the bastards come at us.'

XXVIII

Nicopolis
The same night

THE FIRST RAMPART fell easily, and even though it had been mauled by the ballistae that was still a surprise, and men poured over it and vanished from sight. The men had dropped the ladders they were carrying because they were not needed, and pressed on. Crispinus was in the observation tower, and could see nothing, but the shouting coming from beyond the breach was confused.

'No use staying here,' he said to his staff and led them down. Nearby, Arrian stood waiting at the head of three hundred soldiers picked from the first cohort. Their task was to wait until the breakthrough, then get into the city and head straight for the gate to the citadel and seize it. All of the city must fall tonight, and a half victory would not do.

'You know what you have to do?' Crispinus asked before he could stop himself. Of course, Arrian knew what to do.

'Yes, my lord. Do you trust the letters?' The question suggested Arrian was as nervous as he was, although he was hiding it well. They had found the first message eventually, deciphered the code because it was one Hadrian was fond of using, but the second one had only been seen a couple of hours ago.

'No idea!' Crispinus said, then stopped because cornu horns were blaring out as the supporting cohorts came out of the musculi and started climbing the rampart. He waited, then leaned forward to shout, because the legionaries were cheering as they went. 'If someone is inside helping us then good. But don't assume anything. Just get me that gateway.'

Arrian nodded, and whatever he said was lost because the leading soldiers were clambering over the rampart, shouting and horns blaring. Crispinus went forward as another cohort was committed, this time auxiliaries, all eager to show that they were as bold as any citizen soldier. Cerialis had told him that volunteers from his own ala were providing the assault parties for his own attack against the other breach. Trailing the half-dozen legionary cavalrymen and the two centurions acting as his escort, the legatus went along the side of the sheds, rather than trying to force his way through. No missiles were coming down from the wall, so he went without risk, apart from falling off the side of the ramp where the space was narrow.

As he drew level with the shed, a cornicen appeared and blasted out his challenge, before realising that the commander was right beside him. Crispinus grinned to reassure the man, and the auxiliaries were around him, a crowd rather than a formation as they climbed the slope of the breach. The stench of the dead from the first assault was stronger, and when someone trod on a corpse and the stomach burst open, Crispinus thought that he might vomit, but somehow managed to keep control.

They reached the rampart, men clustering as they headed for the spots where it had collapsed and was easy to climb.

'Help me up!' Crispinus shouted to his escort, because he did not want to wait. They used a shield, just as Priscus and the others had done, and he struggled to believe that that hopeless attack had been only a few days ago. He clambered onto the shield, let them heave him up and still could barely reach the top of the parapet, so leaped and almost fell over onto the walkway, dropping his sword. The legatus fumbled to find the weapon, pushed himself up and stared in horror.

Ahead of him were hundreds and hundreds of his men, with more joining them as the auxiliaries got through and over the rampart. They were trapped, fenced in by a line with walls joining the houses. There were men on all their roofs, more on the new walls, and they were shooting arrows and bolts, or hurling rocks and javelins into the press. The Romans were shouting, but there did not seem to be any real order, and they were pushing uselessly forward. Men fell, and in places they died, but the press of bodies was so tight that they stayed upright. Crispinus heard the whip-crack of a ballista and saw a stone graze along the top of the crowd smashing heads to ruin. He pushed himself up and shouted back over the parapet.

'Petronius!'

'Sir.' The centurion was a short, active man, always eager to do well.

'Get archers. All you can find. I want them up on this rampart.' They were within range of the house tops and higher up, so that ought to give them an advantage.

Petronius ran off, and Crispinus turned to the other centurion. 'Ladders, Decrius. Get men to bring all the ones they have dropped and any you can find. Then get them to the front. You two men!' He pointed to some of his escort. 'Get that one and bring it to me.' He was not sure whether the ladders would be high enough to reach the house tops, but it was worth a try.

A stone slammed into the walkway, so close that he was knocked over and covered in dirt. Crispinus spat to clear his mouth and pushed himself up.

'You all right, sir,' one of his cavalrymen said, his face worried.

'I could do with a bath,' Crispinus shouted, and let the man help him up. The pair with the ladder dragged it over the top, and the legatus beckoned to them to follow him. 'Come on!'

There was a whirring and the cavalryman's head burst like overripe fruit as it was hit by a stone, spraying them all with blood.

'Liber Pater, save me now!' one of the others said, aghast at the sight.

'Go!' Crispinus shouted, and jumped down, running forward. 'To me! To me!'

'Follow the legatus!' one of the men carrying the ladder called out. 'Hispana, follow your legatus!'

Crispinus wished that he had a standard to wave, but had ordered them all to be left in camp rather than risk losing them. He started to push his way through the crowd. Men turned, snarling at him until they saw his ornate cuirass and recognised who it was. 'Come on! Come on!' he repeated.

Arrows flew overhead, coming from behind, which meant that Petronius had not wasted any time and archers were up on the rampart. Crispinus slipped on a patch of blood, but a man broke his fall and lifted him, and he kept pushing forward.

'Come on! Hispana, follow me!' He had a deep voice, and years of training helped make it carry.

'Hispana! Hispana!' men took up the cry.

Crispinus headed for the nearest of the houses, and was already getting close. A bolt from a ballista went through the helmet of a legionary ahead of him and burst out the other side. Another man fell beside him, an arrow in his neck.

'Hispana!' Even the auxiliaries took up the cry. 'Hispana!'

'There!' Crispinus shouted, pointing to the wall of the house.

The two men with the ladder went to the spot, started to raise it, until one was hit by a tile and knocked to the ground, head bloody. The ladder fell, but men behind them caught it and pushed it up. Crispinus tried to reach it, until one of his escort pushed him back.

'Not your job, sir!' The cavalryman went to the ladder himself and started to climb. Behind them men threw pila and anything else they had up at the roof as a deluge of tiles, stones and amphorae came down. The cavalryman covered his head with his shield, shaking with the blows, but staying on, and the ladder was only a little short. He passed a row of windows, filled up with mud bricks by the defenders. A man on the roof leaned out, javelin poised to throw, until a pilum drove deep into his body. He swayed and fell onto the Romans.

Crispinus followed the cavalryman, not willing to wait any longer, and there was a centurion coming behind him and he struggled to remember the man's name for he was one of the auxiliaries rather than his own men. In front the cavalryman had reached the top rung, so was head and shoulders above the wall surrounding the flat roof. A defender swung his shield, making the trooper duck, but the Roman recovered and thrust with his spatha into the man's groin. Another came at him, driving a spear so that it burst through the boards of the cavalryman's shield, and he struggled for balance, let the shield go, hacked at the man's side, and, grabbing the top of the wall, jumped, falling and rolling onto the roof. The spearman was struggling to free his weapon, but another man hacked at the sprawled figure. The legionary cavalryman rolled out of the way, and was on his back and thrust two-handed up into the man's belly.

'Push me!' Crispinus was a short man, and even at the top of the ladder the wall loomed above him.

'Sir?'

'Push my arse!' he shouted back at the centurion behind him, who obliged, shoving hard, and Crispinus managed to get his left arm over the wall, and hauled himself over. The cavalryman was on one knee, parrying and cutting to keep three enemies back, and another defender came at the legatus, head bare, mouth wide to howl at him as he hacked with a curved kopis sword. Crispinus parried, felt his arm numb as sparks flew from the blades. He stepped to the side, cutting wildly and with a dull crack the blade of the other man's sword snapped and the gladius hit him on the head, drawing blood, without going deep. The Nicopolitan stared at his broken sword, and Crispinus had all the time in the world to raise his arm again and slash harder, cutting into the bone.

The cavalryman's left arm hung limp, blood seeping from a gash, and there was another wound below his knee, but still he fought, and, with a sweep, cut through the leg of one of his opponents. Crispinus went to his side, droplets of blood flicking from his gladius as he swept in great arcs that would have caused apoplexy in any drillmaster. The centurion was over the wall, and another ladder was against the house, legionaries rushing up it. A slash sheared off the cavalryman's right hand, which still clutched the handle of his spatha, and blood pumped over Crispinus as he stepped forward and put all his weight behind a lunge to spit the Nicopolitan. His blade stuck, but men were rushing forward on either side of him and the remaining defenders screamed as they were cut down or flung bodily off the roof. Letting the dying man sink down, Crispinus pressed hard with one boot and dragged the gladius free.

A legionary spun around, an arrow sticking from his eye.

The wall joining on to this house was a little lower than the roof, and a man was trying to get up until the centurion went over and punched him in the face with his scutum. Another arrow came, this one slamming into the shield. There were already a dozen men on the rooftop, so with a bellow for them to follow him, the centurion vaulted over and started to fight his way along the wall. Legionaries followed.

Crispinus spotted the archer on the next house along, then saw a legionary who still had a pilum. 'Kill him!' The archer shot at him, and he dodged so that it skidded past, close enough to feel the air move.

The legionary took a couple of paces across the roof and flung the heavy javelin. As the archer was about to nock another arrow, the stubby, pyramid-shaped point struck him below the ribs, and the weight of the shaft drove the slim shank through his body.

'Well done! I'll buy you a drink when this is over!' Crispinus called, then gasped because a hammer had struck him in the back and he was flung forward, the pain worse than anything he had ever known, and he barely felt it when he slammed into the wall. His hands clutched his chest, and the cuirass was dented. Something was in his back.

'Oh shit!' the legionary swore.

Two men held him upright, because the bolt from the ballista meant that they could not sit him against the wall. Crispinus saw their concerned faces, then heard trumpets and cheers that were surely Roman coming from behind them, not from the direction of the breach.

'It's all all right,' he tried to say, but his whole body hurt. Then the darkness opened up around him.

★ ★ ★

Cerialis' attack started late, and took a while to clear the breach itself because the spoil had created a steep slope that would have been hard to climb even if no one had been shooting at the storming party. One hundred troopers from ala Brittanica led, determined to show that on horse or foot they were as good as any soldiers in the army. Legionaries followed, tasked with heading along the walls on either side to take the towers, which did not seem at all weakened by the collapse of the main wall. After them came three hundred legionaries and as many auxiliary infantry, all of them volunteers. They had a long ladder for every twenty men because archers on the top of the siege tower had seen the construction of the second line.

The Britons led, and suffered the worst of the casualties as they spilled over into the city and were struck by the artillery and dozens of archers. They kept going, numbers thinned, and some tried to force their way through the lines of stakes, while others went for the houses, standing on other men's shoulders as they tried and failed to climb. Yet they did not withdraw, and soon Cerialis and the reserves arrived, bringing ladders. Each house was stormed one by one, and the last to hold out was in the centre, where Simon and fifteen of his men refused to give in. They threw back three attacks, killing anyone who managed to get up, and tipping their bodies down. By that time only Simon was on his feet, and he was bleeding from several small wounds.

Cerialis' men were streaming into the city, and a tribune was leading several hundred men towards the other breach to take the enemy from the rear. A fresh cohort was coming through the breach to follow them, but Cerialis could not make himself leave until this last house was taken, even though he knew that it no longer mattered.

'Give up!' he shouted in his rather stilted Greek. 'You will be treated well – you and all your men. You are brave and I honour you.'

'Fight me, Roman!' Simon roared the challenge. 'I'll let you come up.' His shield hung in ruin, his sword was notched and bent, his helmet gone and face smeared with blood.

Some of the archers had come forward and one sent an arrow which punched through Simon's scale shirt. A second man loosed and hit him only an inch or two away from the other arrow. Simon's eyes widened and he fell back.

'I wish you had not done that,' Cerialis lied.

EPILOGUE

The next morning

NICOPOLIS BURNED. SOSIUS, or men he had hired for the task, had prepared carefully and piled up pitch and oil ready to ignite, and the fires burned quickly. The sudden strong winds made everything far worse, spreading the blaze from street to street. Outside the citadel, whose walls had held back the flames, three-quarters of the city was in ruin. The fickle wind had dropped after a few hours, so that the next day thick smoke rose and hung above the remains.

Marcus Atilius Crispinus, legatus of Legio VIIII Hispana, burned on his own pyre behind his main camp. Given the heat, and the heavy losses, Cerialis had decided to hold the funeral straightaway, so that the ashes could be gathered and sent back to the family. Two hundred legionaries paraded, along with several score from other units, and if some showed dents to their armour and scars on their faces, they had wiped the dirt away and done their best to wash down their shields. There were so many dead, and many more wounded who would surely die unless they were brought in and treated, even before anyone thought about dealing with the enemy, that Cerialis could only give so much attention to the fallen legatus.

The prefect was the most senior officer left, even if he took care to show every respect to Arrian as the acting commander of the legion. Once the defences behind each breach had been taken, there was no real resistance, for by then the defenders could see that the city was blazing. Cerialis had met with Arrian as he led his men along the cardo, and they had raced to the citadel gates to find Sentius and his men in place. An hour later, the strategoi, including Athenodorus whose head was bandaged, and some other leading men, came to surrender. The others had been killed or had fled, along with their families.

Many died, and only the raging fires held back the sack of the city as legionaries and auxiliaries alike slipped off into the alleys to see what they could find. The men who had led the assault were bloodied, filled with rage and angry at having seen so many comrades die. Some were exhausted and simply sank down to sleep, while some took such pride in their discipline that they stayed at their posts or even tried to fight the fires. Most went off on their own or in little groups, and many of these murdered, raped and stole as the mood took them and opportunity offered. Men who had been in reserve, or left to guard the camps or man the outposts, followed them into the city, through the breaches or the now opened gates. They were not wild, but they were tired and angry and plenty of them joined in the sack. So did the galearii and other slaves, many of the camp followers and traders, villagers still outside the city, and even some of the citizens when they saw the chance. Alongside the roaring of the flames, were screams of pain and the sobs of women and girls.

The Nicopolitans fled whenever they had the chance, through the little doors in the curtain wall, and the great gates once these were open and the remaining Romans had come in. Some were caught as they tried to get out, and more than a few women accepted a legionary or auxiliary as protector rather than be at the mercy of all. Others did not get the chance. On the plains around the city the picket line was thin because many men had abandoned their posts. Those with bad luck ran into soldiers, who stripped them of their valuables or did far worse. The truly unlucky met with bandits or slavers during the days that followed.

Domitius carried John on his back, leading Sara. Ferox had been true to his word and taken him to the family's house, only to find it already on fire, and Simon and several servants lying dead. Someone had robbed them and killed them, and old John had arrived afterwards. They found him sobbing, but were able to save him and a few valuables the old man had hidden. It was not much, but Ferox sent Bran and Vindex to escort them, while he went out to fetch men and horses. He never asked whether they had had to fight, but the group had escaped, and he had met them at the agreed spot with a few of his men, given them food, three donkeys and his best wishes.

'He is gone then,' Cerialis said as the funeral pyre began to burn down. 'This deserter who helped us.'

'Yes. Carried the old man out on his back, like Aeneas and Anchises.'

The prefect smiled at the reference. 'Only this time it was the Trojans not the Greeks storming a city... Was the woman pretty?'

'Domitius thought so. I guess most men would. Said that they might go to Egypt. It's quiet there and she has relatives.'

'A happy outcome, then,' Cerialis said bitterly. He had turned and was staring at the thick black smoke hanging over the city, a hand shading his eyes. 'Well, they told us to take it and that is what we have done.'

'That's what soldiers always have to do, sir.' Ferox did not add that he did not want to do it anymore, least of all for another of Hadrian's schemes. Saying it out loud would not make something come true, and he was not sure how much the prefect understood about the campaign and the ambition behind it all. Still, Cerialis would write the despatch to Hadrian to tell of his success, and it would probably arrive before the acting governor's successor put in an appearance. What Trajan would think was anyone's guess.

Flavius Cerialis stared at him, as if sensing his thoughts, until at long last he beckoned to his cornicularius, who brought over a writing tablet. The prefect sighed. 'The noble Crispinus' freedman tells me that he was left with orders for you. From the acting governor, the even more noble Hadrian, no less.' Cerialis shook his head. 'I say orders because apparently there were two sets. One to be opened in the case of failure and retreat and the other – no doubt always expected to be true – if we captured Nicopolis.'

Ferox had rarely heard the prefect sound so bitter or so weary.

'The acting governor is a deep man and methodical in his actions.' Cerialis held up the tablet to show that it remained sealed. 'This is the one to be handed to you in case of victory – you will see that even I have no idea of its contents. Perhaps Crispinus knew, perhaps not. The other set has been burned in accordance with the acting governor's instructions. All this was detailed in a covering instruction. It also says that the senior officer present – which must have seemed ominous to poor Crispinus – was to give them to you and watch as you read them, although you are not obliged to reveal the contents. So here we are.' Cerialis held out the little tablet.

Ferox hesitated.

'Neither of us have much of a choice,' Cerialis said.

Ferox nodded and took the orders. He did not think that his face betrayed any emotion as he read the three short sentences.

'Bad news?' Cerialis was genuinely sympathetic.

'No,' Ferox said. 'And that is what worries me.'

Two cohorts of legionaries and several hundred auxiliaries remained at Nicopolis, living in the unscathed buildings of the citadel. The rest of the army went back across the Euphrates, apart from when they needed to escort a supply convoy to the garrison. There was almost no food left in the ruined city, and with the population of the villages swollen by refugees, stripping the land bare would simply have caused a famine.

'We are supposed to be allies,' Arrian told the tribune left in command, repeating it over and over again. 'Never forget that.'

Hadrian never again saw Nicopolis, and was replaced by the properly appointed legatus at the start of June. Trajan did go to the city, just once, when he led his armies south at the start of the next year. By then King Abgarus of Osrhoene had realised that the Romans were coming and done everything to prove his loyalty and support, which as all could see had been demonstrated when his children aided the Romans against the rebels of Nicopolis. Arbandes went with him to meet with Trajan, and the youth's good looks and enthusiasm helped smooth the diplomatic path, since it was so convenient for everyone. By this time Azátē had married the king of Adiabene, an arrangement encouraged by Rome. She bore him a son, and in spite of a number of older boys, from his other wives, it was her child who succeeded him.

Hadrian did not join the emperor on his campaigns. Trajan approved his actions with regards to Nicopolis, at least in public. Privately he thought the decisions were reckless, presumptuous in a governor, let alone one merely acting as a replacement. More than anything else, he simply did not like Hadrian. 'Send the little shit to Antioch with the women,' he told his close advisors, and they found some diplomatic tasks for him to perform there – not least amusing the imperial women. Hadrian did as he was told and waited.

Sosius was nowhere to be seen after Nicopolis had fallen. Ferox said little about him, since he was not sure how much Cerialis or anyone else apart from Crispinus had been told about Hadrian's agent. The letters so embarrassing to Hadrian were never made public, and since the houses of two officers were robbed and the men and several of their household found murdered by the thieves, most likely Sosius had arranged things in his usual style. In the longer run, there was far less peculation in the army in Syria, and that was something, although it probably had far more to do with Trajan's presence in the region, and his close attention to military administration and discipline.

Domitius had told them what he had learned from Caecilius, and gone on his way. He married Sara, and they were happy. Ferox was never sure whether or not they had gone to Egypt.

In July orders arrived for Ferox and the remaining Brigantes to return to Britannia. They did not come directly from Hadrian, but there was little doubt that he was behind them. For the moment at least, Ferox was free. That did not mean that Hadrian's schemes were at an end and Ferox was too old to believe that it was really over. Roman senators tended to stay ambitious as long as there was breath left in their bodies, so no doubt Hadrian would call on him again, whenever it suited his purpose. Yet if this was just a lull before more storms, then all the more reason to make the most of it.

The journey was slow and difficult. With so much of the army moving to support Trajan's drive down the Euphrates and

Tigris valleys, no one in authority was that interested in helping a ragtag irregular unit make its way in the opposite direction. Nothing was straightforward, but nearly all of them made it in the end.

Most Nicopolitans had lost their homes. Workshops and warehouses were destroyed, goods and tools lost or stolen. Few were keen on living under the eyes of a Roman garrison. A few years later when the legionaries left, they slighted more of the defences. No one ever bothered to repair them, for the population who had stayed numbered no more than a few hundred and it never grew beyond that. People moved to better, safer cities, sometimes far afield. A century later the city was abandoned altogether and forgotten.

In the lands around it, the farms and little villages remained and life went on. Folk spoke and lived the way their fathers and fathers' fathers had done, tending their flocks, tilling the hard earth, and cherishing every drop of rain.

HISTORICAL NOTE

*T*HE *CITY* IS a novel, and although I have done my best to depict the era and its setting as accurately as possible, it is only fair to give the reader an idea of where the history stops and the fiction begins. In the Historical Note to *The Fort*, the predecessor to this story, I explained that, in spite of the fact that Trajan's Dacian Wars were waged on a very large scale and involved a significant proportion of the Roman army, they are very poorly recorded. Narrative sources for them are meagre, while the scenes depicted on Trajan's Column are stylised and very hard to understand without knowledge of the story they tell. The situation with Trajan's Parthian expedition from AD 114–117 is far worse, although it appears to have involved even more troops. Almost everything, from the most basic chronology of the operations, to routes involved, battles and sieges, has been lost and reconstructions vary immensely. What we tend to have are hints, such as a victory arch built by Trajan outside Dura Europos which might commemorate a battle fought and won there or nearby or more generally celebrate a victorious campaign.

The essence of what happened is that after almost a century of peace between Rome and Parthia, interrupted by a good deal of posturing, and a limited war under Nero fought over succession to the throne of Armenia, Trajan launched a grand attack into Mesopotamia. It is not clear why he did this. The political situation in Parthia appears to have been chaotic, with several rivals battling to become king of kings. Friction began in the kingdoms allied to both Rome and Parthia, most notably yet another disputed succession to Armenia. Trajan intervened, but the time and effort taken to gather so many legions in the theatre suggest that from the start he was considering a larger campaign. Some would like to see an emperor desperate for glory, perhaps even an ageing man trying to recapture the vigour of youth. Eventually, following the Tigris and Euphrates, he captured the great Parthian cities of Ctesiphon and Seleucia, and reached the Persian Gulf. The emperor was said to have watched a ship setting sail for India and wept because he was too old to match Alexander the Great and reach that distant land.

Whatever his initial intentions, Trajan overran a good deal of territory, creating a number of new provinces, and installed a friendly candidate as king of kings. For all the wishful talk of Alexander, there is no sign that he planned to destroy or take over the Parthian empire, which was still left with the bulk of its territory. Even so, this was not to be. In AD 116 rebellions broke out in many parts of the conquered territory. This was partly a natural reaction to foreign occupation, although it is also quite possible that the outbreaks were coordinated, or at least encouraged by one of the remaining rivals to the king of kings. To make matters more difficult for the Romans, the Jewish population of Egypt, Cyrenaica and Cyprus rebelled in a war that was noted for its ferocity. Stretched too thinly, and with an emperor whose health was now failing badly, the Romans suffered defeats and began to retreat. Trajan tried and failed to capture the desert city of Hatra. In AD 117 he was beginning his journey back to Rome when he fell ill and died.

Hadrian succeeded him, in circumstances we shall discuss later, and abandoned most, but not all, of the conquered territory. No major aggressive wars were launched during his reign, and several frontiers saw a degree of fortification and entrenchment, most notably the building of Hadrian's Wall, that can be seen as indicating a more defensive posture. In the longer run, there would be another major conflict when the Parthians attacked the Roman provinces at the very end of the reign of Antoninus Pius and twice under Septimius Severus a generation later. In each case the fighting shifted in favour of the Romans, who again took Ctesiphon and Seleucia. After each conflict the Romans kept control of more territory. The senator and historian Dio Cassius argued that the major gains under Septimius Severus were provocative and actually made the frontier more rather than less vulnerable.

The City is set against the early stages of Trajan's eastern campaigns. While it is possible to argue over the precise chronology, Trajan did go to Antioch, he did spend time making offerings in temples there and nearby, and Hadrian did accompany him on at least one of these visits, even though the story of the emperor collapsing is invented. After that, he travelled to Zeugma and then north to where a large force had concentrated for the intervention in Armenia. As described in the story, the Armenian king began by adopting a defiant stance during negotiations, but as the Romans advanced into the kingdom he backed down. On many occasions in the past kings had made formal submission to Roman commanders who then responded by making a show of restoring them to power and honour. For whatever reason, Trajan acted differently, deposing the king, who was killed in mysterious circumstances soon afterwards. Trajan's main army then divided into several columns which pushed into neighbouring kingdoms, although only a few anecdotes are preserved about these. In one, a Roman commander issued snowshoes to his soldiers, allowing them to fight effectively in the snow of the high mountains. In another snippet, a city named Adenystrae (location unknown) was captured when a centurion and some soldiers being held in its prison managed to escape and open the gates to the besiegers, providing inspiration for Ferox's and Sentius' exploits at the end of our story.

There is almost no detail in our meagre sources of fighting between Roman forces and those of the Arsacid king of Parthia, although presumably a good deal of this occurred, especially when Trajan's men advanced towards the great Parthian cities. However, it is no coincidence that the bulk of the material refers to negotiation and conflict with individual kings or cities like Hatra. Within the Roman Empire were several autonomous kingdoms, even if the number of these had fallen since the early days of the Principate. On the borders were even more of these states, while the Parthian title of king of kings was not simply an honour but a reality, for the Arsacid king was overlord of many lesser kingdoms and states. His influence, let alone control, over these varied a great deal depending on the circumstances, and the strength and ambitions of everyone involved. Scholars are apt to speak of pro-Roman or pro-Parthian monarchs in Armenia and elsewhere, simplifying what was a very complex relationship. Alliance with one empire did not necessarily mean hostility to the other, and it was perfectly possible to maintain friendly relations with both.

Most of the time, neither the Roman emperor nor the Arsacid king of Parthia wanted very much from allied kings. They favoured stability; both wanted local kings not to be hostile to them or their interests, but otherwise had no real interest in how they ran their kingdoms. Everyone benefitted from the trade that passed through these lands, especially the luxuries coming from India and ultimately China, such as silk and spices. Yet by their nature, these states tended to be unstable, for there was rarely any firm system of succession, and any member of the royal family could become ruler. This was also a problem for the Parthians, exacerbated by the practices of polygamy and the royal harem, which meant that there tended to be a lot of potential successors around. One Parthian king murdered thirty brothers to ensure his succession, and such bloodletting was not unusual. Most of the periods of friction between Rome and Parthia began with an internal power struggle in Armenia or one of the other kingdoms. This, and the wider background of Trajan's aggressive response to concerns of this sort, provide the context for our story.

The kingdom of Osrhoene was real and was ruled at the time of our story by King Abgarus VII. Traditionally, Osrhoene came more under Parthian than Roman influence, but again we should not see this as a simple choice between one or the other. As with Armenia, the first embassy sent by the king to Trajan strongly asserted his independence, and only gradually did it become clear that the emperor wanted a much stronger commitment. Eventually, Abgarus agreed to support and aid the Romans, and presumably did so during the campaigns that followed. His son Arbandes appears to have been sent more than once as envoy, and in the longer run Dio believed that his youthful charm and good looks softened Trajan's attitude. Later, at a feast held near the capital Edessa, the youth performed a local war dance in front of Trajan and his guests. While this provided inspiration for the story, everything else is invented, including Azátē.

The city of Nicopolis is another fiction, although as stated at the start there were a number of cities of this name in the Hellenistic world. Alexander the Great formed a sort of punishment battalion of men suspected of disloyalty or other crimes, but they are mentioned just once in our sources and no hint given of their ultimate fate. Alexander's campaigns made the spread of Greek language and culture much more rapid throughout the Near and Middle East. Yet this was a region where civilisation had very old roots, and the Greek layer co-existed with older and more recent sets of thought, belief and language. Cities like Nicopolis tended to have Greek institutions, such as magistrates and councils, but very mixed communities. Best known is Dura-Europos on the Euphrates in northern Syria, a heavily excavated site, which unfortunately suffered from looting and deliberate destruction in the recent conflict.

Large Jewish communities were present in many cities, including Dura, and formed a significant group in Seleucia and Babylon. The destruction of the Temple in Jerusalem severely disrupted Jewish customs, most obviously by bringing an end to animal sacrifice. Yet the people and the faith adapted and survived, and even in areas which archaeologically show little trace of distinctive practices in the second century AD, became openly Jewish in lifestyle in later periods, which strongly suggests that there was more continuity than material culture reveals. At Dura-Europos there was a substantial synagogue, decorated with colourful paintings showing scenes such as the crossing of the Jordan into Canaan. While conflicting with the very rare depiction of the human form in Second Temple Judaea, these still testify to a vibrant and confident community, living alongside Gentile neighbours. There is evidence for considerable interest in and sympathy for Jewish practices from several dynasties in the region, with some royalty even converting.

Dura-Europos also provided evidence for one of the earliest Christian meeting places to be known, which included wall paintings and a baptistry, although it is less grand than the synagogue. Being a Christian was illegal in the Roman Empire, and one of the best sources for Roman attitudes to the cult comes from a letter written only a few years before our story by Pliny, then legate of Bithynia, and Trajan's reply to him. While doing his rounds and holding assizes in the cities, Pliny was confronted with a number of Christians arrested by the local authorities. He investigated the matter, discovered no hint of the crimes gossip associated with this secret religion – anyone who met in secret was viewed with suspicion in the Roman world, and stories circulated of incest and cannibalism. Pliny found only 'excessive superstition' (*prava superstitio*), but understood that, by law, being a Christian was punishable by death. Therefore he asked each suspect three times whether or not he or she was a Christian. If they said no, and then performed a sacrifice to the imperial cult and reviled the name of Christ, they were set free. The crime was being a Christian at that moment, not having been one in the past. Non-citizens who refused to do this were executed – Pliny felt that they deserved this for unreasonable stubbornness as much as anything else, but the principle was that people should obey a direct order from the emperor's representative. Roman citizens were sent to Rome for trial because they had the right to appeal to the emperor. Trajan's reply is equally instructive, for after approving Pliny's decisions, he tells him that he was not to go looking for Christians. If the local authorities were worried by them and arrested them, then the system had to take its course. Otherwise, the empire was really not bothered. Most of the time the same thing was true of local communities, but at times of crisis, such as natural disasters, epidemics or even economic problems, the Christians offered a convenient scapegoat as a group of odd outsiders.

This brings us to Domitius. A feature of several accounts of martyrdoms of Roman soldiers is the clear implication that they had been Christian for some time more or less openly and no one was that concerned, until suddenly it became an issue, for instance when there was a competition for promotion. The attitude of Pliny, and most Romans, was that public gestures were important and private beliefs and practices on the whole no one else's business. Hence the assumption that anyone sensible would simply lie when accused, perform any ritual necessary, and then get on with their lives. Several martyrdom accounts are critical of members of the Church who did just that, and celebrate the ones who refused, like Domitius. Outside the empire, Christianity was not illegal, at least most of the time, but even within the empire mass persecutions were rare. It is harder to say too much about Christian practices and doctrine in this period, for the probability is that these varied from group to group. When writing the novel I did wonder how much access many Christians had to the Gospels and other Scriptures. Books were expensive, having to be copied by hand, so extensive collections tended to be something only the wealthy could possess, which suggests that more was learned by listening than reading. Thus in the story, Domitius has read only a little in borrowed manuscripts, and relies far more on sermons he has heard and conversations with other believers.

Desertion was always a problem for a professional army with a harsh discipline and enlistment for twenty-five years. Fear of punishment appears to have been a common motive for flight, but we should also note that one first-century AD commander was seen as especially severe for executing men recaptured after deserting for the first time. As always, I have tried to represent the Roman army and how it worked as accurately as possible, but must once again emphasise that there is so much that scholars do not know, since many aspects of day-to-day practice have not been preserved in our sources. Novels like this allow me to try out ideas based on lifelong study of the army and the empire, but must remain guesses.

Legio VIIII Hispana is famous as the legion that supposedly disappeared in what later became Scotland, inspiring among other things Rosemary Sutcliffe's famous children's adventure, *The Eagle of the Ninth*. (The BBC TV dramatisation of the story was one of the things that first inspired my fascination with all things Roman.) While the legion did cease to exist sometime in the first half of the second century AD, we do not know what happened, or whether it was destroyed and never reformed or disbanded for other reasons. The odds are against the legion being destroyed in Britain, but evidence for its activities are so limited that we do not really know where it was or what it was doing at the time of our story. I made it *the* legion in our story because its name is well known, it has a connection with Britannia like many of our characters, and I wondered whether some readers would see the name and anticipate that this would be the story of its demise. For those interested in the evidence for the fate of the VIIII Hispana and a good deal more about how we understand the Roman army and the evidence for it, I recommend Duncan Campbell, *The Fate of the Ninth: the curious disappearance of one of Rome's legions* (2018).

In *The Fort*, Ferox and the rest of them were stuck inside a Roman army base defending it against a far more numerous enemy. In *The City*, I wanted to look at the other side of things and show the Roman army besieging a well-defended stronghold – in this a case a community caught up in machinations on either side through no fault of its own. In the late Republic and under the Principate, the Romans developed a highly sophisticated and very effective system for taking strongholds. Even so, this remained one of the most difficult operations in ancient warfare, and sometimes the legions failed, as they did at Hatra. While fictional, I have done my best to show how the Romans and defenders went about these things, the cat-and-mouse game as each tried to outwit the other, and the slow pace with sudden dramatic shifts in the balance between the two sides.

It was normal for defenders in the ancient world to come out from behind their walls and fight in the open during the early stages of a siege. Keeping close to the walls, sheltered by the support of archers and perhaps artillery, they might well dispute the ground outside for many days. This was a statement of confidence, which was important for morale, and at the same time meant that the attackers would not be in position to start constructing siege works for some time. Once the attackers had managed to drive in the defenders, then they could start preparing to go over, through or under the walls. Direct assaults without preparation rarely succeeded unless the defences were very weak or the defenders stretched too thinly. Therefore, it was a struggle between the attackers constructing siege works and mobile towers, rams and the like, and the defenders devising counter measures or launching sallies to destroy the siege works. At the same time both faced problems of supply, especially as the days dragged onwards. One of the reasons Hatra repulsed Trajan and later Septimius Severus was the great difficulty of supplying a large force in such arid conditions. Almost everything in the story is based on something actually attested in the period, with just a few taken from other eras. For instance the Romans did calculate the distance from a siege ramp to the wall by throwing a plumb-line. At times assaults also failed, and Roman soldiers refused to attack, for sieges were highly stressful and direct attacks costly, especially among the men inclined to be bold and take the lead.

The fate of a city that was stormed was rarely pleasant. Occasionally commanders were able to restrain their men, although even Julius Caesar would not let his soldiers enter one town that surrendered near the end of the day, for fear that he would not be able to control the legionaries once darkness fell. There is no evidence for a rule, let alone a law, that once the ram touched the wall, the defenders could expect to suffer a sack. In practice this tended to happen, and apart from the often callous attitudes of the ancient world towards other human beings, there was an assumption that the horror of a sack would help to deter other strongholds from resisting in the future. For me there is an air of tragedy about this story, as the Nicopolitans get caught up in someone else's war and suffer appallingly as a result. Sadly that was too often the fate of communities in the ancient world, but not wishing to make an adventure story too grim, I decided against a graphic description of the sack itself.

Finally, we come to Hadrian, whose role in these years is unclear. He did spend some time in Athens before the eastern campaigns began, and since a senator needed permission to travel outside Italy, this must have been with Trajan's approval. There is no sign that the trip was made in any official capacity, so that it represented something of a holiday, or at least an episode of private life rather than public career. He had joined Trajan at Antioch, accompanying him on the visit to the shrine of Zeus Casius, but it is unclear in what capacity, and there is no direct evidence that he became one of the emperor's *comites* or companions and he does not appear to have gone to Armenia. A spell as governor or acting governor of Syria has been conjectured, and, although this is little more than a guess, the possibility worked for this story. Hadrian does not appear to have taken direct part in any of the main campaigns or accompanied Trajan to Ctesiphon. By the end of the war, he does appear to have been legate of Syria, but the appointment may well have been recent and probably a result of sending the experienced legatus off to deal with a crisis on the Danube. The appointment, and nomination for a second consulship, suggest Hadrian was back in some favour, but fell short of a full endorsement.

Hadrian was not with Trajan when the latter died. For whatever reasons Trajan had not marked anyone out as favoured successor. Perhaps this was a political gesture, showing that he had faith in the Senate to choose the best candidate, or it may have been more personal, from a man who struggled to come to terms with age and did not wish to think about his own death. His widow, Plotina, immediately announced that on his deathbed, her husband had adopted Hadrian and thus named him as the next *princeps*.

Hadrian acted quickly, and already had a number of significant supporters, unless these men simply sniffed the wind and guessed that it was best to win his favour. Lusius Quietus, the dashing Moor who had won Trajan's favour in Dacia and the eastern campaigns, was swiftly dismissed from the governorship of Judaea. There were several other arrests, and Quietus was among the handful of men who died in the months to come. Whether Hadrian gave the orders or supporters acted on their own initiative is impossible to say, but the executions left a bitter taste with most senators. Some later criticised Hadrian for abandoning some of Trajan's conquests and not adding more territory to the empire, but it was these deaths, combined with his unfortunate manner, that meant that he was not remembered as a popular or good emperor by Rome's elite. First and foremost, our literary sources judge every Roman emperor on how they treated the senatorial class.

GLOSSARY

Agoranomos: official in many Greek cities whose task was to supervise business and maintain order in the Agora or marketplace. This included assigning space to temporary stalls, inspecting the weights, scales and measures used by traders.

ala: a regiment of auxiliary cavalry, roughly the same size as a cohort of infantry. There were two types: *ala quingenaria* consisting of 512 men divided into 16 *turmae*; and *ala milliaria* consisting of 768 men divided into 24 *turmae*.

Armenia: ancient kingdom, which had briefly dominated the wider region in the first century BC, but subsequently found itself between the Roman and Parthian empires. Its kings came from the Parthian royal family, but also had ties to the Romans and constantly had to struggle to control a fractious aristocracy able to take refuge in strongholds in this rugged land. A number of the conflicts between Rome and Parthia began in a dispute over succession to the throne of Armenia.

Arsacids: taking their name from their founder, Arsaces, the dynasty that ruled Parthia – and Armenia – was known as the Arsacids. Since kings were polygamous and sometimes chose successors from the offspring of their harem, there were usually a lot of princes with a claim to the throne at any one time. This led to frequent power struggles and civil wars. There appear to have been three rival Parthian kings at the time of our story.

auxilia/auxiliaries: over half of the Roman army was recruited from non-citizens from all over (and even outside) the empire. These served as both infantry and cavalry and gained citizenship at the end of their twenty-five years of service.

Batavians: an offshoot of the Germanic Chatti, who fled after a period of civil war, the Batavians settled on what the Romans called the Rhine island in modern Netherlands. Famous as warriors, their only obligation to the empire was to provide soldiers to serve in Batavian units of the *auxilia*. Writing around the time of our story, the historian Tacitus described them as 'like armour and weapons - only used in war'.

Berytus: the modern city of Beirut, had been refounded as a colony for Roman army veterans. Their descendants provided many recruits for the legions.

Brigantes: a large tribe or group of tribes occupying much of what would become northern England. Several sub-groups are known, including the Textoverdi and Carvetii (whose name may mean 'stag people').

burgus: a small outpost manned by detached troops rather than a formal unit.

caligae: hobnailed boots worn by soldiers.

canabae: the civilian settlements which rapidly grew up outside almost every Roman fort. The community had no formal status and was probably under military jurisdiction.

carrobalista: a light bolt-shooting catapult or scorpio mounted on a cart.

centurion: a grade of officer rather than a specific rank, each legion had some sixty centurions, while each auxiliary cohort had between six and ten. They were highly educated men and were often given posts of great responsibility. While a minority were commissioned after service in the ranks, most

were directly commissioned or served only as junior officers
before reaching the centurionate.

centurio regionarius: a post attested in the Vindolanda tablets,
as well as elsewhere in Britain and other provinces. They
appear to have been officers on detached service placed in
control of an area. A large body of evidence from Egypt
shows them dealing with criminal investigations as well as
military and administrative tasks.

cataphract: a cavalryman who wore heavy armour, protecting
arms and legs as well as body. Some had helmets with masks
to cover their faces. Usually, the horse was also armoured.
The primary weapon was the two-handed *kontos* or lance,
backed by a sword. Some may also have carried bows.
Parthian cataphracts were famous and combined with the
more numerous horse archers proved formidable in open
battle.

clarissima femina: literally 'most distinguished woman', this
was an honorific for a female member of the senatorial class.

cohort: the principal tactical unit of the legions. The first cohort
consisted of 800 men in five double-strength centuries,
while cohorts two to ten were composed of 480 men in six
centuries of 80. Auxiliaries were either formed in milliary
cohorts of 800 or more often quingeniary cohorts of 480.
Cohortes equitatae or mixed cohorts added 240 and 120
horsemen respectively. These troopers were paid less and
given less-expensive mounts than the cavalry of the *alae*.

commilito (pl. *commilitones*): literally 'fellow soldier' or
'comrade', this was a familiar form of address used most
often by men of similar rank. However, Julius Caesar was
noted for addressing his men in this way. Most emperors
felt it was too familiar and did not use it, but some – and
probably some senior officers – did.

consilium: the council of officers and other senior advisors routinely employed by a Roman governor or senator to guide him in making decisions.

contubernium (pl. *contubernia*): the group of eight soldiers assigned to share a tent on campaign and who may also have shared a pair of rooms in a permanent barrack block.

curator: (i) title given to soldier placed in charge of an outpost such as a *burgus* who may or may not have held formal rank; (ii) the second in command to a decurion in a cavalry *turma*.

decurion: the cavalry equivalent to a centurion, but considered to be junior to them. He commanded a *turma*.

dolabra: the military pickaxe issued to most, if not all, Roman soldiers. It is remarkably similar in shape and size to the tool employed by many modern armies. One famous first-century general claimed that 'wars are won with the pickaxe' for such was the importance of marching camps, fortifications, and siege works in Roman warfare. Trajan's Column depicts some soldiers using them as weapons and this is also mentioned in our literary sources.

duplicarius: a 'double-pay man' was a junior NCO equivalent in the auxilia.

equestrian: the social class just below the Senate. There were many thousand equestrians (*eques*, pl. *equites*) in the Roman Empire, compared to six hundred senators, and a good proportion of equestrians were descendants of aristocracies within the provinces. Those serving in the army followed a different career path to senators.

fabrica (pl. *fabricae*): was a workshop set up by the army to make or maintain/repair equipment. Those in permanent bases, especially legionary fortresses, were often large.

hastatus posterior: the most junior of the six centurions in a legionary cohort.

Gades: modern Cadiz in Spain, originally founded by the Carthaginians and a thriving and wealthy community in the Roman period.

galearii (sing. *galearius*): slaves owned by the army, given basic uniform – the name means 'helmet-wearer' – and training and tasked with fatigues and assisting with the baggage train.

gladius: Latin word for sword, which by modern convention specifically refers to the short sword used by all legionaries and most auxiliary infantry. By the end of the first century most blades were less than 2 feet long.

lancea: a type of javelin or light spear, which could be thrown or thurst.

legate (provincial): the governor of a military province like Britain was a *legatus Augusti*, the representative of the emperor. He was a distinguished senator and usually at least in his forties.

legate (legionary): the commander of a legion was a *legatus legionis* and was a senator at an earlier stage in his career than the provincial governor. He would usually be in his early thirties.

legion: originally the levy of the entire Roman people summoned to war, legion or *legio* became the name for the most important unit in the army. In the last decades of the first century BC, legions became permanent with their own numbers and usually names and titles. In AD 98 there were twenty-eight legions, but the total was soon raised to thirty.

lixae: were camp followers, mainly slaves, forming part of an army on campaign.

Lugdunum: Lyons in France.

medicus: an army medical orderly or junior physician.

musculus: a mobile covered shed employed in sieges to protect soldiers as they got closer to the enemy wall. The name meant 'little mouse', so presumably began as a nickname.

omnes ad stercus: a duty roster of the first century AD from a century of a legion stationed in Egypt has some soldiers assigned *ad stercus*, literally to the 'dung' or 'shit'. This probably meant a fatigue party cleaning the latrines – or just possibly mucking out the stables. From this I have invented *omnes ad stercus* as 'everyone to the latrines' or 'we're all in the shit'.

optio: the second in command of a century of eighty men and deputy to a centurion.

Osrhoene: kingdom on the left bank of the Euphrates with its capital at Edessa which emerged in the break-up of the Seleucid empire. Its kings owed loyalty to the Parthian king of kings, but also maintained friendly relations with Rome. Most of the time, neither side intervened in its domestic affairs.

pilum: the heavy javelin carried by Roman legionaries. It was about 6 to 7 feet long. The shaft was wooden, topped by a slim iron shank ending in a pyramid-shaped point (much like the bodkin arrow used by longbowmen). The shank was not meant to bend. Instead the aim was to concentrate all of the weapon's considerable weight behind the head so that it would punch through armour or shield. If it hit a shield, the head would go through, and the long iron shank gave it the reach to continue and strike the man behind. Its effective range was probably some 15 to16 yards.

praesidium: the term meant 'garrison', and could be employed for a small outpost or a full-sized fort.

prefect (*praefectus*): the commander of most auxiliary units was called a prefect (although a few unit COs held the title tribune). These were equestrians, who first commanded a cohort of auxiliary infantry, then served as equestrian tribune in a legion, before going on to command a cavalry *ala*. There was also a *praefectus castrorum*, or 'prefect of the camp', who after the legate – and depending on opinion the broad-stripe senatorial tribune – was next in command of the legion.

primus pilus: the senior centurion out of 59 or 60 in a legion. This was a post of immense prestige, usually held for a single year. Afterwards men automatically gained equestrian status and some went on to higher posts in imperial service.

princeps: the emperor was supposed to be merely the first citizen, and first senator or princeps rather than a monarch.

princeps posterior: the third most senior centurion in the prestigious first cohort of a legion.

procurator: an imperial official who oversaw the tax and financial administration of a province. Although junior to a legate, a procurator reported directly to the emperor.

pugio: the Roman army dagger. There is little evidence for its use by auxiliaries in this era.

sacramentum: the military oath taken by soldiers when they joined the army and renewed periodically, especially on the accession of a new emperor. Obedience and loyalty was sworn to the state and the emperor.

Saka: a nomadic people from the Steppes, who were believed to be kin – or at least similar in culture, lifestyle and style of warfare – to the Sarmatians. At times they fought against the Parthians, but also were frequently recruited by them.

scorpion (*scorpio*, pl. *scorpiones*): a light torsion catapult or *ballista* with a superficial resemblance to a large crossbow. They shot a heavy bolt with considerable accuracy and tremendous force to a range beyond bowshot. Julius Caesar describes a bolt from one of these engines going through the leg of an enemy cavalryman and pinning him to the saddle.

seplasiarius (or *seplasiario*): military pharmascist working in a fort's hospital.

signifer: a standard-bearer, specifically one carrying a century's standard or *signum* (pl. *signa*).

Silures: a tribe or people occupying what is now South Wales. They fought a long campaign before being overrun by the Romans. Tacitus described them as having curly hair and darker hair or complexions than other Britons, and suggested that they looked more like Spaniards (although since he misunderstood the geography of Britain he also believed that their homeland was closer to Spain than Gaul).

spatha: another Latin term for sword, which is now conventional to employ for the longer blades used mainly by horsemen in this period.

stationarii: soldiers detached from their parent units and stationed as garrison elsewhere, often in a small outpost.

Strategos (pl. *Strategoi*): originally a name for a general or senior army officer, in most Greek city-states these were elected posts. Over time, many evolved to take on civil responsibilities, especially when actual warfare became less and less common.

tesserarius: the third in command of a century after the *optio* and *signifer*, the title originally came from their responsibility for overseeing sentries. The watchword for each night was written on a *tessera* or tablet.

thetatus: in some Roman army documents, the death of a soldier was indicated by the Greek letter theta. From this came the slang word *thetatus*, meaning dead.

tribune: each legion had six tribunes. The most senior was

the broad-stripe tribune (*tribunus laticlavius*), who was a young aristocrat at an early stage of a senatorial career. Such men were usually in their late teens or very early twenties. There were also five narrow-stripe or junior tribunes (*tribuni angusticlavii*).

Triclina: the three couches arranged in a u-shape at a formal Roman dinner party. The open end was to permit the dishes to be brought in and replaced for each course.

Zeugma: major city and legionary base in the old kingdom of Commagene. It guarded one of the most important crossing places on the Euphrates.

CAST OF CHARACTERS

Names with an asterisk (*) are real, though their characters have been embellished for the story. Appearance in other novels is noted as follows:

V = *Vindolanda*
ES = *The Encircling Sea*
B = *Brigantia*
TS = *The Fort*

ABGARUS VII* The royal family of Osrhoene named all its kings Abgarus (or Agbar) and ruled from the capital Edessa. Physically closer to the centres of Parthian power, the kingdom was more heavily under Parthian influence than Roman. However, it was independent, one of the patchwork of kingdoms through which the Parthian king of kings controlled his empire. At first Abgarus VII attempted to placate Trajan without committing to support him, and the Roman emperor was dissatisfied with the initial embassy sent from Osrhoene. Once it became clear that Trajan was determined to assert Roman dominance over the wider region, by force if necessary, Abgarus became far more friendly and managed to placate the emperor. Osrhoene allied with Rome but changed sides during the spate of rebellions late in 116.

It did not go well, and Edessa was sacked by Lusius Quietus. Abgarus VII was either killed in the fighting or died shortly afterwards.

APHRODITE An elderly freedwoman working in Sara's workshop.

APOLLODORUS A guard in the prison at Nicopolis. As a Christian, he is kinder to his charges, especially his fellow believer, Domitius.

ARBANDES*, prince of Osrhoene. A son of Abgarus VII, Arbandes led an embassy to Trajan, but the terms brought from his father failed to please Trajan. Later, after the king submitted to Rome, Trajan was said to have enjoyed watching Arbandes perform a war dance at a feast.

ARRIAN (LUCIUS FLAVIUS ARRIANUS)* Born into a locally important family in Nicomedia in Bithynia, Arrian is best known for his subsequent career as an author and historian, most notably producing the most complete and sober surviving account of Alexander the Great's campaigns. His early career is not recorded in detail, but he appears to have followed the pattern for equestrians serving as officers. Hence, in our story, he has already commanded an auxiliary cohort and is now one of the five equestrian tribunes in Legio VIIII Hispana. There is debate over whether or not he took any part in Trajan's eastern expedition, but he was the right age, and this is certainly possible, while he also later wrote a history of the Parthians, which only survives in brief fragments. Under Hadrian he was elevated to the senatorial order and governed the province of Cappadocia, repulsing an invasion by the nomadic Alans.

ATHENODORUS Nicopolitan aristocrat currently elected to the post of Strategos or senior magistrate with military as well as civil responsibility.

AZÁTĒ, princess of Osrhoene. The favoured daughter of King Abgarus VII, Azátē's fate, like that of most royal women, was to be married as a means of strengthening her father's political influence. Small, intelligent, and as determined and unscrupulous as any of the men of her family, she is determined to work the system in her own favour. In the past she has shown particular generosity to the people of Nicopolis and has personal ties with the city's Jewish community.

BRAN A member of the Novantae tribe of northern Britannia, Bran, as a boy, was part of a raid launched on the coast of the Roman province. Captured by Ferox, he took an oath to serve him. While still young, he went to one of the islands in the far north to train as a warrior in the strict cult presided over by 'the Mother', before returning to follow Ferox. Slim, agile and very skilful, he is a formidable fighter, especially as an individual. Apart from his oath to Ferox, he has sworn vengeance on Sosius. *ES, TF*

BRENNUS One of the Brigantians serving in the irregular unit under Ferox. He is a one-eyed veteran after a wound suffered in an earlier fight. The name means 'great king' and was a common one among the Celtic tribes. *V*

BRUTTIUS PRAESENS, CAIUS* The legatus of Legio VI Ferrata. A fragment of a lost history records that he issued his men with snow shoes to allow them to operate during the winter in the highlands of Armenia.

CERIALIS, FLAVIUS* Attested in the Vindolanda writing tablets as the commander of cohors VIIII Batavorum at the fort in the early years of the second century, there is no evidence outside these documents concerning him. His name is revealing and suggests a connection to the rebellion of the Batavians in AD 70. Flavius was the family name of Vespasian, which suggests that he or a father/grandfather was given Roman citizenship for loyalty to Rome or changing sides at an opportune moment during this conflict. The commander mainly responsible for suppressing the revolt was Petilius Cerialis – hence Flavius from the emperor and Cerialis from the commander. In one of the writing tablets, he is referred to as king, suggesting that he belonged to the royal family of the Batavians (though the editors of the texts are more inclined to see this as sycophancy). *V, ES, B, TF*

CLAUDIA ENICA Daughter of the king and queen of the Brigantes – the largest tribe in northern Britain – and granddaughter of the famous Queen Cartimandua, Claudia Enica is both a fine Roman lady and the leader of her tribe. Slim and beautiful, she has the fiery red hair of her family. Trained as a warrior on an island far to the north, and educated in Gaul and Rome, she lives between two worlds. Married to Ferox – to his continuing amazement – they have been kept apart for years by the machinations of Hadrian. Claudia Enica hopes to gain formal recognition as monarch of her tribe by the Romans, and Ferox does his best to help her and most of all protect her and their children.

CLODIUS SECUNDUS (probably an assumed name). A legionary of Legio VIIII Hispana, Clodius has served for fifteen years and has a long record of offences and dereliction of duty. He enlisted in Londinium, but his origins are unknown.

CRISPINUS, M. ATILIUS The senator appointed to command Legio VIIII Hispana as its legatus legionis, Crispinus is old for the role. Born into a distinguished family, the ambitious Crispinus began his career with great hopes. As a young broad-stripe tribune, he first encountered Ferox near Vindolanda, though his father had already met the centurion during Domitian's Dacian campaigns. Clever, perhaps over clever, Crispinus became involved in a series of intrigues in Britannia, culminating in an attempted rebellion led by Claudia Enica's brother. Taken prisoner by the rebels, he suffered badly. For a long time, as a result of this, or suspicion that he had genuinely joined the rebels, he was declared mad and retired from public life for over a decade. This new command offers a chance to rehabilitate himself. *V, ES, B*

CUNOMINUS One of the Brigantian warriors in the irregular unit commanded by Ferox.

DOMITIUS (CAIUS DOMITIUS CLEMENS) The son and grandson of soldiers, Domitius comes from the Roman colony at Berytus, so has lived in a military atmosphere most of his life, even before he joined the legions. A good soldier, he rose to the rank of *optio ad spem* – i.e. a centurion's deputy with the promise of promotion to centurion when a vacancy arose. At some point he became a Christian, but it was much later before he was denounced for belonging to this illegal cult. At the start of our story, he is a deserter, trying to cross the frontier and leave the Roman Empire.

DUCCIUS A tesserarius (with the optio and signifier, one of the key sub-commanders in a century) who happens upon the misbehaviour of one of the legion's pickets.

FELIX, JULIUS A young legionary serving in VIIII Hispana. He is one of the trio caught out in misconduct while on picket duty.

FEROX, TITUS FLAVIUS Born a prince of the Silures, his father was killed fighting against the Romans, so that he was raised by his grandfather, the 'Lord of the Hills', who was the closest thing the Silures had to a king. When the tribe finally gave in after decades of war against Rome, Ferox was sent to be educated in Gaul and later in Rome. At the age of eighteen he was granted Roman citizenship and commissioned as legionary centurion, serving in the wars against Dacians, Sarmatians and Germanic peoples on the Danube under the Emperor Domitian. Thus began a chequered career, which saw him often decorated for valour and as often in disgrace for his staunch and frequently inconvenient adherence to the truth. Involvement in the investigation after the failed coup by Saturninus left him bitter and depressed, not helped when the woman he loved vanished. Sent to the area around Vindolanda, because he was a nuisance everywhere else, he was forgotten because he had ceased to hold any political importance as hostage. In the years that followed, he encountered Vindex, Crispinus, Cerialis and Sulpicia Lepidina. Since then, he has served against the Dacians and in many other provinces as well as beyond the frontiers. *V, ES, B, TF*

GELLIUS EXORATUS, CAIUS The prefect in charge of cohors IIII Callaececorum Lucensium equitata, Exoratus is an equestrian from Spain and probably the only Spaniard in this regiment originally raised there, but long since posted to the eastern provinces. Although, in his first posting, he is a capable young officer.

HADRIAN* (PUBLIUS AELIUS HADRIANUS, Roman emperor (117–138)) Like Trajan, Hadrian came from the elite of the city of Italica in Spain. His father was Trajan's cousin, and when he died at a young age, Trajan became one of the young Hadrian's guardians. Hadrian served as senatorial tribune with the legions, held a number of other posts, accompanied Trajan to the First Dacian War (101–102) and commanded a legion and then a province during the Second Dacian War (105–106). However, the favour shown to him by the emperor stopped well short of marking him out as a likely successor, and the relationship between the two men appears to have lacked warmth. After time in Athens, where he served as city magistrate, Hadrian played some limited role in Trajan's eastern expedition – hence the pretext for our story – and by 117 was legate of Syria. When Trajan's widow announced that the dying emperor had adopted him, Hadrian acted swiftly and ruthlessly to secure power. As emperor, he governed well and spent much of his reign travelling to visit almost all the provinces of the empire. He never succeeded in winning the affection of the senatorial order. *TF*

HERACLIDES A young citizen of Nicopolis and member of one its prominent families, Heraclides encountered Ferox during the fighting in front of the walls.

INDIKE Born in India, as a child, Indike became a slave and was traded into the Roman Empire. Years later, she was a dancer in an inn in Londinium in Britannia. Won in a game of dice by an ally of Ferox, she was subsequently granted her freedom and chose to marry Philo. She is small, delicately featured and elegant in her movements. *B, TF*

JOHN Sara's grandfather, originally lived in Jotopata in Galilee. As a young man he took part in the great rebellion against Nero, fighting to defend his home city, and later in the unsuccessful defence of Jerusalem. He escaped with his family and later settled in Nicopolis where his daughter married Simon the Elder.

LABERIUS MAXIMUS, MANIUS* A senator who for many years enjoyed Trajan's favour. He served with distinction in the First Dacian War and was the emperor's fellow consul in 103. However, at some point, he was sent into exile for an offence that is not recorded. He was executed early in Hadrian's reign. *TF*

LUCIUS A legionary serving in Legio VIIII Hispana.

MATIDIA* Trajan's niece and mother of Hadrian's wife, Sabina. Trajan displayed great affection for her, not least granting her the title Augusta on the death of her mother. She was in turn fond of Hadrian and assisted him politically.

MEMNON An aristocrat from Nicopolis, Memnon is the senior Strategos or magistrate at the time of our story.

MESSALINUS, L. VALERIUS A tribune heavily involved in the organised corruption among the Syrian provincial army. Shortly before our story begins, he was killed by Ferox.

NICAEA A diminutive, young and very capable freedwoman working in Sara's workshop.

PAUSANIAS A former sailor who at some point converted to Christianity, Pausanias became a gifted preacher. More experienced in the wider world than many, his wisdom, kindness and authority had a powerful influence on Domitius.

PHILO Once the slave and now the freedman of Ferox, Philo is a Jew from Alexandria. He is obsessively neat and highly efficient in everything he does, and has always had higher aspirations for Ferox's standing than the centurion feels able to maintain. *V, ES, B, TF*

PLOTINA, POMPEIA* The wife of Trajan, she belonged to a senatorial family with roots in Gallia Narbonensis. No negative stories survive about her in our sources, suggesting that she performed the role of imperial consort to the satisfaction of the senatorial elite. She was believed to be instrumental in securing the accession of Hadrian after the death of her husband.

PRISCUS A legionary of VIIII Hispana and one of a trio on picket duty found to be misbehaving.

QUIETUS, LUSIUS* A member of the Mauretanian royal family, Lusius (sic) Quietus had a chequered career, including exile under Domitian. During Trajan's Dacian Wars, he rose to prominence commanding a large contingent of Moorish light cavalry, fighting in their traditional style. Trajan rewarded him with admission to the senatorial order and employed him as one of his main field commanders in the eastern campaigns. After Trajan's death, he was imprisoned and subsequently executed. Hadrian's involvement in his fall from power was never proven, but was widely suspected and seems certain.

RUFUS, M. CORNELIUS From a well-to-do family in Tarraco (modern Tarragona) in Spain, Rufus has recently been directly commissioned into Legio VIIII Hispana. He is now one of the most junior centurions in the legion, specifically the hastatus prior in the fifth cohort. An eager, slightly short-sighted young man, he has a particular enthusiasm for engineering.

SARA A Jewish woman in her late twenties, but still unmarried, belonging to a moderately prosperous merchant family in Nicopolis. She is intelligent and very capable, taking on the main burden of supervising the family business as well as her own workshop.

SENTIUS, CAIUS A centurion in the third cohort of Legio VIIII Hispana, Sentius is stolid, determined and lacking in imagination.

SIMON THE ELDER Sara's father. He specialises in trading in inscribed gemstones, and many hours of working on them has caused his eyesight to deteriorate. A widower, he is content to let his daughter make most of the key decisions for the family.

SIMON THE YOUNGER Sara's brother is slightly older than her. He is a bold, restless man, who has spent the last few years travelling to the trading posts on the borders with

China. Although suspicious of Romans in general and Domitius in particular, he is a fair man, whose main concern is to protect his family – and after that, his city.

SOSIUS A shadowy agent of Hadrian, the shaven-headed, former slave Sosius is clever, determined and utterly ruthless. Ferox first encountered him in *The Fort*. TF

SULPICIA LEPIDINA* The wife of Flavius Cerialis appears in the Vindolanda writing tablets, which reveal aspects of their day-to-day life during his command of the cohort stationed at the fort in northern Britain. Nothing else is known about her, and it is an invention in the stories to make her the daughter of a senator. In these novels, she is a major character, friend to Claudia Enica, and in the past briefly Ferox's lover. *V, ES, B, TF*

TRAJAN* (MARCUS ULPIUS TRAIANUS, Roman emperor (98-117)) Trajan's father was a relation and early supporter of Vespasian, the ultimate winner in the civil war following the death of Nero. The family came from Italica in Spain and claimed descent from the original Roman colonists. The son had a good career under the Flavian emperors and demonstrated eager loyalty to Domitian, its unpopular final member. After Domitian's murder, the Senate accepted the elderly Nerva as emperor, and the latter subsequently adopted Trajan as son, the choice aided by the fact that Trajan was currently commander of a major provincial army. Trajan went down in history as a military emperor and spent more of his reign on campaign than any ruler since Augustus. His conquest of Dacia was celebrated in grand style. However, his subsequent eastern expedition began well, only to be beset by widespread rebellion, and he died on his way back to Rome. Trajan was remembered with great reverence by Rome's elite as a good ruler who listened to the advice of the senatorial aristocracy and treated them with great respect. *TF*

VINDEX From the Carvetii – a group akin to the Brigantes, but proud of their independence – Vindex is the son of their chieftain. His mother was not married to his father, so his status is ambiguous. Even so, he was appointed to command a unit of scouts sent to serve alongside the Roman army, during which time he encountered Ferox, and has been by his side almost ever since. *V, ES, B, TF*

About the Author

ADRIAN GOLDSWORTHY studied
at Oxford, where his doctoral thesis examined
the Roman army. He went on to become
an acclaimed historian of Ancient Rome.
He is the author of numerous works of
non fiction, including *Caesar*, *Pax Romana*,
Hadrian's Wall and *Philip and Alexander*.
He is also the author of the Vindolanda series,
set in Roman Britain, which first introduced
readers to centurion Flavius Ferox.